William Morris

The Story of Sigurd the Volsung and the Fall of the Niblungs

William Morris

The Story of Sigurd the Volsung and the Fall of the Niblungs

ISBN/EAN: 9783744742726

Printed in Europe, USA, Canada, Australia, Japan

Cover: Foto ©Andreas Hilbeck / pixelio.de

More available books at **www.hansebooks.com**

THE STORY

OF

SIGURÐ THE VOLSUNG

AND THE

FALL OF THE NIBLUNGS.

BY

WILLIAM MORRIS,

AUTHOR OF 'THE EARTHLY PARADISE.'

FIFTH EDITION.

LONDON:
REEVES AND TURNER, 196 STRAND.
1893.

CONTENTS.

BOOK II.

REGIN.

BOOK III.

BRYNHILD.

BOOK IV.

GUDRUN.

THE STORY

OF

SIGURD THE VOLSUNG

AND THE

FALL OF THE NIBLUNGS.

BOOK I.

SIGMUND.

IN THIS BOOK IS TOLD OF THE EARLIER DAYS OF THE VOLSUNGS, AND OF SIGMUND THE FATHER OF SIGURD, AND OF HIS DEEDS, AND OF HOW HE DIED WHILE SIGURD WAS YET UNBORN IN HIS MOTHER'S WOMB.

Of the dwelling of King Volsung, and the wedding of Signy his daughter.

THERE was a dwelling of Kings ere the world was waxen old ;
  Dukes were the door-wards there, and the roofs were thatched with gold ;
Earls were the wrights that wrought it, and silver nailed its doors ;
Earls' wives were the weaving-women, queens' daughters strewed its floors,
And the masters of its song-craft were the mightiest men that cast
The sails of the storm of battle adown the bickering blast.
There dwelt men merry-hearted, and in hope exceeding great
Met the good days and the evil as they went the way of fate :
There the Gods were unforgotten, yea whiles they walked with men,
Though e'en in that world's beginning rose a murmur now and again
Of the midward time and the fading and the last of the latter days,

And the entering in of the terror, and the death of the People's Praise.

Thus was the dwelling of Volsung, the King of the Midworld's Mark,
As a rose in the winter season, a candle in the dark ;
And as in all other matters 'twas all earthly houses' crown,
And the least of its wall-hung shields was a battle-world's renown,
So therein withal was a marvel and a glorious thing to see,
For amidst of its midmost hall-floor sprang up a mighty tree,
That reared its blessings roofward, and wreathed the roof-tree dear
With the glory of the summer and the garland of the year.
I know not how they called it ere Volsung changed his life,
But his dawning of fair promise, and his noontide of the strife,
His eve of the battle-reaping and the garnering of his fame,
Have bred us many a story and named us many a name ;
And when men tell of Volsung, they call that war-duke's tree,
That crownèd stem, the Branstock ; and so was it told unto me.

So there was the throne of Volsung beneath its blossoming bower,
But high o'er the roof-crest red it rose 'twixt tower and tower,
And therein were the wild hawks dwelling, abiding the dole of their lord ;
And they wailed high over the wine, and laughed to the waking sword.

Still were its boughs but for them, when lo on an even of May
Comes a man from Siggeir the King with a word for his mouth to say :
" All hail to thee King Volsung, from the King of the Goths I come :
He hath heard of thy sword victorious and thine abundant home ;
He hath heard of thy sons in the battle, the fillers of Odin's Hall ;
And a word hath the west-wind blown him, (full fruitful be its fall !)
A word of thy daughter Signy the crown of womanhood :
Now he deems thy friendship goodly, and thine help in the battle good,
And for these will he give his friendship and his battle-aid again :
But if thou wouldst grant his asking, and make his heart full fain,
Then shalt thou give him a matter, saith he, without a price,

—Signy the fairer than fair, Signy the wiser than wise."

Such words in the hall of the Volsungs spake the Earl of Siggeir the Goth,
Bearing the gifts and the gold, the ring, and the tokens of troth.
But the King's heart laughed within him and the King's sons deemed it good ;
For they dreamed how they fared with the Goths o'er ocean and acre and wood,
Till all the north was theirs, and the utmost southern lands.

But nought said the snow-white Signy as she sat with folded hands
And gazed at the Goth-king's Earl till his heart grew heavy and cold,
As one that half remembers a tale that the elders have told,
A story of weird and of woe : then spake King Volsung and said :

" A great king woos thee, daughter ; wilt thou lie in a great king's bed,
And bear earth's kings on thy bosom, that our name may never die ? "

A fire lit up her face, and her voice was e'en as a cry :
" I will sleep in a great king's bed, I will bear the lords of the earth,
And the wrack and the grief of my youth-days shall be held for nothing worth."

Then would he question her kindly, as one who loved her sore,
But she put forth her hand and smiled, and her face was flushed no more
" Would God it might otherwise be ! but wert thou to will it not,
Yet should I will it and wed him, and rue my life and my lot."

Lowly and soft she said it ; but spake out louder now :
" Be of good cheer, King Volsung ! for such a man art thou,
That what thou dost well-counselled, goodly and fair it is,
And what thou dost unwitting, the Gods have bidden thee this :
So work all things together for the fame of thee and thine.
And now meseems at my wedding shall be a hallowed sign,
That shall give thine heart a joyance, whate'er shall follow after."

She spake, and the feast sped on, and the speech and the song and the laughter
Went over the words of boding as the tide of the norland main
Sweeps over the hidden skerry, the home of the shipman's bane.

So wendeth his way on the morrow that Earl of the Gothland King,
Bearing the gifts and the gold, and King Volsung's tokening,
And a word in his mouth moreover, a word of blessing and hail,
And a bidding to King Siggeir to come ere the June-tide fail ·
And wed him to white-hand Signy and bear away his bride,
While sleepeth the field of the fishes amidst the summer-tide.

So on Mid-Summer Even ere the undark night began
Siggeir the King of the Goth-folk went up from the bath of the swan
Unto the Volsung dwelling with many an Earl about ;
There through the glimmering thicket the linkèd mail rang out,
And sang as mid the woodways sings the summer-hidden ford :
There were gold-rings God-fashioned, and many a Dwarf-wrought sword,
And many a Queen-wrought kirtle and many a written spear ;
So came they to the acres, and drew the threshold near,
And amidst of the garden blossoms, on the grassy, fruit-grown land,
Was Volsung the King of the Wood-world with his sons on either hand ;
Therewith down lighted Siggeir the lord of a mighty folk,
Yet showed he by King Volsung as the bramble by the oak,
Nor reached his helm to the shoulder of the least of Volsung's sons.
And so into the hall they wended, the Kings and their mighty ones ;
And they dight the feast full glorious, and drank through the death of the day,
Till the shadowless moon rose upward, till it wended white away ;
Then they went to the gold-hung beds, and at last for an hour or twain
Were all things still and silent, save a flaw of the summer rain.

But on the morrow noontide when the sun was high and bare,
More glorious was the banquet, and now was Signy there,
And she sat beside King Siggeir, a glorious bride forsooth ;

Ruddy and white was she wrought as the fair-stained sea-beast's tooth,
But she neither laughed nor spake, and her eyes were hard and cold,
And with wandering side-long looks her lord would she behold.
That saw Sigmund her brother, the eldest Volsung son,
And oft he looked upon her, and their eyes met now and anon,
And ruth arose in his heart, and hate of Siggeir the Goth,
And there had he broken the wedding, but for plighted promise and troth.
But those twain were beheld of Siggeir, and he deemed of the Volsung kin,
That amid their might and their malice small honour should he win;
Yet thereof made he no semblance, but abided times to be
And laughed out with the loudest, amid the hope and the glee.
And nought of all saw Volsung, as he dreamed of the coming glory,
And how the Kings of his kindred should fashion the round world's story.

So round about the Branstock they feast in the gleam of the gold;
And though the deeds of man-folk were not yet waxen old,
Yet had they tales for songcraft, and the blossomed garth of rhyme;
Tales of the framing of all things and the entering in of time
From the halls of the outer heaven; so near they knew the door.
Wherefore uprose a sea-king, and his hands that loved the oar
Now dealt with the rippling harp-gold, and he sang of the shaping of earth,
And how the stars were lighted, and where the winds had birth,
And the gleam of the first of summers on the yet untrodden grass.
But e'en as men's hearts were hearkening some heard the thunder pass
O'er the cloudless noontide heaven; and some men turned about
And deemed that in the doorway they heard a man laugh out.
Then into the Volsung dwelling a mighty man there strode,
One-eyed and seeming ancient, yet bright his visage glowed:
Cloud-blue was the hood upon him, and his kirtle gleaming-grey
As the latter morning sundog when the storm is on the way:
A bill he bore on his shoulder, whose mighty ashen beam
Burnt bright with the flame of the sea and the blended silver's gleam.
And such was the guise of his raiment as the Volsung elders had told

Was borne by their fathers' fathers, and **the first** that warred in the wold.

So strode he to the Branstock nor greeted any **lord,**
But forth from his cloudy raiment he drew a gleaming sword,
And smote it deep in the tree-bole, and the wild hawks overhead
Laughed 'neath the naked heaven as at last he spake and said :
" Earls of the Goths, and Volsungs, abiders on the earth,
Lo there amid the Branstock a blade of plenteous worth !
The folk **of the war-wand's** forgers wrought never better steel
Since first the **burg of heaven uprose for** man-folk's weal.
Now let the man among you whose heart **and hand may shift**
To pluck it from the oakwood e'en take **it for my gift.**
Then ne'er, but his own heart falter, its point and edge shall fail
Until the night's beginning **and the ending** of the tale.
Be merry Earls of the Goth-folk, **O Volsung Sons** be wise,
And reap the **battle-acre that ripening for you lies :**
For they told me in the wild wood, **I heard on** the mountain **side,**
That the shining house of heaven is wrought exceeding wide,
And that there the Early-comers shall have abundant rest
While Earth grows scant of great ones, and fadeth from its best,
And fadeth from its midward and groweth poor and vile :—
All hail to thee King Volsung ! farewell for a little while ! **"**

So sweet his speaking **sounded, so** wise his words did seem,
That moveless all men sat there, as in a happy dream
We stir not lest **we waken ;** but there his speech had end,
And slowly down the hall-floor, and outward did he wend ;
And none would cast him a question or follow on his ways,
For they knew that the gift was Odin's, a sword for the world to praise.

But now spake Volsung the King : **" Why sit ye** silent and still ?
Is the Battle-Father's visage a token of terror and ill ?
Arise O Volsung Children, Earls of the Goths arise,

And set your hands to the hilts as mighty men and wise !
Yet deem it not too easy ; for belike a fateful blade
Lies there in the heart of the Branstock for a fated warrior made."

Now therewith spake King Siggeir : " King Volsung give me a grace
To try it the first of all men, lest another win my place
And mere chance-hap steal my glory and the gain that I might win."

Then somewhat laughed King Volsung, and he said : O Guest, begin ;
Though herein is the first as the last, for the Gods have long to live,
Nor hath Odin yet forgotten unto whom the gift he would give."

Then forth to the tree went Siggeir, the Goth-folk's mighty lord,
And laid his hand on the gemstones, and strained at the glorious sword
Till his heart grew black with anger ; and never a word he said
As he wended back to the high-seat : but Signy waxed blood-red
When he sat him adown beside her ; and her heart was nigh to break
For the shame and the fateful boding : and therewith King Volsung spake :

" Thus comes back empty-handed the mightiest King of Earth,
And how shall the feeble venture ? yet each man knows his worth ;
And today may a great beginning from a little seed upspring
To o'erpass many a great one that hath the name of King :
So stand forth free and unfree ; stand forth both most and least :
But first ye Earls of the Goth-folk, ye lovely lords we feast."

Upstood the Earls of Siggeir, and each man drew anigh
And deemed his time was coming for a glorious gain and high ;
But for all their mighty shaping and their deeds in the battle-wood,
No looser in the Branstock that gift of Odin stood.
Then uprose Volsung's homemen, and the fell-abiding folk ,
And the yellow-headed shepherds came gathering round the Oak,
And the searchers of the thicket and the dealers with the oar

And the least and the worst of them all was a mighty man of war.
But for all their mighty shaping, and the struggle and the strain
Of their hands, the deft in labour, they tugged thereat in vain ;
And still as the shouting **and** jeers, and the names of men and the laughter
Beat backward from gable to gable, and rattled o'er roof-tree and rafter,
Moody and still sat Siggeir ; for he said : "They have trained me here
As a mock for their woodland bondsmen ; and yet shall they buy it dear."

Now the tumult sank a little, and men cried on Volsung the King
And his sons, the hedge of battle, to try the fateful thing.
So Volsung laughed, and answered : "I will set me to the toil,
Lest these my guests of the Goth-folk should deem I fear the foil.
Yet nought am I ill-sworded, and the oldest friend is best ;
And this, my hand's first fellow, will I bear to the grave-mound's rest,
Nor wield meanwhile another : Yea this **shall** I have in hand
When mid the host of Odin in the Day of Doom I stand."

Therewith from his belt of battle he raised the golden sheath,
And showed the peace-strings glittering about the hidden death :
Then he laid his hand on the Branstock, and cried : "O tree beloved,
I thank thee of thy good-heart that so little thou art moved :
Abide thou thus, green bower, when I am dead and gone
And the **best of** all my kindred a better day hath won !"

Then **as** a young man laughed he, and on the hilts of gold
His hand, the battle-breaker, took fast and certain hold,
And long he **drew and** strained him, but mended not the tale,
Yet none the more thereover his mirth of heart did fail ;
But he wended to the high-seat and thence began to cry :

"Sons I have gotten and cherished, now stand ye forth to try ;
Lest Odin tell in God-home how from the way he strayed,
And how to the man he would not he gave away his blade."

So therewithal rose Rerir, and wasted might and main ;
Then Gunthiof, and then Hunthiof, they wearied them in vain ;
Nought was the might of Agnar ; nought Helgi could avail ;
Sigi the tall and Solar no further brought the tale,
Nor Geirmund the priest of the temple, nor Gylfi of the wood.

At last by the side of the Branstock Sigmund the Volsung stood,
And with right hand wise in battle the precious sword-hilt caught,
Yet in a careless fashion, as he deemed it all for nought :
When lo, from floor to rafter went up a shattering shout,
For aloft in the hand of Sigmund the naked blade shone out
As high o'er his head he shook it : for the sword had come away
From the grip of the heart of the Branstock, as though all loose it lay.
A little while he stood there mid the glory of the hall,
Like the best of the trees of the garden, when the April sunbeams fall
On its blossomed boughs in the morning, and tell of the days to be ;
Then back unto the high-seat he wended soberly ;
For this was the thought within him ; Belike the day shall come
When I shall bide here lonely amid the Volsung home,
Its glory and sole avenger, its after-summer seed.
Yea, I am the hired of Odin, his workday will to speed,
And the harvest-tide shall be heavy.—What then, were it come and past
And I laid by the last of the sheaves with my wages earned at the last ?

He lifted his eyes as he thought it, for now was he come to his place,
And there he stood by his father and met Siggeir face to face,
And he saw him blithe and smiling, and heard him how he spake :
"O best of the sons of Volsung, I am merry for thy sake
And the glory that thou hast gained us ; but whereas thine hand and heart
Are e'en now the lords of the battle, how lack'st thou for thy part
A matter to better the best ? Wilt thou overgild fine gold
Or dye the red rose redder ? So I prithee let me hold
This sword that comes to thine hand on the day I wed thy kin.

For at home have I a store-house ; there is mountain-gold therein
The weight of a war-king's harness ; there is silver plenteous store;
There is iron, and huge-wrought amber, that the southern men love sore,
When they sell me the woven wonder, the purple born of the sea;
And it hangeth up in that bower ; and all this is a gift for thee :
But the sword that came to my wedding, methinketh it meet and right,
That it lie on my knees in the council and stead me in the fight."

But Sigmund laughed and answered, and he spake a scornful word :
"And if I take twice that treasure, will it buy me Odin's sword,
And the gift that the Gods have given ? will it buy me again to stand
Betwixt two mightiest world-kings with a longed-for thing in mine hand
That all their might hath missed of ? when the purple-selling men
Come buying thine iron and amber, dost thou sell thine honour then?
Do they wrap it in bast of the linden, or run it in moulds of earth ?
And shalt thou account mine honour as a matter of lesser worth ?
Came the sword to thy wedding, Goth-king, to thine hand it never came,
And thence is thine envy whetted to deal me this word of shame."

Black then was the heart of Siggeir, but his face grew pale and red,
Till he drew a smile thereover, and spake the word and said :
" Nay, pardon me, Signy's kinsman ! when the heart desires o'ermuch
It teacheth the tongue ill speaking, and my word belike was such.
But the honour of thee and thy kindred, I hold it even as mine,
And I love you as my heart-blood, and take ye this for a sign.
I bid thee now King Volsung, and these thy glorious sons,
And thine earls and thy dukes of battle and all thy mighty ones,
To come to the house of the Goth-kings as honoured guests and dear
And abide the winter over ; that the dusky days and drear
May be glorious with thy presence, that all folk may praise my life,
And the friends that my fame hath gotten ; and that this my new-wed wife
Thine eyes may make the merrier till she bear my eldest born."

Then speedily answered Volsung : " No king of the earth might scorn
Such noble bidding, Siggeir ; and surely will I come
To look upon thy glory and the Goths' abundant home.
But let two months wear over, for I have many a thing
To shape and shear in the Woodland, as befits a people's king :
And thou meanwhile here abiding of all my goods shalt be free,
And then shall we twain together roof over the glass-green sea
With the sides of our golden dragons ; and our war-hosts' blended shields
Shall fright the sea-abiders and the folk of the fishy fields."

Answered the smooth-speeched Siggeir : " I thank thee well for this,
And thy bidding is most kingly ; yet take it not amiss
That I wend my ways in the morning ; for we Goth-folk know indeed
That the sea is a foe full deadly, and a friend that fails at need,
And that Ran who dwells thereunder will many a man beguile :
And I bear a woman with me ; nor would I for a while
Behold that sea-queen's dwelling ; for glad at heart am I
Of the realm of the Goths and the Volsungs, and I look for long to lie
In the arms of the fairest woman that ever a king may kiss.
So I go mine house to order for the increase of thy bliss,
That there in nought but joyance all we may wear the days
And that men of the time hereafter the more our lives may praise."

And for all the words of Volsung e'en so must the matter be,
And Siggeir the Goth and Signy on the morn shall sail the sea.
But the feast sped on the fairer, and the more they waxed in disport
And the glee that all men love, as they knew that the hours were short.
Yet a boding heart bare Sigmund amid his singing and laughter ;
And somewhat Signy wotted of the deeds that were coming after ;
For the wisest of women she was, and many a thing she knew ;   [do,
She would hearken the voice of the midnight till she heard what the Gods would
And her feet fared oft on the wild, and deep was her communing
With the heart of the glimmering woodland. where never a fowl may sing.

So fair sped on the feasting amid the gleam of the **gold,**
Amid the wine and the joyance ; and many **a tale** was told
To the harp-strings of that wedding, **whereof the latter days**
Yet hold a little glimmer to wonder at and praise.
Then the undark night drew over, and faint the high stars shone,
And there on the beds blue-woven the slumber-tide they won ;
Yea while on the brightening mountain the herd-boy watched his sheep,
Yet soft on the breast of Signy King Siggeir lay asleep.

How the Volsungs fared to the Land of the Goths, and of the
*fall of **King** Volsung.*

Now or ever the sun shone houseward, **unto King** Volsung's bed
Came Signy stealing **barefoot, and she spake the** word and said :
"**Awake and hearken, my father, for though the** wedding be done,
And I am the **wife of the Goth-king, yet the** Volsungs are **not gone.**
So I come as a dream of the night, with a word that the Gods would say,
And think thou thereof in the day-tide, and let Siggeir go on his way
With **me** and the gifts and the gold, but do ye abide **in** the land,
Nor trust in the guileful heart and the murder-loving hand,
Lest the kin of the Volsungs perish, and the world be **nothing worth.**"

So came **the word unto** Volsung, and wit in his heart had birth ;
And he sat upright in the bed and kissed her on the lips ;
But he said : "My **word is given, it** is gone like the spring-tide ships :
To death or to life must **I** journey when the months are come to an end.
Yet my sons my words shall hearken, and shall nowise with me wend."

Then she answered, speaking swiftly : "Nay, have thy sons with thee ;
Gather an host together and a mighty company,
And meet the guile and the-death-snare with battle and with wrack."

He said : " Nay, my troth-word plighted e'en so should I draw aback :
I shall go a guest, as my word was ; of whom shall I be afraid ?
For an outworn elder's ending shall no mighty moan be made."

Then answered Signy, weeping : " I shall see thee yet again
When the battle thou arrayest on the Goth-folks' strand in vain.
Heavy and hard are the Norns : but each man his burden bears ;
And what am I to fashion the fate of the coming years ?"

She wept and she wended back to the Goth-king's bolster blue,
And Volsung pondered awhile till slumber over him drew ;
But when once more he wakened, the kingly house was up,
And the homemen gathered together to drink the parting cup :
And grand amid the hall-floor was the Goth king in his gear,
And Signy clad for faring stood by the Branstock dear
With the earls of the Goths about her : so queenly did she seem,
So calm and ruddy coloured, that Volsung well might deem
That her words were a fashion of slumber, a vision of the night.
But they drank the wine of departing, and brought the horses dight,
And forth abroad the Goth-folk and the Volsung Children rode,
Nor ever once would Signy look back to that abode.

So down over acre and heath they rode to the side of the sea,
And there by the long-ships' bridges was the ship-host's company.
Then Signy kissed her brethren with ruddy mouth and warm,
Nor was there one of the Goth-folk but blessed her from all harm ;
Then sweet she kissed her father and hung about his neck,
And sure she whispered him somewhat ere she passed forth toward the deck,
Though nought I know to tell it : then Siggeir hailed them fair,
And called forth many a blessing on the hearts that bode his snare.
Then were the gangways shipped, and blown was the parting horn,
And the striped sails drew with the wind, and away was Signy borne
White on the shielded long ship, a grief in the heart of the gold ;

Nor once would she turn **her about the strand of her** folk to behold.

Thenceforward dwelt the Volsungs in exceeding glorious state,
And merry lived King Volsung, abiding the day of his fate ;
But when the months aforesaid were well-nigh worn away
To his sons and his folk of counsel he fell these words to say :
" Ye mind you of Signy's wedding and of my plighted troth
To go in two months' wearing to the house of Siggeir the Goth :
Nor will I hide how Signy then spake a warning word
And did me to wit that her husband was a grim and guileful lord,
And would draw us to our undoing for envy and despite
Concerning the Sword of Odin, and for dread of the Volsung might.
Now wise is Signy my daughter and knoweth nought but sooth :
Yet are there seasons and times when for longing and self-ruth
The hearts of women wander, and this maybe **is such ;**
Nor for her word of Siggeir will **I trow it overmuch,**
Nor altogether doubt it, since the woman is wrought so wise ;
Nor **much** might my heart love Siggeir for all his kingly guise.
Yet, shall a king hear murder when a king's mouth blessing saith ?
So maybe he is bidding me honour, and maybe he is bidding me death :
Let him do after his fashion, and I will do no less.
In peace will I go to his bidding let the spae-wrights ban or bless ;
And no man now or hereafter of Volsung's blenching shall tell.
But ye, sons, in the land shall tarry, and heed the realm right well,
Lest **the** Volsung Children fade, and the wide world worser grow."

But with one voice cried all men, that they one and all would go
To gather the Goth-king's honour, or let one fate go over all
If he bade them to battle and murder, till each by each should fall.
So spake the sons of his body, and the **wise in** wisdom and war.
Nor yet might it otherwise be, though Volsung bade full sore
That he go in some ship of the merchants with his life alone in his hand ;
With such love he loved his kindred, and the people of his land.

But at last he said :

     "So be it ; for in vain I war with fate,
Who can raise up a king from the dunghill and make the feeble great.
We will go, a band of friends, and be merry whatever **shall come,**
And the Gods, mine own forefathers, shall take counsel of our **home.**"

So now, when all things were ready, in the first **of the autumn tide**
Adown unto the swan-bath the Volsung Children ride ;
And lightly go a shipboard, a goodly company,
Though the tale thereof **be scanty and their ships no more than three** :
But kings' sons dealt with the sail-sheets and **earls and dukes of war**
Were the halers of the hawsers and the tuggers at the oar.
So they drew the bridges shipward, and left the land behind,
And fair astern of the longships sprang up **a following wind ;**
So swift o'er Ægir's acre those mighty sailors ran,
And speedier than all other ploughed down the furrows wan.
And they came to the land of the Goth-folk on the even **of a day ;**
And lo by the inmost skerry a skiff with a sail of grey
That as they neared the foreshore ran Volsung's ship **aboard,**
And there was come white-hand Signy with her latest warning word.

"O strange," she said, "**meseemeth, O sweet, your gear to see,**
And the well-loved Volsung faces, **and the hands that cherished me.**
But short is the time that is left **me for the work I have to win,**
Though nought it be but the speaking of a word ere the worst begin.
For that which I spake aforetime, the seed of a boding drear,
It hath sprung, **it** hath blossomed and born rank harvest of the spear ;
Siggeir hath dight the death-snare ; he hath spread the **shielded net.**
But ye come ere the hour appointed, and he looks not to **meet you yet.**
Now blest be the wind that wafted your sails here **over-soon,**
For thus have I won me seaward 'twixt the twilight **and** the moon,
To pray you for all the world's sake turn back from the murderous shore.
—**Ah** take me hence, my **father,** to see my land **once more !**"

Then sweetly Volsung kissed her : "**Woe am I for thy sake,**
But earth the word hath hearkened, that yet unborn I spake ;
How I ne'er would turn me backward from the sword or the fire of bale ;
—I have held that word till today, and today shall I change the tale ?
And look on these thy brethren, how goodly and great are they,
Wouldst thou have the maidens mock them, when this pain **hath** past away
And they sit at the feast hereafter, that they feared the deadly stroke ?
Let us do our day's work deftly for the praise and the glory of folk ;
And **if the** Norns will have it that the Volsung kin shall fail,
Yet I know of the deed that dies not, and the name that shall ever avail."

But she wept as one sick-hearted : "Woe's me for the hope of the morn !
Yet send me not back unto Siggeir and the evil days and the scorn :
Let me bide the death as ye bide it, and let a woman feel
That hope of the death of battle and the **rest of the** foeman's steel."

"**Nay nay,**" he said, "go backward : **this too** thy fate will **have ;**
For **thou art** the wife of a king, and many a matter may'st save.
Farewell ! as the days win over, as sweet as a tale shall it grow,
This day when our hearts were hardened ; and our glory thou shalt know,
And the love wherewith we loved thee mid the battle and the wrack."

She kissed them and departed, and mid the dusk fared back,
And she **sat** that eve in the high-seat ; and I deem that Siggeir knew
The way that **her feet had wended,** and the deed she went to do :
For the man was grim and guileful, and he knew that the snare was laid
For the mountain bull unblenching and the lion unafraid.

But when the sun on the morrow shone over earth and sea
Ashore went the Volsung Children a goodly company,
And toward King Siggeir's dwelling o'er heath and holt they went.
But when they came to the topmost of a certain grassy bent,
Lo there lay the land before them as thick with shield and spear

As the rich man's wealthiest acre with the harvest of the year.
There bade King Volsung tarry and dight the wedge-array;
"For duly," he said, "doeth Siggeir to meet his guests by the way.
So shield by shield they serried, nor ever hath been **told**
Of any host of battle more glorious with the gold;
And there stood the high King Volsung in the very **front of war**;
And lovelier was his visage than ever heretofore,
As he rent apart the peace-strings that his brand of battle bound
And the bright blade gleamed **to the heavens, and he cast the sheath to the**
[ground.

Then up the steep came the Goth-folk, and the **spear-wood drew** anigh,
And earth's face shook beneath them, yet cried they **never a cry;**
And the Volsungs stood all silent, although forsooth at whiles
O'er the faces grown earth-weary would play the flickering smiles,
And swords would clink and rattle: not long **had they to bide,**
For soon that flood of murder flowed round the hillock-side;
Then at last the edges mingled, and if men forebore the shout,
Yet the din of steel and iron in the grey clouds rang about;
But how to tell of King Volsung, and the valour of his folk!
Three times the wood of battle before their edges broke;
And the shield-wall, sorely dwindled and reft of the ruddy gold,
Against the drift of the war-blast for the fourth time yet did **hold.**
But men's shields were waxen heavy with **the weight of shafts they bore,**
And **the** fifth time many a champion cast earthward Odin's door
And gripped the sword two-handed; and in sheaves the spears came on.
And at last the host of the Goth-folk within the shield-wall won,
And wild **was** the work within it, and oft and o'er again
Forth brake **the** sons of Volsung, **and drave** the foe in vain;
For the driven throng still thickened, till it might not give aback.
But fast abode King Volsung amid the shifting wrack
In the place where once was **the forefront:** for he said: "My feet are old,
And if I wend on further there is nought more to behold
Than this that I see about me."—Whiles drew his foes away

C

And stared across the corpses that before his sword-edge lay.
But nought he followed after : then needs must they in front
Thrust on by the thickening spear-throng come up to bear the brunt,
Till all his limbs were weary and his body rent and torn :
Then he cried : " Lo now, Allfather, is not the swathe well shorn ?
Wouldst thou have me toil for ever, nor win the wages due ?"

And mid the hedge of foemen his blunted sword he threw,
And, laid like the oars of a longship the level war-shafts pressed
On 'gainst the unshielded elder, and clashed amidst his breast,
And dead he fell, thrust backward, and rang on the dead men's gear :
But still for a certain season durst no man draw anear.
For 'twas e'en as a great God's slaying, and they feared the wrath of the sky ;
And they deemed their hearts might harden if awhile they should let him lie.

Lo, now as the plotting was long, so short is the tale to tell
How a mighty people's leaders in the field of murder fell.
For but feebly burned the battle when Volsung fell to field,
And all who yet were living were borne down before the shield :
So sinketh the din and the tumult ; and the earls of the Goths ring round
That crown of the Kings of battle laid low upon the ground,
Looking up to the noon-tide heavens from the place where first he stood :
But the songful sing above him and they tell how his end is as good
As the best of the days of his life-tide ; and well as he was loved
By his friends ere the time of his changing, so now are his foemen moved
With a love that may never be worsened, since all the strife is o'er,
And the warders look for his coming by Odin's open door.

But his sons, the stay of battle, alive with many a wound,
Borne down to the earth by the shield-rush amid the dead lie bound,
And belike a wearier journey must those lords of battle bide
Ere once more in the Hall of Odin they sit by their father's side.
Woe's me for the boughs of the Branstock and the hawks that cried on the fight !

Woe's me for the fireless hearthstones and the hangings of delight,
That the women dare not look on lest they see them sweat with blood !
Woe's me for the carven pillars where the spears of the Volsungs stood !
And who next shall shake the locks, or the silver door-rings meet ?
Who shall pace the floor beloved, worn down by the Volsung feet ?
Who shall fill the gold with the wine, or cry for the triumphing ?
Shall it be kindred or foes, or thief, or thrall, or king ?

Of the ending of all Volsung's Sons save Sigmund only, and of how he
abideth in the wild wood.

So there the earls of the Goth-folk lay Volsung 'neath the grass
On the last earth he had trodden ; but his children bound must pass,
When the host is gathered together, amidst of their array
To the high-built dwelling of Siggeir ; for sooth it is to say,
That he came not into the battle, nor faced the Volsung sword.

So now as he sat in his high-seat there came his chiefest lord,
And he said : " I bear thee tidings of the death of the best of the brave,
For thy foes are slain or bondsmen ; and have thou Sigmund's glaive,
If a token thou desirest ; and that shall be surely enough.
And I do thee to wit, King Siggeir, that the road was exceeding rough,
And that many an earl there stumbled, who shall evermore lie down.
And indeed I deem King Volsung for all earthly kingship's crown."

Then never a word spake Siggeir, save : " Where be Volsung's sons ? "
And he said : " Without are they fettered, those battle-glorious ones :
And methinks 'twere a deed for a king, and a noble deed for thee,
To break their bonds and heal them, and send them back o'er the sea,
And abide their wrath and the bloodfeud for this matter of Volsung's slaying.'

" Witless thou waxest," said Siggeir, " nor heedest the wise man's saying ;

' Slay thou the wolf by the house-door, lest he slay thee in the wood.'
Yet since I am the overcomer, and my days henceforth shall be good,
I will quell them with no death-pains ; let the young men smite them down,
But let me not behold them when my heart is angrier grown."

E'en as he uttered the word was Signy at the door,
And with hurrying feet she gat her apace to the high-seat floor,
As wan as the dawning-hour, though never a tear she had
And she cried: " I pray thee, Siggeir, now thine heart is merry and glad
With the death and the bonds of my kinsmen, to grant me this one prayer,
This one time and no other ; let them breathe the earthly air
For a day, for a day or twain, ere they wend the way of death,
For 'sweet to eye while seen,' the elders' saying saith."

Quoth he : " Thou art mad with sorrow ; wilt thou work thy friends this woe ?
When swift and untormented e'en I would let them go :
Yet now shalt thou have thine asking, if it verily is thy will :
Nor forsooth do I begrudge them a longer tide of ill."

She said : " I will it, I will it—O sweet to eye while seen !"

Then to his earl spake Siggeir : " There lies a wood-lawn green
In the first mile of the forest ; there fetter these Volsung men
To the mightiest beam of the wild-wood, till Queen Signy come again
And pray me a boon for her brethren, the end of their latter life."

So the Goth-folk led to the woodland those gleanings of the strife,
And smote down a great-boled oak-tree, the mightiest they might find,
And thereto with bonds of iron the Volsungs did they bind,
And left them there on the wood-lawn, mid the yew-trees' compassing,
And went back by the light of the moon to the dwelling of the king.

But he sent on the morn of the morrow to see how his foemen fared,

For now as he thought thereover, o'ermuch he deemed it dared
That he saw not the last of the Volsungs laid dead before his feet.
Back came his men ere the noontide, and he deemed their tidings sweet;
For they said: "We tell thee, King Siggeir, that Geirmund and Gylfi are gone.
And we deem that a beast of the wild-wood this murder grim hath done,
For the bones yet lie in the fetters gnawed fleshless now and white;
But we deemed the eight abiding sore minished of their might."

So wore the morn and the noontide, and the even 'gan to fall,
And watchful eyes held Signy at home in bower and hall.

And again came the men in the morning, and spake: "The hopples hold
The bare white bones of Helgi, and the bones of Solar the bold:
And the six that abide seem feebler than they were awhile ago."

Still all the day and the night-tide must Signy nurse her woe
About the house of King Siggeir, nor any might she send:
And again came the tale on the morrow: "Now are two more come to an end.
For Hunthiof dead and Gunthiof, their bones lie side by side,
And the four that are left, us seemeth, no long while will abide."

O woe for the well-watched Signy, how often on that day
Must she send her helpless eyen adown the woodland way!
Yet silent in her bosom she held her heart of flame.
And again on the morrow morning the tale was still the same:

"We tell thee now, King Siggeir, that all will soon be done;
For the two last men of the Volsungs, they sit there one by one,
And Sigi's head is drooping, but somewhat Sigmund sings;
For the man was a mighty warrior, and a beater down of kings.
But for Rerir and for Agnar, the last of them is said,
Their bones in the bonds are abiding, but their souls and lives are sped."

That day from **the eyes** of the watchers nought Signy strove to depart,
But ever she sat in the high-seat **and nursed the** flame in **her** heart.
In the sight of all people she **sat, with** unmoved face and wan,
And to no man gave she a word, nor looked on any man.
Then the dusk and the dark drew **over, but** stirred she never a whit,
And the word of Siggeir's sending, she gave no heed to it.
And there on the morrow morning must he sit him down by her side,
When unto the council of elders folk came from far and wide.
And there came Siggeir's woodmen, and their voice in the hall arose:

"There is no man left **on** the tree-beam : **some** beast hath devoured thy foes ;
There is nought left there but the **bones, and the** bonds that the Volsungs
[bound."
No word spake the earls of the Goth-folk, but the hall rang out with a sound,
With the wail and the cry of Signy, as she stood upright on her **feet,**
And thrust all people from her, and fled to **her** bower as fleet
As the hind **when she first is smitten ; and** her maidens **fled away,**
Fearing her face and her eyen : **no** less at the death of the day
She rose up amid the silence, **and** went her ways alone,
And no man watched her or hindered, **for** they deemed the story done.
So she **went 'twixt** the yellow acres, **and** the green meads of the sheep,
And or ever she reached the wild-wood the night was waxen **deep**
No man **she had to lead her, but** the path was trodden well
By those messengers **of murder,** the men with the tale to tell ;
And the beams of the high white moon gave a glimmering day through night
Till she came where **that lawn of the woods** lay **wide in** the flood of light.
Then she looked, and **lo, in** its midmost a mighty man there stood,
And laboured the earth of the green-sward with a truncheon torn from the wood;
And behold, it was Sigmund the Volsung : but she cried and had no fear :

" **If thou** art living, Sigmund, what **day's work** dost thou **here**
In the midnight and the forest ? **but** if thou art nought but a ghost,
Then where are those Volsung brethren, of whom thou wert best and most ?"

Then he turned about unto her, and his raiment was fouled and torn,
And his eyen were great and hollow, as a famished man forlorn ;

But he cried : " Hail, Sister Signy ! I looked for thee before,
Though what should a woman compass, she one alone and no more,
When all we shielded Volsungs did nought in Siggeir's land ?
O yea, I am living indeed, and this labour of mine hand
Is to bury the bones of the Volsungs ; and lo, it is well-nigh done.
So draw near, Volsung's daughter, and pile we many a stone
Where lie the grey wolf's gleanings of what was once so good."

So she set her hand to the labour, and they toiled, they twain in the wood
And when the work was over, dead night was beginning to fail :
Then spake the white-hand Signy : " Now shalt thou tell the tale
Of the death of the Volsung brethren ere the wood thy wrath shall hide,
Ere I wend me back sick-hearted in the dwelling of kings to abide."

He said : " We sat on the tree, and well ye may wot indeed
That we had some hope from thy good-will amidst that bitter need.
Now none had 'scaped the sword-edge in the battle utterly,
And so hurt were Agnar and Helgi, that, unhelped, they were like to die ;
Though for that we deemed them happier : but now when the moon shone bright,
And when by a doomed man's deeming 'twas the midmost of the night,
Lo, forth from yonder thicket were two mighty wood-wolves come,
Far huger wrought to my deeming than the beasts I knew at home :
Forthright on Gylfi and Geirmund those dogs of the forest fell,
And what of men so hoppled should be the tale to tell ?
They tore them midst the irons, and slew them then and there,
And long we heard them snarling o'er that abundant cheer.
Night after night, O my sister, the story was the same,
And still from the dark and the thicket the wild-wood were-wolves came
And slew two men of the Volsungs whom the sword edge might not end.
And every day in the dawning did the King's own woodmen wend

To behold those craftsmen's carving and rejoice King Siggeir's heart.
And so was come last midnight, when I must play my part :
Forsooth when those first were murdered my heart was as blood and fire ;
And I deemed that my bonds must burst with my uttermost desire
To free my naked hands, that the vengeance might be wrought ;
But now was I wroth with the Gods, that had made the Volsungs for nought
And I said : in the Day of their Doom a man's help shall they miss ;
I will be as a wolf of the forest, if their kings must come to this ;
Or if Siggeir indeed be their king, and their envy has brought it about
That dead in the dust lies Volsung, while the last of his seed dies out.
Therewith from out the thicket the grey wolves drew anigh,
And the he-wolf fell on Sigi, but he gave forth never a cry,
And I saw his lips that they smiled, and his steady eyes for a space ;
And therewith was the she-wolf's muzzle thrust into my very face.
The Gods helped not, but I helped ; and I too grew wolfish then ;
Yea I, who have borne the sword-hilt high mid the kings of men,
I, lord of the golden harness, the flame of the Glittering Heath,
Must snarl to the she-wolf's snarling, and snap with greedy teeth.
While my hands with the hand-bonds struggled ; my teeth took hold the first
And amid her mighty writhing the bonds that bound me burst,
As with Fenrir's Wolf it shall be : then the beast with the hopples I smote,
When my left hand stiff with the bonds had got her by the throat.
But I turned when I had slain her, and there lay Sigi dead,
And once more to the night of the forest the fretting wolf had fled.
In the thicket I hid till the dawning, and thence I saw the men,
E'en Siggeir's heart-rejoicers, come back to the place again
To gather the well-loved tidings : I looked and I knew for sooth
How hate had grown in my bosom and the death of my days of ruth :
Though unslain they departed from me, lest Siggeir come to doubt.
But hereafter, yea hereafter, they that turned the world about,
And raised Hell's abode o'er God-home, and mocked all men-folk's worth—
Shall my hand turn back or falter, while these abide on earth,
Because I once was a child, and sat on my father's knees ;

But long methinks shall Siggeir bide merrily at ease
In the high-built house of the Goths, with his shielded earls around,
His warders of day and of night-tide, and his world of peopled ground,
While his foe is a swordless outcast, a hunted beast of the wood,
A wolf of the holy places, where men-folk gather for good.
And didst thou think, my sister, when we sat in our summer bliss
Beneath the boughs of the Branstock, that the world was like to this?"

As the moon and the twilight mingled, she stood with kindling eyes,
And answered and said: "My brother, thou art strong, and thou shalt be wise:
I am nothing so wroth as thou art with the ways of death and hell,
For thereof had I a deeming when all things were seeming well.
In sooth overlong it may linger; the children of murder shall thrive,
While thy work is a weight for thine heart, and a toil for thy hand to drive;
But I wot that the King of the Goth-folk for his deeds shall surely pay,
And that I shall live to see it: but thy wrath shall pass away,
And long shalt thou live on the earth an exceeding glorious king,
And thy words shall be told in the market, and all men of thy deeds shall sing:
Fresh shall thy memory be, and thine eyes like mine shall gaze
On the day unborn in the darkness, the last of all earthly days,
The last of the days of battle, when the host of the Gods is arrayed
And there is an end for ever of all who were once afraid.
There as thou drawest thy sword, thou shalt think of the days that were,
And the foul shall still seem foul, and the fair shall still seem fair;
But thy wit shall then be awakened, and thou shalt know indeed
Why the brave man's spear is broken, and his war-shield fails at need;
Why the loving is unbelovèd; why the just man falls from his state;
Why the liar gains in a day what the soothfast strives for late.
Yea, and thy deeds shalt thou know, and great shall thy gladness be;
As a picture all of gold thy life-days shalt thou see,
And know that thou too wert a God to abide through the hurry and haste;
A God in the golden hall, a God on the rain-swept waste,
A God in the battle triumphant, a God on the heap of the slain:

And thine hope shall arise and blossom, and thy love shall be quickened again :
And then shalt thou see before thee the face of **all earthly ill ;**
Thou shalt drink of the cup of awakening that thine hand hath **holpen to fill ;**
By the side of the sons of Odin shalt thou fashion a tale to be told
In the hall of the happy Baldur : nor there shall the tale grow old
Of the days before the changing, e'en those that over **us pass.**
So harden thine heart, O brother, and set thy brow as the brass !
Thou shalt do, and thy deeds shall be goodly, and the day's work shall be done
Though nought but the wild deer see it.   Nor yet shalt thou be alone
For ever-more in thy waiting ; **for** belike a fearful friend
The long days for thee may fashion, to help thee ere the end.
But now shalt thou bide **in the** wild-wood, and make thee a lair therein :
Thou art here in the midst of thy foemen, and from them thou well mayst win
Whatso thine heart desireth ; **yet be thou** not too bold,
Lest the tale of the wood-abider too oft **to the** king be told.
Ere many days are departed again shall **I see** thy face,
That I may wot full surely of thine abiding-place
To send thee help and comfort ; but when that hour is o'er
It were good, O last of the Volsungs, that I see thy face no more,
If so indeed it may be : but the Norns must fashion all,
And what the dawn hath fated on the hour of noon shall fall."

Then she kissed him and departed, for the day was nigh at **hand,**
And by then she had left the woodways green lay the horse-fed land
Beneath the new-born **daylight,** and as she brushed the **dew**
Betwixt the yellowing acres, all heaven o'erhead was blue.
And at last on that dwelling of Kings the golden sunlight lay,
And the morn and the noon and the even built up another day.

Of the birth and fostering of **Sinfiotli,** *Signy's* **Son.**

So wrought is **the** will of King Siggeir, and he weareth **Odin's** sword

And it lies on his knees in the council and hath no other lord :
And he sendeth earls o'er the sea-flood to take King Volsung's land,
And those scattered and shepherdless sheep must come beneath his hand.
And he holdeth the milk-white Signy as his handmaid and his wife,
And nought but his will she doeth, nor raiseth a word of strife ;
So his heart is praising his wisdom, and he deems him of most avail
Of all the lords of the cunning that teacheth how to prevail.

Now again in a half-month's wearing goes Signy into the wild,
And findeth her way by her wisdom to the dwelling of Volsung's child.
It was e'en as a house of the Dwarfs, a rock, and a stony cave,
In the heart of the midmost thicket by the hidden river's wave.
There Signy found him watching how the white-head waters ran,
And she said in her heart as she saw him that once more she had seen a man.
His words were few and heavy, for seldom his sorrow slept,
Yet ever his love went with them ; and men say that Signy wept
When she left that last of her kindred : yet wept she never more
Amid the earls of Siggeir, and as lovely as before
Was her face to all men's deeming : nor aught it changed for ruth,
Nor for fear nor any longing ; and no man said for sooth
That she ever laughed thereafter till the day of her death was come.

So is Volsung's seed abiding in a rough and narrow home ;
And wargear he gat him enough from the slaying of earls of men,
And gold as much as he would ; though indeed but now and again
He fell on the men of the merchants, lest, wax he overbold,
The tale of the wood-abider too oft to the king should be told.
Alone in the woods he abided, and a master of masters was he
In the craft of the smithying folk ; and whiles would the hunter see,
Belated amid the thicket, his forge's glimmering light,
And the boldest of all the fishers would hear his hammer benight.
Then dim waxed the tale of the Volsungs, and the word mid the wood-folk rose
That a King of the Giants had wakened from amidst the stone-hedged close,

Where they slept in the heart of the mountains, and had come adown to dwell
In the cave whence the Dwarfs were departed, and they said: It is aught but
To come anigh to his house-door, or wander wide in his woods,   [well
For a tyrannous lord he is, and a lover of gold and of goods.

So win the long years over, and still sitteth Signy there
Beside the King of the Goth-folk, and is waxen no less fair,
And men and maids hath she gotten who are ready to work her will,
For the worship of her fairness, and remembrance of her ill.

So it fell on a morn of springtide, as Sigmund sat on the sward
By that ancient house of the Dwarf-kind and fashioned a golden sword,
By the side of the hidden river he saw a damsel stand,
And a manchild of ten summers was holding by her hand.
And she cried :
        "O Forest-dweller ! harm not the child nor me,
For I bear a word of Signy's, and thus she saith to thee :
' I send thee a man to foster ; if his heart be good at need
Then may he help thy workday ; but hearken my words and heed ;
If thou deem that his heart shall avail not, thy work is over-great
That thou weary thy heart with such-like: let him wend the ways of his fate."

And no more word spake the maiden, but turned and gat her gone,
And there by the side of the river the child abode alone :
But Sigmund stood on his feet, and across the river he went,
For he knew how the child was Siggeir's, and of Signy's fell intent.
So he took the lad on his shoulder, and bade him hold his sword,
And waded back to his dwelling across the rushing ford :
But the youngling fell a prattling, and asked of this and that,
As above the rattle of waters on Sigmund's shoulder he sat !
And Sigmund deemed in his heart that the boy would be bold enough.
So he fostered him there in the woodland in life full hard and rough
For the space of three months' wearing ; and the lad was deft and strong,

Yet his sight was a grief to Sigmund because of his father's wrong.

On a morn to the son of King Siggeir Sigmund the Volsung said :
" I go to the hunting of deer, bide thou and bake our bread
Against I bring the venison."
                                        So forth he fared on his way,
And came again with the quarry about the noon of day ;
Quoth he : " Is the morn's work done?" But the boy said nought for a space,
And all white he was and quaking as he looked on Sigmund's face.

"Tell me, O Son of the Goth-king," quoth Sigmund, "how thou hast fared?
Forsooth, is the baking of bread so mighty a thing to be dared ?"

Quoth the lad : "I went to the meal-sack, and therein was something quick,
And it moved, and I feared for the serpent, like a winter ashen stick
That I saw on the stone last even : so I durst not deal with the thing."

Loud Sigmund laughed, and answered : "I have heard of that son of a king,
Who might not be scared from his bread for all the worms of the land."
And therewith he went to the meal-sack and thrust therein his hand,
And drew forth an ash-grey adder, and a deadly worm it was :
Then he went to the door of the cave and set it down in the grass,
While the King's son quaked and quivered : then he drew forth his sword from
And said :   [the sheath,
        "Now fearest thou this, that men call the serpent of death ?"

Then said the son of King Siggeir : " I am young as yet for the war,
Yet e'en such a blade shall I carry ere many a month be o'er."

Then abroad went the King in the wind, and leaned on his naked sword
And stood there many an hour, and mused on Signy's word.
But at last when the moon was arisen, and the undark night begun,
He sheathed the sword and cried : " Come forth, King Siggeir's son,

Thou shalt wend from out of the wild-wood **and no** more will I foster thee."

Forth came the son of Siggeir, and quaked his face to see,
But thereof nought Sigmund noted, but bade him wend with him.
So they went through the summer night-tide by many a wood-way dim,
Till they came to a certain wood-lawn, and Sigmund lingered there,
And spake as his feet brushed o'er it : "The June flowers blossom fair."
So they came to the skirts of the forest, and the meadows of the neat,
And the earliest wind **of** dawning blew over them soft and sweet :
There stayed Sigmund the Volsung, and said :

                    " King Siggeir's son,
Bide here till the birds are singing, and the day is well begun ;
Then go to the house of the Goth-king, **and** find thou Signy the Queen,
And tell unto no man else the things thou hast heard and seen :
But to her shalt thou tell what thou wilt, and say this word withal :
'**Mother, I come** from the wild-wood, and he saith, whatever befal
Alone will I abide there, nor have such fosterlings ;
For the sons of the Gods may help me, but never the sons of Kings.'
Go, then, with this word in thy mouth—or do thou after thy fate,
And, if thou wilt, betray me !—and repent it early and late."

Then he turned his back on the acres, and away to the woodland strode ;
But the boy scarce bided the sunrise ere he went the homeward road ;
So he came **to** the house of the Goth-kings, and spake with Signy the Queen,
Nor told he to any other the things he had heard and seen,
For the heart **of a king's son had** he.

                    But Signy hearkened his word ;
And long she pondered **and** said : What **is** it my heart hath feared ?
And how shall it be with earth's people if **the** kin of the Volsungs die,
And King Volsung unavenged in his mound by the sea-strand lie ?
I have given my best and bravest, as my heart's blood I would **give,**
And my **heart and** my fame and my body, that the name of Volsung might live.
Lo the first gift cast aback : and how shall it be with the last,—

—If I find out the gift for the giving before the hour be passed?"

Long while she mused and pondered while day was thrust on day,
Till the king and the earls of the strangers seemed shades of the dreamtide
And gone seemed all earth's people, save that woman mid the gold   [grey
And that man in the depths of the forest in the cave of the Dwarfs of old.
And once in the dark she murmured: "Where then was the ancient song
That the Gods were but twin-born once, and deemed it nothing wrong
To mingle for the world's sake, whence had the Æsir birth,
And the Vanir and the Dwarf-kind, and all the folk of earth?"

Now amidst those days that she pondered came a wife of the witch-folk there,
A woman young and lovesome, and shaped exceeding fair,
And she spake with Signy the Queen, and told her of deeds of her craft,
And how the might was with her her soul from her body to waft
And to take the shape of another and give her fashion in turn.
Fierce then in the heart of Signy a sudden flame 'gan burn,
And the eyes of her soul saw all things, like the blind, whom the world's last fire
Hath healed in one passing moment 'twixt his death and his desire.
And she thought: "Alone I will bear it; alone I will take the crime;
On me alone be the shaming, and the cry of the coming time.
Yea, and he for the life is fated and the help of many a folk,
And I for the death and the rest, and deliverance from the yoke."

Then wan as the midnight moon she answered the woman and spake:
"Thou art come to the Goth-queen's dwelling, wilt thou do so much for my
And for many a pound of silver and for rings of the ruddy gold,   [sake,
As to change thy body for mine ere the night is waxen old?"

Nought the witch-wife fair gainsaid it, and they went to the bower aloft
And hand in hand and alone they sung the spell-song soft:
Till Signy looked on her guest, and lo, the face of a queen
With the steadfast eyes of grey, that so many a grief had seen:

But the guest held forth a mirror, and Signy shrank aback
From the laughing lips and the eyes, and the hair of crispy black,
But though she shuddered and sickened, the false face changed no whit ;
But ruddy and white it blossomed and the smiles played over it ;
And the hands were ready to cling, and beckoning lamps were the eyes,
And the light feet longed for the dance, and the lips for laughter and lies.

So that eve in the mid-hall's high-seat was the shape of Signy the Queen,
While swiftly the feet of the witch-wife brushed over the moonlit green,
But the soul mid the gleam of the torches, her thought was of gain and of gold ;
And the soul of the wind-driven woman, swift-foot in the moonlight cold,
Her thoughts were of men's lives' changing, and the uttermost ending of earth,
And the day when death should be dead, and the new sun's nightless birth.

Men say that about that midnight King Sigmund wakened and heard
The voice of a soft-speeched woman, shrill-sweet as a dawning bird :
So he rose, and a woman indeed he saw by the door of the cave
With her raiment wet to her midmost, as though with the river-wave :
And he cried : "What wilt thou, what wilt thou ? be thou womankind or fay,
Here is no good abiding, wend forth upon thy way !"

She said : " I am nought but a woman, a maid of the earl-folk's kin :
And I went by the skirts of the woodland to the house of my sister to win,
And have strayed from the way benighted : and I fear the wolves and the wild
By the glimmering of thy torchlight from afar was I beguiled.
Ah, slay me not on thy threshold, nor send me back again
Through the rattling waves of thy ford, that I crossed in terror and pain ;
Drive me not to the night and the darkness, for the wolves of the wood to
I am weak and thou art mighty : I will go at the dawning hour."   [devour.

So Sigmund looked in her face and saw that she was fair ;
And he said : "Nay, nought will I harm thee, and thou mayst harbour here,
God wot if thou fear'st not me, I have nought to fear thy face :

Though this house be the terror of men-folk, thou shalt find it as safe a place
As though I were nought but thy brother; and then mayst thou tell, if thou wilt,
Where **dwelleth the dread** of the woodland, the bearer **of many a guilt,**
Though meseems for so goodly a woman it were all too ill a deed
In reward for the wood-wight's guesting to betray him in his need."

So he took the hand of the woman and **straightway led her in**
Where days agone the Dwarf-kind would their deeds of smithying win:
And he kindled the half-slaked embers, and gave her **of his cheer**
Amid **the gold and the** silver, and the fight-won raiment **dear;**
And soft was her voice, and she sung him **sweet tales of yore agone,**
Till **all his heart was softened;** and the man was all **alone,**
And in many wise she wooed him; **so they parted not that night,**
Nor slept till **the** morrow morning, when **the woods were waxen** bright
And high above the tree-boughs shone the **sister of** the moon,
And hushed were the water-ouzels with the coming of the noon
When she stepped from the bed of Sigmund, and left the Dwarf's abode;
And turned to the dwellings of men, and the ways **where the** earl-folk rode.
But **next morn from** the **house of** the Goth-king **the witch-wife went** her ways
With gold and goods and **silver, such store as a queen might praise.**

But no long while with Sigmund dwelt **remembrance of that night;**
Amid his kingly longings and his many deeds of might
It fled like the dove in the forest or the down upon the **blast:**
Yet heavy and sad were the years, **that** even in suchwise passed,
As here **it is written** aforetime.
                              Thence were ten years **worn by**
When unto that hidden river a man-child drew anigh,
And he looked **and** beheld how **Sigmund wrought on a helm** of gold
By the crag and **the** stony dwelling where the Dwarf-kin wrought of old.
Then the boy cried: "Thou art **the** wood-wight of whom my mother spake;
Now will I come to thy dwelling."
                              So the rough stream did he take,

And the welter of the waters rose up to his chin and more;
But so stark and strong he waded that he won the further shore:
And he came and gazed on Sigmund: but the Volsung laughed, and said:
" As fast thou runnest toward me as others in their dread
Run over the land and the water: what wilt thou, son of a king?"

But the lad still gazed on Sigmund, and he said: " A wondrous thing!
Here is the cave and the river, and all tokens of the place:
But my mother Signy told me none might behold that face,
And keep his flesh from quaking: but at thee I quake not aught:
Sure I must journey further, lest her errand come to nought:
Yet I would that my foster-father should be such a man as thou."

But Sigmund answered and said: " Thou shalt bide in my dwelling now;
And thou mayst wot full surely that thy mother's will is done
By this token and no other, that thou lookedst on Volsung's son
And smiledst fair in his face: but tell me thy name and thy years:
And what are the words of Signy that the son of the Goth-king bears?"

" Sinfiotli they call me," he said, " and ten summers have I seen;
And this is the only word that I bear from Signy the Queen,
That once more a man she sendeth the work of thine hands to speed,
If he be of the Kings or the Gods thyself shalt know in thy need."

So Sigmund looked on the youngling and his heart unto him yearned;
But he thought: "Shall I pay the hire ere the worth of the work be earned?
And what hath my heart to do to cherish Siggeir's son;
A brand belike for the burning when the last of its work is done?"

But there in the wild and the thicket those twain awhile abode,
And on the lad laid Sigmund full many a weary load,
And thrust him mid all dangers, and he bore all passing well,
Where hardihood might help him; but his heart was fierce and fell;

And ever said Sigmund the Volsung: The lad hath plenteous part
In the guile and malice of Siggeir, and in Signy's hardy heart:
But why should I cherish and love him, since the end must come at last?

Now a summer and winter and spring o'er those men of the wilds had pass'd,
And summer was there again, when the Volsung spake on a day:
"I will wend to the wood-deer's hunting, but thou at home shalt stay,
And deal with the baking of bread against the even come."

So he went and came on the hunting and brought the venison home,
And the child, as ever his wont was, was glad of his coming back,
And said: "Thou hast gotten us venison, and the bread shall nowise lack."

"Yea," quoth Sigmund the Volsung, "hast thou kneaded the meal that was
                                                           [yonder?"
"Yea, and what other?" he said; "though therein forsooth was a wonder:
For when I would handle the meal-sack therein was something quick,
As if the life of an eel-grig were set in an ashen stick:
But the meal must into the oven, since we were lacking bread,
And all that is kneaded together, and the wonder is baked and dead."

Then Sigmund laughed and answered: "Thou hast kneaded up therein
The deadliest of all adders that is of the creeping kin:
So tonight from the bread refrain thee, lest thy bane should come of it."

For here, the tale of the elders doth men a marvel to wit,
That such was the shaping of Sigmund among all earthly kings,
That unhurt he handled adders and other deadly things,
And might drink unscathed of venom: but Sinfiotli so was wrought,
That no sting of creeping creatures would harm his body aught.

But now full glad was Sigmund, and he let his love arise
For the huge-limbed son of Signy with the fierce and eager eyes;

And all deeds of the sword he learned him, and showed him feats of war
Where sea and forest mingle, and up from the ocean's shore
The highway leads to the market, and men go up and down,
And the spear-hedged wains of the merchants fare oft to the Goth-folk's town.
Sweet then Sinfiotli deemed it to look on the bale-fires' light,
And the bickering blood-reeds' tangle, and the fallow blades of fight.
And in three years' space were his war-deeds far more than the deeds of a man:
But dread was his face to behold ere the battle-play began,
And grey and dreadful his face when the last of the battle sank.
And so the years won over, and the joy of the woods they drank,
And they gathered gold and silver, and plenteous outland goods.

But they came to a house on a day in the uttermost part of the woods
And smote on the door and entered, when a long while no man bade;
And lo, a gold-hung hall, and two men on the benches laid
In slumber as deep as the death; and gold rings great and fair
Those sleepers bore on their bodies, and broidered southland gear,
And over the head of each there hung a wolf-skin grey.

Then the drift of a cloudy dream wrapt Sigmund's soul away,
And his eyes were set on the wolf-skin, and long he gazed thereat,
And remembered the words he uttered when erst on the beam he sat,
That the Gods should miss a man in the utmost Day of Doom,
And win a wolf in his stead; and unto his heart came home
That thought, as he gazed on the wolf-skin and the other days waxed dim,
And he gathered the thing in his hand, and did it over him;
And in likewise did Sinfiotli as he saw his fosterer do.
Then lo, a fearful wonder, for as very wolves they grew
In outward shape and semblance, and they howled out wolfish things,
Like the grey dogs of the forest; though somewhat the hearts of kings
Abode in their bodies of beasts. Now sooth is the tale to tell,
That the men in the fair-wrought raiment were kings' sons bound by a spell
To wend as wolves of the wild-wood, for each nine days of the ten,

And to lie all spent for a season when they gat their shapes of men.

So Sigmund and his fellow rush forth from the golden place;
And though their kings' hearts bade them the backward way to trace
Unto their Dwarf-wrought dwelling, and there abide the change,
Yet their wolfish habit drave them wide through the wood to range,
And draw nigh to the dwellings of men and fly upon the prey.

And lo now, a band of hunters on the uttermost woodland way,
And they spy those dogs of the forest, and fall on with the spear,
Nor deemed that any other but woodland beasts they were,
And that easy would be the battle : short is the tale to tell ;
For every man of the hunters amid the thicket fell.

Then onwards fare those were-wolves, and unto the sea they turn,
And their ravening hearts are heavy, and sore for the prey they yearn :
And lo, in the last of the thicket a score of the chaffering men,
And Sinfiotli was wild for the onset, but Sigmund was wearying then
For the glimmering gold of his Dwarf-house, and he bade refrain from the folk,
But wrath burned in the eyes of Sinfiotli, and forth from the thicket he broke ;
Then rose the axes aloft, and the swords flashed bright in the sun,
And but little more it needed that the race of the Volsungs was done,
And the folk of the Gods' begetting : but at last they quelled the war,
And no man again of the sea-folk should ever sit by the oar.

Now Sinfiotli fay weary and faint, but Sigmund howled over the dead,
And wrath in his heart there gathered, and a dim thought wearied his head
And his tangled wolfish wit, that might never understand ;
As though some God in his dreaming had wasted the work of his hand,
And forgotten his craft of creation ; then his wrath swelled up amain
And he turned and fell on Sinfiotli, who had wrought the wrack and the bane.
And across the throat he tore him as his very mortal foe
Till a cold dead corpse by the sea-strand his fosterling lay alow :

Then wearier yet grew Sigmund, and the dim wit seemed to pass
From his heart grown cold and feeble; when lo, amid the grass
There came two weazles bickering, and one bit his mate by the head,
Till she lay there dead before him: then he sorrowed over her dead:
But no long while he abode there, but into the thicket he went,
And the wolfish heart of Sigmund knew somewhat his intent:
So he came again with a herb-leaf and laid it on his mate,
And she rose up whole and living and no worser of estate
Than ever she was aforetime, and the twain went merry away.

Then swiftly rose up Sigmund from where his fosterling lay,
And a long while searched the thicket, till that three-leaved herb he found,
And he laid it on Sinfiotli, who rose up hale and sound
As ever he was in his life-days.   But now in hate they had
That hapless work of the witch-folk, and the skins that their bodies clad.
So they turn their faces homeward and a weary way they go,
Till they come to the hidden river, and the glimmering house they know.

There now they abide in peace, and wend abroad no more
Till the last of the nine days perished, and the spell for a space was o'er,
And they might cast their wolf-shapes: so they stood on their feet upright
Great men again as aforetime, and they came forth into the light
And looked in each other's faces, and belike a change was there
Since they did on the bodies of wolves, and lay in the wood-wolves' lair,
And they looked, and sore they wondered, and they both for speech did yearn.

First then spake out Sinfiotli: "Sure I had a craft to learn,
And thou hadst a lesson to teach, that I left the dwelling of kings,
And came to the wood-wolves' dwelling; thou hast taught me many things
But the Gods have taught me more, and at last have abased us both,
That of nought that lieth before us our hearts and our hands may be loth.
Come then, how long shall I tarry till I fashion something great?
Come, Master, and make me a master that I do the deeds of fate."

Heavy was **Sigmund's visage** but fierce did his eyen glow,
" This is the deed of thy mastery ;—we twain shall slay my foe—
And how **if the foe were thy** father ?"—
Then he telleth him Siggeir's tale :
And saith : " Now think upon it ; how shall thine heart avail
To bear the curse that cometh if thy life endureth long—
The man that slew his father and amended wrong with **wrong ?**
Yet if the Gods have made thee a man unlike all men,
(For thou startest not, nor palest), can I forbear it then,
To use the thing they **have fashioned lest** the Volsung seed should **die**
And unavenged **King Volsung in** his mound by **the sea-strand lie ?"**

Then loud laughed out Sinfiotli, and he said : **" I wot indeed**
That Signy **is my** mother, and her will I help **at need :**
Is **the fox of the** King-folk **my father,** that adder of the brake,
Who gave me never a blessing, and many a cursing spake ?
Yea, have I in sooth a father, save him that cherished my life,
The Lord of the Helm of Terror, the King of **the Flame of Strife ?**
Lo now my hand **is ready to strike what stroke** thou wilt,
For I am the sword of the Gods : and **thine hand shall hold the hilt."**

Fierce glowed the eyes of King Sigmund, for **he knew the time was come**
When the curse King Siggeir fashioned at **last shall seek him home :**
And of what shall **follow after, be it** evil days, or bliss,
Or praise, or the cursing of all men,—the Gods shall see **to this.**

Of the slaying of Siggeir the Goth-king.

So there are those kings abiding, **and they think of nought but the day**
When the time at last shall serve them, to wend on the perilous way.
And so in the first of winter, when nights grow long and mirk,
They fare unto Siggeir's dwelling and seek wherein **to lurk.**

And by hap 'twas the tide of twilight, ere the watch of the night was set
And the watch of the day was departed, as Sinfiotli minded yet.
So now by a passage he wotted they gat them into the bower
Where lay the biggest wine-tuns, and there they abode the hour:
Anigh to the hall it was, but no man came thereto,
But now and again the cup-lord when King Siggeir's wine he drew:
Yea and so nigh to the feast-hall, that they saw the torches shine
When the cup-lord was departed with King Siggeir's dear-bought wine,
And they heard the glee of the people, and the horns and the beakers' din,
When the feast was dight in the hall and the earls were merry therein.
Calm was the face of Sigmund, and clear were his eyes and bright;
But Sinfiotli gnawed on his shield-rim, and his face was haggard and white:
For he deemed the time full long, ere the fallow blades should leap
In the hush of the midnight feast-hall o'er King Siggeir's golden sleep.

Now it fell that two little children, Queen Signy's youngest-born,
Were about the hall that even, and amid the glee of the horn
They played with a golden toy, and trundled it here and there,
And thus to that lurking-bower they drew exceeding near,
When there fell a ring from their toy, and swiftly rolled away
And into the place of the wine-tuns, and by Sigmund's feet made stay;
Then the little ones followed after, and came to the lurking-place
Where lay those night-abiders, and met them face to face,
And fled, ere they might hold them, aback to the thronging hall.

Then leapt those twain to their feet lest the sword and the murder fall
On their hearts in their narrow lair and they die without a stroke;
But e'en as they met the torch-light and the din and tumult of folk,
Lo there on the very threshold did Signy the Volsung stand,
And one of her last-born children she had on either hand;
For the children had cried: "We have seen them—those two among the wine,
And their hats are wide and white, and their garments tinkle and shine."
So while men ran to their weapons, those children Signy took,

And went to meet her kinsmen : then once more did Sigmund look
On the face of his father's daughter, and kind of heart he grew,
As the clash of the coming battle anigh the doomed men drew :
But **wan and** fell was Signy ; and she cried :

" **The end is near !**

—And thou with the smile on thy face and the joyful eyes and clear !
But with these thy two betrayers first stain the edge of fight,
For why should the fruit of my body **outlive** my soul tonight ?"

But he cried in the front of the spear-hedge ; " Nay this shall be far from **me**
To slay thy children sackless, though my death belike they be.
Now men will be dealing, sister, and old the night is grown,
And **fair in the** house of my fathers the benches **are bestrown."**

So she stood aside and gazed : but Sinfiotli taketh **them up**
And breaketh each tender body as a drunkard breaketh a cup ;
With a dreadful voice he crieth, and casteth them down the hall,
And the Goth-folk sunder before them, and at Siggeir's **feet they fall.**

But the fallow blades leapt naked, and on the battle came,
As the tide of the winter ocean sweeps up to the beaconing **flame.**
But firm in the midst of onset Sigmund the Volsung stood,
And stirred no more for the sword-**strokes than the oldest oak of the wood**
Shall shake to the herd-boys' whittles : white danced his war-flame's gleam,
And oft to men's beholding his eyes of God would **beam**
Clear from the sword-blades' tangle, and often for a space
Amazed the garth of murder stared deedless on his face ;
Nor back nor forward moved he : but fierce Sinfiotli **went**
Where the spears were set the thickest, and sword **with sword was blent ;**
And great was the death before him, till he slipped in the blood and fell :
Then the shield-garth compassed Sigmund, and short is the tale to tell ;
For they bore him down unwounded, and bonds about him cast :
Nor sore hurt is Sinfiotli, but is hoppled strait and fast.

Then the Goth-folk went to slumber when the hall was washed from blood:
But a long while wakened Siggeir, for fell and fierce was his mood,
And all the days of his kingship seemed nothing worth as then
While fared the son of Volsung as well as the worst of men,
While yet that son of Signy lay untormented there:
Yea the past days of his kingship seemed blossomless and bare
Since all their might had failed him to quench the Volsung kin.

So when the first grey dawning a new day did begin,
King Siggeir bade his bondsmen to dight an earthen mound
Anigh to the house of the Goth-kings amid the fruit-grown ground:
And that house of death was twofold, for 'twas sundered by a stone
Into two woeful chambers: alone and not alone
Those vanquished thralls of battle therein should bide their hour,
That each might hear the tidings of the other's baleful bower,
Yet have no might to help him. So now the twain they brought
And weary-dull was Sinfiotli, with eyes that looked at nought.
But Sigmund fresh and clear-eyed went to the deadly hall,
And the song arose within him as he sat within its wall;
Nor aught durst Siggeir mock him, as he had good will to do,
But went his ways when the bondmen brought the roofing turfs thereto.

And that was at eve of the day; and lo now, Signy the white
Wan-faced and eager-eyed stole through the beginning of night
To the place where the builders built, and the thralls with lingering hands
Had roofed in the grave of Sigmund and hidden the glory of lands,
But over the head of Sinfiotli for a space were the rafters bare.
Gold then to the thralls she gave, and promised them days full fair
If they held their peace for ever of the deed that then she did:
And nothing they gainsayed it; so she drew forth something hid,
In wrappings of wheat-straw winded, and into Sinfioli's place
She cast it all down swiftly; then she covereth up her face
And beneath the winter starlight she wended swift away.

But her gift do the thralls deem victual, and the thatch on the hall they lay,
And depart, they too, to their slumber, now dight was the dwelling of death.

Then Sigmund hears Sinfiotli, how he cries through the stone and saith:
"Best unto babe is mother, well sayeth the elder's saw;
Here hath Signy sent me swine's-flesh in windings of wheaten straw."

And again he held him silent of bitter words or of sweet;
And quoth Sigmund, "What hath betided? is an adder in the meat?"
Then loud his fosterling laughed: "Yea, a worm of bitter tooth,
The serpent of the Branstock, the sword of thy days of youth!
I have felt the hilts aforetime; I have felt how the letters run
On each side of the trench of blood and the point of that glorious one.
O mother, O mother of kings! we shall live and our days shall be sweet!
I have loved thee well aforetime, I shall love thee more when we meet."

Then Sigmund heard the sword-point smite on the stone wall's side,
And slowly mid the darkness therethrough he heard it gride
As against it bore Sinfiotli: but he cried out at the last:
"It biteth, O my fosterer! it cleaves the earth-bone fast!
Now learn we the craft of the masons that another day may come
When we build a house for King Siggeir, a strait unlovely home."

Then in the grave-mound's darkness did Sigmund the king upstand,
And unto that saw of battle he set his naked hand;
And hard the gift of Odin home to their breasts they drew;
Sawed Sigmund, sawed Sinfiotli, till the stone was cleft atwo,
And they met and kissed together: then they hewed and heaved full hard
Till lo, through the bursten rafters the winter heavens bestarred!
And they leap out merry-hearted; nor is there need to say
A many words between them of whither was the way.

For they took the night-watch sleeping, and slew them one and all

And then on the winter fagots they made them haste to fall,
They pile the oak-trees cloven, and when the oak-beams fail
They bear the ash and the rowan, and build a mighty bale
About the dwelling of Siggeir, and lay the torch therein.
Then they drew their swords and watched it till the flames began to win
Hard on to the mid-hall's rafters, and those feasters of the folk,
As the fire-flakes fell among them, to their last of days awoke.
By the gable-door stood Sigmund, and fierce Sinfiotli stood
Red-lit by the door of the women in the lane of blazing wood:
To death each doorway opened, and death was in the hall.

Then amid the gathered Goth-folk 'gan Siggeir the king to call:
"Who lit the fire I burn in, and what shall buy me peace?
Will ye take my heaped-up treasure, or ten years of my fields' increase,
Or half of my father's kingdom?   O toilers at the oar,
O wasters of the sea-plain, now labour ye no more!
But take the gifts I bid you, and lie upon the gold,
And clothe your limbs in purple and the silken women hold!"

But a great voice cried o'er the fire: "Nay, no such men are we,
No tuggers at the hawser, no wasters of the sea:
We will have the gold and the purple when we list such things to win
But now we think on our fathers, and avenging of our kin.
Not all King Siggeir's kingdom, and not all the world's increase
For ever and for ever, shall buy thee life and peace.
For now is the tree-bough blossomed that sprang from murder's seed;
And the death-doomed and the buried are they that do the deed;
Now when the dead shall ask thee by whom thy days were done,
Thou shalt say by Sigmund the Volsung, and Sinfiotli, Signy's son."

Then stark fear fell on the earl-folk, and silent they abide
Amid the flaming penfold; and again the great voice cried,
As the Goth-king's golden pillars grew red amidst the blaze:

" Ye women of the Goth-folk, come forth upon your ways ;
And thou, **Signy**, O my sister, come **forth** from death and hell,
That beneath the boughs of the Branstock once more **we twain may dwell.**"

Forth came the white-faced women and passed Sinfiotli's sword,
Free by the glaive of Odin the trembling pale ones poured,
But amid their hurrying terror came never Signy's feet ;
And the pearls of the throne of **Siggeir** shrunk in the fervent heat.

Then the men of war surged outward to the twofold doors of bane,
But there **played** the sword of Sigmund amidst the fiery lane
Before the gable door-way, **and by** the woman's door
Sinfiotli sang to the sword-edge amid the bale-fire's roar,
And back again to the burning the earls of the Goth-folk shrank
And the light low licked the tables, and the wine of Siggeir drank.

Lo now to the woman's doorway, the steel-watched bower of flame,
Clad in her queenly raiment King Volsung's **daughter came**
Before Sinfiotli's sword-point ; and she said : **"O mightiest son,**
Best now is our departing in the day my grief hath won,
And the many days of toiling, and the travail **of my womb,**
And the hate, and the fire of longing : **thou, son, and this day of the** doom
Have long been as one to my heart ; and now shall I leave you both,
And well **ye may** wot of the slumber my heart is nothing loth ;
And **all** the more, **as,** meseemeth, **thy** day shall not be long
To weary thee with labour and mingle wrong with **wrong.**
Yea, and I wot that the daylight thine eyes had never **seen**
Save for a great king's murder and the shame of a mighty queen.
But let thy soul, I charge thee, o'er all these things **prevail**
To make thy short day glorious and **leave** a goodly **tale.**"

She kissed him and departed, and unto Sigmund went
As now against the dawning grey grew the winter bent :

As the night and the morning mingled he saw her face once more,
And he deemed it fair and ruddy as in the days of yore;
Yet fast the tears fell from her, and the sobs upheaved her breast:
And she said: "My youth was happy; but this hour belike is best
Of all the days of my life-tide, that soon shall have an end.
I have come to greet thee, Sigmund, then back again must I wend,
For his bed the Goth-king dighteth: I have lain therein, time was,
And loathed the sleep I won there: but lo, how all things pass,
And hearts are changed and softened, for lovely now it seems.
Yet fear not my forgetting: I shall see thee in my dreams
A mighty king of the world 'neath the boughs of the Branstock green,
With thine earls and thy lords about thee as the Volsung fashion hath been.
And there shall all ye remember how I loved the Volsung name,
Nor spared to spend for its blooming my joy, and my life, and my fame.
For hear thou: that Sinfiotli, who hath wrought out our desire,
Who hath compassed about King Siggeir with this sea of a deadly fire,
Who brake thy grave asunder—my child and thine he is,
Begot in that house of the Dwarf-kind for no other end than this;
The son of Volsung's daughter, the son of Volsung's son.
Look, look! might another helper this deed with thee have done?"

And indeed as the word she uttereth, high up the red flames flare
To the nether floor of the heavens: and yet men see them there,
The golden roofs of Siggeir, the hall of the silver door
That the Goths and the Gods had builded to last for evermore.

She said: "Farewell, my brother, for the earls my candles light,
And I must wend me bedward lest I lose the flower of night."

And soft and sweet she kissed him, ere she turned about again,
And a little while was Signy beheld of the eyes of men;
And as she crossed the threshold day brightened at her back,
Nor once did she turn her earthward from the reek and the whirling wrack,

But fair in the fashion of Queens passed on to the heart of the hall.

And then King Siggeir's roof-tree upheaved for its utmost fall,
And its huge walls clashed together, and its mean and lowly things
The fire of death confounded with the tokens of the kings.
A sign for many people on the land of the Goths it lay,
A lamp of the earth none needed, for the bright sun brought the day.

How Sigmund cometh to the Land of the Volsungs again, and of the
death of Sinfiotli his Son.

Now Sigmund the king bestirs him, and Sinfiotli, Sigmund's son,
And they gather a host together, and many a mighty one ;
Then they set the ships in the sea-flood and sail from the stranger's shore,
And the beaks of the golden dragons see the Volsungs' land once more :
And men's hearts are fulfilled of joyance ; and they cry, The sun shines now
With never a curse to hide it, and they shall reap that sow !
Then for many a day sits Sigmund 'neath the boughs of the Branstock green,
With his earls and lords about him as the Volsung wont hath been.
And oft he thinketh on Signy and oft he nameth her name,
And tells how she spent her joyance and her lifedays and her fame
That the Volsung kin might blossom and bear the fruit of worth
For the hope of unborn people and the harvest of the earth.
And again he thinks of the word that he spake that other day,
How he should abide there lonely when his kin was passed away,
Their glory and sole avenger, their after-summer seed.

And now for their fame's advancement, and the latter days to speed,
He weddeth a wife of the King-folk ; Borghild she had to name ;
And the woman was fair and lovely and bore him sons of fame ;
Men call them Hamond and Helgi, and when Helgi first saw light,
There came the Norns to his cradle and gave him life full bright,

And called him Sunlit Hill, Sharp Sword, and Land of Rings,
And bade him be lovely and great, and a joy in the tale of kings.
And he waxed up fair and mighty, **and no** worser than **their word,**
And sweet are the tales of his life-days, and the wonders of his sword,
And the Maid of the Shield that he wedded, and how he changed his life,
And of marvels wrought in the gravemound where he rested from the strife.

But **the tale of** Sinfiotli telleth, that wide in the world **he went,**
And many **a** wall of ravens the edge of his warflame rent;
And oft he drave the war-prey and wasted many a land:
Amidst King **Hunding's** battle he strengthened Helgi's hand;
And he went before **the** banners amidst the steel-grown wood,
When the sons of Hunding gathered and Helgi's hope withstood:
Nor **less he** mowed the war-swathe in Helgi's glorious day
When **the kings** of the hosts at the **Wolf-crag** set the battle in **array.**
Then **at home by** his father's high-seat **he wore** the winter **through;**
And the marvel of all men he was for the deeds whereof they knew,
And the deeds whereof none wotted, and the deeds to follow after.

And **yet** but a little while he loved the song and the laughter,
And the wine that was drunk in peace, and the swordless lying down,
And the deedless day's uprising and the ungirt golden gown.
And **he** thought of the word of his mother, that his day should not be long
To weary his soul with labour or mingle wrong with wrong;
And his heart was exceeding hungry o'er all men to prevail,
And make his short day glorious and leave a goodly tale.

So when green leaves were lengthening and the spring was come again
He set his ships in the sea-flood and sailed across the main;
And the brother of Queen Borghild was his fellow in the war,
A **king of hosts** hight Gudrod; and each to each they swore,
And plighted troth for the helping, and the parting of the prey.

Now a long way over the sea-flood they went ashore on a day
And fought with a mighty folk-king, and overcame at last:
Then wide about his kingdom the net of steel they cast,
And the prey was great and goodly that they drave unto the strand.
But a greedy heart is Gudrod, and a king of griping hand,
Though nought he blench from the battle; so he speaks on a morning fair,
And saith

   "Upon the foreshore the booty will we share
If thou wilt help me, fellow, before we sail our ways."

Sinfiotli laughed, and answered: "O'ershort methinks the days
That two kings of war should chaffer like merchants of the men:
I will come again in the even and look on thy dealings then,
And take the share thou givest."

    Then he went his ways withal,
And drank day-long in his warship as in his father's hall;
And came again in the even: now hath Gudrod shared the spoil,
And throughout that day of summer not light had been his toil:
Forsooth his heap was the lesser; but Sinfiotli looked thereon,
And saw that a goodly getting had Borghild's brother won.
Clean-limbed and stark were the horses, and the neat were fat and sleek,
And the men-thralls young and stalwart, and the women young and meek;
Fair-gilt was the harness of battle, and the raiment fresh and bright,
And the household stuff new-fashioned for lords' and earls' delight.
On his own then looked Sinfiotli, and great it was forsooth,
But half-foundered were the horses, and a sight for all men's ruth
Were the thin-ribbed hungry cow-kind; and the thralls both carle and quean
Were the wilful, the weak, and the witless, and the old and the ill-beseen;
Spoilt was the harness and house-gear, and the raiment rags of cloth.

Now Sinfiotli's men beheld it and grew exceeding wroth,
But Sinfiotli laughed and answered: "The day's work hath been meet:
Thou hast done well, war-brother, to sift the chaff from the wheat

Nought have kings' sons to meddle with **the refuse** of the earth,
Nor shall warriors burden their long-ships with things of nothing worth."

Then he cried across the sea-strand **in a voice** exceeding great :
" Depart, ye thralls of the battle; ye have nought **to** do to wait !
Old, young, and good, and evil, depart and share the spoil,
That burden of the battle, that spring and seed of toil.
—But thou king of the greedy heart, thou king of the thievish grip,
What now wilt thou bear to the sea-strand and set within my ship
To buy thy life from the **slaying** ?   Unmeet for kings to hear
Of a king the breaker of troth, of a king the stealer **of gear."**

Then **mad-wroth** waxed **King Gudrod, and he cried : "Stand** up, my men !
And slay this wood-abider lest **he slay his** brothers again !"

But **no sword leapt from** its sheath, and his **men shrank** back in dread :
Then Sinfiotli's brow grew **smoother, and at last he spake and said :**
" Indeed thou art very brother **of my father** Sigmund's wife :
Wilt thou do so much for thine honour, wilt thou do so much **for** thy life,
As to bide my sword **on** the island in the pale of the hazel wands ?
For I know thee no battle-blencher, but a valiant man of thine hands."

Now nought **King** Gudrod gainsayeth, and men dight the hazelled field,
And there **on** the morrow morning they clash **the** sword and shield,
And the **fallow blades are leaping :** short is the tale to tell,
For **with the third** stroke **stricken** to field King Gudrod fell.
So there in the holm they lay **him ;** and plenteous store of gold
Sinfiotli lays beside him amid **that** hall of mould ;
"For he gripped," saith the **son** of Sigmund, "and gathered for **such a** day."

Then Sinfiotli **and** his fellows o'er the **sea-flood sail** away,
And come to the land of the Volsungs : but Borghild heareth the tale,
And into the hall she cometh with eager face and pale

As the kings were feasting together, and glad was Sigmund grown
Of the words of Sinfiotli's battle, and the tale of his great renown :
And there sat the sons of Borghild, and they hearkened and were glad
Of their brother born in the wild-wood, **and the crown of fame he had.**

So she stood before King Sigmund, and spread her hands abroad :
"I charge thee now, King Sigmund, as thou art the Volsungs' lord,
To tell me of my brother, why cometh he not from the sea ?"

Quoth Sinfiotli : "**Well thou** wottest and the tale **hath come to thee :**
The white swords met in the island ; bright there **did the war-shields shine,**
And **there thy brother abideth, for his hand was worser than mine.**"

But she heeded him never a whit, but cried on Sigmund and said :
"I charge thee now, King Sigmund, as thou art the lord of my bed,
To drive this wolf of the King-folk from out thy guarded land ;
Lest all we of thine house and kindred should fall beneath his hand."

Then spake King Sigmund the Volsung : "**When** thou **hast heard the tale,**
Thou shalt know that somewhat **thy** brother of his oath **to my son did fail ;**
Nor fell the man all sackless : nor yet need Sigmund's son
For any slain in sword-field to any **soul atone.**
Yet for the love I bear thee, and because thy **love I know,**
And because the man was mighty, **and far afield would go,**
I will lay down **a** mighty weregild, **a heap of the ruddy gold.**"

But no word answered Borghild, **for** her heart was grim and **cold ;**
And she went from the hall of the feasting, and lay **in her bower a while ;**
Nor speech she **took,** nor gave it, **but brooded deadly guile.**
And now again on the morrow to **Sigmund the king she** went,
And she saith that her wrath hath failed her, **and that** well is she content
To **take** the king's atonement ; **and she** kissed him **soft** and sweet,
And she **kissed** Sinfiotli his son, and sat **down in the** golden seat

All merry and glad by seeming, and blithe to most and least.
And again she biddeth King Sigmund that he hold a funeral feast
For her brother slain on the island; and nought he gainsayeth her will.

And so on an eve of the autumn do men the beakers fill,
And the earls are gathered together 'neath the boughs of the Branstock green;
There gold-clad mid the feasting went Borghild, Sigmund's Queen,
And she poured the wine for Sinfiotli, and smiled in his face and said:
" Drink now of this cup from mine hand, and bury we hate that is dead."

So he took the cup from her fingers, nor drank but pondered long
O'er the gathering days of his labour, and the intermingled wrong.

Now he sat by the side of his father; and Sigmund spake a word:
" O son, why sittest thou silent mid the glee of earl and lord?"

" I look in the cup," quoth Sinfiotli, "and hate therein I see."

" Well looked it is," said Sigmund; "give thou the cup to me,"
And he drained it dry to the bottom; for ye mind how it was writ
That this king might drink of venom, and have no hurt of it.
But the song sprang up in the hall, and merry was Sigmund's heart,
And he drank of the wine of King-folk and thrust all care apart.

Then the second time came Borghild and stood before the twain,
And she said: " O valiant step-son, how oft shall I say it in vain,
That my hate for thee hath perished, and the love hath sprouted green?
Wilt thou thrust my gift away, and shame the hand of a queen?"

So he took the cup from her fingers, and pondered over it long,
And thought on the labour that should be, and the wrong that amendeth
[wrong.
Then spake Sigmund the King: "O son, what aileth thine heart,

When the earls of men are merry, and thrust all care apart?"

But he said : "I have looked in the cup, and I see the deadly snare."

"Well seen it is," quoth Sigmund, "but thy burden I may bear."
And he took the beaker and drained it, and the song rose up in the hall;
And fair bethought King Sigmund his latter days befall.

But again came Borghild the Queen and stood with the cup in her hand,
And said : "They are idle liars, those singers of every land
Who sing how thou fearest nothing ; for thou losest valour and might,
And art fain to live for ever."
                              Then she stretched forth her fingers white,
And he took the cup from her hand, nor drank, but pondered long
Of the toil that begetteth toil, and the wrong that beareth wrong.

But Sigmund turned him about, and he said : "What aileth thee, son?
Shall our life-days never be merry, and our labour never be done?"

But Sinfiotli said : "I have looked, and lo there is death in the cup."

And the song, and the tinkling of harp-strings to the roof-tree winded up:
And Sigmund was dreamy with wine and the wearing of many a year ;
And the noise and the glee of the people as the sound of the wild woods were,
And the blossoming boughs of the Branstock were the wild trees waving about;
So he said : "Well seen, my fosterling ; let the lip then strain it out."
Then Sinfiotli laughed and answered : " I drink unto Odin then,
And the Dwellers up in God-home, the lords of the lives of men."

He drank as he spake the word, and forthwith the venom ran
In a chill flood over his heart, and down fell the mighty man
With never an uttered death-word and never a death-changed look,
And the floor of the hall of the Volsungs beneath his falling shook.

Then up rose the elder of days with a great and bitter cry
And lifted the head of the fallen, and none durst come anigh
To hearken the words of his sorrow, if any words he said,
But such as the Father of all men might speak over Baldur dead.
And again, as before the death-stroke, waxed the hall of the Volsungs dim,
And once more he seemed in the forest, where he spake with nought but him.

Then he lifted him up from the hall-floor and bore him on his breast,
And men who saw Sinfiotli deemed his heart had gotten rest,
And his eyes were no more dreadful.   Forth fared the Volsung child
With Signy's son through the doorway; and the wind was great and wild,
And the moon rode high in the heavens, and whiles it shone out bright,
And whiles the clouds drew over.   So went he through the night,
Until the dwellings of man-folk were a long while left behind.
Then came he unto the thicket and the houses of the wind,
And the feet of the hoary mountains, and the dwellings of the deer,
And the heaths without a shepherd, and the houseless dales and drear.
Then lo, a mighty water, a rushing flood and wide,
And no ferry for the shipless ; so he went along its side,
As a man that seeketh somewhat : but it widened toward the sea,
And the moon sank down in the west, and he went o'er a desert lea.

But lo, in that dusk ere the dawning a glimmering over the flood,
And the sound of the cleaving of waters, and Sigmund the Volsung stood
By the edge of the swirling eddy, and a white-sailed boat he saw,
And its keel ran light on the strand with the last of the dying flaw.
But therein was a man most mighty, grey-clad like the mountain-cloud,
One-eyed and seeming ancient, and he spake and hailed him aloud :

" Now whither away, King Sigmund, for thou farest far to-night ?"

Spake the King : "I would cross this water, for my life hath lost its light,
And mayhap there be deeds for a king to be found on the further shore."

" My senders," quoth the shipman, " bade me waft a great king o'er,
So set thy burden a shipboard, for the night's face looks toward day."

So betwixt the earth and the water his son did Sigmund lay;
But lo, when he fain would follow, there was neither ship nor man,
Nor aught but his empty bosom beside that water wan,
That whitened by little and little as the night's face looked to the day.
So he stood a long while gazing and then turned and gat him away;
And ere the sun of the noon-tide across the meadows shone
Sigmund the King of the Volsungs was set in his father's throne,
And he hearkened and doomed and portioned, and did all the deeds of a king.
So the autumn waned and perished, and the winter brought the spring.

*Of the last battle of King Sigmund, **and the death of him.***

Now is Queen Borghild driven from the Volsung's bed and board,
And unwedded sitteth Sigmund an exceeding mighty lord,
And fareth oft to the war-field, and addeth fame to fame:
And where'er are the great ones told of his sons shall the people name;
But short was their day of harvest and their reaping of renown,
And while men stood by to marvel they gained their latest crown.
So Sigmund alone abideth of all the Volsung seed,
And the folk that the Gods had fashioned lest the earth should lack a deed.
And he said: "The tree was stalwart, but its boughs are old and worn.
Where now are the children departed, that amidst my life were born?
I know not the men about me, and they know not of my ways:
I am nought but a picture of battle, and a song for the people to praise.
I must strive with the deeds of my kingship, and yet when mine hour is come
It shall meet me as glad as the goodman when he bringeth the last load home."

Now there was a king of the Islands, whom the tale doth Eylimi call,
And saith he was wise and valiant, though his kingdom were but small:

He had one only daughter that Hiordis had to name,
A woman wise and shapely beyond the praise of fame.
And now saith the son of King Volsung that his time is short enow
To labour the Volsung garden, and the hand must be set to the plough:
So he sendeth an earl of the people to King Eylimi's high-built hall,
Bearing the gifts and the tokens, and this word in his mouth withal:

" King Sigmund the son of Volsung hath sent me here with a word
That plenteous good of thy daughter among all folk he hath heard,
And he wooeth that wisest of women that she may sit on his throne,
And lie in the bed of the Volsungs, and be his wife alone.
And he saith that he thinketh surely she shall bear the kings of the earth,
And maybe the best and the greatest of all who are deemed of worth.
Now hereof would he have an answer within a half-month's space,
And these gifts meanwhile he giveth for the increase of thy grace."

So King Eylimi hearkened the message, and hath no word to say,
For an earl of King Lyngi the mighty is come that very day,
He too for the wooing of Hiordis: and Lyngi's realm is at hand,
But afar King Sigmund abideth o'er many a sea and land:
And the man is young and eager, and grim and guileful of mood.

At last he sayeth: " Abide here such space as thou deemest good,
But tomorn shalt thou have thine answer that thine heart may the lighter be
For the hearkening of harp and songcraft, and the dealing with game and glee."
Then he went to Queen Hiordis' bower, where she worked in the silk and
        the gold
The deeds of the world that should be, and the deeds that were of old.
And he stood before her and said:

                        "I have spoken a word, time was,
That thy will should rule thy wedding ; and now hath it come to pass
That again two kings of the people will woo thy body to bed."

So she rose to her feet and hearkened : "And which be they?" she said.

He spake : "The first is Lyngi, a valiant man and a fair,
A neighbour ill for thy father, if a foe's name he must bear :
And the next is King Sigmund the Volsung of a land far over sea,
And well thou knowest his kindred, and his might and his valiancy,
And the tales of his heart of a God ; and though old he be waxen now,
Yet men deem that the wide world's blossom from Sigmund's loins shall grow.'

Said Hiordis : "I wot, my father, that hereof may strife arise ;
Yet soon spoken is mine answer ; for I, who am called the wise,
Shall I thrust by the praise of the people, and the tale that no ending hath,
And the love and the heart of the godlike, and the heavenward-leading path,
For the rose and the stem of the lily, and the smooth-lipped youngling's kiss,
And the eyes' desire that passeth, and the frail unstable bliss ?
Now shalt thou tell King Sigmund, that I deem it the crown of my life
To dwell in the house of his fathers amidst all peace and strife,
And to bear the sons of his body · and indeed full well I know
That fair from the loins of Sigmund shall such a stem outgrow
That all folk of the earth shall be praising the womb where once he lay
And the paps that his lips have cherished, and shall bless my happy day."

Now the king's heart sore misgave him, but herewith must he be content,
And great gifts to the earl of Lyngi and a word withal he sent,
That the woman's troth was plighted to another people's king.
But King Sigmund's earl on the morrow hath joyful yea-saying,
And ere two moons be perished he shall fetch his bride away.
"And bid him," King Eylimi sayeth, "to come with no small array,
But with sword and shield and war-shaft, lest aught of ill betide."

So forth goes the earl of Sigmund across the sea-flood wide,
And comes to the land of the Volsungs, and meeteth Sigmund the king,
And tells how he sped on his errand, and the joyful yea-saying.

So King Sigmund maketh him ready, and they ride adown to the sea
All glorious of gear and raiment, and a goodly company.
Yet hath Sigmund thought of his father, and the deed he wrought before,
And hath scorn to gather his people and all his hosts of war
To wend to the feast and the wedding: yet are their long-ships ten,
And the shielded folk aboard them are the mightiest men of men.
So Sigmund goeth a shipboard, and they hoist their sails to the wind,
And the beaks of the golden dragons leave the Volsungs' land behind.
Then come they to Eylimi's kingdom, and good welcome have they there,
And when Sigmund looked on Hiordis, he deemed her wise and fair.
But her heart was exceeding fain when she saw the glorious king,
And it told her of times that should be full many a noble thing.

So there is Sigmund wedded at a great and goodly feast,
And day by day on Hiordis the joy of her heart increased;
And her father joyed in Sigmund and his might and majesty,
And dead in the heart of the Isle-king his ancient fear did lie.

Yet, forsooth, had men looked seaward, they had seen the gathering cloud,
And the little wind arising, that should one day pipe so loud.
For well may ye wot indeed that King Lyngi the Mighty is wroth,
When he getteth the gifts and the answer, and that tale of the woman's troth:
And he saith he will have the gifts and the woman herself withal,
Either for loving or hating, and that both those heads shall fall.
So now when Sigmund and Hiordis are wedded a month or more,
And the Volsung bids men dight them to cross the sea-flood o'er,
Lo, how there cometh the tidings of measureless mighty hosts
Who are gotten ashore from their long-ships on the skirts of King Eylimi's
                                                                [coasts.
Sore boded the heart of the Isle-king of what the end should be.
But Sigmund long beheld him, and he said: "Thou deem'st of me
That my coming hath brought thee evil; but put aside such things;
For long have I lived, and I know it, that the lives of mighty kings

Are not cast away, nor drifted like the down before the wind ;
And surely I know, who say it, that never would Hiordis' mind
Have been turned to wed King Lyngi or aught but the Volsung seed.
Come, go we forth to the battle, that shall be the latest **deed**
Of thee and me meseemeth : yea, whether thou live or **die,**
No more shall the brand of Odin **at peace in** his scabbard lie."

And therewith he brake **the peace-strings** and drew the blade of **bale,**
And Death on the **point abided,** Fear sat on the edges pale.

So **men ride adown to** the sea-strand, and the kings their hosts array
When the high noon flooded heaven ; and the men of the Volsungs **lay,**
With King Eylimi's shielded champions mid Lyngi's hosts of war,
As the brown pips lie in the apple when ye **cut it through the core.**

But now when the kings were departed, from the King's house Hiordis went,
And before men joined the battle she came to a woody bent,
Where she lay with one of her maidens the death and the **deeds to behold.**

In the noon sun shone **King Sigmund as an image all of gold,**
And he **stood before the** foremost and the banner of his fame,
And many a thing he remembered, and he called on each **earl by his name**
To do well for the house of the Volsungs, and the **ages yet unborn.**
Then he tossed up the sword of the Branstock, and blew on his father's horn,
Dread of so many a battle, doom-song of so many a **man.**
Then all the earth seemed moving as the hosts of Lyngi ran
On the Volsung men and the Isle-folk like wolves upon the **prey ;**
But sore was their **labour and** toil ere the end of their harvesting day.

On went the Volsung banners, and on went Sigmund **before,**   [floor,
And his sword was the flail of the tiller on the wheat of the wheat-thrashing
And his shield was rent from his arm, and his helm was sheared from his head :
But **who may** draw nigh him to smite for the heap and the rampart of dead ?

White went his hair on the wind like the ragged drift of the cloud,
And his dust-driven, blood-beaten harness was the death-storm's angry shroud,
When the summer sun is departing in the first of the night of wrack;
And his sword was the cleaving lightning, that smites and is hurried aback
Ere the hand may rise against it; and his voice was the following thunder.

Then cold grew the battle before him, dead-chilled with the fear and the
For again in his ancient eyes the light of victory gleamed;   [wonder:
From his mouth grown tuneful and sweet the song of his kindred streamed;
And no more was he worn and weary, and no more his life seemed spent:
And with all the hope of his childhood was his wrath of battle blent;
And he thought: A little further, and the river of strife is passed,
And I shall sit triumphant the king of the world at last.

But lo, through the hedge of the war-shafts a mighty man there came,
One-eyed and seeming ancient, but his visage shone like flame:
Gleaming-grey was his kirtle, and his hood was cloudy blue;
And he bore a mighty twi-bill, as he waded the fight-sheaves through,
And stood face to face with Sigmund, and upheaved the bill to smite.
Once more round the head of the Volsung fierce glittered the Branstock's
The sword that came from Odin; and Sigmund's cry once more   [light,
Rang out to the very heavens above the din of war.
Then clashed the meeting edges with Sigmund's latest stroke,
And in shivering shards fell earthward that fear of worldly folk.
But changed were the eyes of Sigmund, and the war-wrath left his face;
For that grey-clad mighty helper was gone, and in his place
Drave on the unbroken spear-wood 'gainst the Volsung's empty hands:
And there they smote down Sigmund, the wonder of all lands,
On the foemen, on the death-heap his deeds had piled that day.

Ill hour for Sigmund's fellows! they fall like the seeded hay
Before the brown scythes' sweeping, and there the Isle-king fell
In the fore-front of his battle, wherein he wrought right well,

And soon they were nought but foemen who stand upon their feet
On the isle-strand by the ocean where the grass and the sea-sand meet.

And now hath the conquering War-king another deed to do,
And he saith : "Who now gainsayeth King Lyngi come to woo,
The lord and the overcomer and the bane of the Volsung kin ?"
So he fares to the Isle-king's dwelling a wife of the kings to win ;
And the host is gathered together, and they leave the field of the dead ;
And round as a targe of the Goth-folk the moon ariseth red.

And so when the last is departed, and she deems they will come not aback,
Fares Hiordis forth from the thicket to the field of the fateful wrack,
And half-dead was her heart for sorrow as she waded the swathes of the sword.
Not far did she search the death-field ere she found her king and lord
On the heap that his glaive had fashioned : not yet was his spirit past,
Though his hurts were many and grievous, and his life-blood ebbing fast ;
And glad were his eyes and open as her wan face over him hung,
And he spake :
        "Thou art sick with sorrow, and I would thou wert not so young ;
Yet as my days passed shall thine pass ; and a short while now it seems
Since my hand first gripped the sword-hilt, and my glory was but in dreams."

She said : "Thou livest, thou livest ! the leeches shall heal thee still."

"Nay," said he, "my heart hath hearkened to Odin's bidding and will ;
For today have mine eyes beheld him : nay, he needed not to speak :
Forsooth I knew of his message and the thing he came to seek.
And now do I live but to tell thee of the days that are yet to come :
And perchance to solace thy sorrow ; and then will I get me home
To my kin that are gone before me.   Lo, yonder where I stood
The shards of a glaive of battle that was once the best of the good :
Take them and keep them surely.   I have lived no empty days ;
The Norns were my nursing mothers ; I have won the people's praise.

When the Gods for one deed asked me I ever gave them twain ;
Spendthrift of glory I was, and great was my life-days' gain ;
Now these shards have been my fellow in the work the Gods would have,
But today hath Odin taken the gift that once he gave.
I have wrought for the Volsungs truly, and yet have I known full well
That a better one than I am shall bear the tale to tell :
And for him shall these shards be smithied ; and he shall be my son
To remember what I have forgotten and to do what I left undone.
Under thy girdle he lieth, and how shall I say unto thee,
Unto thee, the wise of women, to cherish him heedfully.
Now, wife, put by thy sorrow for the little day we have had ;
For in sooth I deem thou weepest : The days have been fair and glad :
And our valour and wisdom have met, and thou knowest they shall not die :
Sweet and good were the days, nor yet to the Fates did we cry
For a little longer yet, and a little longer to live :
But we took, we twain in our meeting, all gifts that they had to give :
Our wisdom and valour have kissed, and thine eyes shall see the fruit,
And the joy for his days that shall be hath pierced mine heart to the root.
Grieve not for me ; for thou weepest that thou canst not see my face
How its beauty is not departed, nor the hope of mine eyes grown base.
Indeed I am waxen weary ; but who heedeth weariness
That hath been day-long on the mountain in the winter weather's stress,
And now stands in the lighted doorway and seeth the king draw nigh,
And heareth men dighting the banquet, and the bed wherein he shall lie ?"

Then failed the voice of Sigmund ; but so mighty was the man,
That a long while yet he lingered till the dusky night grew wan,
And she sat and sorrowed o'er him, but no more a word he spake.
Then a long way over the sea-flood the day began to break ;
And when the sun was arisen a little he turned his head
Till the low beams bathed his eyen, and there lay Sigmund dead.
And the sun rose up on the earth ; but where was the Volsung kin
And the folk that the Gods had begotten the praise of all people to win ?

*How King Sigmund the Volsung was laid in mound on the sea-side of
the Isle-realm.*

Now Hiordis looked from the dead, and her eyes strayed down to the sea,
And a shielded ship she saw, and a war-dight company,
Who beached the ship for the landing: so swift she fled away,
And once more to the depth of the thicket, wherein her handmaid lay:
And she said: "I have left my lord, and my lord is dead and gone,
And he gave me a charge full heavy, and here are we twain alone,
And earls from the sea are landing: give me thy blue attire,
And take my purple and gold and my crown of the sea-flood's fire,
And be thou the wife of King Volsung when men of our names shall ask,
And I will be the handmaid: now I bid thee to this task,
And I pray thee not to fail me, because of thy faith and truth,
And because I have ever loved thee, and thy mother fostered my youth.
Yea, because my womb is wealthy with a gift for the days to be.
Now do this deed for mine asking and the tale shall be told of thee."

So the other nought gainsaith it and they shift their raiment there:
But well-spoken was the maiden, and a woman tall and fair.

Now the lord of those new-coming men was a king and the son of a king,
King Elf the son of the Helper, and he sailed from war-faring
And drew anigh to the Isle-realm and sailed along the strand;
For the shipmen needed water and fain would go a-land;
And King Elf stood hard by the tiller while the world was yet a-cold:
Then the red sun lit the dawning, and they looked, and lo, behold!
The wrack of a mighty battle, and heaps of the shielded dead,
And a woman alive amidst them, a queen with crownèd head,
And her eyes strayed down to the sea-strand, and she saw that weaponed folk,
And turned and fled to the thicket: then the lord of the shipmen spoke:
" Lo, here shall we lack for water, for the brooks with blood shall run,

Yet wend we ashore to behold it and to wot of the deeds late done."

So they turned their faces to Sigmund, and waded the swathes of the sword.
"O, look ye long," said the Sea-king, "for here lieth a mighty lord
And all these are the deeds of his war-flame, yet hardy hearts, be sure,
That they once durst look in his face or the wrath of his eyen endure ;
Though his lips be glad and smiling as a God that dreameth of mirth.
Would God I were one of his kindred, for none such are left upon earth.
Now fare we into the thicket, for thereto is the woman fled,
And belike she shall tell us the story of this field of the mighty dead."

So they wend and find the women, and bespeak them kind and fair :
Then spake the gold-crowned handmaid : "Of the Isle-king's house we were,
And I am the Queen called Hiordis ; and the man that lies on the field
Was mine own lord Sigmund the Volsung, the mightiest under shield."

Then all amazed were the sea-folk when they hearkened to that word,
And great and heavy tidings they deem their ears have heard :
But again spake out the Sea-king : "And this blue-clad one beside,
So pale, and as tall as a Goddess, and white and lovely eyed ?"

"In sooth and in troth," said the woman, "my serving-maid is this ;
She hath wept long over the battle, and sore afraid she is."

Now the king looks hard upon her, but he saith no word thereto,
And down again to the death-field with the women-folk they go.
There they set their hands to the labour, and amidst the deadly mead
They raise a mound for Sigmund, a mighty house indeed ;
And therein they set that folk-king, and goodly was his throne,
And dight with gold and scarlet : and the walls of the house were done
With the cloven shields of the foemen, and banners borne to field ;
But none might find his war-helm or the splinters of his shield,
And clenched and fast was his right hand, but no sword therein he had :

For Hiordis spake to the shipmen:

"Our lord and master bade
That the shards of his glaive of battle should go with our lady the Queen:
And by them that lie a-dying a many things are seen."

So there lies Sigmund the Volsung, and far away, forlorn   [born
Are the blossomed boughs of the Branstock, and the house where he was
To what end was wrought that roof-ridge, and the rings of the silver door,
And the fair-carved golden high-seat, and the many-pictured floor
Worn down by the feet of the Volsungs? or the hangings of delight,
Or the marvel of its harp-strings, or the Dwarf-wrought beakers bright?
Then the Gods have fashioned a folk who have fashioned a house in vain:
It is nought, and for nought they battled, and nought was their joy and their
                                                                  [pain.
Lo, the noble oak of the forest with his feet in the flowers and grass,
How the winds that bear the summer o'er its topmost branches pass,
And the wood-deer dwell beneath it, and the fowl in its fair twigs sing,
And there it stands in the forest, an exceeding glorious thing:
Then come the axes of men, and low it lies on the ground,
And the crane comes out of the southland, and its nest is nowhere found,
And bare and shorn of its blossoms is the house of the deer of the wood.
But the tree is a golden dragon; and fair it floats on the flood,
And beareth the kings and the earl-folk, and is shield-hung all without ·
And it seeth the blaze of the beacons, and heareth the war-God's shout.
There are tidings wherever it cometh, and the tale of its time shall be told.
A dear name it hath got like a king, and a fame that groweth not old.

Lo, such is the Volsung dwelling; lo, such is the deed he hath wrought
Who laboured all his life-days, and had rest but little or nought,
Who died in the broken battle; who lies with swordless hand
In the realm that the foe hath conquered on the edge of a stranger-land.

How Queen Hiordis is known; and how she abideth in the house of
Elf the son of the Helper.

Now asketh the king of those women where now in the world they will go,
And Hiordis speaks for the twain: "This is now but a land of the foe
And our lady and Queen beseecheth that unto thine house we wend
And that there thou serve her kingly that her woes may have an end."

Fain then was the heart of the folk-king, and he bade aboard forth-right,
And they hoist the sails to the wind and sail by day and by night
Till they come to a land of the people, and a goodly land it is
Where folk may dwell unharried and win abundant bliss,
The land of King Elf and the Helper; and there he bids them abide
In his house that is goodly shapen, and wrought full high and wide:
And he biddeth the Queen be merry, and set aside her woe,
And he doth by them better and better, as day on day doth go.

Now there was the mother of Elf, and a woman wise was she,
And she spake to her son of a morning: "I have noted them heedfully,
Those women thou broughtst from the outlands, and fain now would I wot
Why the worser of the women the goodlier gear hath got."

He said: "She hath named her Hiordis, the wife of the mightiest king,
E'en Sigmund the son of Volsung with whose name the world doth ring."

Then the old queen laughed and answered: "Is it not so, my son,
That the handmaid still gave counsel when aught of deeds was done?"

He said: "Yea, she spake mostly; and her words were exceeding wise,
And measureless sweet I deem her, and dear she is to mine eyes."

But she said: "Do after my counsel, and win thee a goodly queen:

Speak ye to the twain unwary, and the truth shall soon be seen,
And again shall they shift their raiment, if I am aught but a fool."

He said : " Thou sayst well, mother, and settest me well to school."
So he spake on a day to the women, and said to the gold-clad one :
" How wottest thou in the winter of the coming of the sun
When yet the world is darkling ?"

                                           She said : " In the days of my youth
I dwelt in the house of my father, and fair was the tide forsooth,
And ever I woke at the dawning, for folk betimes must stir,
Be the meadows bright or darksome ; and I drank of the whey-tub there
As much as the heart desired ; and now, though changed be the days,
I wake athirst in the dawning, because of my wonted ways."

Then laughed King Elf and answered : "A fashion strange enow,
That the feet of the fair queen's-daughter must forth to follow the plough,
Be the acres bright or darkling !   But thou with the eyes of grey,
What sign hast thou to tell thee, that the night wears into day
When the heavens are mirk as the midnight ?"

                                          Said she, "In the days that were
My father gave me this gold-ring ye see on my finger here,
And a marvel goeth with it : for when night waxeth old
I feel it on my finger grown most exceeding cold,
And I know day comes through the darkness ; and such is my dawning sign."

Then laughed King Elf and answered : " Thy father's house was fine ;
There was gold enough meseemeth—But come now, say the word
And tell me the speech thou spakest awrong mine ears have heard,
And that thou wert the wife of Sigmund the wife of the mightiest King."

No whit she smiled, but answered.   " Indeed thou sayst the thing :
Such a wealth I had in my storehouse that I feared the Kings of men."

He said : " Yet for nought didst thou hide thee ; had I known of the matter
As the daughter of my father had I held thee in good sooth,   [then,
For dear to mine eyes wert thou waxen, and my heart of thy woe was ruth.
But now shall I deal with thee better than thy dealings to me have been :
For my wife I will bid thee to be, and the people's very queen."

She said : " When the son of King Sigmund is brought forth to the light of day
And the world a man hath gotten, thy will shall I nought gainsay.
And I thank thee for thy goodness, and I know the love of thine heart ;
And I see thy goodly kingdom, thy country set apart,
With the day of peace begirdled from the change and the battle's wrack :
'Tis enough, and more than enough since none prayeth the past aback."

Then the King is fain and merry, and he deems his errand sped,
And that night she sits on the high-seat with the crown on her shapely head :
And amidst the song and the joyance, and the sound of the people's praise,
She thinks of the days that have been, and she dreams of the coming days.

So passeth the summer season, and the harvest of the year,
And the latter days of the winter on toward the springtide wear.

BOOK II.

REGIN.

NOW THIS IS THE FIRST BOOK OF THE LIFE AND DEATH OF SIGURD THE VOLSUNG, AND THEREIN IS TOLD OF THE BIRTH OF HIM, AND OF HIS DEALINGS WITH REGIN THE MASTER OF MASTERS, AND OF HIS DEEDS IN THE WASTE PLACES OF THE EARTH.

Of the birth of Sigurd the son of Sigmund.

PEACE lay on the land of the Helper and the house of Elf his son;
    There merry men went bedward when their tide of toil was done,
And glad was the dawn's awakening, and the noon-tide fair and glad:
There no great store had the franklin, and enough the hireling had;
And a child might go unguarded the length and breadth of the land
With a purse of gold at his girdle and gold rings on his hand.
'Twas a country of cunning craftsmen, and many a thing they wrought,
That the lands of storm desired, and the homes of warfare sought.
But men deemed it o'er-well warded by more than its stems of fight,
And told how its earth-born watchers yet lived of plenteous might.
So hidden was that country, and few men sailed its sea,
And none came o'er its mountains of men-folk's company.
But fair-fruited, many-peopled, it lies a goodly strip,
'Twixt the mountains cloudy-headed and the sea-flood's surging lip,
And a perilous flood is its ocean, and its mountains, who shall tell
What things in their dales deserted and their wind-swept heaths may dwell.

Now a man of the Kings, called Gripir, in this land of peace abode:
The son of the Helper's father, though never lay his load

In the womb of the mother of Kings that the Helper's brethren bore ;
But of Giant kin was his mother, of the folk that are seen no more ;
Though whiles as ye ride some fell-road across the heath there comes
The voice of their lone lamenting o'er their changed and conquered homes.
A long way off from the sea-strand and beneath the mountains' feet
Is the high-built hall of Gripir, where the waste and the tillage meet ;
A noble and plentiful house, that a little men-folk fear,
But beloved of the crag-dwelling eagles and the kin of the woodland deer.
A man of few words was Gripir, but he knew of all deeds that had been,
And times there came upon him, when the deeds to be were seen :
No sword had he held in his hand since his father fell to field,
And against the life of the slayer he bore undinted shield :
Yet no fear in his heart abided, nor desired he aught at all,
But he noted the deeds that had been, and looked for what should befall.

Again, in the house of the Helper there dwelt a certain man
Beardless and low of stature, of visage pinched and wan :
So exceeding old was Regin, that no son of man could tell
In what year of the days passed over he came to that land to dwell :
But the youth of King Elf had he fostered, and the Helper's youth thereto,
Yea and his father's father's : the lore of all men he knew,
And was deft in every cunning, save the dealings of the sword :
So sweet was his tongue-speech fashioned, that men trowed his every word ;
His hand with the harp-strings blended was the mingler of delight
With the latter days of sorrow ; all tales he told aright ;
The Master of the Masters in the smithying craft was he ;
And he dealt with the wind and the weather and the stilling of the sea ;
Nor might any learn him leech-craft, for before that race was made,
And that man-folk's generation, all their life-days had he weighed.

In this land abideth Hiordis amid all people's praise
Till cometh the time appointed : in the fulness of the days
Through the dark and the dusk she travailed, till at last in the dawning hour

Have the deeds of the Volsungs blossomed, and born their latest flower ;
In the bed there lieth a **man-child, and his eyes look straight on the sun.**
And lo, **the** hope of the people, and the days of a king are **begun.**

Men say of the serving-women, when they cried **on the** joy of the morn,
When they handled the linen raiment, and washed the king new-born,
When they bore him back unto Hiordis, and the weary and happy breast,
And bade her be glad to behold it, how the best was sprung from **the best.**
Yet they shrank **in their rejoicing before the** eyes of the child,
So bright and dreadful were **they ;** yea though the spring morn smiled,
And a **thousand** birds were singing round the fair familiar home,
And still as on other mornings they saw folk go and come,
Yet the hour seemed awful **to them, and the hearts** within them **burned**
As though of fateful matters their souls were newly learned.

But Hiordis looked on the Volsung, on **her grief and her** fond desire,
And the hope of her heart was quickened, and her joy was a living fire ;
And she said : " Now one of the earthly on the eyes of my child hath gazed
Nor shrunk before their glory, nor stayed her love **amazed :**
I behold thee **as** Sigmund beholdeth,—and **I was the home of thine heart—**
Woe's me for **the day when thou wert not, and the hour when we shall part !"**

Then she held him **a** little season **on her weary and** happy breast
And she told him of Sigmund and Volsung and the best sprung forth from **the**
She spake to the new-born baby as one who might understand,   [best :
And told him of Sigmund's battle, and the dead by **the sea-flood's strand,**
And of all the **wars** passed over, and **the** light with darkness blent.

So she spake, and the sun **rose higher, and** her speech **at last** was spent,
And she gave him back to the **women to bear forth to the** people's kings,
That they too may rejoice in her glory and her day of happy things.

But there sat the Helper of **Men with King Elf and his Earls in the hall,**

And they spake of the deeds that had been, and told of the times to befall,
And they hearkened and heard sweet voices and the sound of harps draw nigh,
Till their hearts were exceeding merry and they knew not wherefore or why:
Then, lo, in the hall white raiment, as thither the damsels came,
And amid the hands of the foremost was the woven gold aflame.

"O daughters of earls," said the Helper, "what tidings then do ye bear?
Is it grief in the merry morning, or joy or wonder or fear?"

Quoth the first: "It is grief for the foemen that the Masters of God-home would
                                                    [grieve."
Said the next: "'Tis a wonder of wonders, that the hearkening world shall
                                                    [believe."
"A fear of all fears," said the third, "for the sword is uplifted on men."

"A joy of all joys," said the fourth, "once come, and it comes not again!"

"Lo, son," said the ancient Helper, "glad sit the earls and the lords!
Lookst thou not for a token of tidings to follow such-like words?"

Saith King Elf: "Great words of women! or great hath our dwelling become."

Said the women: "Words shall be greater, when all folk shall praise our home."

"What then hath betid," said King Elf, "do the high Gods stand in our gate?"

"Nay," said they, "else were we silent, and they should be telling of fate."

"Is the bidding come," said the Helper, "that we wend the Gods to see?"

"Many summers and winters," they said, "ye shall live on the earth, it may
                                                    [be."
Said a young man: "Will ye be telling that all we shall die no more?"

"Nay," they answered, "nay, who knoweth but the change may be hard at
[the door?"
"Come ships from the sea," said an elder, "with all gifts of the Eastland
[gold?"
"Was there less than enough," said the women, "when last our treasure was
[told?"
"Speak then," said the ancient Helper, "let the worst and the best be said."

Quoth they: "'Tis the Queen of the Isle-folk, she is weary-sick on her bed."

Said King Elf: "Yet ye come rejoicing; what more lieth under the tongue?'

They said: "The earth is weary: but the tender blade hath sprung,
That shall wax till beneath its branches fair bloom the meadows green;
For the Gods and they that were mighty were glad erewhile with the Queen."

Said King Elf: "How say ye, women? Of a King new-born do ye tell,
By a God of the Heavens begotten in our fathers' house to dwell?"

"By a God of the Earth," they answered; "but greater yet is the son,
Though long were the days of Sigmund, and great are the deeds he hath done."

Then she with the golden burden to the kingly high-seat stepped
And away from the new-born baby the purple cloths she swept,
And cried: "O King of the people, long mayst thou live in bliss,
As our hearts today are happy! Queen Hiordis sends thee this,
And she saith that the world shall call it by the name that thou shalt name;
Now the gift to thee is given, and to thee is brought the fame."

Then e'en as a man astonied King Elf the Volsung took,
While his feast-hall's ancient timbers with the cry of the earl-folk shook;
For the eyes of the child gleamed on him till he was as one who sees
The very Gods arising mid their carven images:

To his ears there came a murmur of far seas beneath the wind
And the tramp of fierce-eyed warriors through the outland forest blind ;
The sound of hosts of battle, cries round the hoisted shield,
Low talk of the gathered wise-ones in the Goth-folk's holy field :
So the thought in a little moment through King Elf the mighty ran
Of the years and their building and burden, and toil of the sons of man,
The joy of folk and their sorrow, and the hope of deeds to do :
With the love of many peoples was the wise king smitten through,
As he hung o'er the new-born Volsung : but at last he raised his head,
And looked forth kind o'er his people, and spake aloud and said :

"O Sigmund King of Battle ; O man of many days,
Whom I saw mid the shields of the fallen and the dead men's silent praise,
Lo, how hath the dark tide perished and the dawn of day begun !
And now, O mighty Sigmund, wherewith shall we name thy son ?"

But there rose up a man most ancient, and he cried : "Hail Dawn of the Day !
How many things shalt thou quicken, how many shalt thou slay !
How many things shalt thou waken, how many lull to sleep !
How many things shalt thou scatter, how many gather and keep !
O me, how thy love shall cherish, how thine hate shall wither and burn !
How the hope shall be sped from thy right hand, nor the fear to thy left return !
O thy deeds that men shall sing of ! O thy deeds that the Gods shall see !
O SIGURD, Son of the Volsungs, O Victory yet to be !"

Men heard the name and they knew it, and they caught it up in the air,
And it went abroad by the windows and the doors of the feast-hall fair,
It went through street and market ; o'er meadow and acre it went,
And over the wind-stirred forest and the dearth of the sea-beat bent,
And over the sea-flood's welter, till the folk of the fishers heard,
And the hearts of the isle-abiders on the sun-scorched rocks were stirred.

But the Queen in her golden chamber, the name she hearkened and knew ;

And she heard the flock of the women, as back to the chamber they drew,
And the name of Sigurd entered, and the body of Sigurd was come,
And it was as if Sigmund **were** living and she still in her lovely home ;
Of all folk of the world was she well, and a soul fulfilled of rest
As alone in the chamber she wakened and Sigurd cherished **her breast.**

But men feast in the merry noontide, and glad **is the April green**
That a Volsung looks on the sunlight and the night and the darkness have
Earls think of marvellous stories, and along the golden strings   [been.
Flit words of banded **brethren** and names of war-fain Kings :
All the days of the deeds of Sigmund who was born so long **ago ;**
All deeds of the glorious Signy, and her tarrying-tide **of woe ;**
Men tell of the years of Volsung, and how long agone it **was**
That he changed his life in battle, and brought **the tale to pass :**
Then goeth the word of the Giants, and the **world seems waxen old**
For the dimness of King Rerir and the tale **of his** warfare told :
Yet unhushed are the singers' voices, nor yet the harp-strings cease
While yet is left a rumour of the mirk-wood's broken peace,
And of Sigi the very ancient, **and the unnamed Sons of God,**
Of the days when the Lords of Heaven full **oft the world-ways trod**

So stilleth the wind in the even and **the sun sinks down in the sea,**
And **men abide** the morrow and the Victory yet **to be.**

Sigurd getteth to him the horse that is called Greyfell.

Now waxeth the son of Sigmund in might and goodliness,
And soft the days win over, and all men his beauty **bless.**
But amidst the summer season was the Isle-queen Hiordis wed
To King Elf the son of the Helper, and fair their life-days sped.
Peace lay on the land for ever, **and** the fields gave good increase,
And there was Sigurd waxing mid the plenty and the peace.

Now hath the child grown greater, and is keen and eager of wit
And full of understanding, and oft hath he joy to sit
Amid talk of weighty matters when the wise men meet for speech;
And joyous he is moreover and blithe and kind with each.
But Regin the wise craftsmaster heedeth the youngling well,
And before the Kings he cometh, and saith such words to tell.

"I have fostered thy youth, King Elf, and thine O Helper of men,
And ye wot that such a master no king shall see again;
And now would I foster Sigurd; for, though he be none of thy blood,
Mine heart of his days that shall be speaketh abundant good."

Then spake the Helper of men-folk: "Yea, do herein thy will:
For thou art the Master of Masters, and hast learned me all my skill:
But think how bright is this youngling, and thy guile from him withhold;
For this craft of thine hath shown me that thy heart is grim and cold,
Though three men's lives thrice over thy wisdom might not learn;
And I love this son of Sigmund, and mine heart to him doth yearn."

Then Regin laughed, and answered: "I doled out cunning to thee;
But nought with him will I measure: yet no cold-heart shall he be,
Nor grim, nor evil-natured: for whate'er my will might frame,
Gone forth is the word of the Norns, that abideth ever the same.
And now, despite my cunning, how deem ye I shall die?"

And they said he would live as he listed, and at last in peace should lie
When he listed to live no longer; so mighty and wise he was.

But again he laughed and answered: "One day it shall come to pass,
That a beardless youth shall slay me: I know the fateful doom;
But nought may I withstand it, as it heaves up dim through the gloom."

So is Sigurd now with Regin, and he learns him many things;

Yea, all save the craft of battle, that men learned the sons of kings :
The smithying sword and war-coat ; the carving runes aright ;
The tongues of many countries, and soft speech for men's delight ;
The dealing with the harp-strings, and the winding ways of song.
So wise of heart waxed Sigurd, and of body wondrous strong :
And he chased the deer of the forest, and many a wood-wolf slew,
And many a bull of the mountains : and the desert dales he knew,
And the heaths that the wind sweeps over ; and seaward would he fare,
Far out from the outer skerries, and alone the sea-wights dare.

On a day he sat with Regin amidst the unfashioned gold,
And the silver grey from the furnace ; and Regin spake and told
Sweet tales of the days that have been, and the Kings of the bold and wise ;
Till the lad's heart swelled with longing and lit his sunbright eyes.

Then Regin looked upon him : "Thou too shalt one day ride
As the Volsung Kings went faring through the noble world and wide.
For this land is nought and narrow, and Kings of the carles are these,
And their earls are acre-biders, and their hearts are dull with peace."

But Sigurd knit his brows, and in wrathful wise he said :
"Ill words of those thou speakest that my youth have cherished,
And the friends that have made me merry, and the land that is fair and good."

Then Regin laughed and answered : "Nay, well I see by thy mood
That wide wilt thou ride in the world like thy kin of the earlier days :   [praise?
And wilt thou be wroth with thy master that he longs for thy winning the
And now if the sooth thou sayest, that these King-folk cherish thee well,
Then let them give thee a gift whereof the world shall tell :
Yea hearken to this my counsel, and crave for a battle-steed."

Yet wroth was the lad and answered : "I have many a horse to my need,
And all that the heart desireth, and what wouldst thou wish me more ?"

Then Regin answered and said : " Thy kin of the Kings of yore
Were the noblest men of men-folk ; and their hearts would never rest
Whatso of good they had gotten, if their hands held not the best.
Now do thou after my counsel, and crave of thy fosterers here
That thou choose of the horses of Gripir whichso thine heart holds dear."

He spake and his harp was with him, and he smote the strings full sweet,
And sang of the host of the Valkyrs, how they ride the battle to meet,
And the dew from the dear manes drippeth as they ride in the first of the sun,
And the tree-boughs open to meet it when the wind of the dawning is done :
And the deep dales drink its sweetness and spring into blossoming grass,
And the earth groweth fruitful of men, and bringeth their glory to pass.

Then the wrath ran off from Sigurd, and he left the smithying stead
While the song yet rang in the doorway : and that eve to the Kings he said :
" Will ye do so much for mine asking as to give me a horse to my will ?
For belike the days shall come, that shall all my heart fulfill,
And teach me the deeds of a king."

                              Then answered King Elf and spake :
" The stalls of the Kings are before thee to set aside or to take,
And nought we begrudge thee the best." —

                              Yet answered Sigurd again ;
For his heart of the mountains aloft and the windy drift was fain :
" Fair seats for the knees of Kings ! but now do I ask for a gift
Such as all the world shall be praising, the best of the strong and the swift.
Ye shall give me a token for Gripir, and bid him to let me choose
From out of the noble stud-beasts that run in his meadow loose.
But if overmuch I have asked you, forget this prayer of mine,
And deem the word unspoken, and get ye to the wine."

Then smiled King Elf, and answered : " A long way wilt thou ride,
To where unpeace and troubles and the griefs of the soul abide,

Yea unto the death at the last: yet surely shalt thou win
The praise of many a people: so have thy way herein.
Forsooth no more may we hold thee than the hazel copse may hold
The sun of the early dawning, that turneth it all unto gold."

Then sweetly Sigurd thanked them; and through the night he lay
Mid dreams of many a matter till the dawn was on the way;
Then he shook the sleep from off him, and that dwelling of Kings he left
And wended his ways unto Gripir.   On a crag from the mountain reft
Was the house of the old King builded; and a mighty house it was,
Though few were the sons of men that over its threshold would pass:
But the wild ernes cried about it, and the vultures toward it flew,   [through,
And the winds from the heart of the mountains searched every chamber
And about were meads wide-spreading; and many a beast thereon,
Yea some that are men-folk's terror, their sport and pasture won.

So into the hall went Sigurd; and amidst was Gripir set
In a chair of the sea-beast's tooth; and his sweeping beard nigh met
The floor that was green as the ocean, and his gown was of mountain-gold,
And the kingly staff in his hand was knobbed with the crystal cold.

Now the first of the twain spake Gripir: " Hail King with the eyen bright!
Nought needest thou show the token, for I know of thy life and thy light.
And no need to tell of thy message; it was wafted here on the wind,
That thou wouldst be coming to-day a horse in my meadow to find:
And strong must he be for the bearing of those deeds of thine that shall be.
Now choose thou of all the way-wearers that are running loose in my lea,
And be glad as thine heart will have thee and the fate that leadeth thee on,
And I bid thee again come hither when the sword of worth is won,
And thy loins are girt for thy going on the road that before thee lies;
For a glimmering over its darkness is come before mine eyes."

Then again gat Sigurd outward, and adown the steep he ran

And unto the horse-fed meadow: but lo, a grey-clad man,
One-eyed and seeming-ancient, there met him by the way:
And he spake: "Thou hastest, Sigurd; yet tarry till I say
A word that shall well bestead thee: for I know of these mountains well
And all the lea of Gripir, and the beasts that thereon dwell."

"Wouldst thou have red gold for thy tidings? art thou Gripir's horse-herd
Nay sure, for thy face is shining like the battle-eager men   [then?
My master Regin tells of: and I love thy cloud-grey gown,
And thy visage gleams above it like a thing my dreams have known."

"Nay whiles have I heeded the horse-kind," then spake that elder of days,
"And sooth do the sages say, when the beasts of my breeding they praise.
There is one thereof in the meadow, and, wouldst thou cull him out,
Thou shalt follow an elder's counsel, who hath brought strange things about,
Who hath known thy father aforetime, and other kings of thy kin."

So Sigurd said, "I am ready; and what is the deed to win?"

He said: "We shall drive the horses adown to the water-side,
That cometh forth from the mountains, and note what next shall betide."

Then the twain sped on together, and they drave the horses on
Till they came to a rushing river, a water wide and wan;
And the white mews hovered o'er it; but none might hear their cry
For the rush and the rattle of waters, as the downlong flood swept by.
So the whole herd took the river and strove the stream to stem,
And many a brave steed was there; but the flood o'ermastered them:
And some, it swept them down-ward, and some won back to bank,
Some, caught by the net of the eddies, in the swirling hubbub sank;
But one of all swam over, and they saw his mane of grey
Toss over the flowery meadows, a bright thing far away:
Wide then he wheeled about them, then took the stream again

And with the waves' white **horses** mingled his cloudy mane.

Then spake the elder of days : " Hearken now, Sigurd, and hear ;
Time **was when** I gave thy father a gift thou shalt yet **deem dear,**
And this **horse is a** gift **of** my giving :—heed nought where thou **mayst ride :**
For I have seen thy fathers in **a** shining house **abide,**
And on earth they thought of its threshold, and **the** gifts **I had to give ;**
Nor prayed for a little longer, **and a** little longer to live."

Then forth he **strode to the mountains, and fain was** Sigurd **now**
To ask him many a matter : but dim did his bright shape grow,
As a man from the litten doorway fades into the dusk of night ;
And the sun in the high-noon shone, and the world was exceeding bright.

So Sigurd turned to the river **and stood by the wave-wet strand,**
And the grey horse swims to his feet and lightly leaps aland,
And the youngling looks **upon him,** and deems none beside him good.
And indeed, **as** tells the **story, he** was come of Sleipnir's **blood,**
The tireless horse of Odin : cloud-grey he was **of hue,**
And it seemed as Sigurd backed him that **Sigmund's son he knew,**
So glad he went beneath him.   Then **the youngling's song arose**
As he brushed through the noon-tide blossoms of Gripir's mighty **close,**
Then he singeth the song of Greyfell, the horse that Odin gave,
Who swam through the sweeping river, **and** back through the toppling wave.

Regin telleth **Sigurd of his kindred, and of the Gold that was accursed**
from ancient days.

Now yet the days pass over, **and more than words may tell**
Grows Sigurd strong and lovely, **and all children love him well.**
But oft he looks on the mountains and many a time is fain
To know of what lies beyond them, and learn of the wide world's gain.

And he saith : " I dwell in a land that is ruled by none of my blood ;
And my mother's sons are waxing, and fair kings shall they be and good :
And their servant or their betrayer—not one of these will I be.
Yet needs must I wait for a little till Odin calls for me."

Now again it happed on a day that he sat in Regin's hall
And hearkened many tidings of what had chanced to fall,
And of kings that sought their kingdoms o'er many a waste and wild,
And at last saith the crafty master :
                         " Thou art King Sigmund's child :
Wilt thou wait till these kings of the carles shall die in a little land,
Or wilt thou serve their sons and carry the cup to their hand ;
Or abide in vain for the day that never shall come about,
When their banners shall dance in the wind and shake to the war-gods' shout?"

Then Sigurd answered and said : " Nought such do I look to be.
But thou, a deedless man, too much thou eggest me :
And these folk are good and trusty, and the land is lovely and sweet,
And in rest and in peace it lieth as the floor of Odin's feet :
Yet I know that the world is wide, and filled with deeds unwrought ;
And for e'en such work was I fashioned, lest the songcraft come to nought,
When the harps of God-home tinkle, and the Gods are at stretch to hearken
Lest the hosts of the Gods be scanty when their day hath begun to darken,
When the bonds of the Wolf wax thin, and Loki fretteth his chain.
And sure for the house of my fathers full oft my heart is fain,
And meseemeth I hear them talking of the day when I shall come,
And of all the burden of deeds, that my hand shall bear them home.
And so when the deed is ready, nowise the man shall lack :
But the wary foot is the surest, and the hasty oft turns back."

Then answered Regin the guileful : " The deed is ready to hand,
Yet holding my peace is the best, for well thou lovest the land ;
And thou lovest thy life moreover, and the peace of thy youthful days,

And why should the full-fed feaster his hand to the rye-bread raise?
Yet they say that Sigmund begat thee and he looked to fashion a man.
Fear nought; he lieth quiet in his mound by the sea-waves wan."

So shone the eyes of Sigurd, that the shield against him hung
Cast back their light as the sunbeams; but his voice to the roof-tree rung:
"Tell me, thou Master of Masters, what deed is the deed I shall do?
Nor mock thou the son of Sigmund lest the day of his birth thou rue."

Then answered the Master of Sleight: "The deed is the righting of wrong,
And the quelling a bale and a sorrow that the world hath endured o'erlong,
And the winning a treasure untold, that shall make thee more than the kings;
Thereof is the Helm of Aweing, the wonder of earthly things,
And thereof is its very fellow, the War-coat all of gold,
That has not its like in the heavens, nor has earth of its fellow told."

Then answered Sigurd the Volsung: "How long hereof hast thou known?
And what unto thee is this treasure, that thou seemest to give as thine own?"

"Alas!" quoth the smithying master, "it is mine, yet none of mine,
Since my heart herein avails not, and my hand is frail and fine—
It is long since I first came hither to seek a man for my need;
For I saw by a glimmering light that hence would spring the deed,
And many a deed of the world: but the generations passed,
And the first of the days was as near to the end that I sought as the last;
Till I looked on thine eyes in the cradle: and now I deem through thee,
That the end of my days of waiting, and the end of my woes shall be."

Then Sigurd awhile was silent; but at last he answered and said:
"Thou shalt have thy will and the treasure, and shalt take the curse on thine
If a curse the gold enwrappeth: but the deed will I surely do,   [head
For today the dreams of my childhood hath bloomed in my heart anew:
And I long to look on the world and the glory of the earth

And to deal in the dealings of men, and garner the harvest of worth.
But tell me, thou Master of Masters, where lieth this measureless wealth ;
Is it guarded by swords of the earl-folk, or kept by cunning and stealth?
Is it over the main sea's darkness, or beyond the mountain wall?
Or e'en in these peaceful acres anigh to the hands of all?"

Then Regin answered sweetly : " Hereof must a tale be told :
Bide sitting, thou son of Sigmund, on the heap of unwrought gold,
And hearken of wondrous matters, and of things unheard, unsaid,
And deeds of my beholding ere the first of Kings was made.

" And first ye shall know of a sooth, that I never was born of the race
Which the masters of God-home have made to cover the fair earth's face ;
But I come of the Dwarfs departed ; and fair was the earth whileome
Ere the short-lived thralls of the Gods amidst its dales were come :—
And how were we worse than the Gods, though maybe we lived not as long?
Yet no weight of memory maimed us ; nor aught we knew of wrong.
What felt our souls of shaming, what knew our hearts of love ?
We did and undid at pleasure, and repented nought thereof.
—Yea we were exceeding mighty—bear with me yet, my son ;
For whiles can I scarcely think it that our days are wholly done.
And trust not thy life in my hands in the day when most I seem
Like the Dwarfs that are long departed, and most of my kindred I dream.

" So as we dwelt came tidings that the Gods amongst us were,
And the people came from Asgard : then rose up hope and fear,
And strange shapes of things went flitting betwixt the night and the eve,
And our sons waxed wild and wrathful, and our daughters learned to grieve.
Then we fell to the working of metal, and the deeps of the earth would know,
And we dealt with venom and leechcraft, and we fashioned spear and bow,
And we set the ribs to the oak-keel, and looked on the landless sea ;
And the world began to be such-like as the Gods would have it to be.
In the womb of the woeful earth had they quickened the grief and the gold.

" It was Reidmar the Ancient begat me ; and now was he waxen old,
And a covetous man and a king ; and he bade, and I built him a hall,
And a golden glorious house ; and thereto his sons did he call,
And he bade them be evil and wise, that his will through them might be
      wrought.
Then he gave unto Fafnir my brother the soul that feareth nought,
And the brow of the hardened iron, and the hand that may never fail,
And the greedy heart of a king, and the ear that hears no wail.

" But next unto Otter my brother he gave the snare and the net,
And the longing to wend through the wild-wood, and wade the highways wet :
And the foot that never resteth, while aught be left alive
That hath cunning to match man's cunning or might with his might to strive.

" And to me, the least and the youngest, what gift for the slaying of ease ?
Save the grief that remembers the past, and the fear that the future sees ;
And the hammer and fashioning-iron, and the living coal of fire ;
And the craft that createth a semblance, and fails of the heart's desire ;
And the toil that each dawning quickens and the task that is never done ;
And the heart that longeth ever, nor will look to the deed that is won.

" Thus gave my father the gifts that might never be taken again ;
Far worse were we now than the Gods, and but little better than men.
But yet of our ancient might one thing had we left us still :
We had craft to change our semblance, and could shift us at our will
Into bodies of the beast-kind, or fowl, or fishes cold ;
For belike no fixèd semblance we had in the days of old,
Till the Gods were waxen busy, and all things their form must take
That knew of good and evil, and longed to gather and make.

" So dwelt we, brethren and father ; and Fafnir my brother fared
As the scourge and compeller of all things, and left no wrong undared :
But for me, I toiled and I toiled ; and fair grew my father's house ;

But writhen and foul **were the hands that had made it glorious;**
And the love of **women left me, and** the fame of sword and **shield :**
And **the sun and the winds** of heaven, and the fowl and the grass of the field
Were grown as the tools of my smithy; and all the world I knew,
And the glories that lie beyond it, and whitherward all things **drew ;**
And myself a little fragment amidst it all I saw,
Grim, cold-heart, and unmighty as the tempest-driven straw.
—Let be.—For Otter my brother saw seldom field or fold,
And he oftenest used **that custom,** whereof e'en now I told,
And would shift his shape with the wood-beasts and the things of land and sea;
And he knew what joy their hearts had, and what they longed to be,
And their dim-eyed understanding, and his wood-craft waxed so great,
That he seemed the king of the creatures and their very mortal fate.

" **Now as the years won over** three **folk** of the heavenly halls
Grew aweary of sleepless sloth, and the day that nought befalls;
And they fain would look on the earth, and their latest handiwork,
And turn the fine gold over, lest a flaw therein should lurk.
And the three were the heart-wise Odin, the Father of the Slain,
And Loki, the World's Begrudger, who maketh all labour vain,
And **Hænir, the** Utter-Blameless, who wrought the hope of man,
And his heart and inmost yearnings, when first the work began ;—
—The God that was aforetime, **and** hereafter yet shall be,
When the new light yet undreamed of shall shine o'er earth and sea.

" Thus about the **world** they wended and deemed it fair and good,
And they loved their life-days dearly : so came they to the wood,
And the lea without a shepherd and the dwellings of the deer,
And unto a mighty water that **ran** from a fathomless mere.
Now that flood my brother Otter **had** haunted many a day
For its plenteous fruit of fishes; and there on the bank he lay
As the Gods came wandering **thither ;** and he slept, and in his dreams
He saw the downlong river, and **its** fishy-peopled streams,

And the swift smooth heads of its forces, and its swirling wells and deep,
Where hang the poisèd fishes, and their watch in the rock-halls keep.
And so, as he thought of it all, and its deeds and its **wanderings,**
Whereby it ran to the sea down the road **of scaly things,**
His body was changed with his thought, as **yet was the wont of our kind,**
And he grew but an Otter indeed ; and his eyes were sleeping and **blind**
The while he devoured the prey, a golden **red-flecked trout.**
Then passed by Odin and Hænir, nor cumbered their souls with **doubt ;**
But Loki lingered a little, and guile **in his heart arose,**
And he saw through the shape of the Otter, and **beheld a chief of his foes,**
A king of the free and the careless : so he called up **his baleful might,**
And gathered his godhead together, and tore a shard outright
From the rock-wall of the river, and across its green wells cast ;
And roaring over the waters that bolt of evil passed,
And smote my brother Otter that his heart's life fled away,
And bore his man's shape with it, and beast-like there he lay,
Stark dead on the sun-lit blossoms : but the Evil God rejoiced,
And because of the sound of his singing the wild grew many-voiced.

"Then the three Gods waded the river, and **no word Hænir spake,**
For his thoughts were set on God-home, and the day **that is ever awake.**
But Odin laughed in his **wrath, and murmured : 'Ah, how long,**
Till the iron shall **ring on** the anvil for the shackles of thy wrong !'

"Then Loki takes up the quarry, and **is e'en as a man again ;**
And the three wend on through the wild-wood till they come to a grassy plain
Beneath the untrodden mountains ; **and lo a noble house,**
And a hall with great craft fashioned, and made full glorious ;
But night on the earth was falling ; so scantly might they see
The wealth of its smooth-wrought **stonework and its** world of imagery :
Then Loki bade turn thither since **day** was at an end,
And into that noble dwelling the lords of God-home wend ;
And the porch was fair and mighty, and so smooth-wrought was its gold,

That the mirrored stars of heaven therein might ye behold:
But the hall, what words shall tell it, how fair it rose aloft,
And the marvels of its windows, and its golden hangings soft,
And the forest of its pillars! and each like the wave's heart shone,
And the mirrored boughs of the garden were dancing fair thereon.
—Long years agone was it builded, and where are its wonders now?

"Now the men of God-home marvelled, and gazed through the golden glow,
And a man like a covetous king amidst of the hall they saw;
And his chair was the tooth of the whale, wrought smooth with never a flaw;
And his gown was the sea-born purple, and he bore a crown on his head,
But never a sword was before him: kind-seeming words he said,
And bade rest to the weary feet that had worn the wild so long.
So they sat, and were men by seeming; and there rose up music and song,
And they ate and drank and were merry: but amidst the glee of the cup
They felt themselves tangled and caught, as when the net cometh up
Before the folk of the firth, and the main sea lieth far off;
And the laughter of lips they hearkened, and that hall-abider's scoff,
As his face and his mocking eyes anigh to their faces drew,
And their godhead was caught in the net, and no shift of creation they knew
To escape from their man-like bodies; so great that day was the Earth.

"Then spake the hall-abider: 'Where then is thy guileful mirth,
And thy hall-glee gone, O Loki?   Come, Hænir, fashion now
My heart for love and for hope, that the fear in my body may grow,
That I may grieve and be sorry, that the ruth may arise in me,
As thou dealtst with the first of men-folk, when a master-smith thou wouldst
And thou, Allfather Odin, hast thou come on a bastard brood?   [be.
Or hadst thou belike a brother, thy twin for evil and good,
That waked amidst thy slumber, and slumbered midst thy work?
Nay, Wise-one, art thou silent as a child amidst the mirk?
Ah, I know ye are called the Gods, and are mighty men at home,
But now with a guilt on your heads to no feeble folk are ye come,

To a folk that need you nothing : time was when we knew you not :
Yet e'en then fresh was the winter, and the summer sun was hot,
And the wood-meats stayed our hunger, and the water quenched our thirst,
Ere the good and the evil wedded and begat the best and the worst.
And how if today I undo it, that work of your fashioning,
If the web of the world run backward, and the high heavens lack a King?
—Woe's me ! for your ancient mastery shall help you at your need :
If ye fill up the gulf of my longing and my empty heart of greed,
And slake the flame ye have quickened, then may ye go your ways
And get ye back to your kingship and the driving on of the days
To the day of the gathered war-hosts, and the tide of your Fateful Gloom.
Now nought may ye gainsay it that my mouth must speak the doom,
For ye wot well I am Reidmar, and that there ye lie red-hand
From the slaughtering of my offspring, and the spoiling of my land ;
For his death of my wold hath bereft me and every highway wet.
—Nay, Loki, naught avails it, well-fashioned is the net.
Come forth, my son, my war-god, and show the Gods their work,
And thou who mightst learn e'en Loki, if need were to lie or lurk!'

" And there was I, I Regin, the smithier of the snare,
And high up Fafnir towered with the brow that knew no fear,
With the wrathful and pitiless heart that was born of my father's will,
And the greed that the Gods had fashioned the fate of the earth to fulfill.

" Then spake the Father of Men   ' We have wrought thee wrong indeed,
And, wouldst thou amend it with wrong, thine errand must we speed ;
For I know of thine heart's desire, and the gold thou shalt nowise lack,
—Nor all the works of the gold.   But best were thy word drawn back,
If indeed the doom of the Norns be not utterly now gone forth.'

" Then Reidmar laughed and answered : ' So much is thy word of worth !
And they call thee Odin for this, and stretch forth hands in vain,
And pray for the gifts of a God who giveth and taketh again !

It was better in times past over, when we prayed for nought at all,
When no love taught us beseeching, and we had no troth to recall.
Ye have changed the world, and it bindeth with the right and the wrong ye
        have made,
Nor may ye be Gods henceforward save the rightful ransom be paid.
But perchance ye are weary of kingship, and will deal no more with the earth?
Then curse the world, **and** depart, and sit in your changeless mirth ;
And there shall be no more kings, and battle and murder shall fail,
And the world shall laugh and long not, nor weep, nor fashion the tale.'

"So spake Reidmar the Wise ; but the wrath burned through his word,
And wasted his heart of wisdom ; and there was Fafnir the Lord,
And there was Regin the Wright, and they raged at their father's back :
And all these cried out together with the voice of the sea-storm's wrack ;
'O hearken, Gods of the Goths ! ye shall die, and we shall be Gods,
And rule your men belovèd with bitter-heavy **rods,**
And make them beasts beneath us, save today ye do our will,
And pay us the ransom of blood, and our hearts with the gold fulfill.'

"But Odin spake in answer, and his voice was awful and cold :
'Give righteous doom, O Reidmar ! say what ye will of the Gold !'

"Then Reidmar laughed in his heart, and his wrath and his wisdom fled,
And nought but his greed abided ; and he spake from his throne and said :

"'Now hearken the doom I shall speak ! Ye stranger-folk shall be free
When ye give me the Flame of the Waters, the gathered Gold of the Sea,
That Andvari hideth rejoicing in the wan realm pale as the grave ;
And the Master of Sleight shall fetch it, and the hand that never gave,
And the heart that begrudgeth for ever shall gather and give and rue.
—Lo this is the doom of the wise, and no doom shall be spoken anew.'

"Then **Odin spake :** 'It is well ; the Curser shall seek for the curse ;

And the Greedy shall cherish the evil—and the seed of the Great they shall
[nurse.'
"No word spake Reidmar the great, for the eyes of his heart were turned
To the edge of the outer desert, so sore for the gold he yearned.
But Loki I loosed from the toils, and he goeth his way abroad ;
And the heart of Odin he knoweth, and where he shall seek the Hoard.

"There is a desert of dread in the uttermost part of the world,
Where over a wall of mountains is a mighty water hurled,
Whose hidden head none knoweth, nor where it meeteth the sea ;
And that force is the Force of Andvari, and an Elf of the Dark is he.
In the cloud and the desert he dwelleth amid that land alone ;
And his work is the storing of treasure within his house of stone.
Time was when he knew of wisdom, and had many a tale to tell
Of the days before the Dwarf-age, and of what in that world befell :
And he knew of the stars and the sun, and the worlds that come and go
On the nether rim of heaven, and whence the wind doth blow,
And how the sea hangs balanced betwixt the curving lands,
And how all drew together for the first Gods' fashioning hands.
But now is all gone from him, save the craft of gathering gold,
And he heedeth nought of the summer, nor knoweth the winter cold,
Nor looks to the sun nor the snowfall, nor ever dreams of the sea,
Nor hath heard of the making of men-folk, nor of where the high Gods be
But ever he gripeth and gathereth, and he toileth hour by hour,
Nor knoweth the noon from the midnight as he looks on his stony bower,
And saith : 'It is short, it is narrow for all I shall gather and get ;
For the world is but newly fashioned, and long shall its years be yet.'

"There Loki fareth, and seeth in a land of nothing good,
Far off o'er the empty desert, the reek of the falling flood
Go up to the floor of heaven, and thither turn his feet
As he weaveth the unseen meshes and the snare of strong deceit ;
So he cometh his ways to the water, where the glittering foam-bow glows,

And the huge flood leaps the rock-wall and a green arch over it throws.
There under the roof of water he treads the quivering floor,
And the hush of the desert is felt amid the water's roar,
And the bleak sun lighteth the wave-vault, and tells of the fruitless plain,
And the showers that nourish nothing, and the summer come in vain.

"There did the great Guile-master his toils and his tangles set,
And as wide as was the water, so wide was woven the net;
And as dim as the Elf's remembrance did the meshes of it show;
And he had no thought of sorrow, nor spared to come and go
On his errands of griping and getting till he felt himself tangled and caught:
Then back to his blinded soul was his ancient wisdom brought,
And he saw his fall and his ruin, as a man by the lightning's flame
Sees the garth all flooded by foemen; and again he remembered his name;
And e'en as a book well written the tale of the Gods he knew,
And the tale of the making of men, and much of the deeds they should do.

"But Loki took his man-shape, and laughed aloud and cried:
'What fish of the ends of the earth is so strong and so feeble-eyed,
That he draweth the pouch of my net on his road to the dwelling of Hell?
What Elf that hath heard the gold growing, but hath heard not the light winds tell
That the Gods with the world have been dealing and have fashioned men for
        the earth?
Where is he that hath ridden the cloud-horse and measured the ocean's girth,
But seen nought of the building of God-home nor the forging of the sword:
Where then is the maker of nothing, the earless and eyeless lord?

In the pouch of my net he lieth, with his head on the threshold of Hell!'
"Then the Elf lamented, and said: 'Thou knowst of my name full well:
Andvari begotten of Oinn, whom the Dwarf-kind called the Wise,
By the worst of the Gods is taken, the forge and the father of lies.'

"Said Loki: 'How of the Elf-kind, do they love their latter life,

When their weal is all departed, and they lie alow in the strife?'

"Then Andvari groaned and answered: 'I know what thou wouldst have,
The wealth mine own hands gathered, the gold that no man gave.'

"'Come forth,' said Loki, 'and give it, and dwell in peace henceforth—
Or die in the toils if thou listest, if thy life be nothing worth.'

"Full sore the Elf lamented, but he came before the God,
And the twain went into the rock-house and on fine gold they trod,
And the walls shone bright, and brighter than the sun of the upper air.
How great was that treasure of treasures : and the Helm of Dread was there;
The world but in dreams had seen it ; and there was the hauberk of gold ;
None other is in the heavens, nor has earth of its fellow told.

"Then Loki bade the Elf-king bring all to the upper day,
And he dight himself with his Godhead to bear the treasure away :
So there in the dim grey desert before the God of Guile,
Great heaps of the hid-world's treasure the weary Elf must pile,
And Loki looked on laughing : but, when it all was done,
And the Elf was hurrying homeward, his finger gleamed in the sun :
Then Loki cried : 'Thou art guileful : thou hast not learned the tale
Of the wisdom that Gods hath gotten and their might of all avail.
Hither to me ! that I learn thee of a many things to come ;
Or despite of all wilt thou journey to the dead man's deedless home.
Come hither again to thy master, and give the ring to me ;
For meseems it is Loki's portion, and the Bale of Men shall it be.'

"Then the Elf drew off the gold-ring and stood with empty hand
E'en where the flood fell over 'twixt the water and the land,
And he gazed on the great Guile-master, and huge and grim he grew ;
And his anguish swelled within him, and the word of the Norns he knew ;
How that gold was the seed of gold to the wise and the shapers of things,

The hoarders of hidden treasure, and the unseen glory of rings;
But the seed of woe to the world and the foolish wasters of men,
And grief to the generations that die and spring again:
Then he cried:
                  'There farest thou Loki, and might I load thee worse
Than with what thine ill heart beareth, then shouldst thou bear my curse
But for men a curse thou bearest: entangled in my gold,
Amid my woe abideth another woe untold.
Two brethren and a father, eight kings my grief shall slay;
And the hearts of queens shall be broken, and their eyes shall loathe the day.
Lo, how the wilderness blossoms! Lo, how the lonely lands
Are waving with the harvest that fell from my gathering hands!'

"But Loki laughed in silence, and swift in Godhead went,
To the golden hall of Reidmar and the house of our content.
But when that world of treasure was laid within our hall
'Twas as if the sun were minded to live 'twixt wall and wall,
And all we stood by and panted.   Then Odin spake and said:

"'O Kings, O folk of the Dwarf-kind, lo, the ransom duly paid!
Will ye have this sun of the ocean, and reap the fruitful field,
And garner up the harvest that earth therefrom shall yield?'

"So he spake; but a little season nought answered Reidmar the wise,
But turned his face from the Treasure, and peered with eager eyes
Endlong the hall and athwart it, as a man may chase about
A ray of the sun of the morning that a naked sword throws out;
And lo from Loki's right-hand came the flash of the fruitful ring,
And at last spake Reidmar scowling:
                                    'Ye wait for my yea-saying
That your feet may go free on the earth, and the fear of my toils may be done;
That then ye may say in your laughter: The fools of the time agone!
The purblind eyes of the Dwarf-kind! they have gotten the garnered sheaf

And have let their Masters depart with the Seed of Gold and of Grief:
O Loki, friend of Allfather, cast down Andvari's ring,
Or the world shall yet turn backward and the high heavens lack a king.'

"Then Loki drew off the Elf-ring and cast it down on the heap,
And forth as the gold met gold did the light of its glory leap:
But he spake: 'It rejoiceth my heart that no whit of all ye shall lack,
Lest the curse of the Elf-king cleave not, and ye 'scape the utter wrack.'

"Then laughed and answered Reidmar: 'I shall have it while I live,
And that shall be long, meseemeth: for who is there may strive
With my sword, the war-wise Fafnir, and my shield that is Regin the Smith?
But if indeed I should die, then let men-folk deal therewith,
And ride to the golden glitter through evil deeds and good.
I will have my heart's desire, and do as the high Gods would.'

"Then I loosed the Gods from their shackles, and great they grew on the floor
And into the night they gat them; but Odin turned by the door,
And we looked not, little we heeded, for we grudged his mastery;
Then he spake, and his voice was waxen as the voice of the winter sea:

"'O Kings, O folk of the Dwarfs, why then will ye covet and rue?
I have seen your fathers' fathers and the dust wherefrom they grew;
But who hath heard of my father or the land where first I sprung?
Who knoweth my day of repentance, or the year when I was young?
Who hath learned the names of the Wise-one or measured out his will?
Who hath gone before to teach him, and the doom of days fulfill?
Lo, I look on the Curse of the Gold, and wrong amended by wrong,
And love by love confounded, and the strong abased by the strong;
And I order it all and amend it, and the deeds that are done I see,
And none other beholdeth or knoweth; and who shall be wise unto me?
For myself to myself I offered, that all wisdom I might know,
And fruitful I waxed of works, and good and fair did they grow;

And I knew, and I wrought and fore-ordered ; and evil sat by my side,
And myself by myself hath been doomed, and I look for the fateful tide ;
And I deal with the generations, and the men mine hand hath made,
And myself by myself shall be grieved, lest the world and its fashioning fade.'

" They went and the Gold abided : but the words Allfather spake,
I call them back full often for that golden even's sake,
Yet little that hour I heard them, save as wind across the lea ;
For the gold shone up on Reidmar and on Fafnir's face and on me.
And sore I loved that treasure: so I wrapped my heart in guile,
And sleeked my tongue with sweetness, and set my face in a smile,
And I bade my father keep it, the more part of the gold,
Yet give good store to Fafnir for his goodly help and bold,
And deal me a little handful for my smithying-help that day.
But no little I desired, though for little I might pray ;
And prayed I for much or for little, he answered me no more
Than the shepherd answers the wood-wolf who howls at the yule-tide door:
But good he ever deemed it to sit on his ivory throne,
And stare on the red rings' glory, and deem he was ever alone :
And never a word spake Fafnir, but his eyes waxed red and grim
As he looked upon our father, and noted the ways of him.

" The night waned into the morning, and still above the Hoard
Sat Reidmar clad in purple ; but Fafnir took his sword,
And I took my smithying-hammer, and apart in the world we went ;
But I came aback in the even, and my heart was heavy and spent ;
And I longed, but fear was upon me and I durst not go to the Gold ;
So I lay in the house of my toil mid the things I had fashioned of old ;
And methought as I lay in my bed 'twixt waking and slumber of night
That I heard the tinkling metal and beheld the hall alight,
But I slept and dreamed of the Gods, and the things that never have slept,
Till I woke to a cry and a clashing and forth from the bed I leapt,
And there by the heaped-up Elf-gold my brother Fafnir stood,

And there at his feet lay Reidmar and reddened the Treasure with blood;
And e'en as I looked on his eyen they glazed and whitened with death,
And forth on the torch-litten hall he shed his latest breath.

"But I looked on Fafnir and trembled for he wore the Helm of Dread,
And his sword was bare in his hand, and the sword and the hand were red
With the blood of our father Reidmar, and his body was wrapped in gold,
With the ruddy-gleaming mailcoat of whose fellow hath nought been told,
And it seemed as I looked upon him that he grew beneath mine eyes:
And then in the mid-hall's silence did his dreadful voice arise:

"'I have slain my father Reidmar, that I alone might keep
The Gold of the darksome places, the Candle of the Deep.
I am such as the Gods have made me, lest the Dwarf-kind people the earth,
Or mingle their ancient wisdom with its short-lived latest birth.
I shall dwell alone henceforward, and the Gold and its waxing curse,
I shall brood on them both together, let my life grow better or worse.
And I am a King henceforward and long shall be my life,
And the Gold shall grow with my longing, for I shall hide it from strife,
And hoard up the Ring of Andvari in the house thine hand hath built.
O thou, wilt thou tarry and tarry, till I cast thy blood on the guilt?
Lo, I am a King for ever, and alone on the Gold shall I dwell
And do no deed to repent of and leave no tale to tell.'

"More awful grew his visage as he spake the word of dread,
And no more durst I behold him, but with heart a-cold I fled;
I fled from the glorious house my hands had made so fair,
As poor as the new-born baby with nought of raiment or gear:
I fled from the heaps of gold, and my goods were the eager will,
And the heart that remembereth all, and the hand that may never be still.

"Then unto this land I came, and that was long ago
As men-folk count the years; and I taught them to reap and to sow,

H

And a famous man I became: but that generation died,
And they said that Frey had taught them, and a God my name did hide.
Then I taught them the craft of metals, and the sailing of the sea,
And the taming of the horse-kind, and the yoke-beasts' husbandry,
And the building up of houses; and that race of men went by,
And they said that Thor had taught them; and a smithying-carle was I.
Then I gave their maidens the needle and I bade them hold the rock,
And the shuttle-race gaped for them as they sat at the weaving-stock.
But by then these were waxen crones to sit dim-eyed by the door,
It was Freyia had come among them to teach the weaving-lore.
Then I taught them the tales of old, and fair songs fashioned and true,
And their speech grew into music of measured time and due,
And they smote the harp to my bidding, and the land grew soft and sweet:
But ere the grass of their grave-mounds rose up above my feet,
It was Bragi had made them sweet-mouthed, and I was the wandering scald;
Yet green did my cunning flourish by whatso name I was called,
And I grew the master of masters—Think thou how strange it is
That the sword in the hands of a stripling shall one day end all this!

"Yet oft mid all my wisdom did I long for my brother's part,
And Fafnir's mighty kingship weighed heavy on my heart
When the Kings of the earthly kingdoms would give me golden gifts
From out of their scanty treasures, due pay for my cunning shifts.
And once—didst thou number the years thou wouldst think it long ago—
I wandered away to the country from whence our stem did grow.
There methought the fells grown greater, but waste did the meadows lie,
And the house was rent and ragged and open to the sky.
But lo, when I came to the doorway, great silence brooded there,
Nor bat nor owl would haunt it, nor the wood-wolves drew anear.
Then I went to the pillared hall-stead, and lo, huge heaps of gold,
And to and fro amidst them a mighty Serpent rolled:
Then my heart grew chill with terror, for I thought on the wont of our race,
And I, who had lost their cunning, was a man in a deadly place,

A feeble man and a swordless in the lone destroyer's fold ;
For I knew that the Worm was Fafnir, the Wallower on the Gold.

"So I gathered my strength and fled, and hid my shame again
Mid the foolish sons of men-folk ; and the more my hope was vain,
The more I longed for the Treasure, and deliv'rance from the yoke :
And yet passed the generations, and I dwelt with the short-lived folk.

"Long years, and long years after, the tale of men-folk told
How up on the Glittering Heath was the house and the dwelling of gold,
And within that house was the Serpent, and the Lord of the Fearful Face :
Then I wondered sore of the desert; for I thought of the golden place
My hands of old had builded ; for I knew by many a sign
That the Fearful Face was my brother, that the blood of the Worm was mine
This was ages long ago, and yet in that desert he dwells,
Betwixt him and men death lieth, and no man of his semblance tells ;
But the tale of the great Gold-wallower is never the more outworn.
Then came thy kin, O Sigurd, and thy father's father was born,
And I fell to the dreaming of dreams, and I saw thine eyes therein,
And I looked and beheld thy glory and all that thy sword should win ;
And I thought that thou shouldst be he, who should bring my heart its rest,
That of all the gifts of the Kings thy sword should give me the best.

"Ah, I fell to the dreaming of dreams ; and oft the gold I saw,
And the golden-fashioned Hauberk, clean-wrought without a flaw,
And the Helm that aweth the world ; and I knew of Fafnir's heart
That his wisdom was greater than mine, because he had held him apart,
Nor spilt on the sons of men-folk our knowledge of ancient days,
Nor bartered one whit for their love, nor craved for the people's praise.

"And some day I shall have it all, his gold and his craft and his heart
And the gathered and garnered wisdom he guards in the mountains apart
And then when my hand is upon it, my hand shall be as the spring

To thaw his winter away and the fruitful tide to bring.
It shall grow, it shall grow into summer, and I shall be he that wrought,
And my deeds shall be remembered, and my name that once was nought;
Yea I shall be Frey, and Thor, and Freyia, and Bragi in one:
Yea the God of all that is,—and no deed in the wide world done,   [yoke
But the deed that my heart would fashion: and the songs of the freed from the
Shall bear to my house in the heavens the love and the longing of folk.
And there shall be no more dying, and the sea shall be as the land,
And the world for ever and ever shall be young beneath my hand."

Then his eyelids fell, and he slumbered, and it seemed as Sigurd gazed
That the flames leapt up in the stithy and about the Master blazed,
And his hand in the harp-strings wandered and the sweetness from them
Then unto his feet leapt Sigurd and drew his stripling's sword,   [poured.
And he cried: "Awake, O Master, for, lo, the day goes by,
And this too is an ancient story, that the sons of men-folk die,
And all save fame departeth.   Awake! for the day grows late,
And deeds by the door are passing, nor the Norns will have them wait."

Then Regin groaned and wakened, sad-eyed and heavy-browed,
And weary and worn was he waxen, as a man by a burden bowed:
And he spake: "Hast thou hearkened, Sigurd, wilt thou help a man that is old
To avenge him for his father? Wilt thou win that Treasure of Gold
And be more than the Kings of the earth? Wilt thou rid the earth of a wrong
And heal the woe and the sorrow my heart hath endured o'erlong?"

Then Sigurd looked upon him with steadfast eyes and clear,
And Regin drooped and trembled as he stood the doom to hear:
But the bright child spake as aforetime, and answered the Master and said:
. "Thou shalt have thy will, and the Treasure, and take the curse on thine
[head."

*Of the forging of the Sword that is called The **Wrath of Sigurd.***

Now again came Sigurd to Regin, **and said: "Thou hast taught me a task**
Whereof **none knoweth** the ending: and a gift **at thine hands I ask."**

Then answered **Regin the Master: "The world must be wide indeed**
If my hand may **not reach across** it for aught thine heart may need."

"**Yea wide is the world,"** said Sigurd, "and soon spoken **is thy word;**
But this gift thou shalt nought gainsay me: for I bid thee forge me a sword."

Then spake the Master of Masters, and his voice **was sweet and soft:**
"Look forth abroad, O Sigurd, and note **in the heavens** aloft
How the dim white moon of the daylight hangs round as the Goth-God's shield,
Now for thee first rang mine anvil when **she** walked the heavenly field
A slim and lovely lady, and the old moon lay on her arm:
Lo, here is a sword I have wrought thee with many a spell and **charm**
And all the craft of the Dwarf-kind; **be** glad **thereof and sure;**
Mid many a storm of battle full well shall **it endure."**

Then Sigurd looked on the slayer, and never a word would speak:
Gemmed were the hilts and golden, **and the blade was** blue and bleak,
And runes of the Dwarf-kind's cunning each side the trench **were scored:**
But soft and sweet spake Regin: **"How likest** thou the **sword?"**

Then Sigurd laughed and answered: "The work is proved by the deed;
See **now** if this be **a traitor to fail me** in my need."

Then Regin trembled and shrank, so bright his eyes outshone
As he turned about to the anvil, and smote the sword thereon;
But the shards fell shivering earthward, and Sigurd's heart grew wroth
As the steel-flakes tinkled **about** him: "Lo, there the right-hand's troth!

Lo, there the golden glitter, and the word that soon is spilt."
And down amongst the ashes he cast the glittering hilt,
And turned his back on Regin and strode out through the door,
And for many a day of spring-tide came back again no more.
But at last he came to the stithy and again took up the word:
"What hast thou done, O Master, in the forging of the sword?"

Then sweetly Regin answered: "Hard task-master art thou,
But lo, a blade of battle that shall surely please thee now!
Two moons are clean departed since thou lookedst toward the sky
And sawest the dim white circle amid the cloud-flecks lie;
And night and day have I laboured; and the cunning of old days
Hath surely left my right-hand if this sword thou shalt not praise."

And indeed the hilts gleamed glorious with many a dear-bought stone,
And down the fallow edges the light of battle shone;
Yet Sigurd's eyes shone brighter, nor yet might Regin face
Those eyes of the heart of the Volsungs; but trembled in his place
As Sigurd cried: "O Regin, thy kin of the days of old
Were an evil and treacherous folk, and they lied and murdered for gold;
And now if thou wouldst bewray me, of the ancient curse beware,
And set thy face as the flint the bale and the shame to bear:
For he that would win to the heavens, and be as the Gods on high,
Must tremble nought at the road, and the place where men-folk die."

White leaps the blade in his hand and gleams in the gear of the wall,
And he smites, and the oft-smitten edges on the beaten anvil fall:
But the life of the sword departed, and dull and broken it lay
On the ashes and flaked-off iron, and no word did Sigurd say,
But strode off through the door of the stithy and went to the Hall of Kings,
And was merry and blithe that even mid all imaginings.

But when the morrow was come he went to his mother and spake:

"The shards, the shards of the **sword,** that thou gleanedst for my sake
In the night on the field of slaughter, **in** the tide when my father fell,
Hast thou kept them through sorrow and joyance? hast thou **warded** them
Where **hast** thou laid them, my mother?" [trusty and well?
Then she looked **upon him and** said:
"Art thou wroth, O Sigurd my son, that such **eyes are in thine head?**
And wilt thou be wroth with thy mother? do **I withstand thee at all?"**

"Nay," said **he,** "nought am **I wrathful, but the days rise up like a wall**
Betwixt **my soul and the** deeds, and I strive **to** rend them through.
And **why wilt** thou fear mine eyen? as the sword lies baleful **and blue**
E'en 'twixt the lips of lovers, when they swear **their troth thereon,**
So keen are the eyes ye have fashioned, ye **folk of the** days agone;
For therein is the light of battle, though **whiles it lieth asleep.**
Now give me the sword, **my** mother, **that Sigmund gave thee to** keep."

She said: "I shall give it thee gladly, for fain shall I be of thy praise
When thou knowest my careful keeping of that hope of the earlier days."

So she took his hand **in her** hand, and they **went their ways, they twain;**
Till they came to the treasure of queen-folk, **the** guarded **chamber of gain:**
They were all alone with its riches, and she turned the key **in the gold,**
And lifted the sea-born purple, and the silken **web** unrolled,
And lo, 'twixt her hands and her bosom the shards of Sigmund's **sword;**
No rust-fleck stained **its edges, and the gems** of the ocean's hoard
Were **as** bright **in** the hilts and **glorious,** as when in **the** Volsungs' **hall**
It shone in the eyes of the earl-folk and flashed from the shielded wall.

But Sigurd smiled upon **it, and** he said: **"O Mother of Kings,**
Well hast thou warded the war-glaive for **a mirror of many things,**
And a hope of much fulfilment: well hast thou **given to me**
The message of my fathers, **and** the word of thing **to be:**
Trusty hath been thy warding, **but** its hour is over **now:**

These shards shall be knit together, and shall hear **the** war-wind blow.
They shall shine through the rain of Odin, as the sun come back to the world,
When the heaviest bolt of the thunder amidst **the storm** is **hurled:**
They shall shake **the thrones** of Kings, and shear the **walls of** war,
And undo the knot of treason when the world is darkening o'er.   [the day;
They have shone in the dusk and the night-tide, they shall shine in the dawn and
They have gathered the storm together, they shall chase the clouds away;
They have sheared red gold asunder, they shall gleam o'er the garnered gold
They have ended many a story, they shall fashion a tale to be told:
They have lived in the wrack of the people; they shall live in the glory of folk
They have stricken **the** Gods in battle, for the Gods shall they strike the
                                                          [stroke."

Then she felt his hands about her as he took the fateful sword,
And he kissed her soft and sweetly; but she answered **never a** word:
So great and fair was he waxen, so glorious was his face,
So young, as the deathless Gods **are, that long in the golden place**
She stood when he was departed: **as** some for-travailed one
Comes over the dark fell-ridges on the birth-tide of the **sun,**
And his gathering sleep falls from him mid the glory **and the blaze;**
And he sees the world grow merry and looks on the lightened ways,
While the ruddy streaks are melting in the day-flood broad and white;
Then the morn-dusk he forgetteth, and the moon-lit waste of night,
And the hall whence he departed with its yellow candles' flare:
So stood the Isle-king's daughter in that treasure-chamber fair.

But swift on his ways went Sigurd, **and to** Regin's house he came,
Where the **Master stood in** the doorway and behind him leapt the flame,
And dark he **looked and** little: **no more** his speech was sweet,
No words on his lip were gathered the Volsung child to greet,
Till he took the sword from Sigurd and the shards of the days of old;
Then he spake:

              " Will nothing serve thee save this blue steel and cold,
The bane of thy father's father, the fate of all his kin,

The baleful blade I fashioned, the Wrath that the Gods would win ? "

Then answered the eye-bright Sigurd : " If thou thy **craft wilt do**
Nought save these battle-gleanings shall be my helper true :
And what if thou **begrudgest,** and my battle-blade be dull,
Yet the hand of the Norns is lifted and the cup is over-full.
Repentst thou ne'er so sorely that thy kin **must lie alow,**
How much soe'er thou longest the **world to overthrow,**
And, doubting the gold and the wisdom, wouldst **even now** appease
Blind hate and **eyeless murder,** and win the world **with these ;**
O'er-late is the time for repenting the word thy lips have said :
Thou shalt have the Gold and the wisdom and take its curse on **thine** head.
I say that thy lips have spoken, and no more with thee it lies
To do the deed or leave it : since thou hast **shown mine eyes**
The world that was aforetime, I **see the world to** be ;
And woe to the tangling thicket, or the wall that hindereth me !
And short is the space I will tarry ; for how if the Worm should die
Ere the first of my strokes be stricken ?   Wilt thou **get to thy mastery**
And knit these shards together that once in the Branstock **stood ?**
But if not and a smith's hands fail me, a king's hand yet shall be good ;
And the Norns have doomed thy brother.   **And** yet **I deem this sword**
Is the slayer of the Serpent, and the scatterer of the Hoard."

Great waxed the gloom of Regin, and he **said : " Thou sayest sooth,**
For none may turn him backward : the sword of a very youth
Shall one day end my cunning, as the Gods my joyance slew,
When nought thereof they were deeming, and another thing would do.
But this sword shall slay the Serpent ; **and** do another deed,
And many an one thereafter till it fail thee in thy **need.**
But as fair and great as thou standeth, yet get thee from mine house,
For in me too might ariseth, and the place is perilous
With the craft that was aforetime, and shall never be again,   [men.
When the hands that have taught thee cunning have failed from the world of

Thou art wroth; **but** thy wrath must slumber till fate its blossom bear;
Not thus were the eyes of Odin when **I** held **him in the** snare.
Depart! **lest** the end overtake **us** ere thy work and mine be done,
But **come** again in the night-tide and the slumber of the sun,
When the sharded moon of April hangs round in the undark May."

Hither and thither a while did the heart of Sigurd sway;
For he feared **no** craft of the Dwarf-kind, nor heeded the ways of Fate,
But his hand wrought e'en as his heart would: and now was he weary with hate
Of the hatred and scorn of the **Gods, and** the greed of gold and of gain,
And the weaponless hands **of** the stripling **of** the wrath and the rending were
But there stood Regin the Master, and his eyes were on Sigurd's eyes,   [fain.
Though nought belike they beheld him, and his brow was sad and wise;
And the **greed died** out of his visage and he **stood like an image of old.**

So the Norns drew Sigurd **away, and the tide was an even of gold,**
And sweet in the April **even were the** fowl-kind singing their **best;**
And the light of life smote Sigurd, and **the joy that** knows no **rest,**
And the fond unnamed desire, and the hope of hidden things;
And he wended fair and lovely to the house of the feasting Kings.

But now when the moon was at full and the undark May begun,
Went Sigurd **unto** Regin mid the slumber of the sun,
And amidst the fire-hall's pavement the King of the Dwarf-kind stood
Like an image of deeds departed and days that once were good;
And he seemed but faint and weary, and his eyes were dim and dazed
As they met the glory of Sigurd where the fitful candles blazed.
Then he spake:
            " Hail, Son of the Volsungs, the corner-stone is laid,
I have toiled and thou hast desired, and, lo, the fateful blade!"

Then Sigurd **saw it** lying on the ashes slaked and pale,
Like the sun and the lightning mingled mid the even's cloudy bale,

For ruddy and great were the hilts, and the edges fine and wan,
And all adown to the blood-point a very flame there ran
That swallowed the runes of wisdom wherewith its sides were scored.
No sound did Sigurd utter as he stooped adown for his sword,
But it seemed as his lips were moving with speech of strong desire.
White leapt the blade o'er his head, and he stood in the ring of its fire
As hither and thither it played, till it fell on the anvil's strength,
And he cried aloud in his glory, and held out the sword full length,
As one who would show it the world ; for the edges were dulled no whit,
And the anvil was cleft to the pavement with the dreadful dint of it.

But Regin cried to his harp-strings : " Before the days of men
I smithied the Wrath of Sigurd, and now is it smithied again :
And my hand alone hath done it, and my heart alone hath dared
To bid that man to the mountain, and behold his glory bared.
Ah, if the son of Sigmund might wot of the thing I would,
Then how were the ages bettered, and the world all waxen good !
Then how were the past forgotten and the weary days of yore,
And the hope of man that dieth and the waste that never bore !
How should this one live through the winter and know of all increase !
How should that one spring to the sunlight and bear the blossom of peace !
No more should the long-lived wisdom o'er the waste of the wilderness stray ;
Nor the clear-eyed hero hasten to the deedless ending of day.
And what if the hearts of the Volsungs for this deed of deeds were born,
How then were their life-days evil and the end of their lives forlorn ?"

There stood Sigurd the Volsung, and heard how the harp-strings rang,
But of other things they told him than the hope that the Master sang ;
And his world lay far away from the Dwarf-king's eyeless realm
And the road that leadeth nowhere, and the ship without a helm :
But he spake : " How oft shall I say it, that I shall work thy will ?
If my father hath made me mighty, thine heart shall I fulfill
With the wisdom and gold thou wouldest, before I wend on my ways ;

For now hast thou failed me nought, and the sword is the wonder of days."

No word for a while spake Regin ; but he hung his head adown
As a man that pondereth sorely, and his voice once more was grown
As the voice of the smithying-master as he spake : " This Wrath of thine
Hath cleft the hard and the heavy ; it shall shear the soft and the fine :
Come forth to the night and prove it."
                                        So they twain went forth abroad,
And the moon lay white on the river and lit the sleepless ford,
And down to its pools they wended, and the stream was swift and full ;
Then Regin cast against it a lock of fine-spun wool,
And it whirled about on the eddy till it met the edges bared,
And as clean as the careless water the laboured fleece was sheared.

Then Regin spake : " It is good, what the smithying-carle hath wrought :
Now the work of the King beginneth, and the end that my soul hath sought
Thou shalt toil and I shall desire, and the deed shall be surely done :
For thy Wrath is alive and awake and the story of bale is begun."

Therewith was the Wrath of Sigurd laid soft in a golden sheath
And the peace-strings knit around it ; for that blade was fain of death ;
And 'tis ill to show such edges to the broad blue light of day,
Or to let the hall-glare light them, if ye list not play the play.

Of Gripir's Foretelling.

Now Sigurd backeth Greyfell on the first of the morrow morn,
And he rideth fair and softly through the acres of the corn ;
The Wrath to his side is girded, but hid are the edges blue,
As he wendeth his ways to the mountains, and rideth the horse-mead through.
His wide grey eyes are happy, and his voice is sweet and soft,
As amid the mead-lark's singing he casteth song aloft :

Lo, lo, the horse and the rider! So once maybe it was,
When over the Earth unpeopled the youngest God would pass;
But never again meseemeth shall such a sight betide,
Till over a world unwrongful new-born shall Baldur ride.

So he comes to that ness of the mountains, and Gripir's garden steep,
That bravely Greyfell breasteth, and adown by the door doth he leap
And his war-gear rattleth upon him; there is none to ask or forbid
As he wendeth the house clear-lighted, where no mote of the dust is hid,
Though the sunlight hath not entered: the walls are clear and bright,
For they cast back each to other the golden Sigurd's light;
Through the echoing ways of the house bright-eyed he wendeth along,
And the mountain-wind is with him, and the hovering eagles' song;
But no sound of the children of men may the ears of the Volsung hear,
And no sign of their ways in the world, or their will, or their hope or their fear.

So he comes to the hall of Gripir, and gleaming-green is it built
As the house of under-ocean where the wealth of the greedy is spilt;
Gleaming and green as the sea, and rich as its rock-strewn floor,
And fresh as the autumn morning when the burning of summer is o'er.
There he looks and beholdeth the high-seat, and he sees it strangely wrought,
Of the tooth of the sea-beast fashioned ere the Dwarf-kind came to nought;
And he looks, and thereon is Gripir, the King exceeding old,
With the sword of his fathers girded, and his raiment wrought of gold;
With the ivory rod in his right-hand, with his left on the crystal laid,
That is round as the world of men-folk, and after its image made,
And clear is it wrought to the eyen that may read therein of Fate,
Though little indeed be its sea, and its earth not wondrous great.

There Sigurd stands in the hall, on the sheathèd Wrath doth he lean,
All his golden light is mirrored in the gleaming floor and green;
But the smile in his face upriseth as he looks on the ancient King,
And their glad eyes meet and their laughter, and sweet is the welcoming:

And Gripir saith : " Hail Sigurd ! for my bidding hast thou done,
And here in the mountain-dwelling are two Kings of men alone."

But Sigurd spake : " Hail father ! I am girt with the fateful sword
And my face is set to the highway, and I come for thy latest word."

Said Gripir : " What wouldst thou hearken ere we sit and drink the wine?"

"Thy word and the Norns'," said Sigurd, "but never a word of mine."

"What sights wouldst thou see," said Gripir, "ere mine hand shall take thine
                                               [hand ? "
"As the Gods would I see," said Sigurd, "though Death light up the land."

"What hope wouldst thou hope, O Sigurd, ere we kiss, we twain, and depart?"

"Thy hope and the Gods'," said Sigurd, "though the grief lie hard on my
                                             [heart."
Nought answered the ancient wise-one, and not a whit had he stirred
Since the clash of Sigurd's raiment in his mountain-hall he heard ;
But the ball that imaged the earth was set in his hand grown old ;
And belike it was to his vision, as the wide-world's ocean rolled,
And the forests waved with the wind, and the corn was gay with the lark,
And the gold in its nether places grew up in the dusk and the dark,
And its children built and departed, and its King-folk conquered and went,
As over the crystal image his all-wise face was bent :
For all his desire was dead, and he lived as a God shall live,
Whom the prayers of the world hath forgotten, and to whom no hand may give.

But there stood the mighty Volsung, and leaned on the hidden Wrath ;
As the earliest sun's uprising o'er the sea-plain draws a path
Whereby men sail to the Eastward and the dawn of another day,
So the image of King Sigurd on the gleaming pavement lay.

Then great in the hall fair-pillared the voice of Gripir arose,
And it ran through the glimmering house-ways, and forth to the sunny close;
There mid the birds' rejoicing went the voice of an o'er-wise King
Like a wind of midmost winter come back to talk with spring.

But the voice cried: "Sigurd, Sigurd! O great, O early born!
O hope of the Kings first fashioned! O blossom of the morn!
Short day and long remembrance, fair summer of the North!
One day shall the worn world wonder how first thou wentest forth!

"Arise, O Sigurd, Sigurd! in the night arise and go,
Thou shalt smite when the day-dawn glimmers through the folds of God-
[home's foe:
"There the child in the noon-tide smiteth; the young King rendeth apart,
The old guile by the guile encompassed, the heart made wise by the heart.

"Bind the red rings, O Sigurd; bind up to cast abroad!
That the earth may laugh before thee rejoiced by the Waters' Hoard.

"Ride on, O Sigurd, Sigurd! for God's word goes forth on the wind,
And he speaketh not twice over; nor shall they loose that bind:
But the Day and the Day shall loosen, and the Day shall awake and arise,
And the Day shall rejoice with the Dawning, and the wise heart learn of the
[wise.
"O fair, O fearless, O mighty, how green are the garths of Kings,
How soft are the ways before thee to the heart of their war-farings!

"How green are the garths of King-folk, how fair is the lily and rose
In the house of the Cloudy People, 'neath the towers of kings and foes!

"Smite now, smite now in the noontide! ride on through the hosts of men!
Lest the dear remembrance perish, and today come not again.

"Is it day?—But the house is darkling—But the hand would gather and hold,
And the lips have kissed the cloud-wreath, and a cloud the arms enfold.

"In the dusk hath the Sower arisen; in the dark hath he cast the seed,
And the ear is the sorrow of Odin and the wrong, and the nameless need!

"Ah the hand hath gathered and garnered, and empty is the hand,
Though the day be full and fruitful mid the drift of the Cloudy Land!

"Look, look on the drift of the clouds, how the day and the even doth grow
As the long-forgotten dawning that was a while ago!

"Dawn, dawn, O mighty of men! and why wilt thou never awake,
When the holy field of the Goth-folk cries out for thy love and thy sake?

"Dawn, now; but the house is silent, and dark is the purple blood
On the breast of the Queen fair-fashioned; and it riseth up as a flood
Round the posts of the door belovèd; and a deed there lieth therein:
The last of the deeds of Sigurd; the worst of the Cloudy Kin—
The slayer slain by the slain within the door and without.
—O dawn as the eve of the birth-day! O dark world cumbered with doubt!

"Shall it never be day any more, nor the sun's uprising and growth?
Shall the kings of earth lie sleeping and the war-dukes wander in sloth
Through the last of the winter twilight? is the word of the wise-ones said
Till the five-fold winter be ended and the trumpet waken the dead?

"Short day and long remembrance! great glory for the earth!
O deeds of the Day triumphant! O word of Sigurd's worth!
It is done, and who shall undo it of all who were ever alive?
May the Gods or the high Gods' masters 'gainst the tale of the righteous strive,
And the deeds to follow after, and all their deeds increase,
Till the uttermost field is foughten, and Baldur riseth in peace!

"Cry out, O waste, before him ! O rocks of the wilderness, cry !
For tomorn shalt thou see the glory, and the man not made to die !
Cry out, O upper heavens ! O clouds beneath the lift !
For the golden King shall be riding high-headed midst the drift :
The mountain waits and the fire ; there waiteth the heart of the wise
Till the earthly toil is accomplished, and again shall the fire arise ;
And none shall be nigh in the ending and none by his heart shall be laid,
Save the world that he cherished and quickened, and the Day that he wakened
                                          [and made."

So died the voice of Gripir from amidst the sunny close,
And the sound of hastening eagles from the mountain's feet arose,
But the hall was silent a little, for still stood Sigmund's son,
And he heard the words and remembered, and knew them one by one.
Then he turned on the ancient Gripir with eyes that knew no guile
And smiled on the wise of King-folk as the first of men might smile
On the God that hath fashioned him happy ; and he spake :
                              " Hast thou spoken and known
How there standeth a child before thee and a stripling scarcely grown ?
Or hast thou told of the Volsungs, and the gathered heart of these,
And their still unquenched desire for garnering fame's increase ?
E'en so do I hearken thy words : for I wot how they deem it long
Till a man from their seed be arisen to deal with the cumber and wrong.
Bid me therefore to sit by thy side, for behold I wend on my way,
And the gates swing-to behind me, and each day of mine is a day
With deeds in the eve and the morning, nor deeds shall the noontide lack ;
To the right and the left none calleth, and no voice crieth aback."

" Come, kin of the Gods," said Gripir, " come up and sit by my side,
That we twain may be glad as the fearless, and they that have nothing to hide :
I have wrought out my will and abide it, and I sit ungrieved and alone,
I look upon men and I help not ; to me are the deeds long done
As those of today and tomorrow : for these and for those am I glad ;
But the Gods and men are the framers, and the days of my life I have had."

                                          I

Then Sigurd came unto Gripir, and he kissed the wise-one's face,
And they sat in the high-seat together, the child and the elder of days;
And they drank of the wine of King-folk, and were joyful each of each,
And spake for a while of matters that are meet for King-folk's speech;
The deeds of men that have been and Kin of the Kings of the earth;
And Gripir told of the outlands, and the mid-world's billowy girth,
And tales of the upper heaven were mingled with his talk,   [walk,
And the halls where the Sea-Queen's kindred o'er the gem-strewn pavement
And the innermost parts of the earth, where they lie, the green and the blue,
And the red and the glittering gem-stones that of old the Dwarf-kind knew.

Long Sigurd sat and marvelled at the mouth that might not lie,
And the eyes no God had blinded, and the lone heart raised on high,
Then he rose from the gleaming high-seat, and the rings of battle rang
And the sheathèd Wrath was hearkening and a song of war it sang,
But Sigurd spake unto Gripir:
                    "Long and lovely are thy days,
And thy years fulfilled of wisdom, and thy feet on the unhid ways,
And the guileless heart of the great that knoweth not anger nor pain:
So once hath a man been fashioned and shall not be again.
But for me hath been foaled the war-horse, the grey steed swift as the cloud,
And for me were the edges smithied, and the Wrath cries out aloud;
And a voice hath called from the darkness, and I ride to the Glittering Heath;
To smite on the door of Destruction, and waken the warder of Death."

So they kissed, the wise and the wise, and the child from the elder turned;
And again in the glimmering house-ways the golden Sigurd burned;
He stood outside in the sunlight, and tarried never a deal,
But leapt on the cloudy Greyfell with the clank of gold and steel,
And he rode through the sinking day to the walls of the kingly stead,
And came to Regin's dwelling when the wind was fallen dead,
And the great sun just departing: then blood-red grew the west,
And the fowl flew home from the sea-mead, and all things sank to rest.

*Sigurd rideth **to the Glittering Heath.***

Again on the morrow morning doth Sigurd the Volsung ride,
And Regin, the Master of Masters, is faring by his side,
And they leave the dwelling of kings and ride the summer land,
Until at the eve of the day the hills are on either hand :
Then they wend up higher and higher, and over the heaths they fare
Till the moon shines broad on the midnight, and they sleep 'neath the heavens
And they waken and look behind them, and lo, the dawning of day [bare ;
And the little land of the Helper and its valleys far away ;
But the mountains rise before them, a wall exceeding great.

Then spake the Master of Masters : "We have come to the garth and the gate :
There is youth and rest behind thee and many a thing to do,
There is many a fond desire, and each day born anew ;
And the land of the Volsungs to conquer, and many a people's praise :
And for me there is rest it maybe, and the peaceful end of days.
We have come to the garth and the gate ; to the hall-door now shall we win,
Shall we go to look on the high-seat and see what sitteth therein ? "

" Yea, and what else ? " said Sigurd, " was thy tale but mockeries,
And have I been drifted hither on a wind of empty lies ? "

" It was sooth, it was sooth," said Regin, " and more might I have told
Had I heart and space to remember the deeds of the days of old."

And he hung down his head as he spake it, and was silent a little space ;
And when it was lifted again there was fear in the Dwarf-king's face.
And he said : "Thou knowest my thought, and wise-hearted art thou grown :
It were well if thine eyes were blinder, and we each were faring alone,
And I with my eld and my wisdom, and thou with thy youth and thy might ;
Yet whiles I dream I have wrought thee, a beam of the morning bright,

A fatherless motherless glory, to work out my desire;
Then high my hope ariseth, and my heart is all afire
For the world I behold from afar, and the day that yet shall be;
Then I wake and all things I remember and a youth of the Kings I see—
—The child of the Wood-abider, the seed of a conquered King,
The sword that the Gods have fashioned, the fate that men shall sing :—
Ah might the world run backward to the days of the Dwarfs of old,
When I hewed out the pillars of crystal, and smoothed the walls of gold!"

Nought answered the Son of Sigmund; nay he heard him nought at all,
Save as though the wind were speaking in the bights of the mountain-hall :
But he leapt aback of Greyfell, and the glorious sun rose up,
And the heavens glowed above him like the bowl of Baldur's cup,
And a golden man was he waxen; as the heart of the sun he seemed,
While over the feet of the mountains like blood the new light streamed;
Then Sigurd cried to Greyfell and swift for the pass he rode,
And Regin followed after as a man bowed down by a load.

Day-long they fared through the mountains, and that highway's fashioner
Forsooth was a fearful craftsman, and his hands the waters were,
And the heaped-up ice was his mattock, and the fire-blast was his man,
And never a whit he heeded though his walls were waste and wan,
And the guest-halls of that wayside great heaps of the ashes spent.
But, each as a man alone, through the sun-bright day they went,
And they rode till the moon rose upward, and the stars were small and fair,
Then they slept on the long-slaked ashes beneath the heavens bare ;   [seemed
And the cold dawn came and they wakened, and the King of the Dwarf-kind
As a thing of that wan land fashioned; but Sigurd glowed and gleamed
Amid the shadowless twilight by Greyfell's cloudy flank,
As a little space they abided while the latest star-world shrank ;
On the backward road looked Regin and heard how Sigurd drew
The girths of Greyfell's saddle, and the voice of his sword he knew,
And he feared to look on the Volsung, as thus he fell to speak :

"I have seen the Dwarf-folk mighty, I have seen the God-folk weak ;
And now, though our might be minished, yet have we gifts to give.
When men desire and conquer, most sweet is their life to live ;
When men are young and lovely there is many a thing to do,
And sweet is their fond desire and the dawn that springs anew."

"This gift," said the Son of Sigmund, "the Norns shall give me yet,
And no blossom slain by the sunshine while the leaves with dew are wet."

Then Regin turned and beheld him : "Thou shalt deem it hard and strange,
When the hand hath encompassed it all, and yet thy life must change.
Ah, long were the lives of men-folk, if betwixt the Gods and them
Were mighty warders watching mid the earth's and the heaven's hem !
Is there any man so mighty he would cast this gift away,—
The heart's desire accomplished, and life so long a day,
That the dawn should be forgotten ere the even was begun ? "

Then Sigurd laughed and answered : "Fare forth, O glorious sun ;
Bright end from bright beginning, and the mid-way good to tell,
And death, and deeds accomplished, and all remembered well !
Shall the day go past and leave us, and we be left with night,
To tread the endless circle, and strive in vain to smite ?
But thou—wilt thou still look backward ? thou sayst I know thy thought :
Thou hast whetted the sword for the slaying, it shall turn aside for nought.
Fear not ! with the Gold and the wisdom thou shalt deem thee God alone,
And mayst do and undo at pleasure, nor be bound by right nor wrong :
And then, if no God I be waxen, I shall be the weak with the strong."

And his war-gear clanged and tinkled as he leapt to the saddle-stead :
And the sun rose up at their backs and the grey world changed to red,
And away to the west went Sigurd by the glory wreathed about,
But little and black was Regin as a fire that dieth out.
Day-long they rode the mountains by the crags exceeding old,

And the ash that the first of the Dwarf-kind found dull and quenched and cold.
Then the moon in the mid-sky swam, and the stars were fair and pale,
And beneath the naked heaven they slept in an ash-grey dale ;
And again at the dawn-dusk's ending they stood upon their feet,
And Sigurd donned his war-gear nor his eyes would Regin meet.

A clear streak widened in heaven low down above the earth ;
And above it lay the cloud-flecks, and the sun, anigh its birth,
Unseen, their hosts was staining with the very hue of blood,
And ruddy by Greyfell's shoulder the Son of Sigmund stood.

Then spake the Master of Masters : " What is thine hope this morn
That thou dightest thee, O Sigurd, to ride this world forlorn ? "

"What needeth hope," said Sigurd, "when the heart of the Volsungs turns
To the light of the Glittering Heath, and the house where the Waster burns?
I shall slay the Foe of the Gods, as thou badst me a while agone,
And then with the Gold and its wisdom shalt thou be left alone."

[round

" O Child," said the King of the Dwarf-kind, "when the day at last comes
For the dread and the Dusk of the Gods, and the kin of the Wolf is unbound,
When thy sword shall hew the fire, and the wildfire beateth thy shield,
Shalt thou praise the wages of hope and the Gods that pitched the field ? "

" O Foe of the Gods," said Sigurd, "wouldst thou hide the evil thing,
And the curse that is greater than thou, lest death end thy labouring,
Lest the night should come upon thee amidst thy toil for nought?
It is me, it is me that thou fearest, if indeed I know thy thought ;
Yea me, who would utterly light the face of all good and ill,
If not with the fruitful beams that the summer shall fulfill,
Then at least with the world a-blazing, and the glare of the grinded sword."

And he sprang aloft to the saddle as he spake the latest word,

And the Wrath sang loud in the sheath as it ne'er had sung before,
And the cloudy flecks were **scattered like flames on the** heaven's **floor**,
And all was kindled at once, and that trench of the mountains grey
Was filled with the living light as the low sun lit the way :
But Regin turned from the glory with blinded eyes and dazed,
And lo, on the cloudy war-steed how another light there blazed,
And a great voice came from amidst it :
                                        "O Regin, in good sooth,
I have hearkened not nor heeded the words of thy fear and **thy ruth** :
Thou **hast told** thy tale and thy longing, and **thereto I** hearkened **well** :—
Let **it** lead thee up to heaven, let it lead thee **down to** hell,
The deed shall be done tomorrow : thou shalt **have that measureless Gold**,
And devour the garnered wisdom that blessed **thy** realm **of** old,
That hath lain unspent and begrudged **in** the very heart of hate :
With the blood and the might of thy brother thine hunger shalt thou sate ;
And this deed shall be mine and thine; but take heed for what followeth then!
Let each do after his kind ! I shall do the deeds of men ;
I shall harvest the field of their sowing, in the bed of their strewing **shall sleep**;
To them shall I give my life-days, to the Gods my **glory to keep**.
But thou with the wealth and the wisdom that the best of the Gods might praise,
If thou shalt indeed excel them and become the hope **of the days**,
Then me in turn hast thou conquered, **and I shall be in turn**
Thy fashioned brand of the battle through good **and evil to burn,**
Or the flame that sleeps in thy stithy **for the gathered winds to blow,**
When thou listest to do and undo and thine uttermost cunning **to show**.
But indeed I wot full surely that thou shalt follow **thy kind** ;
And for all that cometh after, the Norns shall loose and **bind**."

Then his bridle-reins rang **sweetly**, and the warding-walls of death,
And Regin drew up to him, and the Wrath sang loud in the sheath,
And forth from that trench in the mountains by the westward way they ride;
And little **and** black goes Regin by the golden Volsung's side ;
But no more his head **is** drooping, for he seeth the Elf-king's **Gold** ;

The garnered might and the wisdom e'en now his eyes behold.

So up and up they journeyed, and ever as they went
About the cold-slaked forges, o'er many a cloud-swept bent,
Betwixt the walls of blackness, by shores of the fishless meres,
And the fathomless desert waters, did Regin cast his fears,
And wrap him in desire; and all alone he seemed
As a God to his heirship wending, and forgotten and undreamed
Was all the tale of Sigurd, and the folk he had toiled among,
And the Volsungs, Odin's children, and the men-folk fair and young.

So on they ride to the westward, and huge were the mountains grown
And the floor of heaven was mingled with that tossing world of stone:
And they rode till the noon was forgotten and the sun was waxen low,
And they tarried not, though he perished, and the world grew dark below.
Then they rode a mighty desert, a glimmering place and wide,
And into a narrow pass high-walled on either side
By the blackness of the mountains, and barred aback and in face
By the empty night of the shadow; a windless silent place:
But the white moon shone o'erhead mid the small sharp stars and pale,
And each as a man alone they rode on the highway of bale.

So ever they wended upward, and the midnight hour was o'er,
And the stars grew pale and paler, and failed from the heaven's floor,
And the moon was a long while dead, but where was the promise of day?
No change came over the darkness, no streak of the dawning grey;
No sound of the wind's uprising adown the night there ran:
It was blind as the Gaping Gulf ere the first of the worlds began.

Then athwart and athwart rode Sigurd and sought the walls of the pass,
But found no wall before him; and the road rang hard as brass
Beneath the hoofs of Greyfell, as up and up he trod:
—Was it the daylight of Hell, or the night of the doorway of God?

But lo, at the last a glimmer, and a light from the west there came,
And another and another, like points of far-off flame;
And they grew and brightened and gathered; and whiles together they ran
Like the moonwake over the waters; and whiles they were scant and wan,
Some greater and some lesser, like the boats of fishers laid
About the sea of midnight; and a dusky dawn they made,
A faint and glimmering twilight: So Sigurd strains his eyes,
And he sees how a land deserted all round about him lies
More changeless than mid-ocean, as fruitless as its floor:
Then the heart leaps up within him, for he knows that his journey is o'er,
And there he draweth bridle on the first of the Glittering Heath:
And the Wrath is waxen merry and sings in the golden sheath
As he leaps adown from Greyfell, and stands upon his feet,
And wends his ways through the twilight the Foe of the Gods to meet

Sigurd slayeth Fafnir the Serpent.

Nought Sigurd seeth of Regin, and nought he heeds of him,
As in watchful might and glory he strides the desert dim,
And behind him paceth Greyfell; but he deems the time o'erlong
Till he meet the great gold-warden, the over-lord of wrong.

So he wendeth midst the silence through the measureless desert place,
And beholds the countless glitter with wise and steadfast face,
Till him-seems in a little season that the flames grown somewhat wan,
And a grey thing glimmers before him, and becomes a mighty man,
One-eyed and ancient-seeming, in cloud-grey raiment clad;
A friendly man and glorious, and of visage smiling-glad:
Then content in Sigurd groweth because of his majesty,
And he heareth him speak in the desert as the wind of the winter sea:

"Hail Sigurd! Give me thy greeting ere thy ways alone thou wend!"

Said Sigurd : "Hail ! I greet thee, my friend and my fathers' friend."

"Now whither away," said the elder, "with the Steed and the ancient Sword?"

"To the greedy house," said Sigurd, "and the King of the Heavy Hoard."

"Wilt thou smite, O Sigurd, Sigurd?" said the ancient mighty-one.

" Yea, yea, I shall smite," said the Volsung, "save the Gods have slain the
[sun."
" What wise wilt thou smite," said the elder, " lest the dark devour thy day ? "
[a way."
" Thou hast praised the sword," said the child, "and the sword shall find

" Be learned of me," said the Wise-one, "for I was the first of thy folk."

Said the child : " I shall do thy bidding, and for thee shall I strike the stroke."

Spake the Wise-one : " Thus shalt thou do when thou wendest hence alone :
Thou shalt find a path in the desert, and a road in the world of stone ;
It is smooth and deep and hollow, but the rain hath riven it not,
And the wild wind hath not worn it, for it is but Fafnir's slot,
Whereby he wends to the water and the fathomless pool of old,
When his heart in the dawn is weary, and he loathes the ancient Gold :
There think of the great and the fathers, and bare the whetted Wrath,
And dig a pit in the highway, and a grave in the Serpent's path :
Lie thou therein, O Sigurd, and thine hope from the glooming hide,
And be as the dead for a season, and the living light abide !
And so shall thine heart avail thee, and thy mighty fateful hand,
And the Light that lay in the Branstock, the well-belovèd brand."

Said the child: "I shall do thy bidding, and for thee shall I strike the stroke ;
For I love thee, friend of my fathers, Wise Heart of the holy folk."

So spake the Son of Sigmund, and beheld no man anear,
And again was the night the midnight, and the twinkling flames shone clear
In the hush of the Glittering Heath ; and alone went Sigmund's son
Till he came to the road of Fafnir, and the highway worn by one,
By the drift of the rain unfurrowed, by the windy years unrent,
And forth from the dark it came, and into the dark it went.

Great then was the heart of Sigurd, for there in the midmost he stayed,
And thought of the ancient fathers, and bared the bright blue blade,
That shone as a fleck of the day-light, and the night was all around.
Fair then was the Son of Sigmund as he toiled and laboured the ground ;
Great, mighty he was in his working, and the Glittering Heath he clave,
And the sword shone blue before him as he dug the pit and the grave :
There he hid his hope from the night-tide and lay like one of the dead,
And wise and wary he bided ; and the heavens hung over his head.

Now the night wanes over Sigurd, and the ruddy rings he sees,
And his war-gear's fair adornment, and the God-folk's images;
But a voice in the desert ariseth, a sound in the waste has birth,
A changing tinkle and clatter, as of gold dragged over the earth :
O'er Sigurd widens the day-light, and the sound is drawing close,
And speedier than the trample of speedy feet it goes ;
But ever deemeth Sigurd that the sun brings back the day,
For the grave grows lighter and lighter and heaven o'erhead is grey.

But now, how the rattling waxeth till he may not heed nor hark !
And the day and the heavens are hidden, and o'er Sigurd rolls the dark,
As the flood of a pitchy river, and heavy-thick is the air
With the venom of hate long hoarded, and lies once fashioned fair :
Then a wan face comes from the darkness, and is wrought in manlike wise,
And the lips are writhed with laughter and bleared are the blinded eyes ;
And it wandereth hither and thither, and searcheth through the grave
And departeth, leaving nothing, save the dark, rolled wave on wave

O'er the golden head of Sigurd and the edges of the sword,
And the world weighs heavy **on Sigurd,** and the weary curse of the Hoard :
Him-seemed the grave grew straiter, and his **hope of life grew chill,**
And his heart by the Worm was enfolded, and **the bonds of the** Ancient Ill.
                                                                    [Death ;
Then was Sigurd stirred by his glory, and he **strove** with the swaddling of
He turned in the pit on the highway, and the grave of the Glittering Heath ;
He laughed and smote with the laughter and thrust up over his head.
And smote the venom asunder, and clave the heart of Dread ;
Then he leapt from the pit and the grave, and the rushing river of blood,
And fulfilled with the joy of the War-God on the face of earth he stood
With red sword high uplifted, with wrathful glittering eyes ;
And he laughed at the heavens above him for he saw the **sun arise,**
And Sigurd gleamed **on the desert,** and shone in the new-born light,
And the wind in his raiment wavered, and all the world was bright.

But there was the ancient **Fafnir, and the Face** of Terror lay
On the huddled folds of the Serpent, that were **black** and ashen-grey
In the desert lit by the sun ; and those twain looked each on each,
And forth from the Face of Terror went a sound of dreadful speech :

" Child, child, who art thou that hast smitten ? bright child, of whence is thy
                                                                    [birth ? "
" **I** am called the Wild-thing Glorious, and alone I wend on the earth."
                                                                    Foe ! "
" **Fierce child, and who** was thy father?—Thou hast cleft the heart of the

" **Am I like to** the sons of men-folk, that **my** father **I should know ? "**

"Wert thou born of a nameless wonder? shall the lies to my death-day cling?

"**How lieth Sigurd the Volsung, and the** Son of Sigmund the King?"

"O bitter father of Sigurd !—thou hast cleft mine heart atwain !"

"I arose, and I wondered and wended, and I smote, and I smote not in vain."

"What master hath taught thee of murder ?—Thou hast wasted Fafnir's day."

" I, Sigurd, knew and desired, and the bright sword learned the way."

" Thee, thee shall the rattling Gold and the red rings bring to the bane."

" Yet mine hand shall cast them abroad, and the earth shall gather again."

" I see thee great in thine anger, and the Norns thou heedest not."

"O Fafnir, speak of the Norns and the wisdom unforgot !"

" Let the death-doomed flee from the ocean, him the wind and the weather
                                                    [shall drown."
" O Fafnir, tell of the Norns ere thy life thou layest adown ! "

"O manifold is their kindred, and who shall tell them all ?
There are they that rule o'er men-folk and the stars that rise and fall :
—I knew of the folk of the Dwarfs, and I knew their Norns of old ;
And I fought, and I fell in the morning, and I die afar from the gold :
—I have seen the Gods of heaven, and their Norns withal I know :
They love and withhold their helping, they hate and refrain the blow ;
They curse and they may not sunder, they bless and they shall not blend ;
They have fashioned the good and the evil ; they abide the change and the end."

"O Fafnir, what of the Isle, and what hast thou known of its name,
Where the Gods shall mingle edges with Surt and the Sons of the Flame?'

"O child, O Strong Compeller ! Unshapen is it hight ;

There the fallow blades shall be shaken and the Dark and the Day shall smite,
When the Bridge of the Gods is broken, and their white steeds swim the sea,
And the uttermost field is stricken, last strife of thee and me."

'What then shall endure, O Fafnir, the tale of the battle to tell?"

"I am blind, O Strong Compeller, in the bonds of Death and Hell.
But thee shall the rattling Gold and the red rings bring unto bane."

"Yet the rings mine hand shall scatter, and the earth shall gather again."

"Woe, woe! in the days passed over I bore the Helm of Dread,
I reared the Face of Terror, and the hoarded hate of the Dead:
I overcame and was mighty; I was wise and cherished my heart
In the waste where no man wandered, and the high house builded apart:
Till I met thine hand, O Sigurd, and thy might ordained from of old;
And I fought and fell in the morning, and I die far off from the Gold."

Then Sigurd leaned on his sword, and a dreadful voice went by
Like the wail of a God departing and the War-God's misery;
And strong words of ancient wisdom went by on the desert wind,
The words that mar and fashion, the words that loose and bind;
And sounds of a strange lamenting, and such strange things bewailed,
That words to tell their meaning the tongue of man hath failed.

Then all sank into silence, and the Son of Sigmund stood
On the torn and furrowed desert by the pool of Fafnir's blood,
And the Serpent lay before him, dead, chilly, dull, and grey;
And over the Glittering Heath fair shone the sun and the day,
And a light wind followed the sun and breathed o'er the fateful place,
As fresh as it furrows the sea-plain or bows the acres' face.

Sigurd slayeth Regin the Master of Masters on the Glittering Heath.

There standeth Sigurd the Volsung, and leaneth on his sword,
And beside him now is Greyfell and looks on his golden lord,
And the world is awake and living; and whither now shall they wend,
Who have come to the Glittering Heath, and wrought that deed to its end?
For hither comes Regin the Master from the skirts of the field of death,
And he shadeth his eyes from the sunlight as afoot he goeth and saith:
"Ah, let me live for a while! for a while and all shall be well,
When passed is the house of murder and I creep from the prison of hell."

Afoot he went o'er the desert, and he came unto Sigurd and stared
At the golden gear of the man, and the Wrath yet bloody and bared,
And the light locks raised by the wind, and the eyes beginning to smile,
And the lovely lips of the Volsung, and the brow that knew no guile;
And he murmured under his breath while his eyes grew white with wrath:

"O who art thou, and wherefore, and why art thou in the path?"

Then he turned to the ash-grey Serpent, and grovelled low on the ground,
And he drank of that pool of the blood where the stones of the wild were
And long he lapped as a dog; but when he arose again,   [drowned,
Lo, a flock of the mountain-eagles that drew to the feastful plain;
And he turned and looked on Sigurd, as bright in the sun he stood,
A stripling fair and slender, and wiped the Wrath of the blood.

But Regin cried: "O Dwarf-kind, O many-shifting folk,
O shapes of might and wonder, am I too freed from the yoke,
That binds my soul to my body a withered thing forlorn,
While the short-lived fools of man-folk so fair and oft are born?
Now swift in the air shall I be, and young in the concourse of kings,
If my heart shall come to desire the gain of earthly things."

And he looked and saw how Sigurd was sheathing the Flame of War,
And the eagles screamed in the wind, but their voice came faint from afar:
Then he scowled, and crouched and darkened, and came to Sigurd and spake:
"O child, thou hast slain my brother, and the Wrath is alive and awake."

"Thou sayest sooth," said Sigurd, "thy deed and mine is done:
But now our ways shall sunder, for here, meseemeth, the sun
Hath but little of deeds to do, and no love to win aback."

Then Regin crouched before him, and he spake: "Fare on to the wrack!
Fare on to the murder of men, and the deeds of thy kindred of old!
And surely of thee as of them shall the tale be speedily told.
Thou hast slain thy Master's brother, and what wouldst thou say thereto,
Were the judges met for the judging and the doom-ring hallowed due?"

Then Sigurd spake as aforetime: "Thy deed and mine it was,
And now our ways shall sunder, and into the world will I pass."

But Regin darkened before him, and exceeding grim was he grown,
And he spake: "Thou hast slain my brother, and wherewith wilt thou atone?"

"Stand up, O Master," said Sigurd, "O Singer of ancient days,
And take the wealth I have won thee, ere we wend on the sundering ways.
I have toiled and thou hast desired, and the Treasure is surely anear,
And thou hast wisdom to find it, and I have slain thy fear."

But Regin crouched and darkened: "Thou hast slain my brother," he said.

"Take thou the Gold," quoth Sigurd, "for the ransom of my head!"

Then Regin crouched and darkened, and over the earth he hung;
And he said: "Thou hast slain my brother, and the Gods are yet but young.

Bright Sigurd towered above him, and the Wrath cried out in the sheath,
And Regin writhed against it as the adder turns on death ;   [thrall
And he spake : "Thou hast slain my brother, and today shalt thou be my
Yea a King shall be my cook-boy and this heath my cooking-hall."

Then he crept to the ash-grey coils where the life of his brother had lain,
And he drew a glaive from his side and smote the smitten and slain,
And tore the heart from Fafnir, while the eagles cried o'erhead,
And sharp and shrill was their voice o'er the entrails of the dead.

Then Regin spake to Sigurd : "Of this slaying wilt thou be free?
Then gather thou fire together and roast the heart for me,
That I may eat it and live, and be thy master and more ;
For therein was might and wisdom, and the grudged and hoarded lore :—
—Or else, depart on thy ways afraid from the Glittering Heath."

Then he fell abackward and slept, nor set his sword in the sheath,
But his hand was red on the hilts and blue were the edges bared,
Ash-grey was his visage waxen, and with open eyes he stared
On the height of heaven above him, and a fearful thing he seemed,
As his soul went wide in the world, and of rule and kingship he dreamed.

But Sigurd took the Heart, and wood on the waste he found,
The wood that grew and died, as it crept on the niggard ground,
And grew and died again, and lay like whitened bones ;
And the ernes cried over his head, as he builded his hearth of stones,
And kindled the fire for cooking, and sat and sang o'er the roast
The song of his fathers of old, and the Wolflings' gathering host :
So there on the Glittering Heath rose up the little flame,
And the dry sticks crackled amidst it, and alow the eagles came,
And seven they were by tale, and they pitched all round about
The cooking-fire of Sigurd, and sent their song-speech out :
But nought he knoweth its wisdom, or the word that they would speak :

K

And hot grew the Heart of Fafnir and sang amid **the reek.**

Then Sigurd looketh on Regin, and he deemeth it overlong   [wrong,
That **he** dighteth the dear-bought morsel, and the might for the Master of
So he reacheth his hand to the roast to see if the cooking be o'er ;
But the blood and the fat seethed from it and scalded his finger sore,
And he set his hand to his mouth to quench the fleshly smart,
And he tasted the flesh of the Serpent and the blood of Fafnir's Heart :
Then there came a change upon him, for the speech of fowl he knew,
And wise in the ways of the beast-kind as the Dwarfs of old he grew ;
And he knitted his brows and hearkened, and wrath in his heart arose ;
For he felt beset of evil in a world of many foes.
But the hilts of the Wrath he handled, and Regin's heart he saw,
And how that the Foe of the **Gods the net** of death would draw ;
And his bright eyes flashed and sparkled, and his mouth grew **set and stern**
As he hearkened the **voice of the** eagles, **and their song began to learn.**

For the first cried out in the desert : "O mighty Sigmund's son,
How long wilt thou sit and tarry now the dear-bought roast is done ? "

And the second : "Volsung, arise ! for the horns blow up to the hall,
And dight **are** the purple hangings, and the King to the feasting should fall."

And the third : "**How** great is the feast if the eater eat aright
The Heart of the **wisdom** of old and the after-world's delight ! "

And the fourth: "Yea, what of Regin? shall he scatter wrack o'er the world?
Shall the father be slain by the son, and the brother 'gainst brother be hurled?"

And the fifth : " He hath **taught** a stripling the gifts **of a God** to give :
He hath reared up a King for the slaying, that **he alone** might live."

And the sixth : " He shall waken mighty as a God that scorneth at truth ;

He hath drunk of the blood of the Serpent, and drowned all hope and ruth."

And the seventh : " Arise, O Sigurd, lest the hour be overlate !
For the sun in the mid-noon shineth, and swift is the hand of Fate :
Arise ! lest the world run backward and the blind heart have its will,
And once again be tangled the sundered good and ill ;
Lest love and hatred perish, lest the world forget its tale,
And the Gods sit deedless, dreaming, in the high-walled heavenly vale."

Then swift ariseth Sigurd, and the Wrath in his hand is bare,
And he looketh, and Regin sleepeth, and his eyes wide-open glare ;
But his lips smile false in his dreaming, and his hand is on the sword ;
For he dreams himself the Master and the new world's fashioning-lord.
And his dream hath forgotten Sigurd, and the King's life lies in the pit ;
He is nought ; Death gnaweth upon him, while the Dwarfs in mastery sit.

But lo, how the eyes of Sigurd the heart of the guileful behold,
And great is Allfather Odin, and upriseth the Curse of the Gold,
And the Branstock bloometh to heaven from the ancient wondrous root ;
The summer hath shone on its blossoms, and Sigurd's Wrath is the fruit :
Dread then he cried in the desert : " Guile-master, lo thy deed !
Hast thou nurst my life for destruction, and my death to serve thy need ?
Hast thou kept me here for the net and the death that tame things die ?
Hast thou feared me overmuch, thou Foe of the Gods on high ?
Lest the sword thine hand was wielding should turn about and cleave
The tangled web of nothing thou hadst wearied thyself to weave.
Lo here the sword and the stroke ! judge the Norns betwixt us twain !
But for me, I will live and die not, nor shall all my hope be vain."

Then his second stroke struck Sigurd, for the Wrath flashed thin and white,
And 'twixt head and trunk of Regin fierce ran the fateful light;
And there lay brother by brother a faded thing and wan.
But Sigurd cried in the desert : " So far have I wended on !

Dead are the foes of God-home that would blend the good and the ill;
And the World shall **yet be famous, and the Gods shall** have their will.
Nor shall I **be dead and** forgotten, while the earth grows worse and worse,
With the blind heart king o'er the people, and binding curse with curse."

How Sigurd took to him the Treasure of the Elf Andvari.

Now Sigurd eats of the heart that once in the Dwarf-king lay,
The hoard of the wisdom begrudged, the might of the earlier day.
Then wise of heart was he waxen, but longing in him grew
To sow the seed he had gotten, and till the field he knew.
So he leapeth **aback of Greyfell,** and rideth the desert **bare,**
And the hollow slot of Fafnir, **that led to** the Serpent's **lair.**
Then **long he rode adown it, and the ernes** flew overhead,
And tidings great **and glorious of that Treasure** of old **they said.**
So far o'er the waste he wended, and **when** the night was **come**
He saw the earth-old dwelling, the dread Gold-wallower's home:
On the skirts of the Heath it was builded by a tumbled stony bent;
High went that house to the heavens, down 'neath the earth it went,
Of unwrought iron fashioned for the heart of a greedy king:
'Twas **a** mountain, blind without, and within was its plenishing
But the Hoard of Andvari the ancient, and the sleeping Curse unseen,
The Gold **of the** Gods that spared not and the greedy that have been.

Through **the door** strode Sigurd the Volsung, and the grey moon and the
Fell in **on** the tawny gold-heaps of the ancient hapless Hoard: [sword
Gold gear of hosts unburied, **and** the coin of cities dead,
Great spoil of the ages of **battle,** lay there on the **Serpent's bed:**
Huge blocks from mid-earth quarried, where none but the Dwarfs have mined,
Wide sands of the golden rivers no foot of man may find
Lay 'neath the spoils of the mighty and the ruddy rings of yore:
But amidst **was** the Helm of Aweing that the Fear of earth-folk bore,

And there gleamed a wonder beside it, **the Hauberk all of gold,**
Whose like is not in the heavens nor has earth of its fellow told :
There Sigurd **seeth** moreover Andvari's Ring of **Gain,**
The hope of Loki's finger, the Ransom's utmost grain ;
For it shone on the midmost gold-heap like the first star set in the sky
In the yellow **space of even** when **moon-rise draweth anigh.**
Then laughed the Son of Sigmund, and stooped to the golden land,
And gathered that first of the harvest and set it on his hand ;
And he did on the **Helm of** Aweing, and the Hauberk all of **gold,**
Whose like is not in the heavens nor has earth **of its fellow told :**
Then he praised the day of the Volsungs amid the **yellow light,**
And he set his hand to the labour and put forth his kingly might ;
He dragged forth gold to the moon, on the **desert's** face he laid
The innermost earth's adornment, and rings for **the nameless made ;**
He toiled and loaded Greyfell, and the cloudy war-steed shone
And the gear of Sigurd rattled in the flood of moonlight wan ;
There he toiled and loaded Greyfell, and the Volsung's armour rang
Mid the yellow bed of the Serpent : but without the eagles sang :

" Bind the red rings, O Sigurd ! let the gold **shine free** and clear !
For what hath the Son of the Volsungs the ancient Curse to fear ? "

" Bind the **red rings, O Sigurd ! for thy tale is well begun,**
And the world **shall be good and gladdened by the Gold lit up by the sun."**

" Bind the red **rings, O** Sigurd ! **and** gladden **all thine heart !**
For the world shall make thee merry ere thou and she **depart."**

" Bind the red rings, O Sigurd ! for the ways go green below,
Go green to the dwelling of Kings, and the halls that the Queen-folk know."

" Bind the red rings, O Sigurd ! for what is there bides by the way,
Save the joy of folk to awaken, and the dawn of the merry day ? "

" Bind the red rings, O Sigurd ! for the strife awaits thine hand,
And a plenteous war-field's reaping, and the praise of many a land."

" Bind the red rings, O Sigurd ! But how shall storehouse hold
That glory of thy winning and the tidings to be told ? "

Now the moon was dead, and the star-worlds were great on the heavenly plain,
When the steed was fully laden ; then Sigurd taketh the rein
And turns to the ruined rock-wall that the lair was built beneath,
For there he deemed was the gate and the door of the Glittering Heath,
But not a whit moved Greyfell for aught that the King might do ;
Then Sigurd pondered a while, till the heart of the beast he knew,
And clad in all his war-gear he leaped to the saddle-stead,
And with pride and mirth neighed Greyfell and tossed aloft his head,
And sprang unspurred o'er the waste, and light and swift he went,
And breasted the broken rampart, the stony tumbled bent ;
And over the brow he clomb, and there beyond was the world,
A place of many mountains and great crags together hurled.
So down to the west he wendeth, and goeth swift and light,
And the stars are beginning to wane, and the day is mingled with night ;
For full fain was the sun to arise and look on the Gold set free,
And the Dwarf-wrought rings of the Treasure and the gifts from the floor
                                                        [of the sea.

How Sigurd awoke Brynhild upon Hindfell.

By long roads rideth Sigurd amidst that world of stone,
And somewhat south he turneth ; for he would not be alone,
But longs for the dwellings of man-folk, and the kingly people's speech,
And the days of the glee and the joyance, where men laugh each to each.
But still the desert endureth, and afar must Greyfell fare
From the wrack of the Glittering Heath, and Fafnir's golden lair.
Long Sigurd rideth the waste, when, lo, on a morning of day

From out of the tangled crag-walls, amidst the cloud-land grey
Comes up a mighty mountain, and it is as **though there burns**
A torch amidst of its cloud-wreath ; **so** thither Sigurd turns,
For he deems indeed from its topmost to look on the best of the earth ;
And Greyfell neigheth beneath him, and his heart is **full of mirth.**

So he rideth higher and higher, and the light **grows great and strange,**
And forth from the clouds it flickers, till at noon they gather and change,
And settle thick **on the mountain,** and hide its head from sight ;
But the winds in **a** while are awakened, and day bettereth ere **the night,**
And, lifted a measureless mass o'er the desert crag-walls high,
Cloudless the mountain riseth against the sunset sky,
The sea of the sun grown golden, as it ebbs **from the day's desire ;**
And the light that afar was a **torch is grown a river of fire,**
And the mountain is black above it, and below is it **dark and dun ;**
And there is the head of Hindfell as an island in the sun.

Night falls, but yet rides Sigurd, and hath no thought **of rest,**
For he longs to climb that rock-world and **behold the earth at its best ;**
But now mid the maze of the foot-hills he **seeth** the light no more,
And the stars are lovely and gleaming on the lightless heavenly floor.
So up and up he wendeth till the night is wearing thin ;
And he rideth a **rift** of the mountain, and all **is** dark **therein,**
Till the **stars are** dimmed by dawning **and the wakening world is cold ;**
Then afar in the upper rock-wall a breach doth he behold,
And a flood of light poured inward the doubtful dawning blinds:
So swift **he rideth** thither and the mouth of the breach he **finds,**
And sitteth awhile on Greyfell on the marvellous thing to gaze :
For lo, the side of Hindfell enwrapped by the fervent blaze,
And nought 'twixt earth and heaven save **a** world of flickering flame,
And a hurrying shifting tangle, where the dark rents went and came.

Great groweth the heart of Sigurd with uttermost desire,

And he crieth kind to Greyfell, and they hasten up, and nigher,
Till he draweth rein in the dawning on the face of Hindfell's steep :
But who shall heed the dawning where the tongues of that wildfire leap ?
For they weave a wavering wall, that driveth over the heaven
The wind that is born within it ; nor ever aside is it driven
By the mightiest wind of the waste, and the rain-flood amidst it is nought ;
And no wayfarer's door and no window the hand of its builder hath wrought
But thereon is the Volsung smiling as its breath uplifteth his hair,
And his eyes shine bright with its image, and his mail gleams white and fair,
And his war-helm pictures the heavens and the waning stars behind :
But his neck is Greyfell stretching to snuff at the flame-wall blind,
And his cloudy flank upheaveth, and tinkleth the knitted mail,
And the gold of the uttermost waters is waxen wan and pale.

Now Sigurd turns in his saddle, and the hilt of the Wrath he shifts,
And draws a girth the tighter ; then the gathered reins he lifts,
And crieth aloud to Greyfell, and rides at the wildfire's heart ;
But the white wall wavers before him and the flame-flood rusheth apart,
And high o'er his head it riseth, and wide and wild is its roar
As it beareth the mighty tidings to the very heavenly floor :
But he rideth through its roaring as the warrior rides the rye,
When it bows with the wind of the summer and the hid spears draw anigh
The white flame licks his raiment and sweeps through Greyfell's mane,
And bathes both hands of Sigurd and the hilts of Fafnir's bane,
And winds about his war-helm and mingles with his hair,
But nought his raiment dusketh or dims his glittering gear ;
Then it fails and fades and darkens till all seems left behind,
And dawn and the blaze is swallowed in mid-mirk stark and blind

But forth a little further and a little further on
And all is calm about him, and he sees the scorched earth wan
Beneath a glimmering twilight, and he turns his conquering eyes,
And a ring of pale slaked ashes on the side of Hindfell lies ;

And the world of the waste is beyond it ; and all is hushed and grey,
And the new-risen moon is a-paleing, and the stars grow faint with day.

Then Sigurd looked before him and a Shield-burg there he saw,
A wall of the tiles of Odin wrought clear without a flaw,
The gold by the silver gleaming, and the ruddy by the white ;
And the blazonings of their glory were done upon them bright,
As of dear things wrought for the war-lords new come to Odin's hall.
Piled high aloft to the heavens uprose that battle-wall,
And far o'er the topmost shield-rim for a banner of fame there hung
A glorious golden buckler ; and against the staff it rung
As the earliest wind of dawning uprose on Hindfell's face
And the light from the yellowing east beamed soft on the shielded place.

But the Wrath cried out in answer as Sigurd leapt adown
To the wasted soil of the desert by that rampart of renown ;
He looked but little beneath it, and the dwelling of God it seemed,
As against its gleaming silence the eager Sigurd gleamed :
He draweth not sword from scabbard, as the wall he wendeth around,
And it is but the wind and Sigurd that wakeneth any sound :
But, lo, to the gate he cometh, and the doors are open wide,
And no warder the way withstandeth, and no earls by the threshold abide
So he stands awhile and marvels ; then the baleful light of the Wrath
Gleams bare in his ready hand as he wendeth the inward path :   · [snare,
For he doubteth some guile of the Gods, or perchance some Dwarf-king's
Or a mock of the Giant people that shall fade in the morning air :
But he getteth him in and gazeth ; and a wall doth he behold,
And the ruddy set by the white, and the silver by the gold ;
But within the garth that it girdeth no work of man is set,
But the utmost head of Hindfell ariseth higher yet ;
And below in the very midmost is a Giant-fashioned mound,
Piled high as the rims of the Shield-burg above the level ground ;
And there, on that mound of the Giants, o'er the wilderness forlorn,

A pale grey image lieth, and gleameth in the morn.

So there was Sigurd alone; and he went from the shielded door,
And aloft in the desert of wonder the Light of the Branstock he bore;
And he set his face to the earth-mound, and beheld the image wan,
And the dawn was growing about it; and, lo, the shape of a man
Set forth to the eyeless desert on the tower-top of the world,
High over the cloud-wrought castle whence the windy bolts are hurled.

Now he comes to the mound and climbs it, and will see if the man be dead
Some King of the days forgotten laid there with crownèd head,
Or the frame of a God, it may be, that in heaven hath changed his life,
Or some glorious heart belovèd, God-rapt from the earthly strife:
Now over the body he standeth, and seeth it shapen fair,
And clad from head to foot-sole in pale grey-glittering gear,
In a hauberk wrought as straitly as though to the flesh it were grown:
But a great helm hideth the head and is girt with a glittering crown.

So thereby he stoopeth and kneeleth, for he deems it were good indeed
If the breath of life abide there and the speech to help at need;
And as sweet as the summer wind from a garden under the sun
Cometh forth on the topmost Hindfell the breath of that sleeping-one.
Then he saith he will look on the face, if it bear him love or hate,
Or the bonds for his life's constraining, or the sundering doom of fate.
So he draweth the helm from the head, and, lo, the brow snow-white,
And the smooth unfurrowed cheeks, and the wise lips breathing light;
And the face of a woman it is, and the fairest that ever was born,
Shown forth to the empty heavens and the desert world forlorn:
But he looketh, and loveth her sore, and he longeth her spirit to move,
And awaken her heart to the world, that she may behold him and love.
And he toucheth her breast and her hands, and he loveth her passing sore;
And he saith: "Awake! I am Sigurd;" but she moveth never the more.

Then he looked on his bare bright blade, and he said: "Thou—what wilt thou
For indeed as I came by the war-garth thy voice of desire I knew."   [do?
Bright burnt the pale blue edges for the sunrise drew anear,
And the rims of the Shield-burg glittered, and the east was exceeding clear:
So the eager edges he setteth to the Dwarf-wrought battle-coat
Where the hammered ring-knit collar constraineth the woman's throat;
But the sharp Wrath biteth and rendeth, and before it fail the rings,
And, lo, the gleam of the linen, and the light of golden things:
Then he driveth the blue steel onward, and through the skirt, and out,
Till nought but the rippling linen is wrapping her about;
Then he deems her breath comes quicker and her breast begins to heave,
So he turns about the War-Flame and rends down either sleeve,
Till her arms lie white in her raiment, and a river of sun-bright hair
Flows free o'er bosom and shoulder and floods the desert bare.

Then a flush cometh over her visage and a sigh up-heaveth her breast,
And her eyelids quiver and open, and she wakeneth into rest;
Wide-eyed on the dawning she gazeth, too glad to change or smile,
And but little moveth her body, nor speaketh she yet for a while;
And yet kneels Sigurd moveless her wakening speech to heed,
While soft the waves of the daylight o'er the starless heavens speed,
And the gleaming rims of the Shield-burg yet bright and brighter grow,
And the thin moon hangeth her horns dead-white in the golden glow.

Then she turned and gazed on Sigurd, and her eyes met the Volsung's eyes.
And mighty and measureless now did the tide of his love arise,   [loved,
For their longing had met and mingled, and he knew of her heart that she
As she spake unto nothing but him and her lips with the speech-flood moved:

" O, what is the thing so mighty that my weary sleep hath torn,
And rent the fallow bondage, and the wan woe over-worn?"

He said: " The hand of Sigurd and the Sword of Sigmund's son,

And the heart that the Volsungs fashioned this deed for thee have done."

But she said : **"Where then is Odin that laid me here alow ?**
Long lasteth the grief of the world, and manfolk's tangled woe !"

" He dwelleth above," said Sigurd, " but I on the earth abide,
And I came from the Glittering Heath the waves of thy fire to ride."

But therewith the sun rose upward and lightened all the earth,
And the light flashed up to the heavens from the rims of the glorious girth ;
But they twain arose together, and with both her palms outspread,
And bathed in the light returning, she cried aloud and said :

All hail, **O Day and thy Sons,** and thy kin of the coloured things !
Hail, following Night, and thy Daughter **that leadeth** thy wavering wings !
Look down with unangry eyes on us today alive,
And give us the hearts victorious, **and the gain** for which we strive !
All hail, ye Lords of God-home, and ye Queens of the House of Gold !
Hail, thou dear Earth that bearest, and thou Wealth of field and fold !
Give us, your noble children, the glory of wisdom and speech,
And the hearts and the hands of healing, and the mouths and hands that
                                                            [teach !"
Then they turned and were knit together ; and oft and o'er again
They craved, **and kissed** rejoicing, and their hearts were full and fain.

Then Sigurd looketh upon her, and the words from his heart arise :
" Thou art the fairest of earth, and the wisest of the wise ;
O who art thou that lovest ?   I am Sigurd, e'en as I told ;
I have slain the Foe of the Gods, and gotten the Ancient Gold ;
And great were the gain of thy love, and the gift of mine earthly days,
If we twain should never sunder as we wend on the changing ways.
O who art thou that lovest, thou **fairest of all things** born ?
And what meaneth thy sleep and thy slumber **in** the wilderness forlorn ?"

She said : " **I am she that loveth** : I was born of the earthly folk,
But of old Allfather took me from the Kings and their wedding yoke :
And he called me the Victory-Wafter, and I went and came as he would,
And I chose the slain for his war-host, and the days were glorious and good,
Till the thoughts of my heart overcame me, and **the pride of my wisdom and**
      speech,
And I scorned the earth-folk's Framer and the Lord of the world I must teach :
For the death-doomed I caught from the sword, and the fated life **I slew,**
And I deemed that my deeds were goodly, and that long I should do and undo.
But Allfather came against me and the God in his wrath arose ;   [foes,
And he **cried: 'Thou** hast thought in thy folly that the Gods have friends and
That they wake, and the world wends onward, that they sleep, and the world
     slips back,   [wrack :
That they laugh, and the world's weal waxeth, that they frown and fashion the
Thou hast cast up the curse against me ; **it shall** fall aback on thine head ;
Go back to the sons of repentance, with the children of sorrow wed !
For the Gods are great unholpen, and their grief is seldom seen,
And the wrong that they will and must be is **soon as** it hath not been.'

"Yet I thought: 'Shall **I** wed in the world, shall **I** gather grief on **the earth?**
Then the fearless heart **shall** I wed, and bring the best to birth,
And fashion such tales for the telling, **that Earth shall be** holpen at least,
If the Gods think scorn of its fairness, as they sit at the changeless feast.'

" Then somewhat smiled Allfather ; and he spake : ' So let it be !
The doom thereof abideth ; **the** doom of me and thee.
Yet long shall the time pass **over** ere thy waking-day be born :
Fare forth, and forget and be weary 'neath the Sting of the Sleepful Thorn !'

"**So** I came to the head of Hindfell and the ruddy shields and white,
And the wall of the wildfire wavering around the isle of night ;
And there the Sleep-thorn pierced me, and the slumber on me fell,
And the night of nameless sorrows that hath no tale to tell.

Now I am she that loveth ; and the day is nigh at hand
When I, who have ridden the sea-realm and the regions of the land,
And dwelt in the measureless mountains and the forge of stormy days,
Shall dwell in the house of my fathers and the land of the people's praise ;
And there shall hand meet hand, and heart by heart shall beat,
And the lying-down shall be joyous, and the morn's uprising sweet.
Lo now, I look on thine heart and behold of thine inmost will,
That thou of the days wouldst hearken that our portion shall fulfill ;
But O, be wise of man-folk, and the hope of thine heart refrain !
As oft in the battle's beginning ye vex the steed with the rein,
Lest at last in its latter ending, when the sword hath hushed the horn,
His limbs should be weary and fail, and his might be over-worn.
O be wise, lest thy love constrain me, and my vision wax o'er-clear,
And thou ask of the thing that thou shouldst not, and the thing that thou
        wouldst not hear.

" Know thou, most mighty of men, that the Norns shall order all,
And yet without thine helping shall no whit of their will befall ;
Be wise ! 'tis a marvel of words, and a mock for the fool and the blind ;
But I saw it writ in the heavens, and its fashioning there did I find :
And the night of the Norns and their slumber, and the tide when the world
        runs back,
And the way of the sun is tangled, it is wrought of the dastard's lack.
But the day when the fair earth blossoms, and the sun is bright above,
Of the daring deeds is it fashioned and the eager hearts of love.

" Be wise, and cherish thine hope in the freshness of the days,
And scatter its seed from thine hand in the field of the people's praise ;
Then fair shall it fall in the furrow, and some the earth shall speed,
And the sons of men shall marvel at the blossom of the deed :
But some the earth shall speed not : nay rather, the wind of the heaven
Shall waft it away from thy longing—and a gift to the Gods hast thou given,
And a tree for the roof and the wall in the house of the hope that shall be,

Though it seemeth our very sorrow, **and the grief of thee and me.**

" Strive not with the fools of man-folk : **for** belike **thou shalt overcome ;**
And what then is the gain of thine hunting when thou bearest the quarry home?
Or else shall the fool overcome thee, and what deed thereof shall grow?
Nay, strive with the wise man rather, and increase thy woe and his woe ;
Yet thereof a gain hast thou gotten ; **and the half of** thine heart hast thou won
If thou may'st prevail against him, and his deeds are the deeds thou hast done:
Yea, and if thou fall before him, in him shalt thou live again,
And **thy deeds in his hand** shall blossom, and his heart of thine heart shall be
                 [fain.
"When thou hearest the fool rejoicing, and he saith, 'It is over and past,
And the wrong was better than right, and hate turns into love at the last,
And we strove for nothing at all, and the Gods are fallen asleep ;
For so good is the world a growing that the evil good shall reap : '
Then loosen thy sword in the scabbard and settle the helm on thine head,
For men betrayed are mighty, and great are the wrongfully dead.

"Wilt thou do the deed and repent it? thou hadst better never been born :
Wilt thou do the deed and exalt it? then thy fame shall be outworn :
Thou shalt do the deed and abide it, and sit on thy throne on high,
And look on today and tomorrow as those that never die.

" Love thou the Gods—and withstand them, lest thy fame should fail in the end,
And thou be but their thrall and their bondsmen, who wert born for their
   very friend:
For few things from the Gods are hidden, and the hearts of men they know,
And how that none rejoiceth to quail and crouch alow.

" I have spoken the words, belovèd, to thy matchless glory and worth ;
But thy heart to my heart hath been speaking, though my tongue hath set it
For I am she that loveth, and I know what thou wouldst teach [forth:
From the heart of thine unlearned wisdom, and I needs must speak thy speech.'

Then words were weary and silent, but oft and o'er again
They craved and kissed rejoicing, and their hearts were full and fain.

Then spake the Son of Sigmund: "Fairest, and most of worth,
Hast thou seen the ways of man-folk and the regions of the earth?
Then speak yet more of wisdom; for most meet meseems it is
That my soul to thy soul be shapen, and that I should know thy bliss."

So she took his right hand meekly, nor any word would say,
Not e'en of love or praising, his longing to delay;
And they sat on the side of Hindfell, and their fain eyes looked and loved,
As she told of the hidden matters whereby the world is moved:
And she told of the framing of all things, and the houses of the heaven;
And she told of the star-worlds' courses, and how the winds be driven;
And she told of the Norns and their names, and the fate that abideth the earth;
And she told of the ways of King-folk in their anger and their mirth;
And she spake of the love of women, and told of the flame that burns,
And the fall of mighty houses, and the friend that falters and turns,
And the lurking blinded vengeance, and the wrong that amendeth wrong,
And the hand that repenteth its stroke, and the grief that endureth for long:
And how man shall bear and forbear, and be master of all that is;
And how man shall measure it all, the wrath, and the grief, and the bliss.

" I saw the body of Wisdom, and of shifting guise was she wrought,
And I stretched out my hands to hold her, and a mote of the dust they caught;
And I prayed her to come for my teaching, and she came in the midnight dream—
And I woke and might not remember, nor betwixt her tangle deem:
She spake, and how might I hearken; I heard, and how might I know;
I knew, and how might I fashion, or her hidden glory show?
All things I have told thee of Wisdom are but fleeting images
Of her hosts that abide in the heavens, and her light that Allfather sees:
Yet wise is the sower that sows, and wise is the reaper that reaps,
And wise is the smith in his smiting, and wise is the warder that keeps:

And wise shalt thou be to deliver, and I shall be wise to desire;
—And lo, the tale that is told, and the sword and the wakening fire!
Lo now, I am she that loveth, and hark how Greyfell neighs,
And Fafnir's Bed is gleaming, and green go the downward ways,
The road to the children of men and the deeds that thou shalt do
In the joy of thy life-days' morning, when thine hope is fashioned anew.
Come now, O Bane of the Serpent, for now is the high-noon come,
And the sun hangeth over Hindfell and looks on the earth-folk's home;
But the soul is so great within thee, and so glorious are thine eyes,
And me so love constraineth, and mine heart that was called the wise,
That we twain may see men's dwellings and the house where we shall dwell,
And the place of our life's beginning, where the tale shall be to tell."

So they climb the burg of Hindfell, and hand in hand they fare,
Till all about and above them is nought but the sunlit air,
And there close they cling together rejoicing in their mirth;
For far away beneath them lie the kingdoms of the earth,
And the garths of men-folk's dwellings and the streams that water them,
And the rich and plenteous acres, and the silver ocean's hem,
And the woodland wastes and the mountains, and all that holdeth all;
The house and the ship and the island, the loom and the mine and the stall,
The beds of bane and healing, the crafts that slay and save,
The temple of God and the Doom-ring, the cradle and the grave.

Then spake the Victory-Wafter: "O King of the Earthly Age,
As a God thou beholdest the treasure and the joy of thine heritage,
And where on the wings of his hope is the spirit of Sigurd borne?
Yet I bid thee hover awhile as a lark alow on the corn;
Yet I bid thee look on the land 'twixt the wood and the silver sea
In the bight of the swirling river, and the house that cherished me!
There dwelleth mine earthly sister and the king that she hath wed;
There morn by morn aforetime I woke on the golden bed;

L

There eve by eve I tarried mid the speech and the lays of kings ;
There noon by noon I wandered and plucked the blossoming things ;
The little land of Lymdale by the swirling river's side,
Where Brynhild once was I called in the days ere my father died ;
The little land of Lymdale 'twixt the woodland and the sea,
Where on thee mine eyes shall brighten and thine eyes shall beam on me."

" I shall seek thee there," said Sigurd, "when the day-spring is begun,
Ere we wend the world together in the season of the sun."

" I shall bide thee there," said Brynhild, "till the fulness of the days,
And the time for the glory appointed, and the springing-tide of praise."

From his hand then draweth Sigurd Andvari's ancient Gold ;
There is nought but the sky above them as the ring together they hold,
The shapen ancient token, that hath no change nor end,
No change, and no beginning, no flaw for God to mend :
Then Sigurd cries : "O Brynhild, now hearken while I swear,
That the sun shall die in the heavens and the day no more be fair,
If I seek not love in Lymdale and the house that fostered thee,
And the land where thou awakedst 'twixt the woodland and the sea !"

And she cried : "O Sigurd, Sigurd, now hearken while I swear
That the day shall die for ever and the sun to blackness wear,
Ere I forget thee, Sigurd, as I lie 'twixt wood and sea
In the little land of Lymdale and the house that fostered me !"

Then he set the ring on her finger and once, if ne'er again,
They kissed and clung together, and their hearts were full and fain.

So the day grew old about them and the joy of their desire,
And eve and the sunset came, and faint grew the sunset fire,

And the shadowless death of the day was sweet in the golden tide ;
But the stars shone forth on the world, and the **twilight changed and died** ;
And sure **if the first of man-folk** had been born to that starry night,
And had heard no tale of the sunrise, he had never longed for the **light** :
But Earth longed amidst her slumber, as 'neath the night she **lay,**
And fresh and all abundant abode the deeds of Day.

BOOK III.

BRYNHILD.

Of the Dream of Gudrun the Daughter of Giuki.

AND now of the Niblung people the tale beginneth to tell, [dwell
  How they deal with the wind and the weather; in the cloudy drift they
When the war is awake in the mountains, and they drive the desert spoil,
And their weaponed hosts unwearied through the misty hollows toil;
But again in the eager sunshine they scour across the plain,
And spear by spear is quivering, and rein is laid by rein,
And the dust is about and behind them, and the fear speeds on before,
As they shake the flowery meadows with the fleeting flood of war.
Yea, when they come from the battle, and the land lies down in peace,
No less in gear of warriors they gather earth's increase,
And helmed as the Gods of battle they drive the team afield:
These come to the council of elders with sword and spear and shield,
And shout to their war-dukes' dooming of their uttermost desire:
These never bow the helm-crest before the High-Gods' fire
But show their swords to Odin, and cry on Vingi-Thor
With the dancing of the ring-mail and the smitten shields of war:
Yet though amid their high-tides of the deaths of men they sing,
And of swords in the battle broken, and the fall of many a king,
Yet they sing it wreathed with the flowers and they praise the gift and the gain
Of the war-lord sped to Odin as he rends the battle atwain.
And their days are young and glorious, and in hope exceeding great

With sword and harp and beaker on the skirts of the Norns they wait.

Now the **King** of this folk is Giuki, and he sits in the Niblung hall
When the **song of men** goes roofward and the shields **shine out from the wall;**
And his queen in the high-seat sitteth, the woman overwise,
Grimhild the kin of the God-folk, the wife of the glittering eyes :
And his sons on each **hand are sitting ;** there is Gunnar the **great and fair,**
With the lovely face of a **king 'twixt** the night of his wavy hair :
And **there is the wise-heart Hogni ; and** his lips are **close and thin,**
And grey and awful his eyen, and a many sights they win :
And there is Guttorm the youngest, of the fierce and wandering glance,
And the heart that never resteth till the swords **in the war-wind dance :**
And there is Gudrun his daughter, and light **she stands by the board,**
And fair are her arms in the hall as the beaker's flood is **poured :**
She comes, and the earls keep silence ; she smiles, and men rejoice ;
She **speaks,** and the harps **unsmitten** thrill faint **to** her queenly voice.

So blossom the days of the Niblungs, and great is **their hope's increase**
'Twixt the merry days of battle and the tide of their guarded peace :
There is many a noon of joyance, and many an eve's delight,
And many a deed for the doing 'twixt the morning and the **night.**

Now betimes on **a** morning **of** summer that Giuki's daughter arose,
Alone went the fair-armed Gudrun to her flowery garden-close ;
And she went by the bower of women, and her damsels saw her thence,
And her nurse went down **to meet her** as she came by the rose-hung fence,
And she saw that her eyes were **heavy** as she trod with doubtful feet
Betwixt the rose and the lily, nor blessed the blossoms **sweet :**
And she spake :
   " What ails thee, **daughter, as** one asleep to tread
O'er the grass of the merry summer and the daisies white and red ?
And to have no heart for the harp-play, or the needle's mastery,
Where the gold and the silk are framing the Swans of the Goths on the sea,

And helms and shields of warriors, and Kings on the hazelled isle?
Why hast thou no more joyance on the damsels' glee to smile?
Why biddest thou not to the wild-wood with horse and hawk and hound?
Why biddest thou not to the heathland and the eagle-haunted ground
To meet thy noble brethren as they ride from the mountain-road?
Hast thou deemed the hall of the Niblungs a churlish poor abode?
Wouldst thou wend away from thy kindred, and scorn thy fosterer's praise?
—Or is this the beginning of love and the first of the troublous days?"

Then spake the fair-armed Gudrun: "Nay, nought I know of scorn
For the noble kin of the Niblungs, or the house where I was born;
No pain of love hath smit me, and no evil days begin,
And I shall be fain tomorrow of the deeds that the maidens win:
But if I wend the summer in dull unlovely seeming,
It comes of the night, O mother, and the tide of last night's dreaming."

Then spake the ancient woman: "Thy dream to me shalt thou show;
Such oft foretell but the weather, and the airts whence the wind shall blow."

Blood-red was waxen Gudrun, and she said: "But little it is:
Meseems I sat by the door of the hall of the Niblungs' bliss,
And from out of the north came a falcon, and a marvellous bird it was;
For his feathers were all of gold, and his eyes as the sunlit glass,
And hither and thither he flew about the kingdoms of Kings,
And the fear of men went with him, and the war-blast under his wings:
But I feared him never a deal, nay, hope came into my heart,
And meseemed in his war-bold ways I also had a part;
And my eyes still followed his wings as hither and thither he swept
O'er the doors and the dwellings of King-folk; till the heart within me leapt,
For over the hall of the Niblungs he hung a little space,
Then stooped to my very knees, and cried out kind in my face:
And fain and full was my heart, and I took him to my breast,
And fair methought was the world and a home of infinite rest."

Her speech dropped dead as she spake, and her eyes from the nurse she turned,
But now and again thereafter the flush in her fair cheek burned,
And her eyes were dreamy and great, as of one who looketh afar.

But the nurse laughed out and answered : "Such the dreams of maidens are ;
And if thou hast told me all 'tis a goodly dream, forsooth :
For what should I call this falcon save a glorious kingly youth,
Who shall fly full wide o'er the world in fame and victory,
Till he hangs o'er the Niblung dwelling and stoops to thy very knee ?
And fain and full shall thine heart be, when his cheek shall cherish thy breast,
And fair things shalt thou deem of the world as a place of infinite rest."

But cold grew the maiden's visage : " God wot thou hast plenteous lore
In the reading of dreams, my mother ; but thou lovest thy fosterling sore,
And the good and the evil alike shall turn in thine heart to good ;
Wise too is my mother Grimhild, but I fear her guileful mood,
Lest she love me overmuch, and fashion all dreams to ill.
Now who is the wise of woman, who herein hath measureless skill ?
For her forthright would I find, how far soever I fare,
Lest I wend like a fool in the world, and rejoice with my feet in the snare."

Quoth the nurse : " Though the dream be goodly and its reading easy and
It is nought but a little matter if thy golden wain be dight,   [light,
And thou ride to the land of Lymdale, the little land and green,
And come to the hall of Brynhild, the maid and the shielded Queen,
The Queen and the wise of women, who sees all haps to come :
And 'twill be but light to bid her to seek thy dream-tale home ;
Though surely shall she arede it in e'en such wise as I ;
And so shall the day be merry and the summer cloud go by."

"Thou hast spoken well," said Gudrun, " let us tarry now no whit ;
For wise in the world is the woman, and knoweth the ways of it."

So they make the yoke-beasts ready, and dight the wains for the way,
And the maidens gather together, and their bodies they array,
And gird the laps of the linen, and do on the dark-blue gear,
And bind with the leaves of summer the wandering of their hair:
Then they drive by dale and acré, o'er heath and holt they wend,
Till they come to the land of the waters, and the lea by the woodland's end;
And there is the burg of Brynhild, the white-walled house and long,
And the garth her fathers fashioned before the days of wrong.
So fare their feet on the earth by the threshold of the Queen,
And Brynhild's damsels abide them, for their goings had been seen;
And the mint and the blossomed woodruff they strew before their feet,
And their arms of welcome take them, and they kiss them soft and sweet,
And they go forth into the feast-hall, the many-pillared house;
Most goodly were its hangings and its webs were glorious
With tales of ancient fathers, and the Swans of the Goths on the sea,
And weaponed Kings on the island, and great deeds yet to be;
And the host of Odin's Choosers, and the boughs of the fateful Oak,
And the gush of Mimir's Fountain, and the Midworld-Serpent's yoke.

So therein the maidens enter, but Gudrun all out-goes,
As over the leaves of the garden shines the many-folded rose:
Amidst and alone she standeth; in the hall her arms shine white,
And her hair falls down-behind her like a cloak of the sweet-breathed night,
As she casts her cloak to the earth, and the wind of the flowery tide
Runs over her rippling raiment and stirs the gold at her side.
But she stands and may scarce move forward, and a red flush lighteth her face
As her eyes seek out Queen Brynhild in the height of the golden place.

But lo, as a swan on the sea spreads out her wings to arise
From the face of the darksome ocean when the isle before her lies,
So Brynhild arose from her throne and the fashioned cloths of blue
When she saw the Maid of the Niblungs, and the face of Gudrun knew;
And she gathers the laps of the linen, and they meet in the hall, they twain,

And she taketh her hands in her hands and kisseth her sweet and fain :
And she saith : " Hail, sister and queen ! for we deem thy coming kind :
Though **forsooth the** hall of Brynhild is no weary way to find :
How fare the kin of the Niblungs ? is thy mother happy and hale,
And the ancient of days, **thy** father, the King **of all avail ?"**

" It is well with my house," said Gudrun, "and my brethren's days are fair,
And my mother's **morns** are joyous, and her eves have done with **care ;**
And my father's heart is happy, and the Niblung glory grows,
And the **land in peace is lying** 'neath the lily and the rose :
But love **and the mirth** of summer have moved **my** heart to come
To look on thy measureless beauty, and seek thy glory home."

" O be thou welcome !" said Brynhild ; "it is good when queen-folk meet.
Come now, O goodly sister, and sit in my golden **seat :**
There are lovely hours before us, and the half of the summer day ;
And what is the night of summer that eve should drive thee away ? "

So they sat, they twain, in the high-seat ; and the maidens bore them wine,
And they handled Dwarf-wrought treasures with their fingers fair and fine,
And lovely they were together, and they marvelled each at each :
Yet oft was Gudrun silent, and she faltered in her speech,
As they matched great Kings and their war-deeds, and told of times that were,
And their fathers' fathers' doings, and the deaths of war-lords dear.
And at last the twain sat silent, and spake **no** word at all,
And the western sky waxed ruddy, for the sun drew near its fall ;
And the speech of the murmuring maidens, and the voice of the toil of folk,
Died out in the hall of **Brynhild as the** garden-song **awoke.**

Then Brynhild took up the **word, and her voice was soft** as she said :
" We have told of the best of King-folk, the living and the dead ;
But hast thou heard, my sister, how the world grows fair with the word
Of a King from the mountains coming, a great and marvellous lord,

Who hath slain the Foe of the Gods, and the King that was wise from of old;
Who hath slain the great Gold-wallower, and gotten the ancient Gold;
And the hand of victory hath he, and the overcoming speech,
And the heart and the eyes triumphant, and the lips that win and teach?"

Then met the eyes of the women, and Brynhild's word died out,
And bright flushed Gudrun's visage, and her lips were moved with doubt.
But again spake Brynhild the wise:
                "He is come of a marvellous kin,
And of men that never faltered, and goodly days shall he win:
Yea now to this land is he coming, and great shall be his fame;
He is born of the Volsung King-folk, and Sigurd is his name."

Then all the heart laughed in her, but the speech of her lips died out,
And red and pale waxed Gudrun, and her lips were moved with doubt,
Till she spake as **a Queen of the Earth:**
                "Sister, the day grows late,
And meseemeth the watch of the earl-folk looks oft from the Niblung **gate**
For the gleam of our golden wains and the dust-cloud thin and soft;
But nought shall they now behold them till the moon-lamp blazeth aloft.
Farewell, and have thanks for thy welcome and thy glory that I have seen,
And I bid thee come to the Niblungs while the summer-ways are green,
That we thine heart may gladden as thou gladdenedst ours today."

And she **rose** and kissed her sweetly as one that wendeth away:
But Brynhild looked upon her and said: "Wilt thou depart,
And leave the word unspoken that lieth on thine heart?"

Then Gudrun faltered and spake: "Yea, hither I came **in** sooth,
With a dream for thine eyes of wisdom, and a prayer for thine heart of ruth:
But young in the world am I waxen, and the scorn of folk I fear
When I speak to the ears of the wise, and a maiden's dream they hear."

"I shall mock thee nought," said Brynhild ; "yet who shall say indeed
But my heart shall fear thee rather, nor help thee in thy need?"

Then spake the daughter of Giuki : "Lo, this was the dream I dreamed :
For without by the door of the Niblungs I sat in the morn, as meseemed ;
Then I saw a falcon aloft, and a glorious bird he was,
And his feathers glowed as the gold, and his eyes as the sunlit glass :
Hither and thither he flew about the kingdoms of Kings,
And fear was borne before him, and death went under his wings :
Yet I feared him not, but loved him, and mine eyes must follow his ways,
And the joy came into my heart, and hope of the happy days :
Then over the hall of the Niblungs he hung a little space
And stooped to my very knees, and cried out kind in my face ;
And fain and full was my heart, and I took him to my breast,
And I cherished him soft and warm, for I deemed I had gotten the best."

So speaketh the Maid of the Niblungs, and speech her lips doth fail,
And she gazeth on Brynhild's visage, and seeth her waxen pale,
As she saith : "'Tis a dream full goodly, and nought hast thou to fear ;
Some glory of Kings shall love thee and thine heart shall hold him dear."

Again spake the daughter of Giuki : "Not yet hast thou hearkened all :
For meseemed my breast was reddened, as oft by the purple and pall,
But my heart was heavy within it, and I laid my hand thereon,
And the purple of blood enwrapped me, and the falcon I loved was gone."

Yet pale was the visage of Brynhild, and she said : "Is it then so strange
That the wedding-lords of the Niblungs their lives in the battle should change?
Thou shalt wed a King and be merry, and then shall come the sword,
And the edges of hate shall be whetted and shall slay thy love and thy lord,
And dead on thy breast shall he fall : and where then is the measureless moan?
From the first to the last shalt thou have him, and scarce shall he die alone.
Rejoice, O daughter of Giuki ! there is worse in the world than this :

He shall die, and thou shalt remember the days of his glory and bliss."

"I woke, and I wept," said Gudrun, "for the dear thing I had loved:
Then I slept, and again as aforetime were the gates of the dream-hall moved,
And I went in the land of shadows; and lo I was crowned as a queen,
And I sat in the summer-season amidst my garden green;
And there came a hart from the forest, and in noble wise he went,
And bold he was to look on, and of fashion excellent
Before all beasts of the wild-wood; and fair gleamed that glorious-one,
And upreared his shining antlers against the very sun.
So he came unto me and I loved him, and his head lay kind on my knees,
And fair methought the summer, and a time of utter peace.
Then darkened all the heavens and dreary grew the tide,
And medreamed that a queen I knew not was sitting by my side,
And from out of the din and the darkness, a hand and an arm there came,
And a golden sleeve was upon it, and red rings of the Queen-folk's fame:
And the hand was the hand of a woman: and there came a sword and a thrust
And the blood of the lovely wood-deer went wide about the dust.
Then I cried aloud in my sorrow, and lo, in the wood I was,
And all around and about me did the kin of the wild-wolves pass,
And I called them friends and kindred, and upreared a battle-brand,
And cried out in a tongue that I knew not, and red and wet was my hand.
Lo now, the dream I have told thee, and nought have I held aback.
O Brynhild, what wilt thou tell me of treason and murder and wrack?"

Long Brynhild stood and pondered and weary-wise was her face,
And she gazed as one who sleepeth, till thus she spake in a space:
"One dream in twain hast thou told, and I see what I saw e'en now,
But beyond is nought but the darkness and the measureless midnight's flow:
Thy dream is all areded; I may tell thee nothing more:
Thou shalt live and love and lose, and mingle in murder and war.
Is it strange, O child of the Niblungs, that thy glory and thy pain
Must be blent with the battle's darkness and the unseen hurrying bane?

Do ye, of all folk on the earth, pray God for the changeless peace,
And not for the battle triumphant and the fruit of fame's increase?
For the rest, thou mayst not be lonely in thy welfare or thy woe,
But hearts with thine heart shall be tangled : but the queen and the hand
    thou shalt know,
When we twain are wise together; thou shalt know of the sword and the wood,
Thou shalt know of the wild-wolves' howling and thy right-hand wet with
When the day of the smith is ended, and the stithy's fire dies out,   [blood,
And the work of the master of masters through the feast-hall goeth about."

They stand apart by the high-seat, and each on each they gaze
As though they forgat the summer, and the tide of the passing days,
And abode the deeds unborn and the Kings' deaths yet to be,
As the merchant bideth deedless the gold in his ships on the sea.

At last spake the wise-heart Brynhild : " O glorious Niblung child !
The dreams and the word we have hearkened, and the dreams and the word
    have been wild.
Thou hast thy life and thy summer, and the love is drawing anear ;
Take these to thine heart to cherish, and deem them good and dear,
Lest the Norns should mock our knowledge and cast our fame aside,
And our doom be empty of glory as the hopeless that have died.
Farewell, O Niblung Maiden ! for day on day shall come
Whilst thou shalt live rejoicing mid the blossom of thine home.
Now have thou thanks for thy greeting and thy glory that I have seen ;
And come thou again to Lymdale while the summer-ways are green."

So the hall-dusk deepens upon them till the candles come arow,
And they drink the wine of departing and gird themselves to go ;
And they dight the dark-blue raiment and climb to the wains aloft
While the horned moon hangs in the heaven and the summer wind blows soft.
Then the yoke-beasts strained at the collar, and the dust in the moon arose,
And they brushed the side of the acre and the blooming dewy close ;

Till at last, when the moon was sinking and the night was waxen late,
The warders of the earl-folk looked forth from the Niblung gate,
And saw the gold pale-gleaming, and heard the wain-wheels crush
The weary dust of the summer amidst the midnight hush.

So came the daughter of Giuki from the hall of Brynhild the queen
When the days of the Niblungs blossomed and their hope was springing green.

How the folk of Lymdale met Sigurd the Volsung in the woodland.

Full fair was the land of Lymdale, and great were the men thereof,
And Heimir the King of the people was held in marvellous love ;
And his wife was the sister of Brynhild, and the Queen of Queens was she ;
And his sons were noble striplings, and his daughters sweet to see ;
And all these lived on in joyance through the good days and the ill,
Nor would shun the war's awaking ; but now that the war was still
They looked to the wethers' fleeces and what the ewes would yield,
And led their bulls from the straw-stall, and drave their kine afield ;
And they dealt with mere and river and all waters of their land,
And cast the glittering angle, and drew the net to the strand,
And searched the rattling shallows, and many a rock-walled well,
Where the silver-scaled sea-farers, and the crook-lipped bull-trout dwell.
But most when their hearts were merry 'twas the joy of carle and quean
To ride in the deeps of the oak-wood, and the thorny thicket green :
Forth go their hearts before them to the blast of the strenuous horn,
Where the level sun comes dancing down the oaks in the early morn :
There they strain and strive for the quarry, when the wind hath fallen dead
In the odorous dusk of the pine-wood, and the noon is high o'erhead :
There oft with horns triumphant their rout by the lone tree turns,
When over the bison's lea-land the last of sunset burns ;
Or by night and cloud all eager with shaft on string they fare,
When the wind from the elk-mead setteth, or the wood-boar's tangled lair :

For the wood is their barn and their storehouse, and their bower and feasting-
And many an one of their warriors in the woodland war shall fall.   [hall,

So now in the sweet spring season, on a morn of the sunny tide
Abroad are the Lymdale people to the wood-deers' house to ride :
And they **wend towards** the sun's uprising, and over the **boughs he comes,**
And the merry wind is with him, and stirs the woodland homes ;   [glades,
But their horns to his face **cast clamour,** and their hooves shake down the
And the hearts of their **hounds** are eager, and oft they redden **blades ;**
Till at last in the noon they tarry in a daisied wood-lawn green,
And good **and** gay is their raiment, and their spears are sharp **and sheen,**
And they crown themselves with the oak-leaves, and sit, both most and **least,**
And there on the forest venison and the ancient wine they feast ;
Then they wattle the twigs of the thicket to bear their spoil away,
And the toughness of the beech-boughs with the woodbine overlay :
With the voice of their merry labour the hall of the oakwood rings,
For fair they are and joyous as the first God-fashioned Kings.

Now they gather their steeds together, that ere the moon is born
The candles of King Heimir may shine on harp and horn :
But as they stand by the stirrup and hand on rein is laid,
All eyes are turned to beholding the eastward-lying glade,
For thereby comes something glorious, as though an earthly sun
Were lit by the orb departing, lest the day should be wholly done ;
Lo now, as they stand astonied, a wonder they behold,
For a warrior cometh riding, and his gear is all of gold ;
And grey is the steed and mighty beneath that lord of war,
And a treasure of gold he beareth, and the gems of the ocean's floor :
Now they deem the war-steed wondrous and the treasure strange they deem,
But so exceeding glorious doth the harnessed rider seem,
That men's hearts are all exalted as he draweth nigh and nigher,
And there are they abiding in fear and great desire :
For they look on the might of his limbs, and his waving locks **they see,**

And his glad eyes clear as the heavens, and the wreath of the summer tree
That girdeth the dread of his war-helm, and they wonder at his sword,
And the tinkling rings of his hauberk, and the rings of the ancient Hoard :
And they say: Are the Gods on the earth? did the world change yesternight?
Are the sons of Odin coming, and the days of Baldur the bright?

But forth stood Heimir the ancient, and of Gods and men was he chief
Of all who have handled the harp ; and he stood betwixt blossom and leaf,
And thrust his spear in the earth and cast abroad his hands :
" Hail, thou that ridest hither from the North and the desert lands !
Now thy face is turned to our hall-door and thereby must be thy way ;
And, unless the time so presseth that thou ridest night and day,
It were good that thou lie in my house, and hearken the clink of the horn,
Whether peace in thy hand thou bear us, or war on thy saddle be borne ;
Whether wealth thou seek, or friends, or kin, or a maiden lost,
Or hast heart for the building of cities nor wilt hold thee aback for the cost :
If fame thou wilt have among King-folk, to the land of the Kings art thou come,
Or wouldst thou adown to the sea-flood, thou must pass by the garth of our
Yea art thou a God from the heavens, who wilt deem me little of worth, [home.
And art come for the wrack of my realm and wilt cast King Heimir forth,
Thou knowest I fear thee nothing, and no worse shall thy welcome be :
Or art thou a wolf of the hearth, none here shall meddle with thee :—
Yet lo, as I look on thine eyen, and behold thy hope and thy mirth,
Meseems thou art better than these, some son of the Kings of the Earth."

Then spake the treasure-bestrider,—for his horse e'en now had he reined
By the King and the earls of the people where the boughs of the thicket
"Yea I am a son of the Kings; but my kin have passed away,   [waned :—
And once were they called the Volsungs, and the sons of God were they :
I am young, but have learned me wisdom; I am lone, but deeds have I done;
I have slain the Foe of the Gods, and the Bed of the Worm have I won.
But meseems that the earth is lovely, and that each day springeth anew
And beareth the blossom of hope, and the fruit of deeds to do.

And herein thou sayest the sooth, that I seek the fame of Kings,
And with them would I do and undo and be heart of their warfarings :
And for this o'er the Glittering Heath to the kingdoms of earth am I come,
And over the head of Hindfell, and I seek the earl-folk's home
That is called the lea of Lymdale 'twixt the wood and the water-side ;
For men call it the gate of the world where the Kings of Men abide :
Nor the least of God-folk am I, nor the wolf of the Kings accursed,
But Sigurd the son of Sigmund in the land of the Helper nursed :
And I thank thee, lord, for thy bidding, and tonight will I bide in thine hall,
And fare on the morrow to Lymdale and the deeds thenceforward to fall."

Then Sigurd leapt from Greyfell, and men were marvelling there
At the sound of his sweet-mouthed wisdom, and his body shapen fair.
But Heimir laughed and answered : "Now soon shall the deeds befall,
And tonight shalt thou ride to Lymdale and tonight shalt thou bide in my hall :
For I am the ancient Heimir, and my cunning is of the harp,
Though erst have I dealt in the sword-play while the edge of war was sharp."

Then Sigurd joyed to behold him, for a god-like King he was,
And amid the men of Lymdale did the Son of Sigmund pass ;
And their hearts are high uplifted, for across the air there came
A breath of his tale half-spoken and the tidings of his fame ;
And their eyes are all unsatiate of gazing on his face,
For his like have they never looked on for goodliness and grace.

So they bear him the wine of welcome, and then to the saddle they leap
And get them forth from the wood-ways to the lea-land of the sheep,
And the bull-fed Lymdale meadows ; and thereover Sigurd sees
The long white walls of Heimir amidst the blossomed trees :
Then the slim moon rises in heaven, and the stars in the tree-tops shine,
But the golden roof of Heimir looks down on the torch-lit wine,
And the song of men goes roofward in praise of Sigmund's Son,
And a joy to the Lymdale people is his glory new-begun.

How Sigurd met Brynhild in Lymdale.

So there abideth Sigurd with the Lymdale forest-lords
In mighty honour holden, and in love beyond all words,
And thence abroad through the people there goeth a rumour and breath
Of the great Gold-wallower's slaying, and the tale of the Glittering Heath,
And a word of the ancient Treasure and Greyfell's gleaming Load ;
And the hearts of men grew eager, and the coming deeds abode.
But warily dealeth Sigurd, and he wends in the woodland fray
As one whose heart is ready and abides a better day :
In the woodland fray he fareth, and oft on a day doth ride
Where the mighty forest wild-bulls and the lonely wolves abide ;
For as then no other warfare do the lords of Lymdale know,
And the axe-age and the sword-age seem dead a while ago,
And the age of the cleaving of shields, and of brother by brother slain,
And the bitter days of the whoredom, and the hardened lust of gain ;
But man to man may hearken, and he that soweth reaps,
And hushed is the heart of Fenrir in the wolf-den of the deeps.

Now is it the summer-season, and Sigurd rideth the land,
And his hound runs light before him, and his hawk sits light on his hand,
And all alone on a morning he rides the flowery sward
Betwixt the woodland dwellings and the house of Lymdale's lord ;
And he hearkens Greyfell's going as he wends adown the lea,
And his heart for love is craving, and the deeds he deems shall be ;
And he hears the Wrath's sheath tinkling as he rides the daisies down,
And he thinks of his love laid safely in the arms of his renown.
But lo, as he rides the meadows, before him now he sees
A builded burg arising amid the leafy trees,
And a white-walled house on its topmost with a golden roof-ridge done,
And thereon the clustering dove-kind in the brightness of the sun.

So Sigurd stayed to behold it, for the heart within him laughed,
But e'en then, as the arrow speedeth from the mighty archer's draught,
Forth fled the falcon unhooded from the hand of Sigurd the King,
And up, and over the tree-boughs he shot with steady wing:
Then the Volsung followed his flight, for he looked to see him fall
On the fluttering folk of the doves, and he cried the backward call
Full oft and over again; but the falcon heeded it nought,
Nor turned to his kingly wrist-perch, nor the folk of the pigeons sought,
But flew up to a high-built tower, and sat in the window a space,
Crying out like the fowl of Odin when the first of the morning they face,
And then passed through the open casement as an erne to his eyrie goes.

Much marvelled the Son of Sigmund, and rode to the fruitful close:
For he said: Here a great one dwelleth, though none have told me thereof,
And he shall give me my falcon, and his fellowship and love.
So he came to the gate of the garth, and forth to the hall-door rode,
And leapt adown from Greyfell, and entered that fair abode;
For full lovely was it fashioned, and great was the pillared hall,
And fair in its hangings were woven the deeds that Kings befall,
And the merry sun went through it and gleamed in gold and horn;
But afield or a-fell are its carles, and none labour there that morn,
And void it is of the maidens, and they weave in the bower aloft,
Or they go in the outer gardens 'twixt the rose and the lily soft:
So saith Sigurd the Volsung, and a door in the corner he spies
With knots of gold fair-carven, and the graver's masteries:
So he lifts the latch and it opens, and he comes to a marble stair,
And aloft by the same he goeth through a tower wrought full fair.
And he comes to a door at its topmost, and lo, a chamber of Kings,
And his falcon there by the window with all unruffled wings.

But a woman sits on the high-seat with gold about her head,
And ruddy rings on her arms, and the grace of her girdle-stead;
And sunlit is her rippled linen, and the green leaves lie at her feet,

And e'en as a swan on the billow where the firth and the out-sea meet.
On the dark blue cloths she sitteth, so fair and softly made
Are her limbs by the linen hidden, and so white is she arrayed.
But a web of gold is before her, and therein by her shuttle wrought
The early days of the Volsungs and the war by the sea's rim fought,
And the crowned queen over Sigmund, and the Helper's pillared hall,
And the golden babe uplifted to the eyes of duke and thrall;
And there was the slender stripling by the knees of the Dwarf-folk's lord,
And the gift of the ancient Gripir, and the forging of the Sword;
And there were the coils of Fafnir, and the hooded threat of death,
And the King by the cooking-fire, and the fowl of the Glittering Heath;
And there was the headless King-smith and the golden halls of the Worm,
And the laden Greyfell faring through the land of perished storm;
And there was the head of Hindfell, and the flames to the sky-floor driven;
And there was the glittering shield-burg, and the fallow bondage riven;
And there was the wakening woman and the golden Volsung done,
And they twain o'er the earthly kingdoms in the lonely evening sun:
And there were fells and forests, and towns and tossing seas,
And the Wrath and the golden Sigurd for ever blent with these,
In the midst of the battle triumphant, in the midst of the war-kings' fall,
In the midst of the peace well-conquered, in the midst of the praising hall.

There Sigurd stood and marvelled, for he saw his deeds that had been,
And his deeds of the days that should be, fair wrought in the golden sheen;
And he looked in the face of the woman, and Brynhild's eyes he knew,
But still in the door he tarried, and so glad and fair he grew,
That the Gods laughed out in the heavens to see the Volsung's seed;
And the breeze blew in from the summer and over Brynhild's weed,
Till his heart so swelled with the sweetness that the fair word stayed in his
      mouth,
And a marvel beloved he seemeth, as a ship new-come from the south:
And still she longed and beheld him, nor foot nor hand she moved
As she marvelled at her gladness, and her love so well beloved.

But at last through the sounds of summer the voice of Sigurd came,
And it seemed as a silver trumpet from the house of the fateful fame;
And he spake: "Hail, lady and queen! hail, fairest of all the earth!
Is it well with the hap of thy life-days, and thy kin and the house of thy birth?"

She said: "My kin is joyous, and my house is blooming fair,
And dead, both root and branches, is the tree of their travail and care."

He spake: "I have longed, I have wondered if thy heart were well at ease,
If the hope of thy days had blossomed and born thee fair increase."

"O have thou thanks," said Brynhild, "for thine heart that speaketh kind!
Yea, the hope of my days is accomplished, and no more there is to find."

And again she spake in a space: "The road hath been weary and long,
But well hast thou ridden it, Sigurd, and the sons of God are strong."

He said: "I have sought, O Brynhild, and found the heart of thine home;
And no man hath asked or holpen, and all unbidden I come."

She said: "O welcome hither! for the heart of the King I knew,
And thine hope that overcometh, and thy will that nought shall undo."

"Unbidden I came," he answered, "yet it is but a little space
Since I heard thy voice on the mountain, and thy kind lips cherished my face."

She rose from the dark-blue raiment, and trembling there she stood,
And no word her lips had gotten that her heart might deem it good:
And his heart went forth to meet her, yet nought he moved for a while,
Until the God-kin's laughter brake blooming from a smile
And he cried: "It is good, O Brynhild, that we draw exceeding near,
Lest Odin mock Kings' children that the doom of fate they fear."

Then forth she stepped from the high-seat, and forth from the threshold he
Till both their **bodies mingling seemed one glory** and the same,   [came,
And far o'er all fulfilment did the souls within them long,
As at breast and at lips of the faithful the earthly love strained strong ;
And fresh from the deeps of the summer the breeze across them blew,
But nought of the earth's desire, or the lapse of time they knew.

Then apart, **but exceeding** nigh, for a little while they stand,
Till Brynhild toucheth her lord, and taketh his hand in her hand,   ˊ
And she leadeth **him through the** chamber, and sitteth down in her seat ;
And him she setteth beside her, and she saith :
                                   " It is right and meet
That thou sit in this throne of my fathers, since thy gift today I have :
Thou hast given it altogether, nor **aught** from me wouldst save ;
And thou knowest the tale of women, how oft it haps on a day
That of such gifts men repent them, and their **lives are cast away.**"

He said : " I have cast it away as the tiller casteth the seed,
That the summer may better the spring-tide, and the autumn winter's need :
For what were the fruit of our lives if apart they needs must pass,
And men shall say hereafter : Woe worth the hope that was ! "

She said: " That day shall dawn the best of all earthly days
When we sit, we twain, in the high-seat in the hall of the people's praise :
Or else, what fruit of our life-days, what fruit of our death shall be ?
What fruit, save men's remembrance of the grief of thee and **me ?**"

He said : " It is sharper to bear than the bitter sword in the breast.
O woe, **to think** of it now in **the** days of our gleaning of rest ! "

Said **Brynhild :** " I bid thee remember the word that **I** have sworn,
How the sun shall turn to blackness, and the last day be outworn,
Ere I **forget** thee, Sigurd, and the kindness of thy face.**"

And they kissed and the day grew later and noon failed the golden place.
But Sigurd said : "O Brynhild, remember how I swore
That the sun should die in the heavens and day come back no more,
Ere I forget thy wisdom and thine heart of inmost love.
Lo now, shall I unsay it, though the Gods be great above,
Though my life should last for ever, though I die tomorrow morn,
Though I win the realm of the world, though I sink to the thrall-folk's scorn?"

She said : "Thou shalt never unsay it, and thy heart is mine indeed :
Thou shalt bear my love in thy bosom as thou helpest the earth-folk's need :
Thou shalt wake to it dawning by dawning; thou shalt sleep and it shall not
       be strange :
There is none shall thrust between us till our earthly lives shall change.
Ah, my love shall fare as a banner in the hand of thy renown,
In the arms of thy fame accomplished shall it lie when we lay us adown.
O deathless fame of Sigurd ! O glory of my lord !
O birth of the happy Brynhild to the measureless reward !"

So they sat as the day grew dimmer, and they looked on days to come,
And the fair tale speeding onward, and the glories of their home ;
And they saw their crownèd children and the kindred of the kings,
And deeds in the world arising and the day of better things :
All the earthly exaltation, till their pomp of life should be passed,
And soft on the bosom of God their love should be laid at the last.

But when words have a long while failed them, and the night is nigh at hand,
They arise in the golden glimmer, and apart and anigh they stand :
Then Brynhild stooped to the Wrath, and touched the hilts of the sword,
Ere she wound her arms round Sigurd and cherished the lips of her lord :
Then sweet were the tears of Brynhild, and fast and fast they fell,
And the love that Sigurd uttered, what speech of song may tell?

But he turned and departed from her, and her feet on the threshold abode

As he went through the pillared feast-hall, and forth to the night he rode:
So he turned toward the dwelling of Heimir and his love and his fame seemed one,
And all full-well accomplished, what deeds soe'er were done:
And the love that endureth for ever, and the endless hope he bore,
As he faced the change of Heaven and the chance of worldly war.

Of Sigurd's riding to the Niblungs.

What aileth the men of Lymdale, that their house is all astir?
Shall the hunt be up in the forest, or hath the shield-hung fir
Brought war from the outer ocean to their fish-belovèd stream?
Or have the piping shepherds beheld the war-gear gleam
Adown the flowery sheep-dales? or betwixt the poplars grey
Have the neat-herds seen the banners of the drivers of the prey?

No, the forest shall be empty of the Lymdale men this morn,
And the wells of the Lymdale river have heard no battle-horn,
Nor the sheep in the flowery hollows seen any painted shield,
And nought from the fear of warriors bide the neat-herds from the field;
Yet full is the hall of Heimir with eager earls of war,
And the long-locked happy shepherds are gathered round the door,
And the smith has left his stithy, and the wife has left her rock,
And the **bright thrums** hang unwinded by the maiden's weaving-stock:
And there is the wife and the maiden, the elder and the boy;
And scarce shall you tell what moves them, much sorrow or great joy.

But lo, as they gather and hearken by the door of Heimir's hall,
The wave of a mighty music on the souls of men doth fall,
And they bow their heads and hush them, because for a dear guest's sake
Is Heimir's hand in the harp-strings and the ancient song is awake,
And the words of the Gods' own fellow, and the hope of days gone by;

Then deep is that song-speech laden with the deeds that draw anigh,
And many a hope accomplished, and many an unhoped change,
And things of all once spoken, now grown exceeding strange;
Then keen as the battle-piercer the stringèd speech arose,
And the hearts of men went with it, as of them that meet the **foes;**
Then soared the song triumphant as o'er the world well won,
Till sweet and soft it ended as a rose falls 'neath the sun;
But thereafter was there silence till the earls cast up the shout,
And the whole house clashed and glittered as the tramp of men bore out,
And folk **fell back before them;** then forth the earl-folk pour,
And forth comes Heimir the Ancient and stands by his fathers' door:
And then is the feast-hall empty and none therein abides:
For forth on the cloudy Greyfell the Son of Sigmund rides,
And the Helm of Awe he beareth, and the Mail-coat all of gold,
That hath not its like in the heavens nor has earth of its fellow told,
And the Wrath to his side is girded, though the peace-strings wind it round,
Yet oft and again it singeth, and strange is its sheathèd sound:
But beneath the King in his war-gear and beneath the wondrous Sword
Are the red rings of the Treasure, and the gems of Andvari's Hoard,
And light goes Greyfell beneath it, and oft and o'er again
He neighs out hope of battle, for the heart of the beast is fain.

So there sitteth Sigurd the Volsung, and is dight to ride his ways,
For the world lies fair before him and the field of the people's praise;
And he kisseth the ancient Heimir, and haileth the folk of the land,
And he crieth kind and joyous as the reins lie loose in his hand:
" Farewell, O folk of Lymdale, and your joy of the summer-tide!
For the acres whiten, meseemeth, and the harvest-field is wide:
Who knows of the toil that shall be, when the reaping-hook gleams grey,
And the knees of the strong are loosened in the afternoon of day?
Who knows of the joy that shall be, when the reaper cometh again,
And his sheaves are crowned with the blossoms, and the song goes up from
But now let the Gods look to it, to hinder or to speed!   [the wain?

But the love and the longing I know, and I know the hand and the deed."

And he gathered the reins together, and set his face to the road,
And the glad steed neighed beneath him as they fared from the King's abode,
And out past the dewy closes; but the shouts went up to the sky,
Though some for very sorrow forbore the farewell cry,
Nor was any man but heavy that the godlike guest should go;
And they craved for that glad heart guileless, and that face without a foe.
But Greyfell fareth onward, and back to the dusky hall
Now goeth the ancient Heimir, and back to bower and stall,
And back to hammer and shuttle go earl and carle and quean;
And piping in the noontide adown the hollows green
Go the yellow-headed shepherds amidst the scattered sheep;
And all hearts a dear remembrance and a hope of Sigurd keep.

But forth by dale and lealand doth the Son of Sigmund wend,
Till far away lies Lymdale and the folk of the forest's end;
And he rides a heath unpeopled and holds the westward way,
Till a long way off before him come up the mountains grey;
Grey, huge beyond all telling, and the host of the heapèd clouds,
The black and the white together, on that rock-wall's coping crowds;
But whiles are rents athwart them, and the hot sun pierceth through,
And there glow the angry cloud-caves 'gainst the everlasting blue,
And the changeless snow amidst it; but down from that cloudy head
The scars of fires that have been show grim and dusky-red;
And lower yet are the hollows striped down by the scanty green,
And lingering flecks of the cloud-host are tangled there-between,
White, pillowy, lit by the sun, unchanged by the drift of the wind.

Long Sigurd looked and marvelled, and up-raised his heart and his mind;
For he deemed that beyond that rock-wall bode his changèd love and life
On the further side of the battle, and the hope, and the shifting strife:
So up and down he rideth, till at even of the day

A hill's brow he o'ertoppeth that had hid the mountains grey ;
Huge, blacker they showed than aforetime, white hung the cloud-flecks there,
But red was the cloudy crown, for the sun was sinking fair :
A wide plain lay beneath him, and a river through it wound
Betwixt the lea and the acres, and the misty orchard ground ;
But forth from the feet of the mountains a ridgèd hill there ran
That upreared at its hithermost ending a builded burg of man ;
And Sigurd deemed in his heart as he looked on the burg from afar,
That the high Gods scarce might win it, if thereon they fell with war ;
So many and great were the walls, so bore the towers on high
The threat of guarded battle, and the tale of victory.
Then swift he hasteneth downward, lest day be wholly spent
Ere he come to the gate well warded, and the walls' beleaguerment ;
For his heart is eager to hearken what men-folk therein dwell
And the name of that noble dwelling, and the tale that it hath to tell.
So he rides by the tilth of the acres, 'twixt the overhanging trees,
And but seldom now and again a glimpse of the burg he sees,   [bridge ;
Till he comes to the flood of the river, and looks up from the balks of the
Then how was the plain grown little 'neath that mighty burg of the ridge
O'erhung by the cloudy mountains and the ash of another day,
Whereto the slopes clomb upward till the green died out in the grey,
And the grey in the awful cloud-land, where the red rents went and came
Round the snows no summers minish and the far-off sunset flame :
But lo, the burg at the ridge-end ! have the Gods been building again
Since they watched the aimless Giants pile up the wall of the plain,
The house for none to dwell in ?   Or in what days lived the lord
Who 'neath those thunder-forges upreared that battle's ward ?
Or was not the Smith at his work, and the blast of his forges awake,
And the world's heart poured from the mountain for that ancient people's
For as waves on the iron river of the days whereof nothing is told   [sake ?
Stood up the many towers, so stark and sharp and cold ;
But dark-red and worn and ancient as the midmost mountain-sides
Is the wall that goeth about them ; and its mighty compass hides

Full many a dwelling of man whence the reek now goeth aloft,
And the voice of the house-abiders, the sharp sounds blent with the soft :
But one house in the midst is unhidden and high up o'er the wall it goes ;
Aloft in the wind of the mountains its golden roof-ridge glows,
And down mid its buttressed feet is the wind's voice never still ;
And the day and the night pass o'er it and it changes to their will,
And whiles is it glassy and dark, and whiles is it white and dead,
And whiles is it grey as the sea-mead, and whiles is it angry red ;   [storm,
And it shimmers under the sunshine and grows black to the threat of the
And dusk its gold roof glimmers when the rain-clouds over it swarm,
And bright in the first of the morning its flame doth it uplift,
When the light clouds rend before it and along its furrows drift.

Upriseth the heart of Sigurd, but ever he rideth forth
Till he comes to the garth and the gateway built up in the face of the north :
Then e'en as a wind from the mountains he heareth the warders' speech,
As aloft in the mighty towers they clamour each to each :
Then horn to horn blew token, and far and shrill they cried,
And he heard, as the fishers hearken the cliff-fowl over the tide :
But he rode in under the gate, that was long and dark as a cave
Bored out in the isles of the northland by the beat of the restless wave ;
And the noise of the winds was within it, and the sound of swords unseen,
As the night when the host is stirring and the hearts of Kings are keen.
But no man stayed or hindered, and the dusk place knew his smile,
And into the court of the warriors he came forth after a while,
And looked aloft to the hall-roof, high up and grey as the cloud,
For the sun was wholly perished ; and there he crieth aloud :

"Ho, men of this mighty burg, to what folk of the world am I come ?
And who is the King of battles who dwells in this lordly home ?
Or perchance are ye of the Elf-kin ? are ye guest-fain, kind at the board,
Or murder-churls and destroyers to gain and die by the sword ? "

Then the spears in the forecourt glittered and **the swords shone** over the wall,
But the song of smitten harp-strings came faint **from the** cloudy hall.
And he hearkened a voice and a crying : "The house of Giuki the King,
And the Burg of the Niblung people and the heart of **their warfaring."**
There were many men about him, and the wind in the **wall-nook sang,**
And the spears of the Niblungs glittered, and the swords **in the forecourt rang.**
But they looked on his face in **the even,** and they hushed their **voices and**
For fear and **great desire** the hearts of men amazed.   [gazed,

Now **cometh an earl to** King Giuki as he sits in godlike wise
With his sons, the Kings of battle, and his wife of the **glittering eyes,**
And the King cries out at his coming to tell why **the watch-horns blew ;**
But **the earl** saith : " Lord of the people, choose now **what thou wilt do ;**
For here is a strange new-comer, and he saith, **to thee alone**
Will he tell of his name and his kindred, and **the deeds that** his hand hath done.
But he beareth a Helm of Aweing and a Hauberk **all** of gold,
That hath not its like in the heavens nor has earth of its fellow told ;
And strange is all his raiment, and **he beareth a Dwarf-wrought sword,**
And his war-steed beareth beneath him red rings of a mighty Hoard,
And the ancient gems **of the sea-floor: there he sits on his cloud-grey steed,**
And **his eyes are** bright **in the even, and we deem him mighty indeed,**
And our hearts are upraised at his coming; but how shall **I tell thee or say**
If he be a King of the Kings and a lord of the earthly day,
Or if rather the Gods be abroad and he be one of these ?
But forsooth no battle he biddeth, nor craveth he our peace.
So choose herein, King Giuki, **wilt** thou bid the man begone
To his house of the earth **or the** heavens, lest a worser deed be won,
Or wilt thou bid him abide **in** the Niblung peace and love ?
And meseems if thus thou doest, thou shalt never **repent thee thereof."**

Then uprose the King of the Niblungs, and was **clad** in purple and pall,
And his sheathed sword lay in his hand, as he gat him adown the hall,
And abroad through the Niblung doorway ; and a mighty man he **was,**

And wise and ancient of days: so there by the earls doth he pass,
And beholdeth the King on the war-steed and looketh up in his face:
But Sigurd smileth upon him in the Niblungs' fencèd place,
As the King saith: "Gold-bestrider, who into our garth wouldst ride,
Wilt thou tell thy name to a King, who biddeth thee here abide
And have all good at our hands? for unto the Niblungs' home
And the heart of a war-fain people from the weary road are ye come;
And I am Giuki the King: so now if thou nam'st thee a God,
Look not to see me tremble; for I know of such that have trod
Unfeared in the Burg of the Niblungs; nor worser, nor better at all
May fare the folk of the Gods than the Kings in Giuki's hall;
So I bid thee abide in my house, and when many days are o'er,
Thou shalt tell us at last of thine errand, if thou bear us peace or war."

Then all rejoiced at his word till the swords on the bucklers rang,
And adown from the red-gold Treasure the Son of Sigmund sprang,
And he took the hand of Giuki, and kissed him soft and sweet,
And spake: "Hail, ancient of days! for thou biddest me things most meet,
And thou knowest the good from the evil: few days are over and gone
Since my father was old in the world ere the deed of my making was won;
But Sigmund the Volsung he was, full ripe of years and of fame;
And I, who have never beheld him, am Sigurd called of name;
Too young in the world am I waxen that a tale thereof should be told,
And yet have I slain the Serpent, and gotten the Ancient Gold,
And broken the bonds of the weary, and ridden the Wavering Fire.
But short is mine errand to tell, and the end of my desire:
For peace I bear unto thee, and to all the kings of the earth,
Who bear the sword aright, and are crowned with the crown of worth;
But unpeace to the lords of evil, and the battle and the death;
And the edge of the sword to the traitor, and the flame to the slanderous breath:
And I would that the loving were loved, and I would that the weary should sleep,
And that man should hearken to man, and that he that soweth should reap.
Now wide in the world would I fare, to seek the dwellings of Kings,

For with them would I do and undo, and be heart of their warfarings;
So I thank thee, lord, for thy bidding, and here in thine house will I bide,
And learn of thine ancient wisdom till forth to the field we ride."

Glad then was the murmur of folk, for the tidings had gone forth,
And its breath had been borne to the Niblungs, and the tale of Sigurd's worth.

But the King said: "Welcome, Sigurd, full fair of deed and of word!
And here mayst thou win thee fellows for the days of the peace and the sword;
For not lone in the world have I lived, but sons from my loins have sprung,
Whose deeds with the rhyme are mingled, and their names with the people's
                                                    [tongue."
Then he took his hand in his hand, and into the hall they passed,
And great shouts of salutation to the cloudy roof were cast;
And they rang from the glassy pillars, and the Gods on the hangings stirred,
And afar the clustering eagles on the golden roof-ridge heard,
And cried out on the Sword of the Branstock as they cried in the other days:
Then the harps rang out in the hall, and men sang in Sigurd's praise;
And a flood of great remembrance, and the tales of the years gone by
Swept over the soul of Sigurd, and his fathers seemed anigh;
And he looked to the cloudy hall-roof, and anigh seemed Odin the Goth,
And the Valkyrs holding the garland, and the crown of love and of troth;
And his soul swells up exalted, and he deems that high above,
In the glorious house of the heavens, are the outstretched hands of his love;
And she stoops to the cloudy feast-hall, and the wavering wind is her voice,
And her odorous breath floats round him, as she bids her King rejoice.

But now on the daïs he meeteth the kin of Giuki the wise:
Lo, here is the crownèd Grimhild, the queen of the glittering eyes;
Lo, here is the goodly Gunnar with the face of a king's desire;
Lo, here is Hogni that holdeth the wisdom tried in the fire;
Lo, here is Guttorm the youngest, who longs for the meeting swords;
Lo, here, as a rose in the oak-boughs, amid the Niblung lords

Is the Maid of the Niblungs standing, the white-armed Giuki's child;
And all these looked long on Sigurd and their hearts upon him smiled.

So Grimhild greeted the guest, and she deemed him fair and sweet,
And she deemed him mighty of men, and a king for the queen-folk meet.
Then Gunnar the goodly war-king spake forth his greeting and speed,
And deemed him noble and great, and a fellow for kings in their need:
And Hogni gave him his greeting, and none his eyes might dim,
And he smiled as the winter sun on the shipless ocean's rim.
Then greeted him Guttorm the young, and cried out that his heart was glad
That the Volsung lived in their house, that a King of the Kings they had.
Then silent awhile the Maiden, the fair-armed Gudrun, stood,
Yet might all men see by her visage that she deemed his coming good;
But at last the gold she taketh, and before him doth she stand,
And she poureth the wine of King-folk, and stretcheth forth her hand,
And she saith: " Hail, Sigurd the Volsung ! may I see thy joy increase,
And thy shielded sons beside thee, and thy days grown old in peace !"

And he took the cup from her hand, and drank, while his heart rejoiced
At the Niblung Maiden's beauty, and her blessing lovely-voiced;
And he thanked her well for the greeting, and no guile in his heart was grown,
But he thought of his love enfolded in the arms of his renown.

So the Niblungs feast glad-hearted through the undark night and kind,
And the burden of all sorrow seems fallen far behind
On the road their lives have wended ere that happiest night of nights,
And the careless days and quiet seem but thieves of their delights;
For their hearts go forth before them toward the better days to come,
When all the world of glory shall be called the Niblungs' home:
Yea, as oft in the merry season and the morning of the May
The birds break out a-singing for the world's face waxen gay,
And they flutter there in the blossoms, and run through the dewy grass,
As they sing the joy of the spring-tide, that bringeth the summer to pass;

And they deem that for them alone was the earth wrought long ago,
And no hate and no repentance, and no fear to come they know;
So fared the feast of the Niblungs on the eve that Sigurd came
In the day of their deeds triumphant, and the blossom of their fame.

*Of Sigurd's warfaring in the company of the Niblungs, and of his
great fame and glory.*

Now gone is the summer season and the harvest of the year,
And amid the winter weather the deeds of the Niblungs wear;
But nought is their joyance worsened, or their mirth-tide waxen less,
Though the swooping mountain tempest howl round their ridgy ness,
Though a house of the windy battle their streeted burg be grown,
Though the heaped-up, huddled cloud-drift be their very hall-roof's crown,
Though the rivers bear the burden, and the Rime-Gods grip and strive,
And the snow in the mirky midnoon across the lealand drive.

But lo, in the stark midwinter how the war is smitten awake,
And the blue-clad Niblung warriors the spears from the wall-nook take,
And gird the dusky hauberk, and the ruddy fur-coat don,
And draw the yellowing ermine o'er the steel from Welshland won.
Then they show their tokened war-shields to the moon-dog and the stars,
For the hurrying wind of the mountains has borne them tale of wars.
Lo now, in the court of the warriors they gather for the fray,
Before the sun's uprising, in the moonless morn of day;
And the spears by the dusk gate glimmer, and the torches shine on the wall,
And the murmuring voice of women comes faint from the cloudy hall:
Then the grey dawn beats on the mountains mid a drift of frosty snow,
And all men the face of Sigurd mid the swart-haired Niblungs know;
And they see his gold gear glittering mid the red fur and the white,
And high are the hearts uplifted by the hope of happy fight;   [swords,
And they see the sheathed Wrath shimmer mid the restless Welsh-wrought

And their hearts rejoice beforehand o'er the fall of conquered lords :
And they see the Helm of Aweing and the awful eyes beneath,
And they deem the victory glorious, and fair the warrior's death.

So forth through that cave of the gate from the Niblung Burg they fare,
And they turn their backs on the plain, and the mountain-slopes they dare,
And the place of the slaked earth-forges, as the eastering wind shall lead,
And but few swords bide behind them the Niblung Burg to heed.
But lo, in the jaws of the mountains how few and small they seem,
As dusky-strange in the snow-drifts their knitted hauberks gleam :
Lo, now at the mountains' outmost 'neath Sigurd's gleaming eyes
How wide in the winter season the citied lealand lies :
Lo, how the beacons are flaring, and the bell-swayed steeples rock,
And the gates of cities are shaken with the back-swung door-leaves' shock :
And, lo, the terror of towns, and the land that the winter wards,
And over the streets snow-muffled the clash of the Niblung swords.

But the slaves of the Kings are gathered, and their host the battle abides,
And forth in the front of the Niblungs the golden Sigurd rides ;
And Gunnar smites on his right hand, and Hogni smites on the left,
And glad is the heart of Guttorm, and the Southland host is cleft
As the grey bill reapeth the willows in the autumn of the year,
When the fish lie still in the eddies, and the rain-flood draweth anear.

Now sheathed is the Wrath of Sigurd ; for as wax withstands the flame,
So the Kings of the land withstood him and the glory of his fame.
And before the grass is growing, or the kine have fared from the stall,
The song of the fair-speech-masters goes up in the Niblung hall,
And they sing of the golden Sigurd and the face without a foe,
And the lowly man exalted and the mighty brought alow :
And they say, when the sun of summer shall come aback to the land,
It shall shine on the fields of the tiller that fears no heavy hand ;
That the sheaf shall be for the plougher, and the loaf for him that sowed,

Through every furrowed acre where the Son of Sigmund rode.

Full dear was Sigurd the Volsung to all men most and least,
And now, as the spring drew onward, 'twas deemed a goodly feast
For the acre-biders' children by the Niblung Burg to wait,
If perchance the Son of Sigmund should ride abroad by the gate :
For whosoever feared him, no little-one, forsooth,
Would shrink from the shining eyes and the hand that clave out truth
From the heart of the wrack and the battle: it was then, as his gold gear burned
O'er the balks of the bridge and the river, that oft the mother turned,
And spake to the laughing baby : "O little son, and dear,
When I from the world am departed, and whiles a-nights ye hear
The best of man-folk longing for the least of Sigurd's days,
Thou shalt hearken to their story, till they tell forth all his praise,
And become beloved and a wonder, as thou sayest when all is sung,
' And I too once beheld him in the days when I was young.' "

Men say that the white-armed Gudrun, the lovely Giuki's child,
Looked long on Sigurd's visage in the winter weather wild
On the eve of the Kings' departure ; and she bore him wine and spake
"Thou goest to the war, O Sigurd, for the Niblung brethren's sake ;
And so women send their kindred on many a doubtful tide,
And dead full oft on the death-field shall the hope of their lives abide ;
Nor must they fear beforehand, nor weep when all is o'er ;
But thou, our guest and our stranger, thou goest to the war,
And who knows but thine hand may carry the hope of all the earth ;
Now therefore if thou deemest that my prayer be aught of worth,
Nor wilt scorn the child of a Niblung that prays for things to come,
Pledge me for thy glad returning, and the sheaves of fame borne home ! "

He laughed, for his heart was merry for the seed of battle sown,
For the fruit of love's fulfilment, and the blossom of renown ;
And he said : " I look in the wine-cup and I see goodwill therein ;

Be merry, Maid of the Niblungs, for these are the **prayers that win !**"

He drank, and the soul within him to the love and the glory turned,
And all unmoved was her visage, howso her heart-strings yearned.

But again when the bolt of battle on the sleeping kings had been hurled,
And the gold-tipped cloud of the Niblungs had been sped on the winter world,
And once more in that hall of the stories was dight triumphant **feast,**
And in joy of soul past telling sat all men most and least,
There stood the daughter of Giuki by the king-folk's happy board,
And grave and stern was Gudrun as the wine of kings she poured :
But Sigurd smiled upon her, and he said :
                                        " O maid, rejoice
For thy pledge's fair redeeming, and the hope of thy kindly voice !   [wrack
Thou hast prayed for the guest and the stranger, and, lo, from the battle and
Is the hope of the Niblungs blossomed, and **thy brethren's lives come back.**"

She turned **and** looked upon him, and the flush ran over her face,
And died out **as** the summer lightning, that scarce endureth a space ;
But still was her visage troubled, as she said : " Hast thou called me kind
Because I feared for earth's glory when point and edge are blind ?
But now **is the** night as the day, when thou bringest my brethren **home,**
And back in the arms of thy glory the Niblung hope has come."

But his eyes look kind upon her, and the trouble passeth away,
And there in the hall of the Niblungs is dark night as glorious day.

Now spring o'er the winter prevaileth, and the blossoms brighten the field ;
But lo, in the flowery lealands the gleam of spear and shield,
For swift to the tidings of warfare speeds on the Niblung folk,
And the Kings to the sea are riding, and the battle-laden oak.
Now the isle-abiders tremble, and the dwellers by the sea
And the nesses flare with the beacons, and the shepherds leave the **lea,**

As the tale of the golden **warrior speeds on** from isle to isle.
Now spread is the snare of treason, and cast is the net of guile,
And the mirk-wood gleams with the ambush, and venom lurks at the board;
And whiles and again for a little the fair fields gleam with **the sword,**
And the host of the isle-folk gather, **nigh** numberless **of tale :**
But **how** shall its bulk and its writhing the willow-log avail
When the red flame lives amidst it **?** Lo now, the golden man
In the towns from of old time famous, by the temples tall and wan ;
How he wends with the swart-haired Niblungs through the mazes of the streets,
And the **hosts** of the conquered outlands and their uncouth praying meets
There **he wonders at** their life-days **and** their fond imaginings,
As he bears the love of Brynhild through the houses of the kings,
Where his word shall do and undo, and with crowns of kings shall **he deal;**
And he laughs to scorn the treasure where thieves break through and steal,
And the moth and the rust are corrupting : and he thinks the time is long
Till the dawning of love's summer from the cloudy days of wrong.

So they raise and abase and alter, then turn about and ride,
Mid the peace of the sword triumphant, to the shell-strown ocean's **side;**
And they bear their glory away to the mouth of the fishy stream,
And again in the Niblung lealand doth the Welsh-wrought war-gear **gleam,**
And they come to the Burg of the Niblungs and the mighty gate of **war,**
And betwixt the gathered maidens through its dusky depths they pour,
And with war-helms **done with blossoms round the** Niblung hall they **sing**
In the windless cloudless even and the ending of the spring ;
Yea, they sing **the** song of Sigurd and the face without **a foe,**
And they sing of the prison's rending and the tyrant **laid alow,**
And the golden thieves' abasement, **and** the stilling **of the churl,**
And the mocking of the dastard where the chasing **edges** whirl ;
And they sing of the outland maidens that thronged round Sigurd's hand,
And sung in the streets of the foemen of the war-delivered land ;
And they tell how the ships of the merchants come free and go at their will,
And how wives in peace and safety may crop the vine-clad hill ;

How the maiden sits in her bower, and the weaver sings at his loom,
And forget the kings of grasping and the greedy days of gloom ;
For by sea and hill and township hath the Son of Sigmund been,
And looked on the folk unheeded, and the lowly people seen.

Then into the hall of the Niblungs go the battle-staying earls,
And they cast the spoil in the midmost ; the webs of the out-sea pearls,
And the gold-enwoven purple that on hated kings was bright ;
Fair jewelled swords accursèd that never flashed in fight ;
Crowns of old kings of battle that dastards dared to wear ;
Great golden shields dishonoured, and the traitors' battle-gear ;
Chains of the evil judges, and the false accusers' rings,
And the cloud-wrought silken raiment of the cruel whores of kings.
And they cried : " O King of the people, O Giuki old of years,
Lo, the wealth that Sigurd brings thee from the fashioners of tears !
Take thou the gift, O Niblung, that the Volsung seed hath brought !
For we fought on the guarded fore-shore, in the guileful wood we fought ;
And we fought in the traitorous city, and the murder-halls of kings ;
And Sigurd showed us the treasure, and won us the ruddy rings
From the jaws of the treason and death, and redeemed our lives from the snare,
That the uttermost days might know it, and the day of the Niblungs be fair :
And all this he giveth to thee, as the Gods give harvest and gain,
And sit in their thrones of the heaven, of the praise of the people fain."

Then Sigurd passed through the hall, and fair was the light of his eyes,
And he came to King Giuki the ancient, and Grimhild the overwise,
And stooped to the elder of days and kissed the war-wise head ;
And they loved him passing sore as a very son of their bed.
But he stood in the sight of the people, and sweet he was to see,
And no foe and no betrayer, and no envier now hath he :
But Gunnar the bright in the battle deems him his earthly friend,
And Hogni is fain of his fellow, howso the day's work end,
And Guttorm the young is joyous of the help and gifts he hath ;

And all these would shine beside him in the glory of his path ;
There is none to hate or hinder, or mar the golden day,
And the light of love flows plenteous, as the sun-beams hide the way.

Now there was the white-armed Gudrun, the lovely Giuki's child,
And her eyes beheld his glory, but her heart was unbeguiled,
And the dear hope fainted in her : I am frail and weak, she saith,
And he so great and glorious with the eyes that look on death !
Yet she comes, and speaks before him as she bears the golden horn :
" The world is glad, O Sigurd, that ever thou wert born,
And I with the world am rejoicing : drink now to the Niblung bliss,
That I, a deedless maiden, may thank thee well for this !"

So he drank of the cup at her bidding and laughed, and said, " Forsooth,
Good-will with the cup is blended, and the very heart of ruth :
Yet meseems thy words are merrier than thine inmost soul this eve ;
Nay, cast away thy sorrow, lest the Kings of battle grieve !"

She smiled and departed from him, and there in the cloudy hall
To the feast of their glad returning the Niblung children fall ;
And far o'er the flowery lealand the shepherds of the plain
Behold the litten windows, and know that Kings are fain.

So fares the tale of Sigurd through all kingdoms of the earth,
And the tale is told of his doings by the utmost ocean's girth ;
And fair feast the merchants deem it to warp their sea-beat ships
High up the Niblung River, that their sons may hear his lips
Shed fair words o'er their ladings and the opened southland bales ;
Then they get them aback to their countries, and tell how all men's tales
Are nought, and vain and empty in setting forth his grace,
And the unmatched words of his wisdom, and the glory of his face.
Came the wise men too from the outlands, and the lords of singers' fame,
That men might know hereafter the deeds that knew his name ;

And all these to their lands departed, and bore aback his love,
And cherished the tree of his glory, and lived glad in the joy thereof.

But men say that howsoever all other folk of earth
Loved Sigmund's son rejoicing, and were bettered of their mirth,
Yet ever the white-armed Gudrun, the dark-haired Niblung Maid,
From the barren heart of sorrow her love upon him laid:
He rejoiceth, and she droopeth; he speaks and hushed is she;
He beholds the world's days coming, nought but Sigurd may she see;
He is wise and her wisdom falters; he is kind, and harsh and strange
Comes the voice from her bosom laden, and her woman's mercies change.
He longs, and she sees his longing, and her heart grows cold as a sword,
And her heart is the ravening fire, and the fretting sorrows' hoard.

Ah, shall she not wander away to the wilds and the wastes of the deer,
Or down to the measureless sea-flood, and the mountain marish drear?
Nay, still shall she bide and behold him in the ancient happy place,
And speak soft as the other women with wise and queenly face.
Woe worth the while for her sorrow, and her hope of life forlorn!
—Woe worth the while for her loving, and the day when she was born!

Of the **Cup** *of evil drink that Grimhild the Wise-wife gave to Sigurd.*

Now again in the latter summer do those Kings of the Niblungs ride
To chase the sons of the plunder that curse the ocean-side:
So over the oaken rollers they run the cutters down
Till fair in the first of the deep are the glittering bows up-thrown;
But, shining wet and steel-clad, men leap from the surfy shore,
And hang their shields on the gunwale, and cast abroad the oar;
Then full to the outer ocean swing round the golden beaks,
And Sigurd sits by the tiller and the host of the spoilers seeks.
But lo, by the rim of the out-sea where the masts of the Vikings sway,

And their bows plunge down to the **sea-floor as they ride** the ridgy way,
And show the slant decks covered with swords from stem to stern :
Hark now, how the horns of battle for the clash of warriors yearn,
And the mighty song of mocking goes up from the thousands of throats,
As down the wind and landward the **raven-banner floats :**
For they see thin streaks and shining o'er the waters' face draw nigh,
And about each streak a foam-wake as the wet oars toss on high ;
And they shout; for the silent Niblungs round those great sea-castles **throng,**
And the eager men unshielded swarm up the heights of wrong.
Then **from bulwark unto** bulwark the Wrath's flame sings and leaps,
And the unsteered manless dragons drift down the weltering deeps,
And the waves toss up a shield-foam, and hushed are the clamorous throats
And dead in the summer even the raven-banner floats,
And the Niblung song goes upward, as the sea-burgs long accursed
Are swept toward the field-folk's houses, and the shores they saddened erst :
Lo there on the poop stands Sigurd mid the black-haired Niblung kings,
And his heart goes forth before him toward the day of better things,
And the burg in the land of Lymdale, and the hands that bide him there.

But now with the spoil of the spoilers mid the Niblungs doth **he fare,**
When the Kings have dight the beacons and the warders of the coast,
That fire may call to fire for the swift redeeming host.
Then **they fare to** the Burg of the people, and leave that lealand free
That **a maid may wend** untroubled by the edges of the **sea ;**
And **glad in the** autumn season they sit them down again
By the shrines of the Gods of the Niblungs, and the hallowed hearths of men.

So there on an eve is Sigurd in the ancient Niblung hall,
Where the cloudy hangings waver and the flickering shadows fall,
And he sits by the Kings on the high-seat, and **wise of men he seems,**
And of many a hidden marvel past thought of man he dreams :
On the Head of Hindfell he thinketh, and how fair the woman was,
And how that his love hath blossomed, and the fruit shall come to **pass ;**

And he thinks of the burg in Lymdale, and how hand met hand in love,
Nor deems him aught too feeble the **heart of the world to move** ;
And more than a God he seemeth, and so steadfast and so great,
That the sea of chance wide-weltering 'neath his will must needs abate.

High riseth the glee of the people, and the song and the clank of the cup
Beat back from pillar to pillar, to the cloud-blue roof go up ;
And men's hearts rejoice in the battle, and the hope of coming days,
Till scarce may they think of their fathers, and the kings of bygone praise.

But Giuki looketh on Sigurd and saith from heart grown fain :
"To sit by the silent wise-one, how mighty is the gain !
Yet we know this long while, Sigurd, that lovely is thy speech ;
Wilt thou tell us the tales of the ancient, **and** the words of masters teach ?
For the joy of our hearts is stormy with mighty battles won,
And sweet shall be their **lulling** with thy tale of deeds agone."

Then they brought the harp to Sigurd, and he looked on the ancient man,
As his hand sank into the strings, and a ripple over them ran,
And **he looked** forth kind o'er the people, and all men on his glory gazed,
And hearkened, hushed and happy, as the King his voice upraised ;
There **he sang** of the works of Odin, and the halls of the heavenly coast,
And the **sons** of God uprising, and the Wolflings' gathering host ;
And **he told** of the birth of Rerir, and of Volsung yet unborn,
All the **deeds** of his father's father, and his battles overworn ;
Then he told of Signy and Sigmund, and the changing of their lives ;
Tales of great kings' departing, and their kindred and their **wives.**
But his song and his fond desire go up to the cloudy roof,
And blend with the eagles' shrilling in the windy night **aloof.**
So he made an end of his story, and he sat and longed full sore
That the days of all his longing as a story might be o'er :
But the wonder of the people, and their love of Sigurd grew,
And green grew the tree of the Volsungs, as the Branstock blossomed anew.

Now up rose Grimhild the wise-wife, and she stood by Sigurd and said:
"There is none of the kings of kingdoms that may match thy goodlihead:
Lo now, thou hast sung of thy fathers; but men shall sing of thee,
And therewith shall our house be remembered, and great shall our glory be.
I beseech thee hearken a little to a faithful word of mine,
When thou of this cup hast drunken; for my love is blent with the wine."

He laughed and took the cup: But therein with the blood of the earth
Earth's hidden might was mingled, and deeds of the cold sea's birth,
And things that the high Gods turn from, and a tangle of strange love,
Deep guile, and strong compelling, that whoso drank thereof
Should remember not his longing, should cast his love away,
Remembering dead desire but as night remembereth day.

So Sigurd looked on the horn, and he saw how fair it was scored
With the cunning of the Dwarf-kind and the masters of the sword;
And he drank and smiled on Grimhild above the beaker's rim,
And she looked and laughed at his laughter; and the soul was changed in him.
Men gazed and their hearts sank in them, and they knew not why it was,
Why the fair-lit hall was darkling, nor what had come to pass:
For they saw the sorrow of Sigurd, who had seen but his deeds erewhile,
And the face of the mighty darkened, who had known but the light of its smile

But Grimhild looked and was merry: and she deemed her life was great,
And her hand a wonder of wonders to withstand the deeds of Fate:
For she saw by the face of Sigurd and the token of his eyes
That her will had abased the valiant, and filled the faithful with lies,
And blinded the God-born seer, and turned the steadfast athwart,
And smitten the pride of the joyous, and the hope of the eager heart;
The hush of the hall she hearkened, and the fear of men she knew,
But all this was a token unto her, and great pride within her grew,
As she saw the days that were coming from the well-spring of her blood;
Goodly and glorious and great by the kings of her kindred she stood,

And faced the sorrow of Sigurd, and her soul of that hour was fain;
For she thought : I will heal the smitten, I will raise up the smitten and slain,
And take heed where the Gods were heedless, and build on where they began,
And frame hope for the unborn children and the coming days of man.

Then she spake aloud to the Volsung : " Hear this faithful word of mine !
For the draught thou hast drunken, O Sigurd, and my love was blent with the
O Sigurd, son of the mighty, thy kin are passed away,   [wine :
But uplift thine heart and be merry, for new kin hast thou gotten today;
Thy father is Giuki the King, and Grimhild thy mother is made,
And thy brethren are Gunnar and Hogni and Guttorm the unafraid.
Rejoice for a kingly kindred, and a hope undreamed before !
For the folk shall be wax in the fire that withstandeth the Niblung war ;
The waste shall bloom as a garden in the Niblung glory and trust,
And the wrack of the Niblung people shall burn the world to dust :
Our peace shall still the world, our joy shall replenish the earth ;
And of thee it cometh, O Sigurd, the gold and the garland of worth !"

But the heart was changed in Sigurd ; as though it ne'er had been
His love of Brynhild perished as he gazed on the Niblung Queen :
Brynhild's belovèd body was e'en as a wasted hearth,
No more for bale or blessing, for plenty or for dearth.
—O ye that shall look hereafter, when the day of Sigurd is done,
And the last of his deeds is accomplished, and his eyes are shut in the sun,
When ye look and long for Sigurd, and the image of Sigurd behold,
And his white sword still as the moon, and his strong hand heavy and cold,
Then perchance shall ye think of this even, then perchance shall ye wonder and
"Twice over, King, are we smitten, and twice have we seen thee die." [cry,

As folk of the summer feasters, who have fallen to feast in the morn,
And have wreathed their brows with roses ere the first of the clouds was born ;
Beneath the boughs were they sitting, and the long leaves twinkled about,
And the wind with their laughter was mingled, nor held aback from their shout,

Amidst of their harp it lingered, from the mouth of their horn went up,
Round the reek of their roast was it breathing, o'er the flickering face of their
—Lo now, why sit they so heavy, and why is their joy-speech dead,   [cup—
Why are the long leaves drooping, and the fair wind hushed o'erhead ?—
Look out from the sunless boughs to the yellow-mirky east,
How the clouds are woven together o'er that afternoon of feast ;
There are heavier clouds above them, and the sun is a hidden wonder,
It rains in the nether heaven, and the world is afraid with the thunder :
E'en so in the hall of the Niblungs, and the holy joyous place,
Sat the earls on the marvel gazing, and the sorrow of Sigurd's face.

Men say that a little after the evil of that night
All waste is the burg of Brynhild, and there springeth a marvellous light
On the desert hard by Lymdale, and few men know for why ;
But there are, who say that a wildfire thence roareth up to the sky
Round a glorious golden dwelling, wherein there sitteth a Queen
In remembrance of the wakening, and the slumber that hath been ;
Wherein a Maid there sitteth, who knows not hope nor rest
For remembrance of the Mighty, and the Best come forth from the Best.

But the hushed Kings sat in the feast-hall, till Grimhild cried on the harp,
And the minstrels' fingers hastened, and the sound rang clear and sharp
Beneath the cloudy roof-tree, but no joyance with it went,
And no voice but the eagles' crying with the stringèd song was blent ;
And as it began, it ended, and no soul had been moved by its voice,
To lament o'er the days passed over, or in coming days to rejoice.
Late groweth the night o'er the people, but no word hath Sigurd said,
Since he laughed o'er the glittering Dwarf-gold and raised the cup to his head :
No wrath in his eyes is arisen, no hope, nor wonder, nor fear ;
Yet is Sigurd's face as boding to folk that behold him anear,
As the mountain that broodeth the fire o'er the town of man's delights,
As the sky that is cursed nor thunders, as the God that is smitten nor smites.

So silent sitteth the Volsung o'er the blindness of the wrong,
But night on the Niblungs waxeth, and their Kings for the morrow long,
And the morrow of tomorrow that the light may be fair to their eyes,
And their days as the days of the joyous : so now from the throne they arise,
And their men depart from the feast-hall, their care in sleep to lay,
But none durst speak with Sigurd, nor ask him, whither away,
As he strideth dumb from amidst them ; and all who see him deem
That he heedeth the folk of the Niblungs but as people of a dream.
So they fall away from about him, till he stands in the forecourt alone ;
Then he fares to the kingly stables, nor knoweth he his own,
Nor backeth the cloudy Greyfell, but a steed of the Kings he bestrides
And forth through the gate of the Niblungs and into the night he rides :
—Yea he with no deed before him, and he in the raiment of peace ;
And the moon in the mid-sky wadeth, and is come to her most increase.

In the deedless dark he rideth, and all things he remembers save one,
And nought else hath he care to remember of all the deeds he hath done :
He hasteneth not nor stayeth ; he lets the dark die out
Ere he comes to the burg of Brynhild and rides it round about ;
And he lets the sun rise upward ere he rideth thence away,
And wendeth he knoweth not whither, and he weareth down the day ;
Till lo, a plain and a river, and a ridge at the mountains' feet
With a burg of people builded for the lords of God-home meet.
O'er the bridge of the river he rideth, and unto the burg-gate comes
In no lesser wise up-builded than the gate of the heavenly homes :
Himseems that the gate-wards know him, for they cry out each to each,
And as whispering winds in the mountains he hears their far-off speech.
So he comes to the gate's huge hollow, and amidst its twilight goes,
And his horse is glad and remembers, and that road of King-folk knows ;
And the winds are astir in its arches with the sound of swords unseen,
And the cries of kings departed, and the battles that have been.

So into a garth of warriors from that dusk he rideth out

And no man stayeth nor hindereth; there he gazeth round about,
And seeth a glorious dwelling, a mighty far-famed place,
As the last of the evening sunlight shines fair on his weary face:
And there is a hall before him, and huge in the even it lies,
A mountain grey and awful with the Dwarf-folk's masteries:
And the houses of men cling round it, and low they seem and frail,
Though the wise and the deft have built them for a long-enduring tale:
There the wind sings loud in the wall-nook, and the spears are sparks on the
And the swords are flaming torches as the sun is hard on his fall: [wall,
He falls, and the even dusketh o'er that sword-renownèd close,
But Sigurd bideth and broodeth for the Niblung house he knows,
And he hath a thought within him that he rideth forth from shame,
And that men have forgotten the greeting and are slow to remember his fame.

But forth from the hall came a shouting, and the voice of many men,
And he deemed they cried "Hail, Sigurd! thou art welcome home again!"
Then he looked to the door of the feast-hall and behold it seemed to him
That its wealth of graven stories with more than the dusk was dim;
With the waving of white raiment and the doubtful gleam of gold.
Then there groweth a longing within him, nor his heart will he withhold;
But he rideth straight to the doorway, and the stories of the door:
And there sitteth Giuki the ancient, the King, the wise of war,
And Grimhild the kin of the God-folk, the wife of the glittering eyes;
And there is the goodly Gunnar, and Hogni the overwise,
And Guttorm the young and the war-fain; and there in the door and the shade,
With eyes to the earth cast downward, is the white-armed Niblung Maid.
But all these give Sigurd greeting, and hail him fair and well;
And King Giuki saith:

          "Hail, Sigurd! what tidings wilt thou tell
Of thy deeds since yestereven? or whitherward wentst thou?"

Then unto the earth leapt the Volsung, and gazed with doubtful brow
On the King and the Queen and the Brethren, and the white-armed Giuki's
                                                        [Child,

Yet amidst all these in a measure of his heavy heart was beguiled :
He spread out his hands before them, and he spake :

                                  "O, what be ye,
Who ask of the deeds of Sigurd, and seek of the days to be ?
Are ye aught but the Niblung children ? for meseems I would ask for a gift,
But the thought of my heart is unstable, and my hope as the winter-drift;
And the words may not be shapen.—But speak ye, men of the earth,
Have ye any new-found tidings, or are deeds come nigh to the birth ?
Are there knots for my sword to sunder ? are there thrones for my hand to
      shake ?   [take ?
And to which of the Gods shall I give, and from which of the Kings shall I
Or in which of the houses of man-folk henceforward shall I dwell ?
O speak, ye Niblung children, and the tale to Sigurd tell !'

None answered a word for a space ; but Gudrun wept in the door,
And the noise of men came outward and of feet that went on the floor.
Then Grimhild stood before him, and took him by the hand,
And she said : " In the hall are gathered the earls of the Niblung land.
Come thou with the Mother of Kings and sit in thy place tonight,
That the cheer of the earls may be bettered, nor the war-dukes lose delight."

" Come, brother and king," said Gunnar, " for here of all the earth
Is the place that may not lack thee, and the folk that loves thy worth."

" Come, Sigurd the wise," said Hogni, " and so shall thy visage cheer
The folk that is bold for tomorrow, and the hearts that know no fear."

"Come, Sigurd the keen," said Guttorm, "for thy sword lies light in the sheath,
And oft shall we ride together to face the fateful death."

No word at all spake Gudrun, as she stood in the doorway dim,
But turned her face from beholding as she reached her hand to him.

Then Sigurd nought gainsaid them, but into the hall he passed,
And great shouts of salutation to the cloudy roof were cast,
And rang back from the glassy pillars, and the woven God-folk stirred,
And afar the clustering eagles on the golden roof-ridge heard,
And cried out on the Sword of the Branstock as they cried in other days;
And the harps rang out in the hall, and men sang in Sigurd's praise.

But he looked to the right and the left, and he knew there was ruin and lack,
And the death of yestereven, and the days that should never come back;
And he strove, but nought he remembered of the matters that he would,
Save that great was the flood of sorrow that had drowned his days of good:
Then he deemed that the sons of the earl-folk, e'en mid their praising word,
Were looking on his trouble as a people sore afeard;
And the gifts that the Gods had given the pride in his soul awoke,
And kindled was Sigurd's kindness by the trouble of the folk;
And he thought: I shall do and undo, as while agone I did,
And abide the time of the dawning, when the night shall be no more hid!
Then he lifted his head like a king, and his brow as a God's was clear,
And the trouble fell from the people, and they cast aside their fear;
And scarce was his glory abated as he sat in the seat of the Kings
With the Niblung brethren about him, and they spake of famous things,
And the dealings of lords of the earth; but he spake and answered again
And thrust by the grief of forgetting, and his tangled thought and vain,
And cast his care on the morrow, that the people might be glad.
Yet no smile there came to Sigurd, and his lips no laughter had;
But he seemeth a king o'er-mighty, who hath won the earthly crown,
In whose hand the world is lying, who no more heedeth renown.

But now speaketh Grimhild the Queen: " Rise, daughter of my folk,
For thou seest my son is weary with the weight of the careful yoke;
Go, bear him the wine of the Kings, and hail him over the gold,
And bless the King for his coming to the heart of the Niblung fold."

Upriseth the white-armed Gudrun, and taketh the cup in her hand;
Dead-pale in the night of her tresses by Sigurd doth she stand,
And strives with the thought within her, and finds no word to speak :
For such is the strength of her anguish, as well might slay the weak;
But her heart is a heart of the Queen-folk and of them that bear earth's kings,
And her love of her lord seems lovely, though sore the torment wrings.
——How fares it with words unspoken, when men are great enow,
And forth from the good to the good the strong desires shall flow?
Are they wasted e'en as the winds, the barren maids of the sky,
Of whose birth there is no man wotteth, nor whitherward they fly?

Lo, Sigurd lifteth his eyes, and he sees her silent and pale,
But fair as Odin's Choosers in the slain kings' wakening dale,
But sweet as the mid-fell's dawning ere the grass beginneth to move ;
And he knows in an instant of time that she stands 'twixt death and love,
And that no man, none of the Gods can help her, none of the days,
If he turn his face from her sorrow, and wend on his lonely ways.
But she sees the change in his eyen, and her queenly grief is stirred,
And the shame in her bosom riseth at the long unspoken word,
And again with the speech she striveth ; but swift is the thought in his heart
To slay her trouble for ever, and thrust her shame apart.
And he saith :
　　　　　　"O Maid of the Niblungs, thou art weary-faced this eve :
Nay, put thy trouble from thee, lest the shielded warriors grieve !
Or tell me what hath been done, or what deed have men forborne,
That here mid the warriors' joyance thy life-joy lieth forlorn ?
For so may the high Gods help me, as nought so much I would,
As that round thine head this even might flit unmingled good !"

He seeth the love in her eyen, and the life that is tangled in his,
And the heart cries out within him, and man's hope of earthly bliss ;
And again would he spare her the speech, as she strives with her longing sore.

" Here are glad men **about us,** and a joyous folk **of war,**
And they that have loved thee for long, and they that have cherished mine
But we twain alone are woeful, as sad folk sitting apart.   [heart ;
Ah, if I thy **soul** might gladden ! **if** thy lips might give me peace !
Then belike were we gladdest of all ; for I love thee more than **these.**
The cup of goodwill that thou bearest, and the greeting thou wouldst say,
Turn these to the **cup of thy love,** and the words of the troth-plighting **day;**
The love that endureth for ever, and the never-dying **troth,**
To face the **Norns' undoing,** and the Gods amid **their wrath."**

Then **he taketh the cup and her** hands, and she boweth meekly adown,
Till she feels the arms of Sigurd round her trembling body thrown :
A little while she doubteth in the mighty slayer's arms
As Sigurd's love unhoped-for **her barren bosom warms ;**
A little while she struggleth **with the fear** of his mighty fame,
That grows with her hope's fulfilment ; ruth rises with wonder and shame ;
For the kindness grows in her soul, as forgotten anguish **dies,**
And her heart feels Sigurd's sorrow in the breast whereon she lies ;
Then the fierce love overwhelms her, and **as wax in the fervent fire**
All dies and is forgotten in the sweetness of desire ;
And **close she** clingeth to Sigurd, as **one** that hath gotten the **best**
And fair **things of the world she deemeth,** as a place of infinite rest.

Of the Wedding of Sigurd the Volsung.

That night sleeps Sigurd the Volsung, and awakes on **the morrow-morn,**
And wots at the first but dimly what thing in his life **hath been born :**
But the sun cometh up in the autumn, and the eve he remembereth,
And the word he hath given to Gudrun to love her to the death ;
And he longs for the Niblung maiden, that her love may cherish his heart,
Lest e'en as a Godhead banished he dwell in the world apart :
The new sun smiteth his body as he leaps from the golden bed,

And doeth on his raiment and is fair apparelled ;
Then he goes his ways through the chambers, and greeteth none at all
Till he comes to the garth and the garden in the nook of the Niblung wall.

Now therein, mid the yellowing leafage, and the golden blossoms spent,
Alone and lovely and eager the white-armed Gudrun went ;
Swift then he hasteneth toward her, and she bideth his drawing near,
And now in the morn she trembleth ; for her love is blent with fear ;
And wonder is all around her, for she deemed till yestereve,
When she saw the earls astonied, and the golden Sigurd grieve,
That on some most mighty woman his joyful love was set ;
And love hath made her humble, and her race doth she forget,
And her noble and mighty heart from the best of the Niblungs sprung,
The sons of the earthly War-Gods of the days when the world was young.
Yea she feareth her love and his fame, but she feareth his sorrow most,
Lest he spake from a heart o'erladen and counted not the cost.
But lo, the love of his eyen, and the kindness of his face !
And joy her body burdens, and she trembleth in her place,
And sinks in the arms that cherish with a faint and eager cry,
And again on the bosom of Sigurd doth the head of Gudrun lie.

Fairer than yestereven doth Sigurd deem his love,
And more her tender wooing and her shame his soul doth move ;
And his words of peace and comfort come easier forth from him,
And woman's love seems wondrous amidst his trouble dim ;
Strange, sweet, to cling together ! as oft and o'er again
They crave and kiss rejoicing, and their hearts are full and fain.

Then a little while they sunder, and apart and anigh they stand,
And Sigurd's eyes grow awful as he stretcheth forth his hand,
And his clear voice saith :
                    "O Gudrun, now hearken while I swear
That the sun shall die for ever and the day no more be fair,

Ere I forget thy pity and thine inmost heart of love !
Yea, though the Kings be mighty, and the Gods be great above,
I will wade the flood and the fire, and the waste of war forlorn,
To look on the Niblung dwelling, and the house where thou wert born."

Strange seemed the words to Sigurd that his gathering love compelled,
And sweet and strange desire o'er his tangled trouble welled.

But bright flashed the eyes of Gudrun, and she said : " King, as for me,
If thou sawest the heart in my bosom, what oath might better thee ?
Yet my words thy words shall cherish, as thy lips my lips have done.
—Herewith I swear, O Sigurd, that the earth shall hate the sun,
And the year desire but darkness, and the blossoms shrink from day,
Ere my love shall fail, belovèd, or my longing pass away ! "

Now they go from the garth and the garden, and hand in hand they come
To the hall of the kings of aforetime, and the heart of the Niblung home.
There they go 'neath the cloudy roof-tree, and on to the high-seat fair,
And there sitteth Giuki the ancient, and the guileful Grimhild is there,
With the swart-haired Niblung brethren ; and all these are exceeding fain,
When they look on Sigurd and Gudrun, and the peace that enwrappeth the
For in her is all woe forgotten, sick longing little seen,   [twain,
And the shame that slayeth pity, and the self-scorn of a Queen ;
And all doubt in love is swallowed, and lovelier now is she
Than a picture deftly painted by the craftsmen over sea ;
And her face is a rose of the morning by the night-tide framed about,
And the long-stored love of her bosom from her eyes is leaping out.
But how fair is Sigurd the King that beside her beauty goes !
How lovely is he shapen, how great his stature shows !
How kind is the clasping right-hand, that hath smitten the battle acold !
How kind are the awful eyen that no foeman durst behold !
How sweet are the lips unsmiling, and the brow as the open day !
What man can behold and believe it, that his life shall pass away ?

So he standeth proud by the high-seat, and the sun through the vast hall pours
And the Gods on the hangings waver as the wind goes by the doors,
And abroad are the sounds of man-folk, and the eagles cry from the roof,
And the ancient deeds of Sigmund seem **fallen** far aloof;
And dead are **t**he fierce days fallen, and the world is soft and sweet,
As the Son of the Volsungs speaketh in noble words and meet:

"O hearken, **King of the** Niblungs, O ancient of the days!
Time was, when alone I wandered, and went on the wasteland ways,
And sore my soul desired the harvest of the sword:
Then I slew the great Gold-wallower, and won the ancient Hoard,
And I turned to the dwellings of men; for I longed for measureless fame,
And to do and undo with the Kings, and the pride of the Kings to tame;
And I longed for the love of the King-folk; but who desired my soul,
Who stayed my feet in his dwelling, **who showed the** weary the goal,
Who drew me forth from the wastes, and the **bitter** kinless dearth,
Till I came to the house of Giuki and the hallowed Niblung hearth?
Count up the deeds and forbearings, count up the words of the days
That show forth the love of the Niblungs and the ancient people's praise.
Nay, number the waves of the sea, and the grains of the yellow sand,
And the drops of the rain in the April, and the blades of the grassy land!
And **what if** one heart of the Niblungs had stored and treasured it all,
And hushed, and moved but softly, lest one grain thereof should fall?
If she feared the barren garden, and the sunless fallow field?
How **then should** the spring-tide labour, and the summer toil **to yield!**
And so may the high Gods help **me, as** I from this day forth
Shall toil for her exalting to the height of worldly worth,
If thou stretch thine hands forth, Giuki, and hail me **for thy** son:
Then there as thou sitt'st in thy grave-mound when thine earthly day is done,
Thou shalt hear of our children's children, **and** the crownèd kin of kings,
And the peace of the Niblung **people in the day** of better things;
And then mayst thou be merry of the eve when Sigurd came,
In the day of the deeds of the Niblungs and the blossom of their fame.

Stretch forth thine hands to thy son : for I bid thy daughter to wife,
And her life shall withhold my death-day, and her death shall stay my life."

Then spoke the ancient Giuki : " Hail, Sigurd, son of mine eld !
And I bless the Gods for the day that mine ancient eyes have beheld :
Now let me depart in peace, since I know for very sooth
That waxen e'en as the God-folk shall the Niblungs blossom in youth.
Come, take thy mother's greeting, and let thy brethren say
How well they love thee, Sigurd, and how fair they deem the day."

Then lowly bendeth Sigurd 'neath the guileful Grimhild's hand,
And he kisseth the Kings of the Niblungs, and about him there they stand,
The war-fain, darkling kindred ; and all their words are praise,
And the love of the tide triumphant, and the hope of the latter days.

Hark now, on the morrow morning how the blast of the mighty horn
From the builded Burg of the Niblungs goes over the acres shorn,
And the roads are gay with the riders, and the bull in the stall is left,
And the plough is alone in the furrow, and the wedge in the bole half-cleft;
And late shall the ewes be folded, and the kine come home to the pail,
And late shall the fires be litten in the outmost treeless dale :
For men fare to the gate of Giuki and the ancient cloudy hall,
And therein are the earls assembled and the kings wear purple and pall,
And the flowers are spread beneath them, and the bench-cloths beaten with
And the walls are strange and wondrous with the noble stories told: [gold ;
For new-hung is the ancient dwelling with the golden spoils of the south,
And men seem merry for ever, and the praise is in each man's mouth,
And the name of Sigurd the Volsung, the King and the Serpent's Bane,
Who exalteth the high this morning and blesseth the masters of gain :
For men drink the bridal of Sigurd and the white-armed Niblung maid,
And the best with the best shall be mingled, and the gold with the gold o'erlaid.

So, fair in the hall is the feasting and men's hearts are uplifted on high,

And they deem that the best of their life-days are surely drawing anigh,
As now, one after other, uprise the scalds renowned,
And their well-belovèd voices awake the hoped-for sound,
In the midmost of the high-tide, and the joy of feasting lords.
Then cometh a hush and a waiting, and the light of many swords
Flows into the hall of Giuki by the doorway of the King,
And amid those flames of battle the war-clad warriors bring
The Cup of daring Promise and the hallowed Boar of Sôn,
And men's hearts grow big with longing and great is the hope-tide grown;
For bright the Son of Sigmund ariseth by the board,
And unwinds the knitted peace-strings that hamper Regin's Sword:
Then fierce is the light on the high-seat as men set down the Cup
Anigh the hand of Sigurd, and the edges blue rise up,
And fall on the hallowed Wood-beast: as a trump of the woeful war
Rings the voice of the mighty Volsung as he speaks the words of yore:

" By the Earth that groweth and giveth, and by all the Earth's increase
That is spent for Gods and man-folk; by the sun that shines on these;
By the Salt-Sea-Flood that beareth the life and death of men;
By the Heavens and Stars that change not, though earth die out again;
By the wild things of the mountain, and the houseless waste and lone;
By the prey of the Goths in the thicket and the holy Beast of Sôn,
I hallow me to Odin for a leader of his host,
To do the deeds of the Highest, and never count the cost:
And I swear, that whatso great-one shall show the day and the deed,
I shall ask not why nor wherefore, but the sword's desire shall speed:
And I swear to seek no quarrel, nor to swerve aside for aught,
Though the right and the left be blooming, and the straight way wend to
And I swear to abide and hearken the prayer of any thrall,   [nought:
Though the war-torch be on the threshold and the foemen's feet in the hall:
And I swear to sit on my throne in the guise of the kings of the earth,
Though the anguish past amending, and the unheard woe have birth.
And I swear to wend in my sorrow that none shall curse mine eyes

For the scowl that quelleth beseeching, and the hate that scorneth the wise.
So help me Earth and Heavens, and the Under-sky and Seas,
And the Stars in their ordered houses, and the Norns that order these !"

And he drank of the Cup of the Promise, and fair as a star he shone,
And all men rejoiced and wondered, and deemed Earth's glory won.

Then came the girded maidens, and the slim earls' daughters poured,
And uprose the dark-haired Gunnar and bare was the Niblung sword ;
Blue it gleamed in the hand of the folk-king as he laid it low on the Beast,
And took oath as the Goths of aforetime in the hush of the people's feast :
" I will work for the craving of Kings, and accomplish the will of the great,
Nor ask what God withstandeth, nor hearken the tales of fate ;
When a King my life hath exalted, and wrought for my hope and my gain,
For every deed he hath done me, thereto shall I fashion twain.
I shall bear forth the fame of the Niblungs through all that hindereth ;
In my life shall I win great glory, and be merry in my death."

So sweareth the lovely war-king and drinketh of the Cup,
And the joy of the people waxeth and their glad cry goeth up.
But again came the girded maidens : earls' daughters pour the wine,
And bare is the blade of Hogni in the feast-hall over the Swine ;
Then he cries o'er the hallowed Wood-beast: "Earth, hearken, how I swear
To beseech no man for his helping, and to vex no God with prayer ;
And to seek out the will of the Norns, and look in the eyes of the curse ;
And to laugh while the love aboundeth, lest the glad world grow into worse ;
Then if in the murder I laugh not, O Earth, remember my name,
And oft tell it aloud to the people for the Niblungs' fated shame ! "

Then he drank of the Cup of the Promise, and all men hearkened and deemed
That his speech was great and valiant, and as one of the wise he seemed.

Then the linen-folded maidens of the earl-folk lift the gold

But the earls look each on the other, and Guttorm's place behold,
And empty it lieth before them ; for the child hath wearied of peace,
And he sits by the oars in the East-seas, and winneth fame's increase.
Nor then, nor ever after, o'er the Holy Beast he spake,
When mighty hearts were exalted for the golden Sigurd's sake.

But now crieth Giuki the Ancient : "O fair sons, well have ye sworn,
And gladdened my latter-ending, and my kingly hours outworn ;
Full fain from the halls of Odin on the world's folk shall I gaze
And behold all hearts rejoicing in the Niblungs' glorious days."

Glad cries of earls rose upward and beat on the cloudy roof,
And went forth on the drift of the autumn to the mountains far aloof:
Speech stirred in the hearts of the singers, and the harps might not refrain,
And they called on the folk of aforetime of the Niblung joy to be fain.

But Sigurd sitteth by Gudrun, and his heart is soft and kind,
And the pity swelleth within it for the days when he was blind ;
And with yet another pity, lest his sorrow seen o'erweigh
Her fond desire's fulfilment, and her fair soul's blooming-day :
And many a word he frameth his kingly fear to hide,
And the tangle of his trouble, that her joy may well abide.
But the joy so filleth Gudrun and the triumph of her bliss,
That oft she sayeth within her : How durst I dream of this ?
How durst I hope for the days wherein I now shall dwell,
And that assurèd joyance whereof no tongue may tell ?

So fares the feast in glory till thin the night doth grow,
And joy hath wearied the people, and to rest and sleep they go :
Then dight is the fateful bride-bed, and the Norns will hinder nought
That the feet of the Niblung Maiden to the chamber of Kings be brought,
And the troth is pledged and wedded, and the Norns cast nought before
The feet of Sigurd the Volsung and the bridal chamber-door.

All hushed was the house of the Niblungs, and they two **were left alone,**
And kind as a man made happy was the golden **Sigurd grown,**
As there in the arms of the mighty he clasped the Niblung Maid ;
But her spirit fainted within her, and her very soul was afraid,
And her mouth was empty of words when their lips were sundered a space,
And in awe and utter wonder she gazed upon his face ;
As one who hath prayed for a God in the dwelling of man **to abide,**
And he comes, and the face unfashioned his ruth and his mercy must hide.
She trembled and wept before him, till at last amidst **her tears**
The joy and the hope of women fell on her unawares,   [blessed,
And she sought the hands that had held her, **and the face that her face had**
And the bosom of Sigurd the Mighty, the hope of her earthly rest.

Then he spake as she hearkened and wondered : " With the Kings of men I
And none but the men of the war-fain our coming swords abode :   [rode,
O, dear was the day of the riding, and the hope of the clashing swords !
O, dear were the deeds of battle, and the fall of Odin's lords,
When I met the overcomers, and beheld **them overcome,**
When we rent the spoil from the spoilers, **and led the chasers home !**
O, sweet was the day of the summer when we won the ancient towns,
And we stood in the golden bowers and took and gave **the crowns** !
And sweet were the suppliant faces, **and the** gifts and the grace **we gave,**
And the life and the wealth unhoped for, and the hope to heal and save :
And sweet was the praise of the Niblungs, and dear was the song that arose
O'er **the** deed assured, accomplished, and the death of the people's foes !
O joyful deeds of the mighty! O wondrous life of a King !
Unto thee alone will I tell it, and his fond imagining,
That but few of the people wot of, as he sits with face unmoved
In the place where kings have perished, in the seat of kings beloved ! "

His kind arms clung about her, and her face to his face he drew ;
" **The** life **of** the kings have **I** conquered, but this is strange and **new** ;
And from out the heart of the striving a lovelier thing is born,

And the love of my love is sweeter and these hours before the morn."

Again she trembled before him and knew not what she feared,
And her heart alone, unhidden, deemed her love too greatly dared ;
But the very body of Sigurd, the wonder of all men,
Cast cherishing arms about her, and kissed her mouth again,
And in love her whole heart melted, and all thought passed away,
Save the thought of joy's fulfilment and the hours before the day ;
She murmured words of loving as his kind lips cherished her breast,
And the world waxed nought but lovely and a place of infinite rest.

But it was long thereafter ere the sun rose o'er their love,
And lit the world of autumn and the pale sky hung above ;
And it stirred the Gods in the heavens, and the Kings of the Goths it stirred,
Till the sound of the world awakening in their latter dreams they heard ;
And over the Burg of the Niblungs the day spread fair and fresh
O'er the hopes of the ancient people and those twain become one flesh.

Sigurd rideth with the Niblungs, and wooeth Brynhild for King Gunnar.

Now it fell on a day of the spring-tide that followed on these things,
That Sigurd fares to the meadows with Gunnar and Hogni the Kings ;
For afar is Guttorm the youngest, and he sails the Eastern Seas,
And fares with war-shield hoisted to win him fame's increase.
So come the Kings to the Doom-ring, and the people's Hallowed Field,
And no dwelling of man is anigh it, and no acre forced to yield :
There stay those Kings of the people alone in weed of war,
And they cut a strip of the greensward on the meadow's daisied floor,
And loosen it clean in the midst, while its ends in the earth abide ;
Then they heave its midmost aloft, and set on either side
An ancient spear of battle writ round with words of worth ;

And these are the posts of the door, whose threshold is **of the earth,**
And the skin of the earth is its lintel : but with war-glaives gleaming bare
The Niblung Kings and Sigurd beneath the earth-yoke fare ;
Then each an arm-vein openeth, and their blended blood falls down
On Earth the fruitful Mother where they rent her **turfy gown :**
And then, when the blood of the Volsungs hath run with the Niblung blood,
They kneel with their hands upon it and swear the brotherhood :
Each man at his brother's bidding to come with the blade in his hand,
Though the fire and the flood should sunder, and the very **Gods withstand**:
Each man to love and cherish his brother's hope and will ;
Each man to avenge his brother when the Norns his fate fulfill :
And now are they foster-brethren, and in such wise have they sworn
As the God-born Goths of aforetime, when the world was newly born.
But among the folk of the Niblungs goes **forth the tale of the same,**
And men deem the tidings a glory and the garland of their fame.

So is Sigurd yet with the Niblungs, and he loveth Gudrun his wife,
And wendeth afield with the brethren to the days of the dooming of life ;
And nought his glory waneth, nor falleth the flood of **praise :**
To every man he hearkeneth, nor gainsayeth any grace,
And glad is the poor in the Doom-ring when he seeth his face mid **the Kings,**
For **the tangle** straighteneth before him, and the maze of crookèd things.
But the **smile is departed from him, and the laugh of Sigurd the** young,
And of few words now is he waxen, and his songs are seldom sung.
Howbeit of all the sad-faced was Sigurd loved the best ;
And men say : **Is the king's heart** mighty beyond all hope of rest ?
Lo, how he beareth the people ! how heavy their woes are grown !
So oft were a God mid the Goth-folk, if he dwelt in the world alone.

Now Giuki the King of the Niblungs must change **his life at the last,**
And they lay him down in the mountains and a great mound over him cast :
For thus had he said in his life-days : "When my hand from the people shall fade,
Up there on the side of the mountains shall the King of the Niblungs be laid,

Whence one seeth the plain of the tillage and the fields where man-folk go;
Then whiles in the dawn's awakening, when the day-wind riseth to blow,
Shall I see the war-gates opening, and the joy of my shielded men
As they look to the field of the dooming: and whiles in the even again
Shall I see the spoil come homeward, and the host of the Niblungs pour
Through the gates that the Dwarf-folk builded and the well-belovèd door."

So there lieth Giuki the King, mid steel and the glimmer of gold,
As the sound of the feastful Niblungs round his misty house is rolled:
But Gunnar is King of the people, and the chief of the Niblung land;
A man beloved for his mercy, and his might and his open hand;
A glorious king in the battle, a hearkener at the doom,
A singer to sing the sun up from the heart of the midnight **gloom.**

On **a** day sit the Kings in the high-seat when Grimhild saith to her son:
" O Gunnar, King belovèd, **a** fair life hast thou won;
On the flood, in the field hast thou wrought, and hung the chambers with gold;
Far abroad mid many a people are the tidings of thee told:
Now do a deed for thy mother and the hallowed Niblung hearth,
Lest the house of the mighty perish, and our tale grow wan with dearth.
If thou do the deed that I bid thee, and wed a wife of the Kings,
No less shalt thou cleave the war-helms and scatter the ruddy rings."

He said: " Meseemeth, mother, thou speaketh not in haste,
But hast sought **and** found beforehand, lest thy fair words fall to waste."

She said: "Thou sayest the sooth; **I** have found the thing I sought:
A Maid for thee is shapen, and a Queen for thee is wrought:
In the waste land hard by Lymdale a marvellous hall is built,
With its roof of the red gold beaten, and its wall-stones over-gilt:
Afar o'er the heath men see it, **but** no man draweth nigher,
For the garth that goeth about it is nought but the roaring fire,
A white wall waving aloft; and no window nor wicket is there,

Whereby the shielded earl-folk or the sons of the merchants may fare :
But few things from me are hidden, **and I** know in that hall of gold
Sits Brynhild, white as a wild-swan where the foamless seas are rolled ;
And the daughter of Kings of the world, and the **sister of Queens is she,**
And wise, and Odin's Chooser, and **the Breath of Victory** :
But for this cause **sitteth she thus** in the ring of the **Wavering Flame,**
That no son of the Kings **will she wed save** the mightiest master **of fame,**
And the man **who knoweth not fear,** and the man foredoomed of fate
To ride **through her Wavering Fire to** the door of her golden gate :
And for **him she** sitteth and waiteth, and him shall she **cherish and love,**
Though **the Kings** of the world should withstand it, and **the Gods that sit**
Speak **thou, O mighty** Gunnar !—nay rather, Sigurd my **son,**   [above.
Say who but the lord of the Niblungs should wed with this glorious one ? "

Long Sigurd gazeth upon her, and slow **he sayeth again** :
" I know thy will, my mother ; of all the sons of men,
Of all the Kings unwedded, and the kindred of the **great,**
It is meet that my brother Gunnar should ride **to her golden gate."**

Then laughed Gunnar and answered : **" May a king of the people fear ?**
May a king of the harp and the hall-glee hold such a **maid but dear ?**
Yet nought have I and my kindred to do with fateful deeds ;
Lo, how **the fair earth** bloometh, **and the field fulfilleth our** needs,
And our swords rust not in our scabbards, and our steeds bide not in the stall,
And oft are the **shields of** the Niblungs drawn clanking down from the wall ;
And I sit by my brother Sigurd, **and** no ill there is **in our life,**
And the harp and the sword is beside me, and I joy in the peace and the strife.
So I live, till at last in the sword-play midst **the** uttermost longing of fame
I shall change my life and **be merry, and leave no hated name.**
Yet nevertheless, my mother, since the word has thus gone forth,
And I wot of thy great desire, **I will** reach at this garland of worth ;
And I bid you, Kings and Brethren, with the wooer of Queens to ride,
That ye **tell of the** thing hereafter, and the deeds that shall betide."

"It were well, O Son," said Grimhild, "in such fellowship to fare ;
But not today nor tomorrow ; the hearts of the Gods would I wear,
And know of the will of the Norns ; for a mighty matter is this,
And a deed all lands shall tell of, and the hope of the Niblung bliss."

So apart for long dwelt Grimhild, and mingled the might of the earth
With the deeds of the chilly sea, and the heart of the cloudland's dearth ;
And all these with the wine she mingled, and sore guile was set therein,
Blindness, and strong compelling for such as dared to win :
And she gave the drink to her sons ; and withal unto Gunnar she spake,
And told him tales of the King-folk, and smote desire awake ;
Till many a time he bethinks him of the Maiden sitting alone,
And the Queen that was shapen for him; till a dream of the night is she grown,
And a tale of the day's desire, and the crown of all his praise :
And the net of the Norns was about him, and the snare was spread in his ways,
And his mother's will was spurring adown the way they would ;
For she was the wise of women and the framer of evil and good.

In the May-morn riseth Gunnar with fair face and gleaming eyes,
And he calleth on Sigurd his brother, and he calleth on Hogni the wise :
"Today shall we fare to the wooing, for so doth our mother bid ;
We shall go to gaze on marvels, and things from the King-folk hid."

So they do on the best of their war-gear, and their steeds are dight for the road,
And forth to the sun neigheth Greyfell as he neighed 'neath the Golden Load :
But or ever they leap to the saddle, while yet in the door they stand,
Thereto cometh Grimhild the wise-wife, and on each head layeth her hand,
As she saith : "Be mighty and wise, as the kings that came before !
For they knew of the ways of the Gods, and the craft of the Gods they bore :
And they knew how the shapes of man-folk are the very images
Of the hearts that abide within them, and they knew of the shaping of these.
Be wise and mighty, O Kings, and look in mine heart and behold
The craft that prevaileth o'er semblance, and the treasured wisdom of old !

I hallow you thus for the **day, and** I hallow you thus for the night,
And I hallow you **thus for** the dawning with my fathers' hidden might.
Go now, for ye bear my will while I sit in the hall **and spin ;**
And tonight shall be the weaving, and tomorn **the web shall ye win."**

So they leap to the saddles aloft, and they ride and speak no word,
But the hills **and the** dales are awakened by the clink of the sheathèd **sword:**
None looks in **the face** of the **other,** but the earth and the **heavens gaze,**
And behold **those kings of battle ride down the dusty ways.**

So they **come to the Waste of Lymdale when the** afternoon is begun,
And afar they see **the flame-blink on the grey sky** under the sun :
And they spur and speak no **word, and no** man to his fellow will turn ;
But they see the hills draw **upward and the** earth beginning to burn :
And they ride, and the eve is coming, and the sun hangs low o'er the earth,
And the red flame roars up to it from the midst of the desert's **dearth.**
None turns or speaks to his brother, but the Wrath gleams bare and red,
And blood-red is the Helm of Aweing **on** the golden Sigurd's **head,**
And bare is the blade of Gunnar, and the first of the **three he rides,**
And the wavering wall is before him and the **golden sun it hides.**

Then the heart **of a king's son failed not,** but he tossed his sword **on high**
And laughed as **he** spurred for the fire, and cried the Niblung cry ;
But the **mare's son saw** and imagined, and the battle-eager steed,
That so oft had pierced the spear-hedge and never failed at need,
Shrank back, and shrieked in his terror, and spite of **spur and rein**
Fled fast as the foals unbitted on Odin's pasturing **plain ;**
Wide **then he** wheeled with Gunnar, **but** with **hand and knee he dealt,**
And the voice of a lord belovèd, till the steed his master felt,
And bore him back to the brethren ; by Greyfell Sigurd stood,
And stared at the heart of the fire, and his helm was red as blood ;
But Hogni sat in his saddle, and watched the flames up-roll ;
And he said : " Thy steed has failed thee that was once the noblest foal

In the pastures of King Giuki ; but since thine heart fails not,
And thou wouldst not get thee backward and say, The fire was hot,
And the voices pent within it were singing nought but death,
Let Sigurd lend thee his steed that wore the Glittering Heath,
And carried the Bed of the Serpent, and the ancient ruddy rings.
So perchance may the mocks be lesser when men tell of the Niblung Kings."

Then Sigurd looked on the twain, and he saw their swart hair wave
In the wind of the waste and the flame-blast, and no answer awhile he gave.
But at last he spake : "O brother, on Greyfell shalt thou ride,
And do on the Helm of Aweing and gird the Wrath to thy side,
And cover thy breast with the war-coat that is throughly woven of gold,
That hath not its like in the heavens nor has earth of its fellow told :
For this is the raiment of Kings when they ride the Flickering Fire,
And so sink the flames before them and the might of their desire."

Then Hogni laughed in his heart, and he said : "This changing were well
If so might the deed be accomplished ; but perchance there is more to tell:
Thou shalt take the war-steed, Gunnar, and enough or nought it shall be :
But the coal-blue gear of the Niblungs the golden hall shall see."

Then Sigurd looked on the speaker, as one who would answer again,
But his words died out on the waste and the fire-blast made them vain.
Then he casteth the reins to his brother, and Gunnar praiseth his gift,
And springeth aloft to the saddle as the fair sun fails from the lift ;
And Sigurd looks on the burden that Greyfell doth uprear,
The huge king towering upward in the dusky Niblung gear :
There sits the eager Gunnar, and his heart desires the deed,
And of nought he recketh and thinketh, but a fame-stirred warrior's need ;
But Greyfell trembleth nothing and nought of the fire doth reck :
Then the spurs in his flank are smitten, and the reins lie loose on his neck,
And the sharp cry springeth from Gunnar—no handbreadth stirred the beast;
The dusk drew on and over and the light of the fire increased,

And still as a shard on the mountain in the sandy dale alone
Was the shape of the cloudy Greyfell, nor moved he more than the stone ;
But right through **the** heart of the fire for ever Sigurd stared,
As he stood in the gold red-litten with the Wrath's thin edges bared.

No word for a **while spake any,** till Gunnar leaped to the earth,
And the anger **wrought within** him, and the fierce words **came to birth :**
" Who **mocketh the King of the** Niblungs **in the** desert land forlorn ?
Is **it thou, O Sigurd the Stranger ? is it** thou, O younger-born ?
Dost thou laugh in the hall, O Mother ? dost thou spin, and laugh at the tale
That has drawn thy son and thine eldest to the sword and the blaze of the bale ?
Or thou, O God of the **Goths, wilt thou hide** and laugh thy fill,
While the **hands of the fosterbrethren the** blood of brothers spill ? "

But the awful voice of Sigurd across the wild went forth :
" How changed are **the** words of Gunnar ! where wend his ways of worth ?
I mock thee not in the desert, as I mocked thee not in the mead,
When I swore beneath the turf-yoke to help thy fondest need :
Nay, strengthen thine heart for the work, for the gift that thy manhood awaits ;
For I **give thee a gift,** O Niblung, that shall overload the Fates,
And how **may a** King sustain it ? but forbear with the dark to strive ;
For thy mother spinneth and worketh, and her craft is awake and alive."

Then Hogni **spake** from the saddle : " The time, and the time is come
To gather the might of our mother, **and** of her that spinneth at home.
Forbear all words, O **Gunnar,** and anigh to Sigurd **stand,**
And face to face behold him, and take his hand in thine hand :
Then be thy will as his will, that **his heart may mingle** with thine,
And the love that he sware 'neath **the earth-yoke with** thine hope may inter-
[twine."
Then the wrath from the Niblung slippeth and the shame that anger hath bred,
And the heavy wings of the dreamtide flit over Gunnar's head :
But he doth by his brother's bidding, and Sigurd's hand he takes,

And he looks in the eyes of the Volsung, though scarce in the desert he wakes.
There Hogni sits in the saddle aloof from the King's desire,
And little his lips are moving, as he stares on the rolling fire,
And mutters the spells of his mother, and the words she **bade him say:**
But the craft of the kings of aforetime on those Kings of the battle **lay;**
Dark night was spread behind them, and the fire flared up before,
And unheard was the wind of the wasteland mid the white flame's wavering
[roar.

Long Sigurd gazeth on Gunnar, till he sees, as through a cloud,
The long black locks of the Niblung, and the King's face set and proud:
Then the face is alone on the dark, and the dusky Niblung mail
Is nought but the night before him: then whiles will the visage fail,
And grow again as he gazeth, black hair and gleaming eyes,
And fade **again** into nothing, as for more **of** vision he tries:
Then all is nought but the night, yea the **waste** of an emptier thing,
And the fire-wall Sigurd forgetteth, nor feeleth the hand of the King:
Nay, what is it now he remembereth? it is nought that aforetime he knew,
And no world is there left him to live in, and no deed to rejoice in or rue;
But frail and alone he fareth, and as one in the sphere-stream's drift,
By the starless empty places that lie beyond the lift:
Then at last is he stayed in his drifting, and he saith, It is blind and dark;
Yet he feeleth the earth at his feet, and there cometh a change and a spark,
And away in an instant of time **is** the mirk of the dreamland rolled,
And there is the fire-lit midnight, and before him an image of gold,
A man in the raiment of Gods, nor fashioned worser **than they:**
Full sad **he gazeth on** Sigurd from the great wide eyes and grey;
And the Helm that Aweth the people is set on the golden hair,
And the Mail of Gold enwraps him, and the Wrath in his hand is bare.

Then Sigurd looks on his arm **and** his hand **in his brother's** hand,
And thereon is the dark grey mail-gear well forged in the southern land;
Then he looks on the sword that he beareth, and, lo, the eager blade
That leaps in the hand of Gunnar when the kings are waxen afraid;

And he turns his face o'er his shoulder, and the raven-locks hang down
From the dark-blue **helm of** the Dwarf-folk, and the rings of the Niblung
[crown.
Then a red flush riseth against him in the face **ne'er seen before,**
Save dimly in the mirror or the burnished targe **of war,**
And the foster-brethren sunder, **and the** clasped **hands** fall apart ;
But a **change cometh over Sigurd,** and the fierce pride **leaps in his heart;**
He knoweth the soul of Gunnar, and the shaping of his **mind ;**
He **seeketh the** words of Sigurd, **and** Gunnar's **voice doth he find,**
As **he cries : "I** know thy bidding ; let the **world** be lief **or loth,**
The child is unborn that shall hearken how **Sigurd rued his oath !**
Well fare thou brother **Gunnar ! what deed shall I do this eve**
That I shall never repent **of,** that thine **heart shall never** grieve ?
What deed shall I do this **even** that none **else** may bring to the birth,
Nay, not the King of **the** Niblungs, and the lord of the best of the earth ?"

The flames rolled **up** to the heavens, and the **stars behind were bright,**
Dark Hogni sat on **his** war-steed, and **stared out into the night,**
And there stood Gunnar the King in Sigurd's **semblance wrapped,**
—**As** Sigurd walking in slumber, for in Grimhild's guile **was he lapped,**
That his heart forgat his glory, **and the ways of** Odin's **lords,**
And the thought was frozen within **him, and the might of spoken words.**

But Sigurd **leapeth on** Greyfell, and the sword in his hand is **bare,**
And the gold **spurs flame on his** heels, and the fire-blast lifteth **his hair ;**
Forth Greyfell **bounds rejoicing, and** they see **the grey wax red,**
As unheard the war-gear **clasheth,** and the flames **meet over his head,**
Yet a while they see him riding, as through the **rye men ride,**
When the word goes forth in the **summer of the kings by the ocean-side ;**
But the fires were slaked **before him** and the **wild-fire** burned no more
Than the **ford** of the summer waters when **the rainy** time is o'er.

Not once turned Sigurd aback, nor looked o'er the ashy ring,

To the midnight wilderness drear and the spell-drenched Niblung King:
But he stayed and looked before him, and lo, a house high-built
With its roof of the red gold beaten, and its wall-stones over-gilt:
So he leapt adown from Greyfell, and came to that fair abode,
And dark in the gear of the Niblungs through the gleaming door he strode:
All light within was that dwelling, and a marvellous hall it was,
But of gold were its hangings woven, and its pillars gleaming as glass,
And Sigurd said in his heart, it was wrought erewhile for a God:
But he looked athwart and endlong as alone its floor he trod,
And lo, on the height of the daïs is upreared a graven throne,
And thereon a woman sitting in the golden place alone;
Her face is fair and awful, and a gold crown girdeth her head;
And a sword of the kings she beareth, and her sun-bright hair is shed
O'er the laps of the snow-white linen that ripples adown to her feet:
As a swan on the billow unbroken ere the firth and the ocean meet,
On the dark-blue cloths she sitteth, in the height of the golden place,
Nor breaketh the hush of the hall, though her eyes be set on his face.

Now he sees this is even the woman of whom the tale hath been told,
E'en she that was wrought for the Niblungs, the bride ordained from of old,
And hushed in the hall he standeth, and a long while looks in her eyes,
And the word he hath shapen for Gunnar to his lips may never arise.

The man in Gunnar's semblance looked long and knew no deed;
And she looked, and her eyes were dreadful, and none would help her need.
Then the image of Gunnar trembled, and the flesh of the War-King shrank:
For he heard her voice on the silence, and his heart of her anguish drank:

"King, King, who art thou that comest, thou lord of the cloudy gear?
What deed for the weary-hearted shall thy strange hands fashion here?"

The speech of her lips pierced through him like the point of the bitter sword,
And he deemed that death were better than another spoken word:

But he clencheth his hand on the war-blade, and setteth his face as the brass,
And the voice of his brother Gunnar from out his lips doth pass :
"When thou lookest on me, O Goddess, thou seest Gunnar the King,
The King and the lord of the Niblungs, and the chief of their warfaring.
But art thou indeed that Brynhild of whom is the rumour and fame,
That she bideth the coming of kings to ride her Wavering Flame,
Lest she wed the little-hearted, and the world grow evil and vile?
For if thou be none other I will speak again in a while."

She said: "Art thou Gunnar the Stranger? O art thou the man that I see?
Yea, verily I am Brynhild : what other is like unto me?
O men of the Earth behold me ! hast thou seen, O labouring Earth,
Such sorrow as my sorrow, or such evil as my birth?"

Then spake the Wildfire's Trampler that Gunnar's image bore :
"O Brynhild, mighty of women, be thou glorious evermore !
Thou seest Gunnar the Niblung, as he sits mid the Niblung lords,
And rides with the gods of battle in the fore-front of the swords.
Now therefore awaken to life ! for this eve have I ridden thy Fire,
When but few of the kings would outface it, to fulfil thine heart's desire.
And such love is the love of the kings, and such token have women to know
That they wed with God's belovèd, and that fair from their bed shall outgrow
The stem of the world's desire, and the tree that shall not be abased,
Till the day of the uttermost trial when the war-shield of Odin is raised.
So my word is the word of wooing, and I bid thee remember thine oath,
That here in this hall fair-builded we twain may plight the troth ;
That here in the hall of thy waiting thou be made a wedded wife,
And be called the Queen of the Niblungs, and awaken unto life."

Hard rang his voice in the hall, and a while she spake no word,
And there stood the Image of Gunnar, and leaned on his bright blue sword:
But at last she cried from the high-seat : " If I yet am alive and awake,
I know no words for the speaking, nor what answer I may make."

She ceased and he answered nothing; and a hush on the hall there lay,
And the moon slipped over the windows as he clomb the heavenly way;
And no whit stirred the raiment of Brynhild: till she hearkened the Wooer's
    voice,
As he said: "Thou art none of the women that swear and forswear and rejoice,
Forgetting the sorrow of kings and the Gods and the labouring earth.
Thou shalt wed with King Gunnar the Niblung and increase his worth with
                            [thy worth.'
And again was there silence a while, and the War-King leaned on his sword
In the shape of his foster-brother; then Brynhild took up the word:
"Hail Gunnar, King of the Niblungs! tonight shalt thou lie by my side,
For thou art the Gods' belovèd, and for thee was I shapen a bride:
For thee, for the King, have I waited, and the waiting now is done;
I shall bear Earth's kings on my bosom and nourish the Niblung's son.
Though women swear and forswear, and are glad no less in their life,
Tonight shall I wed with the King-folk and be called King Gunnar's wife.
Come Gunnar, Lord of the Niblungs, and sit in my fathers' seat!
For for thee alone was it shapen, and the deed is due and meet."

Up she rose exceeding glorious, and it was as when in May
The blossomed hawthorn stirreth with the dawning-wind of day;
But the Wooer moved to meet her, and amid the golden place
They met, and their garments mingled and face was close to face;
And they turned again to the high-seat, and their very right hands met,
And King Gunnar's bodily semblance beside her Brynhild set..

But over his knees and the mail-rings the high King laid his sword,
And looked in the face of Brynhild and swore King Gunnar's word:
He swore on the hand of Brynhild to be true to his wedded wife,
And before all things to love her till all folk should praise her life.
Unmoved did Brynhild hearken, and in steady voice she swore
To be true to Gunnar the Niblung while her life-days should endure;
So she swore on the hand of the Wooer: and they two were all alone,

And they sat a while in the high-seat when the wedding-troth was done,
But no while looked each on the other, and hand fell down from hand,
And no speech there was betwixt them that their hearts might understand.

At last spake the all-wise Brynhild : " Now night is beginning to fade,
Fair-hung is the chamber of Kings, and the bridal bed is arrayed."

He rose and looked upon her : as the moon at her utmost height,
So pale was the visage of Brynhild, and her eyes as cold and bright :   [space,
Yet he stayed, nor stirred from the high-seat, but strove with the words for a
Till she took the hand of the King and led him down from his place,
And forth from the hall she led him to the chamber wrought for her love ;
The fairest chamber of earth, gold-wrought below and above,
And hung were the walls fair-builded with the Gods and the kings of the earth
And the deeds that were done aforetime, and the coming deeds of worth.
There they went in one bed together ; but the foster-brother laid
'Twixt him and the body of Brynhild his bright blue battle-blade,
And she looked and heeded it nothing ; but e'en as the dead folk lie,
With folded hands she lay there, and let the night go by :
And as still lay that Image of Gunnar as the dead of life forlorn,
And hand on hand he folded as he waited for the morn.
So oft in the moonlit minster your fathers may ye see
By the side of the ancient mothers await the day to be.
Thus they lay as brother by sister—and e'en such had they been to behold,
Had he borne the Volsung's semblance and the shape she knew of old.

Night hushed as the moon fell downward, and there came the leaden sleep
And weighed down the head of the War-King, that he lay in slumber deep,
And forgat today and tomorrow, and forgotten yesterday ;
Till he woke in the dawn and the daylight, and the sun on the gold floor lay,
And Brynhild wakened beside him, and she lay with folded hands
By the edges forged of Regin and the wonder of the lands,
The Light that had lain in the Branstock, the hope of the Volsung Tree,

The Sunderer, the Deliverer, the torch of days **to be** :
Then he strove to remember the night and what **deeds** had come to pass,
And what deeds he should do hereafter, and what manner of man he was ;
For there in the golden chamber lay the **dark unwonted gear,**
And beside his cheek on the pillow were long locks of the raven hair :
But at last he remembered the even and the deed he came to do,
And he turned **and spake to** Brynhild as he rose from the bolster blue :

" I give thee thanks, fair woman, for the wedding-troth fulfilled ;
I have come where the Norns have led me, and done as the high Gods willed :
But now give we the gifts of the morning, for I needs must depart to my men
And look on the Niblung children, and rule o'er the people again.
But I thank thee well for thy greeting, and thy glory **that I** have seen,
For but little thereto are those tidings that folk have told of the Queen.
Henceforth with the Niblung people anew beginneth thy life,
And fair days of peace await thee, and fair days of glorious strife.
And my **heart shall be** grieved at thy grief, and be glad of thy well-doing,
And all men shall say thou hast wedded a true heart and a king."

So spake he in semblance of Gunnar, and from off his hand he drew
A ring of the spoils of the Southland, a marvel seen but of few,
And **he set the** ring on her finger, and she turned to her lord and spake :
" I thank **thee,** King, for thy goodwill, and thy pledge of love I take.
Depart with my troth to thy people : but ere full ten days are o'er
I shall **come** to the Sons of the Niblungs, and then shall we part no more
Till the day of the **change of** our life-days, when Odin and Freyia shall call.
Lo, here, my gift of the morning ! 'twas my dearest treasure of all ;
But thou art become its master, and for thee was it fore-ordained,
Since thou art the man of mine oath and the best that the earth hath gained."

And lo, 'twas the Grief of Andvari, and the lack that made him loth,
The last of the God-folk's ransom, the Ring of Hindfell's oath ;
Now on Sigurd's hand it shineth, and long he looketh thereon,

But it gave him back no memories of the days that were bygone.
Then in most exceeding sorrow rose Sigurd from the bed,
And again lay Brynhild silent as an image of the dead.
Then the King did on his war-gear and girt his sword to his side,
And was e'en as an image of Gunnar when the Niblungs dight them to ride.
And she on the bed of the bridal, remembering hope that was,
Lay still, and hearkened his footsteps from the echoing chamber pass.
So forth from the hall goes the Wooer, and slow and slow he goes,
As a conquered king from his city fares forth to meet his foes ;
And he taketh the reins of Greyfell, nor yet will back him there,
But afoot through the cold slaked ashes of yester-eve doth fare,
With his eyes cast down to the earth; till he heareth the wind, and a cry,
And raiseth a face brow-knitted and beholdeth men anigh,
And beholdeth Hogni the King set grey on his coal-black steed,
And beholdeth the image of Sigurd, the King in the golden weed :
Then he stayeth and stareth astonished and setteth his hand to his sword;
Till Hogni cries from his saddle, and his word is a kindly word :

" Hail, brother, and King of the people ! hail, helper of my kin !
Again from the death and the trouble great gifts hast thou set thee to win
For thy friends and the Niblung children, and hast crowned thine earthly fame,
And increased thine exceeding glory and the sound of thy lovèd name."

Nought Sigurd spake in answer but looked straight forth with a frown,
And stretched out his hand to Gunnar, as one that claimeth his own.
Then no word speaketh Gunnar, but taketh his hand in his hand,
And they look in the eyes of each other, and a while in the desert they stand
Till the might of Grimhild prevaileth, and the twain are as yester-morn ;
But sad was the golden Sigurd, though his eyes knew nought of scorn :
And he spake:
               " It is finished, O Gunnar ! and I will that our brotherhood
May endure through the good and the evil as it sprang in the days of the good:
But I bid thee look to the ending, that the deed I did yest'reve

Bear nought for me to repent of, for thine heart of hearts to grieve.
Thou art troth-plight, O King of the Niblungs, to Brynhild Queen of the earth,
She hath sworn thine heart to cherish and increase thy worth with her worth :
She shall come to the house of Gunnar **ere ten days** are past and o'er ;
And thenceforth the life of Brynhild shall part from thy life no more,
Till the doom of our kind shall speed you, and Odin and Freyia shall call,
And ye bide the Day of the Battle, and the uttermost changing of all."

The praise and thanks they gave him ! the words of love they spake ! ·
The tale that the world should **hear of,** deeds done for Sigurd's sake !
They were lovely might you hear **them :** but they lack ; for in very deed
Their sound was clean forgotten in the day of Sigurd's need.

But as yet are those King-folk lovely, and no guile of heart they know,
And, in troth and love rejoicing, by Sigurd's side they go :
O'er heath and holt they hie them, o'er hill and **dale they** ride,
Till they come to the Burg of the Niblungs and **the war-gate** of their pride;
And there is Grimhild the wise-wife, and she sits and spins in the hall.

"Rejoice, O mother," saith Gunnar, "for thy guest hath holpen all
And this eve shall thy sons be merry : but ere ten days are o'er
Here cometh the Maid, and the Queen, the Wise, and the Chooser **of war :**
So wrought is the will of the Niblungs and their blossoming boughs increase,
And joyous strife shall **we dwell** in, and merry days of peace."

So that night in the hall of the ancient they hold high-tide again,
And the Gods on the Southland hangings smile out full fair and fain,
And the song goes up of Sigurd, and the praise of his fame fulfilled,
But his speech in the dead sleep lieth, and the words of his wisdom are chilled :
And men say, the King is careful, **for** he thinks **of the** people's weal,
And his heart is afraid for our trouble, lest the Gods **our** joyance steal.

But that night, when the feast was over, to Gudrun Sigurd came,

And she noted the ring on his finger, and she knew it was nowise the same
As the ring he was wont to carry ; so she bade him tell thereof :
Then he turned unto her kindly, and his words were words of love ;
Nor his life nor his death he heeded, but told her last night's tale :
Yea he drew forth the sword for **his** slaying, and whetted the edges of bale;
For he took that Gold of Andvari, that Curse **of the uttermost land,**
And he spake as a king that loveth, and set it **on her hand ;**
But her heart was exceeding joyous, as he kissed **her sweet and soft,**
And bade her bear it for ever, **that** she might remember him oft
When **his hand** from the world was departed and **he sat** in Odin's **home.**

But no **one** of his words she forgat when the latter days were come,
When the earth was hard for her footsteps, **and** the heavens were darkling
And but e'en as a tale that is told were waxen the years of her love.   [above,
Yea thereof, from the Gold of Andvari, the spark of the waters wan,
Sprang a flame of bitter trouble, and the death of many **a man,**
And the quenching of the kindreds, and the blood **of the broken troth,**
And the Grievous Need of the Niblungs and the **Sorrow of Odin the Goth.**

How **Brynhild was wedded to Gunnar the Niblung.**

So wear the **ten days over, and the** morrow-morn is come,
And the light-foot expectation flits through the Niblung **home,**
And the girded hope is ready, and **all** people are astir,
When the voice of the keen-eyed watchman from the topmost tower they hear:
" **Look** forth from the Burg, O Niblungs, and the war-gate of renown !
For the wind is up in the morning, and the may-blooms fall adown,
And the sun on the earth is shining, and the **clouds are** small and high,
And here is a goodly people and **an army drawing anigh.**"

Then horsed are the sons of the earl-folk, and their robes are glittering-gay,
And they ride o'er the bridge of the river adown the dusty way,

Till they come on a lovely people, and the **maids of war** they meet,
Whose cloaks are blue and broidered, and their girded linen sweet ;
And they ride on the roan and the grey, and the dapple-grey and the red,
And many a bloom of the may-tide on their crispy locks is shed :
Fair, young are the sons of the earl-folk, and they laugh for love **and** glee,
As the lovely-wristed maidens on the summer ways they see.

But lo, mid the sweet-faced fellows there cometh a golden wain,
Like the wain of the sea be-shielded with the signs of the war-god's gain :
Snow-white are its harnessed yoke-beasts, and its bench-cloths are of blue,
Inwrought with the written **wonders that ancient** women knew :
But nought therein **there** sitteth save a crownèd queen alone,
Swan-white on the dark-blue bench-cloths and the carven ivory throne ;
Abashed are sons of the earl-folk of their laughter and their glee,
When the glory of Queen Brynhild on the summer **ways** they see.

But they hear the voice of the woman, and her speech is soft and kind :
" Are ye the sons of the Niblungs, and the folk I came to find,
O young men fair and lovely ? So may your days **be long,**
And grow in **gain** and glory, **and** fail of grief and wrong !"
Then they hailed her sweet and goodly, and back again they rode
By the bridge o'er the rushing river to the gate of their abode ;
And high aloft, half-hearkened, rang the joyance of the horn,
And the cry of the Ancient People from their walls of war was borne
O'er the tilth of the plain, and the meadows, and the sheep-fed slopes that lead
From the God-built wall of the mountains to the blossoms of the mead.

Then up in the wain stood Brynhild, and her voice was sweet as she said :
" Is this the house of Gunnar, and the man I swore to wed ?"

But she hearkened the cry from the gateway **and the** hollow of the door :
" Yea this is the dwelling of Gunnar, and the house of the God of War :
There is none of the world so mighty, be he outland King or Goth,

Save Sigurd the mighty Volsung and the brother of his troth."

Then spake Brynhild and said : "**Lo, a** house of **ancient** Kings,
Wrought for great deeds' fulfilment, and the birth of noble things !
Be the bloom of the earth upon it, and the hope of the heavens above !
May peace and joy abide there, and the full content of love !
And when our days are **done with,** and we lie alow in rest,
May its lords returning homeward still deem they see the best !"

She spake with voice unfaltering, and the golden **wain moved on,**
And **all men** deemed who heard **her** that great gifts their home had won.

So she passed through the dusk of the **doorway,** and the cave of the war-fain
Wherein the echoing horse-hoofs as the sound of swords awoke,   [folk,
And the whispering wind of the may-tide from the cloudy wall smote back,
And cried in the crown of the roof-arch of battle and the wrack ;
And the voice of maidens sounded as kings' cries in the **day of the wrath,**
When the flame is on the threshold and the war-shields strew the path.

So fair in the sun **of the forecourt doth** Brynhild's wain **shine bright,**
And the huge hall riseth before her, and the ernes cry out from its height,
And there by the door of the Niblungs she sees huge warriors stand,
Dark-clad, **by the** shoulders greater than the best of any land,
And she knoweth the chiefs of the Niblungs, the dreaded **dukes of war :**
But one in cloudy raiment stands a very midst the door,
And ruddy and bright is his visage, and his black **locks wave in the wind,**
And she knoweth the King **of the** Niblungs and the **man she came to find:**
Then nought she lingered nor loitered, **but stepped to the earth adown**
With right-hand reached to the **War-God, the wearer of the crown ;**
And she said :
                    "I behold thee, Gunnar, the King of War that rode
Through the waves of the Flickering Fire to the door of mine abode,
To lie **by my side** in the even, and waken in the morn ;

And for this I needs must deem thee the best of all men born,
The highest-hearted, **the greatest, the staunchest of thy love :**
And that such the world yet holdeth, my heart is fain thereof:
And for thee I deem was I fashioned, and for thee **the oath I swore**
In the days of my glory and wisdom, ere the days of youth were o'er.
May the bloom of the earth be upon thee, and the hope of the heavens above,
May the blessing of days be upon thee, and the full content of love !
Mayst thou see our children's children, and the crownèd kin of kings !
May no hope from thine eyes be hidden of the day of better things !
May the fire ne'er stay thy glory, nor the ocean-flood thy fame !
Through ages of all ages may the wide world praise thy name !
Yea oft may the word be spoken when low we lie at **rest ;**
' It befell in the days of Gunnar, the happiest and the best !'
All this may the high Gods give thee, **and thereto a gift I** give,
The body of Queen Brynhild so long as both we live."

With unmoved face, unfaltering, the blessing-words she said,
But the joy sprang up in Gunnar and increased his goodlihead,
And he cast his arms about her and kissed her **on** the mouth,
And he said :

      " The gift is greater than all treasure of the south :
As glad as my heart this moment, so glad may be thy life,
And the world be never weary of the joy of Gunnar's wife !"

She spake no word, and smiled **not,** but she held his hand henceforth.
And he said : " Now take the greetings of my men, **the** most of worth."

Then she turned her face to the war-dukes, and hearkened to their praise,
And she spake in few words sweetly, and blessed their coming days.
Then again spake Gunnar and said : " **Lo,** Hogni my brother is this ;
But Guttorm is far on the East-seas, and seeketh the warrior's bliss ;
A third there is of my brethren, and my house holds none so great ;
In the hall by the side of my sister thy face doth he await."

Then Brynhild turned unto Hogni, and he greeted her fair and well,
And she prayed all blessings upon him, and a tale that the world should tell:
Then again she spake unto Gunnar: "I had deemed ye had been but three
Who sprang from the loins of Giuki; is this fourth akin unto thee,
This hall-abider the mighty?"
                                        He said: "He is nought of our blood,
But the Gods have sent him to usward to work us measureless good:
It is even Sigurd the Volsung, the best man ever born,
The man that the Gods withstand not, my friend, and my brother sworn."

She heard the name, and she changed not, but her feet went forth as he led,
And under the cloudy roof-tree Queen Brynhild bowed her head.
Then, were there a man so ancient as had lived beyond his peers
On the earth, that beareth all things, a twice-told tale of years,
He had heard no sound so mighty as the shout that shook the wall
When Brynhild's feet unhearkened first trod the Niblung hall.
No whit the clamour stirred her; but her godlike eyes she raised
And betwixt the hedge of the earl-folk on the golden high-seat gazed,
And the man that sat by Gudrun: but e'en as the rainless cloud
Ere the first of the tempest ariseth the latter sun doth shroud,
And men look round and shudder, so Grimhild came between
The silent golden Sigurd and the eyes of the mighty Queen,
And again heard Brynhild greeting, and again she spake and said:

"O Mother of the Niblungs, such hap be on thine head,
As thy love for me, the stranger, was past the pain of words!
Mayst thou see thy son's sons glorious in the meeting of the swords!
Mayst thou sleep and doubt thee nothing of the fortunes of thy race!
Mayst thou hear folk call yon high-seat the earth's most happy place!"

Then the Wise-wife hushed before her, and a little fell aside,
And nought from the eyes of Brynhild the high-seat now did hide;
And the face so long desired, unchanged from time agone,

Q

In the house of the Cloudy People from the Niblung high-seat shone :
She stood with her hand in Gunnar's, and all about and around
Were the unfamiliar faces, and the folk that day had found ;
But her heart ran back through the years, and yet her lips did move
With the words she spake on Hindfell, when they plighted troth of love.

Lo, Sigurd fair on the high-seat by the white-armed Gudrun's side,
In the midst of the Cloudy People, in the dwelling of their pride !
His face is exceeding glorious and awful to behold ;
For of all his sorrow he knoweth and his hope smit dead and cold :
The will of the Norns is accomplished, and, lo, they wend on their ways,
And leave the mighty Sigurd to deal with the latter days :
The Gods look down from heaven, and the lonely King they see,
And sorrow over his sorrow, and rejoice in his majesty.
For the will of the Norns is accomplished, and outworn is Grimhild's spell,
And nought now shall blind or help him, and the tale shall be to tell :
He hath seen the face of Brynhild, and he knows why she hath come,
And that his is the hand that hath drawn her to the Cloudy People's home :
He knows of the net of the days, and the deeds that the Gods have bid,
And no whit of the sorrow that shall be from his wakened soul is hid :
And his glory his heart restraineth, and restraineth the hand of the strong
From the hope of the fools of desire and the wrong that amendeth wrong ;
And he seeth the ways of the burden till the last of the uttermost end.
But for all the measureless anguish, and the woe that nought may amend,
His heart speeds back to Hindfell, and the dawn of the wakening day ;
And the hours betwixt are as nothing, and their deeds are fallen away
As he looks on the face of Brynhild ; and nought is the Niblung folk,
But they two are again together, and he speaketh the words he spoke,
When he swore the love that endureth, and the truth that knoweth not change ;
And Brynhild's face drew near him with eyes grown stern and strange.
—Lo, such is the high Gods' sorrow, and men know nought thereof,
Who cry out o'er their undoing, and wail o'er broken love.

Now she stands on the floor of the high-seat, and for e'en so little a space
As men may note delaying, she looketh on Sigurd's face,
Ere she saith :
        "I have greeted many in the Niblungs' house today,
And for thee is the last of my greetings ere the feast shall wear away :
Hail, Sigurd, son of the Volsungs ! hail, lord of Odin's storm !
Hail, rider of the wasteland and slayer of the Worm !
If aught thy soul shall desire while yet thou livest on earth,
I pray that thou mayst win it, nor forget its might and worth."

All grief, sharp scorn, sore longing, stark death in her voice he knew,
But gone forth is the doom of the Norns, and what shall he answer thereto,
While the death that amendeth lingers? and they twain shall dwell for awhile
In the Niblung house together by the hearth that forged the guile ;
Yet amid the good and the guileless, and the love that thought no wrong,
Shall they fashion the deeds to remember, and the fame that endureth for long :
And oft shall he look on Brynhild, and oft her words shall he hear,
And no hope and no beseeching in his inmost heart shall stir.
So he spake as a King of the people in whom all fear is dead,
And his anguish no man noted, as the greeting-words he said :

" Hail, fairest of all things fashioned ! hail, thou desire of eyes !
Hail, chooser of the mightiest, and teacher of the wise !
Hail, wife of my brother Gunnar ! in might may thy days endure,
And in peace without a trouble that the world's weal may be sure ! "

She heard and turned unto Gunnar as a queen that seeketh her place,
But to Gudrun she gave no greeting, nor beheld the Niblung's face.
Then up stood the wife of Sigurd and strove with the greeting-word,
But the cold fear rose in her heart, and the hate within her stirred,
And the greeting died on her lips, and she gazed for a moment or twain
On the lovely face of Brynhild, and so sat in the high-seat again,
And turned to her lord beside her with many a word of love.

But the song sprang up in the hall, and the eagles cried from above,
And forth to the freshness of May went the joyance of the feast :
And Sigurd sat with the Niblungs, and gave ear to most and to least,
And showed no sign to the people of the grief that on him lay ;
Nor seemeth he worser to any than he was on the yesterday.

Of the Contention betwixt the Queens.

So there are all these abiding in the Burg of the ancient folk
Mid the troth-plight sworn and broken, and the oaths of the earthly yoke.
Then Guttorm comes from his sea-fare, and is waxen fierce and strong,
A man in the wars delighting, blind-eyed through right and wrong :
Still Sigurd rides with the Brethren, as oft in the other days,
And never a whit abateth the sound of the people's praise ;
They drink in the hall together, they doom in the people's strife,
And do every deed of the King-folk, that the world may rejoice in their life.

There now is Brynhild abiding as a Queen in the house of the Kings,
And hither and thither she wendeth through the day of queenly things ;
And no man knoweth her sorrow ; though whiles is the Niblung bed
Too hot and weary a dwelling for the temples of her head,
And she wends, as her wont was aforetime, when the moon is riding high,
And the night on the earth is deepest ; and she deemeth it good to lie
In the trench of the windy mountains, and the track of the wandering sheep,
While soft in the arms of Sigurd Queen Gudrun lieth asleep :
There she cries on the lovely Sigurd, and she cries on the love and the oath,
And she cries on the change and the vengeance, and the death to deliver them
But her crying none shall hearken, and her sorrow nought shall know,   [both.
Save the heart of the golden Sigurd, and the man fast bound in woe :
So she wendeth her back in the dawning, toward the deeds and the dwellings of
And she sits in the Niblung high-seat, and is fair and queenly again.   [men,

Close now is her converse with Gudrun, and sore therein she strives
Lest the barren stark contention should mingle in their lives ;
And she humbles her oft before her, as before the Queen of the earth,
The mistress, the overcomer, the winner of all that is worth :
And Gudrun beareth it all, and deemeth it little enow
Though the wife of Sigurd be worshipped: and the scorn in her heart doth
Of every soul save Sigurd : for that tale of the night she bears   [grow,
Scarce hid 'twixt the lips and the bosom ; and with evil eye she hears
Songs sung of the deeds of Gunnar, and the rider of the fire,
Who mocked at the bane of King-folk to win his heart's desire :
But Sigurd's will constraineth, and with seeming words of peace
She deals with the converse of Brynhild, and the days her load increase.

Men tell how the heart-wise Hogni grew wiser day by day ;
He knows of the craft of Grimhild, and how she looketh to sway
The very council of God-home and the Norns' unchanging mind ;
And he saith that well-learned is his mother, but that e'en her feet are blind
Down the path that she cannot escape from: nay oft is she nothing, he saith,
Save a staff for the foredoomed staying, and a sword for the ordered death ;
And that he will be wiser than this, nor thrust his desire aside,
Nor smother the flame of his hatred ; but the steed of the Norns will he ride,
Till he see great marvels and wonders, and leave great tales to be told :
And measureless pride is in him, a stern heart, stubborn and cold.

But of Gunnar the Niblung they say it, that the bloom of his youth is o'er,
And many are manhood's troubles, and they burden him oft and sore.
He dwells with Brynhild his wife, with Grimhild his mother he dwells,
And noble things of his greatness, of his joy, the rumour tells ;
Yet oft and oft of an even he thinks of that tale of the night,
And the shame springs fresh in his heart at his brother Sigurd's might ;
And the wonder riseth within him, what deed did Sigurd there,
What gift to the King hath he given : and he looks on Brynhild the fair,
The fair face never smiling, and the eyes that know no change,

And he deems in the bed of the Niblungs she is but cold and strange;
And the Lie is laid between them, as the sword lay while agone.
He hearkens to Grimhild moreover, and he deems she is driving him on,
He knoweth not whither nor wherefore: but she tells of the measureless Gold,
And the Flame of the uttermost Waters, and the Hoard of the kings of old:
And she tells of kings' supplanters, and the leaders of the war,
Who take the crown of song-craft, and the tale when all is o'er:
She tells of kings' supplanters, and saith: Perchance 'twere well,
Might some tongue of the wise of the earth of those deeds of the night-tide tell:
She tells of kings' supplanters: I am wise, and the wise I know,
And for nought is the sword-edge whetted, save the smiting of the blow:
Old friends are last to sever, and twain are strong indeed,
When one the King's shame knoweth, and the other knoweth his need.

So Gunnar hearkens and hearkens, and he saith, It is idle and worse:
If the oath of my brother be broken, let the earth then see to the curse!
But again he hearkens and hearkens, and when none may hear his thought
He saith in the silent night-tide: Shall my brother bring me to nought?
Must my stroke be a stroke of the guilty, though on sackless folk it fall?
Shall a king sit joy-forsaken mid the riches of his hall?
And measureless pride is in Gunnar, and it blends with doubt and shame,
And the unseen blossom is envy and desire without a name.

But fair-faced, calm as a God who hath none to call his foes,
Betwixt the Kings and the people the golden Sigurd goes;
No knowledge of man he lacketh, and the lore he gained of old
From the ancient heart of the Serpent and the Wallower on the Gold
Springs fresh in the soul of Sigurd; the heart of Hogni he sees,
And the heart of his brother Gunnar, and he grieveth sore for these.
But he seeth the heart of Brynhild, and knoweth her lonely cry
When the waste is all about her, and none but the Gods are anigh:
And he knoweth her tale of the night-tide, when desire, that day doth dull,
Is stirred by hope undying, and fills her bosom full

Of the sighs she may **not utter,** and the prayers that none may heed ;
Though the Gods were once so mighty the smiling world to speed.
And he knows of the day of her burden, **and the measure** of her toil,
And the peerless pride of her heart, and **her scorn of the fall** and **the foil.**
And the shadowy wings **of the Lie, that with hand unwitting he** led
To the Burg of the ancient people, brood over board and bed ;
And the hand of the hero faileth, and seared is the sight of the wise,
And good is at one with evil till the new-born death shall arise.

In the hall sitteth Sigurd by Brynhild, in the council of the **Kings,**
And he hearkeneth her spoken wisdom, and **her word of lovely things :**
In the field they meet, and the wild-wood, **on the acre** and the heath ;
And scarce may he tell if the meeting be worse than the coward's death,
Or better than life of the **righteous : but his love is a flaming fire,**
That hath burnt up all before **it of the things that feed desire.**

The heart of Gudrun he seeth, **her** heart of burning love,
That knoweth of nought but Sigurd **on the earth, in the heavens above,**
Save the **foes that** encompass his life, and **the woman that wasteth away**
'Neath the toil of a love like her love, **and the unrewarded day :**
For hate her eyes hath quickened, and no more is Gudrun blind,
And sure, though dim it may be, she seeth the days behind :
And the shadowy wings of the Lie, that the **hand** unwitting led
To the love and the heart of Gudrun, brood over board and **bed ;**
And for all the hand of the hero and the foresight **of the wise,**
From the heart of a loving woman shall the death **of men arise.**

It was most in these latter **days that his fame went far abroad,**
The helper, the overcomer, **the righteous sundering sword ;**
The loveliest King of the King-folk, the man of sweetest speech,
Whose ear is dull to no man that his helping shall beseech ;
The eye-bright seer of all things, that wasteth every wrong,
The straightener of the crooked, the hammer of the strong :

Lo, such was the Son of Sigmund in the days whereof I tell,
The dread of the **doom** and the battle; and all children loved him well.

Now it happed on a summer season mid the blossom of the year,
When the clouds were high and little, and the sun exceeding clear,
That Queen Brynhild arose in the morning, and longed for the eddying pool,
And the Water of the Niblungs her summer sleep to cool :
So she set her face to the river, where the hawthorn and the rose
Hide the face of the sunlit water from the yellow-blossomed close
And the house-built Burg of the Niblungs; for there by a grassy strand
The shallow water floweth o'er white and stoneless sand
And deepeneth up and outward; and the bank on the further side
Goes high and shear and rocky the water's face to hide   [oft
From the plain and the horse-fed meadow: there the wives of the Niblungs
Would play in the wide-spread water **when the summer** days were soft ;
And thither now goes Brynhild, and the flowery screen doth pass,
When lo, fair linen raiment falls before her on the grass,
And she looks, and there is Gudrun, the white-armed Niblung child,
All bare for the sunny river and the water undefiled.
Round she turned with her face yet dreamy with the love of yesternight,
Till the flush of anger changed it : but Brynhild's face grew white,
Though **soft** she spake and queenly :
                                        " Hail, sister of my lord !
Thou **art** fair in the summer morning 'twixt the river and the sward ! "

Then she disarrayed her shoulders and cast her golden **girth,**
Andshe said: "Thou art sister ofGunnar, and the kin **of the best** of the earth ;
So shalt thou go before me to meet the water cold."

Then, smiling nowise kindly, doth Gudrun her behold,
And she saith : " Thou art wrong, Queen Brynhild, to give the place to me,
For she that is wife of the greatest more than sister-kin shall be.
—Nay, if here were the sister of Sigurd ne'er before me should she go,

Though sister were she surely of the best that the earth-folk know :
Yet I linger not, since thou biddest, for the courteous of women thou art ;
And the love of the night and the morning is heavy at my heart ;
For the best of the world was beside me, while thou layest with Gunnar the
[King."

She laughs and leaps, and about her the glittering waters spring :
But Brynhild laugheth in answer, and her face is white and wan
As swift she taketh the water ; and the bed-gear of the swan
Wreathes long folds round about her as she wadeth straight and swift
Where the white-scaled slender fishes make head against the drift :
Then she turned to the white-armed Gudrun, who stood far down the stream
In the lapping of the west-wind and the rippling shallows' gleam,
And her laugh went down the waters, as the war-horn on the wind,
When the kings of war are seeking, and their foes are fain to find.

But Gudrun cried upon her, and said : " Why wadest thou so
In the deeps and the upper waters, and wilt leave me here below ?"

Then e'en as one transfigured loud Brynhild cried, and said :
"So oft shall it be between us at hall and board and bed ;
E'en so in Freyia's garden shall the lilies cover me,
While thou on the barren footways thy gown-hem folk shall see :
E'en so shall the gold cloths lap me, when we sit in Odin's hall,
While thou shiverest, little hidden, by thy lord, the Helper's thrall,
By the serving-man of Gunnar, who all his bidding doth,
And waits by the door of the bower while his master plighteth the troth :
But my mate is the King of the King-folk who rode the Wavering Fire,
And mocked at the ruddy death to win his heart's desire.
Lo now, it is meet and righteous that ye of the happy days
Should bow the heads and wonder at the wedding all men praise.
O, is it not goodly and sweet with the best of the earth to dwell,
And the man that all shall worship when the tale grows old to tell !
For the woe and the anguish endure not, but the tale and the fame endure,

And as wavering wind is the joyance, but the Gods' renown shall be sure :
It is well, O ye troth-breakers ! there was found a man to ride
Through the waves of my Flickering Fire to lie by Brynhild's side."

Then no word answered Gudrun till she waded up the stream
And stretched forth her hand to Brynhild, and thereon was a golden gleam,
And she spake, and her voice was but little :
                              "Thou mayst know by this token and sign
If the best of the kings of man-folk and the master of masters is thine."

White waxed the face of Brynhild as she looked on the glittering thing :
And she spake : "By all thou lovest, whence haddest thou the ring ?"

Then Gudrun laughed in her glory the face of the Queen to see :
"Thinkst thou that my brother Gunnar gave the Dwarf-wrought ring to me?"

Nought spake the glorious woman, but as one who clutcheth a knife
She turned on the mocking Gudrun, and again spake Sigurd's wife :

" I had the ring, O Brynhild, on the night that followed the morn,
When the semblance of Gunnar left thee in thy golden hall forlorn :
And he, the giver that gave it, was the Helper's war-got thrall,
And the babe King Elf uplifted to the war-dukes in the hall ;
And he rode with the heart-wise Regin, and rode the Glittering Heath,
And gathered the Golden Harvest and smote the Worm to the death :
And he rode with the sons of the Niblungs till the words of men must fail
To tell of the deeds of Sigurd and the glory of his tale :
Yet e'en as thou sayst, O Brynhild, the bidding of Gunnar he did,
For he cloaked him in Gunnar's semblance and his shape in Gunnar's hid :—
Thou all-wise Queen of the Niblungs, was this so hard a part
For the learned in the lore of Regin, who ate of the Serpent's heart ?
—Thus he wooed the bride for Gunnar, and for Gunnar rode the fire ;
And he held thine hand for Gunnar, and lay by thy dead desire.

We have known thee for long, O Brynhild, and great is thy renown ;
In this shalt thou joy henceforward and nought in thy wedding crown."

Now is Brynhild wan as the dead, and she openeth her mouth to speak,
But no word cometh outward : then the green bank doth she seek,
And casteth her raiment upon her, and flees o'er the meadow fair,
As though flames were burning beneath it, and red gleeds the daisies were :
But fair with face triumphant from the water Gudrun goes,
And with many a thought of Sigurd the heart within her glows.

And yet as she walked the meadow a fear upon her came,
What deeds are the deeds of women in their anguish and their shame ;
And many a heavy warning and many a word of fate
By the lips of Sigurd spoken she remembereth overlate ;
Yet e'en to the heart within her she dissembleth all her dread.
Daylong she sat in her bower in glee and goodlihead,
But when the day was departing and the earl-folk drank in the hall
She went alone in the garden by the nook of the Niblung wall ;
There she thought of that word in the river, and of how it were better unsaid,
And she looked with kind words to hide it, as men bury their battle-dead
With the spice and the sweet-smelling raiment : in the cool of the eve she went
And murmured her speech of forgiveness and the words of her intent,
While her heart was happy with love : then she lifted up her face,
And lo, there was Brynhild the Queen hard by in the leafy place ;
Then the smile from her bright eyes faded and a flush came over her cheek
And she said : " What dost thou, Brynhild ? what matter dost thou seek ?"

But the word of Sigurd smote her, and she spake ere the answer came :
" Hard speech was between us, Brynhild, and words of evil and shame ;
I repent, and crave thy pardon : wilt thou say so much unto me,
That the Niblung wives may be merry, as great queens are wont to be ?"

But no word answered Brynhild, and the wife of Sigurd spake :

"Lo, I humble myself before thee for many a warrior's sake,
And yet is thine anger heavy—well then, tell all thy tale,
And the grief that sickens thine heart, that a kindly word may avail."

Then spake Brynhild and said: "Thou art great and livest in bliss,
And the noble queens and the happy should ask better tidings than this
For ugly words must tell it; thou shouldst scarce know what they mean;
Thou, the child of the mighty Niblungs, thou, Sigurd's wedded queen.
It is good to be kindly and soft while the heart hath all its will."

Said the Queen: "There is that in thy word that the joy of my heart would kill.
I have humbled myself before thee, and what further shall I say?"

Then spake Brynhild the Queen: "I spake heavy words today;
And thereof do I repent me; but one thing I beseech thee and crave:
That thou speak but a word in thy turn my life and my soul to save:
—Yea the lives of many warriors, and the joy of the Niblung home,
And the days of the unborn children, and the health of the days to come—
Say thou it was Gunnar thy brother that gave thee the Dwarf-lord's ring,
And not the glorious Sigurd, the peerless lovely King;
E'en so will I serve thee for ever, and peace on this house shall be,
And rest ere my departing, and a joyous life for thee;
And long life for the lovely Sigurd, and a glorious tale to tell.
O speak, thou sister of Gunnar, that all may be better than well!"

But hard grew the heart of Gudrun, and she said: "Hast thou heard the tale
That the wives of the Niblungs lie, lest the joy of their life-days fail?   [lord?
Wilt thou threaten the house of the Niblungs, wilt thou threaten my love and my
—It was Sigurd that lay in thy bed with thee and the edge of the sword;
And he told me the tale of the night-tide, and the bitterest tidings thereof,
And the shame of my brother Gunnar, how his glory was turned to a scoff;
And he set the ring on my finger with sweet words of the sweetest of men,
And no more from me shall it sunder—lo, wilt thou behold it again?"

And her hand gleamed white in the even with the ring of Andvari thereon,
The thrice-cursed burden of greed and the grain from the needy won ;
Then uprose the voice of Brynhild, and she cried to the towers aloft :

"O house of the ancient people, I blessed thee sweet and soft ;
In the day of my grief I blessed thee, when my life seemed evil and long ;
Look down, O house of the Niblungs, on the hapless Brynhild's wrong !
Lest the day and the hour be coming when no man in thy courts shall be left
To remember the woe of Brynhild, and the joy from her life-days reft ;
Lest the grey wolf howl in the hall, and the wood-king roll in the porch,
And the moon through thy broken rafters be the Niblungs' feastful torch."

"O God-folk hearken," cried Gudrun, "what a tale there is to tell !
How a Queen hath cursed her people, and the folk that hath cherished her well!"

"O Niblung child," said Brynhild, "what bitterer curse may be
Than the curse of Grimhild thy mother, and the womb that carried thee ?"

"Ah fool!" said the wife of Sigurd, "wilt thou curse thy very friend ?
But the bitter love bewrays thee, and thy pride that nought shall end."

"Do I curse the accursèd?" said Brynhild, "but yet the day shall come,
When thy word shall scarce be better on the threshold of thine home ;
When thine heart shall be dulled and chilly with e'en such a mingling of might,
As in Sigurd's cup she mingled, and thou shalt not remember aright."

Out-brake the child of the Niblungs: 'A witless lie is this ;
But thou sickenest sore for Sigurd, and the giver of all bliss:
A ruthless liar thou art: thou wouldst cut off my glory and gain,
Though it further thine own hope nothing, and thy longing be empty and vain.
Ah, thou hungerest after mine husband !—yet greatly art thou wed,
And high o'er the kings of the Goth-folk doth Gunnar rear the head."

"Which one of the sons of Giuki," said Brynhild, "durst to ride
Through the waves of my Flickering Fire to lie by Brynhild's side?
Thou shouldst know him, O Sister of Kings; let the glorious name be said,
Lest mine oath in the water be written, and I wake up, vile and betrayed,
In the arms of the faint-heart dastard, and of him that loveth life,
And casteth his deeds to another, and the wooing of his wife."

"Yea, hearken," said she of the Niblungs, "what words the stranger saith!
Hear the words of the fool of love, how she feareth not the death,
Nor to cry the shame on Gunnar, whom the King-folk tremble before:
The wise and the overcomer, the crown of happy war!"

Said Brynhild: "Long were the days ere the Son of Sigmund came;
Long were the days and lone, but nought I dreamed of the shame.
So may the day come, Grimhild, when thine eyes know not thy son!
Think then on the man I knew not, and the deed thy guile hath done!"

Then coldly laughed Queen Gudrun, and she said: "Wilt thou lay all things
On the woman that hath loved thee and the Mother of the Kings?
O all-wise Queen of the Niblungs, was this change too hard a part
For the learned in the lore of Regin, who ate of the Serpent's heart?"

Then was Brynhild silent a little, and forth from the Niblung hall
Came the sound of the laughter of men to the garth by the nook of the wall;
And a wind arose in the twilight, and sounds came up from the plain
Of kine in the dew-fall wandering, and of oxen loosed from the wain,
And the songs of folk free-hearted, and the river rushing by;
And the heart of Brynhild hearkened and she cried with a grievous cry:

"O Sigurd, O my Sigurd, we twain were one, time was,
And the wide world lay before us and the deeds to bring to pass!
And now I am nought for helping, and no helping mayst thou give;
And all is marred and evil, and why hast thou heart to live?"

She held her peace for anguish, and forth from the hall there came
The shouts of the joyous Niblungs, and the sound of Sigurd's name:
And Brynhild turned from Gudrun, and lifted her voice and said:
"O evil house of the Niblungs, may the day of your woe and your dread
Be meted with the measure of the guile ye dealt to me,
When ye sealed your hearts from pity and forgat my misery!"

And she turned to flee from the garden; but her gown-lap Gudrun caught,
And cried: "Thou evil woman, for thee were the Niblungs wrought,
And their day of the fame past telling, that they should heed thy life?
Dear house of the Niblung glory, fair bloom of the warriors' strife,
How well shalt thou stand triumphant, when all we lie in the earth
For a little while remembered in the story of thy worth!"

But the lap of her linen raiment did Brynhild tear from her hold
And spake from her mouth brought nigher, and her voice was low and cold:

"Such pride and comfort in Sigurd henceforward mayst thou find,
Such joy of his life's endurance, as thou leav'st me joy behind!"

But turmoil of wrath wrapt Gudrun, that she knew not the day from the night,
And she hardened her heart for evil as the warriors when they smite:
And she cried: "Thou filled with murder, my love shall blossom and bloom
When thou liest in the hell forgotten! smite thence from the deedless gloom,
Smite thence at the lovely Sigurd, from the dark without a day!
Let the hand that death hath loosened the King of Glory slay!"

So died her words of anger, and her latter speech none heard,
Save the wind of the early night-tide and the leaves by its wandering stirred;
For amidst her wrath and her blindness was the hapless Brynhild gone:
And she fled from the Burg of the Niblungs and cried to the night alone:

'O Sigurd, O my Sigurd, what now shall give me back

One word of thy loving-kindness from the tangle and the wrack?
O Norns, fast bound from helping, O Gods that never weep,
Ye have left stark death to help us, and the semblance of our sleep!
Yet I sleep and remember Sigurd; and I wake and nought is there,
Save the golden bed of the Niblungs, and the hangings fashioned fair:
If I stretch out mine hand to take it, that sleep that the sword-edge gives,
How then shall I come on Sigurd, when again my sorrow lives
In the dreams of the slumber of death? O nameless, measureless woe,
To abide on the earth without him, and alone from earth to go!"

So wailed the wife of Gunnar, as she fled through the summer night,
And unwitting around she wandered, till again in the dawning light
She stood by the Burg of the Niblungs, and the dwelling of her lord.

Awhile bode the white-armed Gudrun on the edge of the daisied sward,
Till she shrank from the lonely flowers and the chill, speech-burdened wind.
Then she turned to the house of her fathers and her golden chamber kind;
And for long by the side of Sigurd hath she lain in light-breathed sleep,
While yet the winds of night-tide round the wandering Brynhild sweep,

Gunnar talketh with Brynhild.

On the morrow awakeneth Gudrun; and she speaketh with Sigurd and saith:
" For what cause is Brynhild heavy, and as one who abideth but death?"

"Yea," Sigurd said, "is it so? as a great queen she goes upon earth,
And thoughtful of weighty matters, and things that are most of worth."

"It was other than this," said Gudrun, "that I deemed her yesterday;
All men would have said great trouble on the wife of Gunnar lay."

"Is it so?" said Sigurd the Volsung, "Ah, I sore misdoubt me then,

'That thereof shall we hear great tidings that shall be for the ruin of men."

"Why grieveth she so," said Gudrun, "a queen so mighty and wise,
The Chooser of the war-host, the desire of many eyes,
The Queen of the glorious Gunnar, the wife of the man she chose?
And she sits by his side on the high-seat, as the lily blooms by the rose."

"Where then in the world was Brynhild," said he, "when she spake that word,
And said that her belovèd was her very earthly lord?"

Then was Sigurd silent a little, and Gudrun spake no more;
For despite the heart of the Niblungs, and her love exceeding sore,
With fear her soul was smitten for the word that Sigurd spake,
And yet more for his following silence; and the stark death seemed to awake
And stride through the Niblung dwelling, and the sunny morn grew dim:
Till, lo, the voice of the Volsung, and the speech came forth from him:

"Hearken, Gudrun my wife; the season is nigh at hand,
Yea, the day is now on the threshold, when thou alone in the land
Shalt answer for Sigurd departed, and shalt say that I loved thee well;
And yet if thou hear'st men say it, then true is the tale to tell,
That Brynhild was my belovèd in the tide and the season of youth;
And as great as is thy true-love, e'en so was her love and her truth.
But for this cause thus have I spoken, that the tale of the night hast thou told,
And cast the word unto Brynhild, and shown her the token of gold.
—A deed for the slaying of many, and the ending of my life,
Since I betrayed her unwitting.—Yet grieve not, Gudrun my wife!
For cloudy of late were the heavens with many a woven lie,
And now is the clear of the twilight, when the slumber draweth anigh.
But call up the soul of the Niblungs, and harden thine heart to bear,
For wert thou not sprung from the mighty, today were thy portion of fear:
Yea, thou wottest it even as I; but I see thine heart arise,
And the soul of the mighty Niblungs, and fair is the love in thine eyes."

Then forth went the King from the chamber to the council of the Kings,
And he sat with the wise in the Doom-ring for the sifting of troublous things,
And rejoiced the heart of the people: and the Wrath kept watch by his side.
And his eyen were nothing dimmer than on many a joyous tide.

But abed lay Brynhild the Queen, as a woman dead she lay,
And no word for better or worse to the best of her folk would she say:
So they bore the tidings to Gunnar, and said: "Queen Brynhild ails
With a sickness whereof none knoweth, and death o'er her life prevails."

Then uprose Gunnar the Niblung, and he went to Brynhild his wife,
And prayed her to strengthen her heart for the glory of his life:
But she gave not a word in answer, nor turned to where he stood,
And there rose up a fear in his heart, and he looked for little of good:
There he bode for a long while silent, and the thought within him stirred
Of wise speech of his mother Grimhild, and many a warning word:
But he spake:

      "Art thou smitten of God, unto whom shall we cast the prayer?
Art thou wronged by one of the King-folk, for whom shall the blades be bare?"

Belike she never heard him; she lay in her misery,
And the slow tears gushed from her eyen and nought of the world would she
But ill thoughts arose in Gunnar, and remembrance of the speech   [see.
Erst spoken low by Grimhild; yet he turned his heart to beseech,
And he spake again:

      "O Brynhild, if I ever made thee glad,
If the glory of the great-ones of my gift thine heart hath had,
As mine heart hath been faithful to thee, as I longed for thy life-days' gain,
Tell now of thy toil and thy trouble that we each of each may be fain!"

Nought spake she, nothing she moved, and the tears were dried on her cheek;
But the very words of Grimhild did Gunnar's memory seek;
He sought and he found and considered; and mighty he was and young,

And he thought of the deeds of his fathers and the tales of the Niblungs sung;
How they bore no God's constraining, and rode through the wrong and the
    right
That the storm of their wrath might quicken, and their tempest carry the light.
The words of his mother he gathered and the wrath-flood over him rolled,
And with it came many a longing, that his heart had never told,
Nay, scarce to himself in the night-tide, for the gain of the ruddy rings,
And the fame of the earth unquestioned and the mastery over kings,
And he sole King in the world-throne, unequalled, unconstrained ;
And with wordless wrath he fretted at the bonds that his glory had chained,
And the bitter anger stirred him, and at last he spake and cried :

"How long, O all-wise Brynhild, like the dead wilt thou abide,
Nor speak to thy lord and thy husband and the man that rode thy Fire,
And mocked at the bane of King-folk to accomplish thy desire ?
I deem thou sickenest, Brynhild, with the love of a mighty-one,
The foe, the King's supplanter, he that so long hath shone
Mid the honour of our fathers, and the lovely Niblung house,
Like a serpent amidst of the treasure that the day makes glorious."

Yet never a word she answered, nor unto the great King turned,
Till through all the patience of King-folk the flame of his anger burned,
And his voice was the rattling thunder, as he cried across the bed :

"O who art thou, fearful woman ? art thou one of the first of the dead ?
Hast thou long ago seen and hated the tide of the Niblung praise,
And clad thee in flesh twice over for the bane of our happy days ?
Art thou come from the far-off country that none may live and behold
For the bane of the King of the Niblungs, and of Sigurd lord of the Gold?"

Then she raised herself on her elbow and turned her eyes on the King :
"O tell me, Gunnar," she said, "that thou gavest Andvari's Ring
To thy sister the white-armed Gudrun !—thou, not thy captain of war,

The son of the God-born Volsungs, the Lord **of the** Treasure of yore !
O swear it that I may live ! that I may be glad in thine hall,
And weave with **the wisdom of women, and broider** the purple and pall,
And look in thy face at the chess-play, and drink of thy carven cup,
And whisper a word in season when the voice of the wise goes up,
And speak thee the speech of kindness by the hallowed Niblung hearth.
O swear it, King of the Niblungs, lest thine honour die of the dearth !
O swear it, lord I have wedded, lest mine honour come to nought,
And I be but a **wretch and a** bondmaid for a year's embracing bought !"

Till **his heart** hath heard her meaning at the golden bed he stares,
And the last of the words she speaketh flit empty past his ears ;
For he knows that the tale of the night-tide hath been told and understood,
And now of her shame was he deeming e'en worse than Brynhild would.
So he turns from her face and the chamber with his glory so undone,
That he saith the Gods did evil when the mighty work they won,
And wrought the Burg of the Niblungs, and fashioned his fathers' **days,**
And led them on to the harvest of the deeds and the people's praise.
And nought he sees to amend it, save the hungry eyeless sword,
And the **war** without hope or **honour,** and the **strife** without reward.

So alone he goeth his ways, and the morn to the noontide falls,
And the sun goeth down **in the** heavens, and fades from the Niblung walls,
And the dusk **and the dark draw** over, and no man the King may see.
But Sigurd **sits** in the hall mid the war-dukes' company :
Alone of the Kings in the Doom-ring, and the council of the wise,
By the street and the wharf and **the** burg-gate he shines in the people's eyes;
Stately and lovely to look on **he** heareth of good and **of ill,**
And he knitteth up and divideth, with life and death **at** his will.

Of the exceeding great grief and mourning of Brynhild.

Now the sun cometh up in the morning and shines o'er holt and heath,
And the wall of the mighty mountains, and the sheep-fed slopes beneath,
And the horse-fed plain and the river, and the acres of the wheat,
And the herbs of bane and of healing, and the garden hedges sweet;
It shines on the sea and the shepherd, and the husbandman's desire;
On the Niblung Burg it shineth and smiteth the vanes afire;
And in Gudrun's bower it shineth, and seeth small joy therein,
For hushed the fair-clad maidens the work of women win;
Then Gudrun looketh about her, and she saith:
        "Why sit ye so,
That I hearken but creak of the loom-stock and the battens' homeward blow?
Why is your joy departed and your sweet speech fallen dumb?
Are the Niblungs fled from the battle, is their war-host overcome?
Have the Norns given forth their shaming? have they fallen in the fight?
Yet the sun shines notwithstanding, and the world around is bright."

Then answered a noble woman, and the wise of maids was she:
"Thou knowest, O lovely lady, that nought of this may be;
Yet with woe that the world shall hearken the glorious house is filled,
On the hearth of all men hallowed the cup of joy is spilled.
—A dread, an untimely hour, an exceeding evil day!"

Then the wife of Sigurd answered: "Arise and go thy way
To the chamber of Queen Brynhild, and bid her wake at last,
For that long have we slept and slumbered, and the deedless night is passed:
Bid her wake to the deeds of queen-folk, and be glad as the world-queens are
When they look on the people that loves them, and thrust all trouble afar.
Let her foster her greatness and glory, and the fame no ages forget,
That tomorn may as yesterday blossom, yea more abundantly yet."

Then arose the light-foot maiden : but she stayed and spake by the door :
" O Gudrun, I durst not behold her, for the days of her joyance are o'er,
And the days of her life are numbered, and her might is waxen weak,
And she lieth as one forsaken, and no word her lips will speak,
Nay, not to her lord that loveth : but all we deem, O Queen,
That the wrath of the Gods is upon her for ancient deeds unseen."

Nought answered the white-armed Gudrun, but the fear in her soul arose,
For she thought of the golden Sigurd, and the compassing of foes,
And great grew the dread of her maidens as they gazed upon her face :
But she rose and looked not backward as she hastened from her place,
And sought the King of the Niblungs by hall and chamber and stair,
And bright was the pure mid-morning and the wind was fresh and fair.

So she came on her brother Gunnar, as he sat apart and alone,
Arrayed in the Niblung war-gear, nor moved he more than the stone
In the jaws of the barren valley and the man-deserted dale ;
On his knees was the breadth of the sunshine, and thereon lay the edges pale,
The war-flame of the Niblungs, the sword that his right hand knew :

White was the fear on her lips, and hard at her heart it drew,
As she spake :
                    "I have found thee, O brother ! O Gunnar, go to her and say
That my heart is grieved with her grief and I mourn for her evil day."

Then Gunnar answered her word, but his words were heavy and slow :
" Thou know'st not the words thou speakest—and wherefore should I go,
Since I am forbidden to share it, the woe or the weal of her heart ?
Look thou on the King of the Niblungs, how he sitteth alone and apart,
Fast bound in the wiles of women, and the web that a traitor hath spun,
And no deed for his hand he knoweth, or to do or to leave undone."

Wan-faced from before him she fled, and she went with hurrying feet,

And no child of man in her going would she look upon or greet,
Till she came unto Hogni the Wise ; and he sat in his war-array,
The coal-blue gear of the Niblungs, and the sword o'er his knees there lay:

She sickened, and said: "What dost thou? what then is the day and the deed,
That the sword on thy knees is naked, and thou clad in the warrior's weed?
Go in, go in to Brynhild, and tell her how I mourn
For the grief whereof none wotteth that hath made her days forlorn."

" It is good, my sister," said Hogni, " to abide in the harness of war
When the days and the days are changing, and the Norns' feet stand by the
I will nowise go in unto Brynhild, lest the evil tide grow worse.   [door.
For what woman will bear the sorrow and burden her soul with a curse
If she may escape it unbidden ? and there are words that wound
Far worse than the bitter edges, though wise in the air they sound.
Bide thou and behold things fated ! Hast thou learned how men may teach
The stars in their ordered courses, or lead the Norns with speech ?"

She stood and trembled before him, nor durst she long behold
The silent face of Hogni and the far-seeing eyes and cold.
So she gat her forth from before him, and Sigurd her husband she sought,
And the speech on her lips was ready, till the chill fear made it nought ;
For apart and alone was he sitting in all his war-gear clad,
And Fafnir's Helm of Aweing, and Regin's Wrath he had,
And over the breast of Sigurd was the Hauberk all of gold
That hath not the like in the heavens nor has earth of its fellow told

But he set her down beside him and said : " What fearest thou then ?
What terror strideth in daylight mid the peace of the Niblung men ?"

She cried: "The Helm and the Sword, and the golden guard of thy breast !"

'So oft, O wife," said Sigurd, "is a war-king clad the best

When the peril quickens before him, and on either hand is doubt ;
Thus men wreathe round the beaker whence the wine shall be soon poured out.
But hope thou not o'ermuch, for the end is not today ;
And fear thou little indeed, for not long shall the sword delay :
But speak, O daughter of Giuki, for thy lips scarce held the word
Ere thou sawest the gleam of my hauberk and the edge of the ancient Sword,
The Light that hath lain in the Branstock, the hope of the Volsung tree,
The Sunderer, the Deliverer, the torch of days to be."

She sighed ; for her heart was heavy for the days but a while agone,
When the death was little dreamed of, and the joy was lightly won ;
And her soul was bitter with anger for the day that Brynhild had led
To the heart of the Niblung glory : but fear thrust on, and she said :
"O my lord, O Sigurd the mighty, an evil day is this,
A chill, an untimely hour for the blooming of our bliss !
Go in to my sister Brynhild, and tell her of very sooth
That my heart for her sorrow sorrows, and is sick for woe and ruth."

"The hour draws nigh," said Sigurd, "for I know of the speech and the word
That is kind in the air to hearken, and is worse than the whetted sword.
Now is Brynhild sore encompassed by a tide of measureless woe,
And amidst and anear, as I see it, she seeth the death-star grow.
Yet belike it is, O Gudrun, that thy will herein shall be done ;
But now depart, I pray thee, and leave thy lord alone :
Heavy and hard shall it be, for a season shall it endure,
But the grief and the sorrow shall perish, and the fame of the Gods is sure."

Yet she sat by his side and spake not, and a while at his glory she gazed,
For his face o'erpassed the brightness that so long the folk had praised,
And she durst not question or touch him, and at last she rose from his side,
And gat her away soft-footed, and wandered far and wide
Through the house and the Burg of the Niblungs ; yet durst she never more
Go look on the Niblung Brethren as they sat in their harness of war.

But the morn to the noon hath fallen, and the afternoon to the eve,
And the beams of the westering sun the Niblung wall-stones leave,
And yet sitteth Sigurd alone; then the sun sinketh down into night,
And the moon ariseth in heaven, and **the earth is** pale with her light
And there sitteth Sigurd the Volsung **in** the gold and the harness of war
That was won from the heart-wise Fafnir and the **guarded Treasure** of yore,
But pale is the Helm of Aweing, and wan are the ruddy rings :
So whiles in a city forsaken ye see the shapes of kings,   [known,
And the lips that the carvers wrought, while their words were remembered and
And the brows **men trembled to** look on in the long-enduring stone,
And their hands **once unforgotten, and their** breasts, the walls of war ;
But now are they hidden marvels to the wise and **the master of lore,**
And he nameth them not, nor knoweth, **and their fear is faded away.**

E'en so sat Sigurd the Volsung till the night waxed moonless and grey,
Till the chill dawn spread o'er the lowland, and the purple fells grew clear
In the cloudless summer dawn-dusk, and the sun was drawing **anear:**
Then reddened the Burg of the Niblungs, and the walls of the ancient folk,
And a wind came down from the mountains **and the living things awoke**
And cried out for need and rejoicing ; till, lo, the rim of the sun
Showed over the **eastern ridges, and the new day was begun ;**
And **the beams rose higher and higher, and white grew the** Niblung wall,
And the spears **on the ramparts glistered and the windows blazed withal,**
And the sunlight flooded the courts, and throughout the chambers streamed:
Then bright as **the flames of the** heaven the Helm of Aweing gleamed,
Then clashed the red rings of **the** Treasure, as Sigurd stood on his feet,
And went through the echoing chambers, as the winds in **the wall-nook beat;**
And there in the earliest morning while the lords **of the** Niblungs lie
'Twixt light sleep and awakening they hear the **clash** go by,
And their dreams are of happy battle, and the songs that follow **fame,**
And the hope of the Gods accomplished, and the tales of the ancient name,
Ere Sigurd came to the Niblungs and faced their **gathered foes.**

But on to the chamber of Brynhild alone in the morning he goes,
And the sun lieth broad across it, and the door is open wide
As the last of the women had left it; then he lifted his voice and cried:

"Awake, arise, O Brynhild! for the house is smitten through
With the light of the sun awakened, and the hope of deeds to do."

She spake: "Art thou come to behold me? thou, the mightiest and the worst
Of the pitiless betrayers, that the hope of my life hath nursed."

He said: "It is I that awake thee, and I give thee the life and the days
For fulfilling the deedful measure, and the cup of the people's praise."

She cried: "O the gifts of Sigurd!—Ah why didst thou cast me aside,   [pride?
That we twain should be dwelling, the strangers, in the house of the Niblung
What life is the death in life? what deeds—where the shame cometh up
Betwixt the speech of the wise-ones and the draught of the welcoming cup;
And the shame and repentance awaketh when the song in the harp is awake?
Where we rise in the morning for nothing, and lie down for no love's sake?
Where thou ridest forth to the battle and the dead hope dulleth thy light,
And with shame thy hand is cumbered when the sword is uplifted to smite?
O Sigurd, what hast thou done, that the gifts are cast aback?
—O nay, no life of repentance!—but the bitter sword and the wrack!"

"O Brynhild, live!" said the Volsung, "for what shall the world be then
When thou from the earth art departed, and the hallowed hearths of men?"

She said: "Woe worth the while for the word that hath come from thy mouth!
As the bitter weltering ocean to the shipman dying of drouth,
E'en so is the life thou biddest, since thou pitiedst not thine own,
Nor thy love, nor the hope of thy life-days, but must dwell as a glory alone!"

"It is truer to tell," said Sigurd, "that mine heart in thy love was enwrapped

Till the evil hour of the darkening, and the eyeless **tangle had** happed :
And thereof shalt thou know, O Brynhild, on one **day** better than I,   [die :
When the stroke of the sword hath been smitten, and the night hath seen me
Then belike in thy fresh-springing wisdom thou shalt **know of the dark and**
          the deed,
And the snare for our feet fore-ordered **from whence they shall never be freed.**
But for me, in the net **I awakened and the toils that unwitting I wove,**
And no tongue may tell **of the sorrow that** I had **for thy wedded love :**
But I dwelt in **the dwelling of kings ; so I** thrust **its seeming apart**
And I laboured **the** field of Odin : and e'en this was **a joy to my heart,**
That we dwelt in one house together, though **a stranger's house it were."**

"O late, and o'erlate !" cried Brynhild—"may the dead folk hearken **and hear?**
All was and today it is not—And the Oath unto Gunnar is sworn,
Shall I live the days twice over, and **the life** thou hast made forlorn ? "

And she heard the words of Hindfell and the oath of the earlier day,
Till the daylight darkened before her, and all **memory passed away,**
And she cried : **"I may live no longer, for the Gods have forgotten the earth,**
And my heart is the forge of sorrow, **and my life is a wasting dearth."**

Then **once again spake Sigurd, once** only **and no more :**
A pillar **of light all golden** he stood on the sunlit floor ;
And his eyes were the eyes of Odin, and his face was the hope of the world,
And his voice was the **thunder of** even when the bolt **o'er the** mountains **is**
The fairest of all **things fashioned** he stood 'twixt **life and death,**   [hurled :
And the Wrath of Regin rattled, and the rings of **the Glittering Heath,**
As **he** cried :
          " I am Sigurd the Volsung, and **belike the tale shall be true**
That **no hand** on the earth may hinder what **my hand would fashion and do :**
And what God or what man **shall gainsay it if our love** be greater **than these,**
The pride and the glory of **Sigurd,** and the latter days' increase ?
O live, live, Brynhild belovèd ! **and** thee on the earth will I wed,

And put away Gudrun the Niblung—and all those shall be as the dead."

But so swelled the heart within him as he cast the speech abroad,
That the golden wall of the battle, the fence unrent by the sword,
The red rings of the uttermost ocean on the breast of Sigurd brake :
And he saw the eyes of Brynhild, and turned from the word she spake :

"I will not wed thee, Sigurd, nor any man alive."

Then Sigurd goes out from before her; and the winds in the wall-nook strive,
And the craving of fowl and the beast-kind with the speech of men is blent,
And the voice of the sons of the Niblungs; and their day's first hour is spent
As he goes through the hall of the War-dukes, and many an earl is astir,
But none durst question Sigurd lest of evil days he hear :
So he comes to his kingly chamber, and there sitteth Gudrun alone,
And the fear in her soul is minished, but the love and the hatred are grown :
She is wan as the moonlit midnight ; but her heart is cold and proud,
And she asketh him nought of Brynhild, and nought he speaketh aloud.

Of the slaying of Sigurd the Volsung.

Ere the noon ariseth Brynhild, and forth abroad she goes,
And sits by the wall of her bower 'twixt the lily and the rose ;
Great dread and sickness is on her, as it shall be once on the morn
When the uttermost sun is arisen 'neath the blast of the world-shaking horn :
Her maidens come and go, but none dares cast her a word ;
From the wall the warders behold her, and turn round to the spear and the
Yea, few dare speak of Brynhild as morning fadeth in noon   [sword ;
In the Burg of the ancient people mid the stir and the glory of June.

Then cometh forth speech from Brynhild, and she calls to her maidens and
" Go tell ye the King of the Niblungs that I am arisen from death, [saith :

And come forth from the uttermost sickness, and with him I needs must speak:
That we look into weighty matters and due deeds for king-folk seek."

So they went and returned not again, and it was but a little space
Ere she looked, and behold, it was Gunnar that stood before her face, [head,
And his war-gear darkened the noon-tide and the grey helm gleamed from his
But his eyes were fearful beneath it: then she gazed on the heavens and said:

"Thou art come, O King of the Niblungs; what mighty deed is to frame
That thou wearest the cloudy harness, and the arms of the Niblung name?"

He spake: "O woman, thou mockest! what King of the people is here?
Are not all kings confounded, and all peoples' shame laid bare?
Shall the Gods grow little to help, or men grow great to amend?
Nay, the hunt is up in the world and the Gods to the forest will wend,
And their hearts are exceeding merry as they ride and drive the prey:
But what if the bear grin on them, and the wood-beast turn to bay?
What now if the whelp of their breeding a wolf of the world be grown,
To cry out in the face of their brightness and mar their glad renown?"

She heeded him not, nor hearkened: but he said: "Thou wert wise of old;
And hither I come at thy bidding: let the thought of thine heart be told."

She said: "What aileth thee, Gunnar? time was thou wert great and glad,
And that was yester-morning: how then is the good turned bad?"

He said: "I was glad in my dreams, and I woke and my glory was dead."

"Hath a God then wrought thee evil, or one of the King-folk?" she said.

He said: "In the snare am I taken, in the web that a traitor hath spun;
And no deed knoweth my right-hand to do or to leave undone."

"I look upon thee," said Brynhild, "I know thy race and thy name,
Yet meseems the deed thou sparest, to amend thine evil and shame."

"Nought, nought," he said, "may amend it, save the hungry eyeless sword,
And the war without hope or honour, and the strife without reward."

"Thou hast spoken the word," said Brynhild, "if the word is enough, it is well.
Let us eat and drink and be merry, that all men of our words may tell !"

"O all-wise woman," said Gunnar, "what deed lieth under the tongue ?
What day for the dearth of the people, when the seed of thy sowing hath
[sprung ?"
She said : "Our garment is Shame, and nought the web shall rend,
Save the day without repentance, and the deed that nought may amend."

"Speak, mighty of women," said Gunnar, "and cry out the name and the deed
That the ends of the Earth may hearken, and the Niblungs' grievous Need."

"To slay," she said, "is the deed, to slay a King ere the morn,
And the name is Sigurd the Volsung, my love and thy brother sworn."

She turned and departed from him, and he knew not whither she went ;
But he took his sword from the girdle and the peace-strings round it rent,
And into the house he gat him, and the sunlit fair abode,
But his heart in the mid-mirk waded, as through the halls he strode,
Till he came to a chamber apart ; and Grimhild his mother was there,
And there was his brother Hogni in the cloudy Niblung gear :   [wait
Him-seemed there was silence between them as of them that have spoken, and
Till the words of their mouths be accomplished by slow unholpen Fate :
But they turned to the door, and beheld him, and he took his sheathèd sword
And cast it adown betwixt them, and it clashed half bare on the board,
And Grimhild spake as it clattered : "For whom are the peace-strings rent ?
For whom is the blood-point whetted and the edge of thine intent ?"

He said : " For the heart of Sigurd ; **and thus all is rent away**
Betwixt this word and his slaying, **save a** little **hour of day.**"

Then spake Hogni and answered : " All lands beneath **the sun**
Shall know and hearken and wonder that such a deed must be done."
[worse
" Speak, brother of Kings," said **Gunnar, " dost thou know deeds better or**
That shall wash us clean from shaming, and redeem our lives from the curse?"

" I am none of the Norns," said Hogni, " nor the **heart of Odin the Goth,**
To avenge the foster-brethren, or broken love and troth :
Thy will is the story fated, nor shall I **look on the deed**
With uncursed hands unreddened, and edges dulled at need."

Again spake Grimhild the wise-wife : " Where then is Guttorm the brave ?
For **he** blent not his blood **with** the Volsung's, **nor** his oath to Sigurd gave,
Nor called on Earth to witness, nor went beneath the yoke ;
And now is he Sigurd's foeman ; and who **may curse his stroke ? "**

Then Hogni laughed and answered : " His feet on the threshold **stand :**
Forged **is thy sword, O Mother, and its** hilts are come to hand,
And **look that thou whet it duly ; for the** Norns are departed now ;
From the blood **of our foster-brother** no branch of bale shall grow ;
Hoodwinked are the Gods of heaven, their sleep-dazed eyes are blind ;
They shall peer and grope through the darkness, and nought therein shall find,
Save the red right hand of Guttorm, and his lips that never **swore ;**
At **the** young man's deed shall they wonder, and all shall be **covered o'er :**
Ho, Guttorm, enter, and hearken to **the counsel of the wise ! "**

Then in through the door strode Guttorm fair-clad **in** hunter's guise,
With no steel save his wood-knife girded ; but his war-fain eyes stared wild,
As he spake: "What words are ye hiding from the youngest Niblung child ?
What work is to win, my brethren, that ye sit in warrior's weed,

And tell me nought of the glory, and cover up the deed ? ”

Then uprose Grimhild the wise-wife, and took the cup again ;
Night-long had she brewed that witch-drink and laboured not in vain.
For therein was the creeping venom, and hearts of things that prey
On the hidden lives of ocean, and never look on day ;
And the heart of the ravening wood-wolf and the hunger-blinded beast
And the spent slaked heart of the wild-fire the guileful cup increased :
But huge words of ancient evil about its rim were scored,
The curse and the eyeless craving of the first that fashioned sword.

So the cup in her hand was gleaming, as she turned unto Guttorm and spake:
“ Be merry, King of the War-fain ! we hold counsel for thy sake :
The work is a God’s son’s slaying, and thine is the hand that shall smite,
That thy name may be set in glory and thy deeds live on in light.”

Forth flashed the flame from his eyen, and he cried : “ Where then is the foe,
This dread of mine house and my brethren, that my hand may lay him alow?”

“ Drink, son,” she said, “and be merry ! and I shall tell his name,
Whose death shall crown thy life-days, and increase thy fame with his fame.”

He drinketh and craveth for battle, and his hand for a sword doth seek,
And he looketh about on his brethren, but his lips no word may speak ;
They speak the name, and he hears not, and again he drinks of the cup
And knows not friend nor kindred, and the wrath in his heart wells up,
That no God may bear unmingled, and he cries a wordless cry,
As the last of the day is departing and the dusk time drawing anigh.

Then Grimhild goes from the chamber, and bringeth his harness of war,
And therewith they array his body, and he drinketh the cup once more,
And his heart is set on the murder, and now may he understand
What soul is dight for the slaying, and what quarry is for his hand.

For again they tell him of Sigurd, and the man he remembereth,
And praiseth his mighty name and his deeds that laughed on death.

Now dusk and dark draw over, and through the glimmering house
They go to the place of the Niblungs, the high hall and glorious ;
For hard by is the chamber of Sigurd : there dight in their harness of war
In their thrones sit Gunnar and Hogni, but Guttorm stands on the **floor**
With his blue blade **naked before** them : the torches flare **from the wall**
And **the woven God-folk waver,** but the hush is deep in the hall,
And those Niblung faces **change** not, though the slow moon slips **from her**
And earth is acold ere dawning, and new winds shake the night.   [height

Now it was in the earliest dawn-dusk that **Guttorm stirred in** his place,
And the mail-rings tinkled upon him, as he turned his helm-hid face,
And went forth from the hall and the high-seat ; but the Kings sat still in their
And hearkened the clash of his going and heeded how it died.   [pride

Slow, all alone goeth Guttorm to Sigurd's chamber **door,**
And all is open before him, and the white moon lies on the **floor**
And **the** bed where Sigurd lieth with Gudrun on his breast,
And light comes her breath from her bosom in the joy of infinite rest.
Then Guttorm stands on the threshold, and his heart of **the murder is fain,**
And **he thinks of the** deeds of Sigurd, and praiseth his greatness **and gain;**
Bright blue is his blade in the moonlight—but lo, how Sigurd lies,
As the carven dead **that die not,** with fair wide-open eyes ;
And their glory gleameth **on** Guttorm, and the hate **in his heart is** chilled,
And he shrinketh aback from the threshold and knoweth not what he willed.

But his brethren heed and hearken, and they **hear the** clash **draw nigh,**
But they stir no whit in their pride, though the lord of all creatures should die
Then they see where cometh Guttorm, but they cast him never a word,
For white 'neath the flickering torches they see his unstained sword ;
But he gazed on those Kings of the kindred, and the beast of war **awoke ;**

And his heart was exceeding wrathful **with** the tarrying of the stroke :
And he strode to the chamber of Sigurd, and again they heeded well
How the clash, in the cloister awakened, by the threshold died and fell.

But Guttorm gazed from the threshold, and the moon was fading away
From the golden bed of Sigurd, and the Niblung woman lay
On the bosom of the Volsung, and her hand lay light on her lord ;
But dread were his eyes wide-open, and they gleamed against the sword,
And Guttorm **shrank from** before them, and back to the hall he came :
There the biding brethren behold him flash wild in the torches' flame,
Nor stir their lips to question ; but their swords on their knees are laid ;
The torches faint in the dawning, **and** they see his unstained blade.

Now dieth moon and candle, and though the day be nigh
The roof of the hall fair-builded seems far **aloof as the** sky,
But a glimmer grows on the pavement and the ernes on the roof-ridge stir
Then the brethren hist **and hearken, for a sound** of feet they hear,
And into the hall of the Niblungs a white thing cometh apace :
But the sword of Guttorm upriseth, and he wendeth from his place,
And the clash of steel goes with him ; yet loud as it may sound
Still more they hear those footsteps light-falling on the ground,
And the hearts of the Niblungs waver, and their pride is smitten acold,
For they look on that latest comer, and Brynhild they behold :
But she **sits by** their side **in silence,** and heeds them nothing more
Than the **grey** soft-footed morning heeds yester-even's war.

But Guttorm clashed in the cloisters and through the silence strode
And scarce on the threshold **of Sigurd** a little while **abode :**
There the moon from the floor **hath** departed and **heaven** without is grey,
And afar in the eastern quarter **faint** glimmer streaks of day.
Close over the head of Sigurd the Wrath gleams wan and bare,
And the Niblung woman stirreth, **and** her brow is knit with fear ;
But the King's closed eyes are hidden, loose lie his empty hands,

There is nought 'twixt the sword of the slayer and the Wonder of all Lands.
Then Guttorm laughed in his war-rage, and his sword leapt up on high,
As he sprang to the bed from the threshold and cried a wordless cry,
And with all the might of the Niblungs through Sigurd's body thrust,
And turned and fled from the chamber, and fell amid the dust,
Within the door and without it, the slayer slain by the slain ;
For the cast of the sword of Sigurd had smitten his body atwain
While yet his cry of onset through the echoing chambers went.

Woe's me ! how the house of the Niblungs by another cry was rent,
The wakening wail of Gudrun, as she shrank in the river of blood
From the breast of the mighty Sigurd : he heard it and understood,
And rose up on the sword of Guttorm, and turned from the country of death,
And spake words of loving-kindness as he strove for life and breath :

"Wail not, O child of the Niblungs ! I am smitten, but thou shalt live,
In remembrance of our glory, mid the gifts the Gods shall give !"

She stayed her cry to hearken, and her heart well nigh stood still :
But he spake : "Mourn not, O Gudrun, this stroke is the last of ill ;
Fear leaveth the House of the Niblungs on this breaking of the morn ;
Mayst thou live, O woman beloved, unforsaken, unforlorn !"

Then he sank aback on the sword, and down to his lips she bent   [spent :
If some sound therefrom she might hearken ; for his breath was well-nigh
"It is Brynhild's deed," he murmured, "and the woman that loves me well;
Nought now is left to repent of, and the tale abides to tell.
I have done many deeds in my life-days, and all these, and my love, they lie
In the hollow hand of Odin till the day of the world go by.
I have done and I may not undo, I have given and I take not again :
Art thou other than I, Allfather, wilt thou gather my glory in vain ?"

There was silence then in the chamber, as the dawn spread wide and grey,

And hushed was the hall of the Niblungs at the entering-in of day.
Long Gudrun hung o'er the Volsung and waited the coming word ;
Then she stretched out her hand to Sigurd and touched her love and her lord,
And the broad day fell on his visage, and she knew she was there alone,
And her heart was wrung with anguish and she uttered a weary moan :
Then Brynhild laughed in the hall, and the first of men's voices was that
Since when on yester-even the kings in the high-seat had sat.

But the wrath of Gunnar was kindled and the words of the king out-brake,
" Woe's me, thou wonder of women ! thou art glad for no man's sake,
Nay not for thine own, meseemeth, for thou bidest here as the dead,
As the pale ones stricken deedless, whose tale of life is sped."

She hearkened him not nor answered ; and day came on apace,
And they heard the anguish of Gudrun and her voice in the ancient place.

" Awake, O House of the Niblungs ! for my kin hath slain my lord.
Awake, awake, to the murder, and the edges of the sword !
Awake, go forth and be merry ! and yet shall the day betide,
When ye stand in the garth of the foemen, and death is on every side,
And ye look about and around you, and right and left ye look
For the least of the hours of Sigurd, and his hand that the battle shook
Then be your hope as mine is, then face ye death and shame
As I face the desolation, and the days without a name !"

And she shrieked as the woe gathered on her, and the sun rose over her head:
" Wake, wake, O men of this house, for Sigurd the Volsung is dead !"

In the house rose rumour and stir, and men stood up in the morn,
And their hearts with doubt were shaken, as if with the Uttermost Horn :
The cry and the calling spread, and shields clashed down from the wall,
And swords in the chamber glittered, and men ran apace to the hall.
Nor knew what man to question, nor who had tidings to give,

Nor what were the days thenceforward wherein the folk should live.
But ever the word is amongst them that Sigurd the Volsung is slain,
And the spears in the hall were tossing as the rye in the windy plain.
But they look aloft to the high-seat and they see the gleam of the gold :
And Gunnar the King of battle, and Hogni wise and cold,
And Brynhild the wonder of women ; and her face is deadly pale,
And the Kings are clad in their war-gear, and bared are the edges of bale.
Then cold fear falleth upon them, but the noise and the clamour abate,
And they look on the war-wise Gunnar and awhile for his word they wait ;
But e'en as he riseth above them, doth a shriek through the tumult ring :

"Awake, O House of the Niblungs, for slain is Sigurd the King !"

Then nothing faltered Gunnar, but he stood o'er the Niblung folk,
And over the hall woe-stricken the words of pride he spoke :

" Mourn now, O Niblung people, for gone is Sigurd our guest,
And Guttorm the King is departed, and this is our day of unrest ;
But all this of the Norns was fore-ordered, and herein is Odin's hand ;
Cast down are the mighty of men-folk, but the Niblung house shall stand :
Mourn then today and tomorrow, but the third day waken and live,
For the Gods died not this morning, and great gifts they have to give."

He spake and awhile was silence, and then did the cry outbreak,
And many there were of the Earl-folk that wept for Sigurd's sake ;
And they wept for their little children, and they wept for those unborn,
Who should know the earth without him and the world of his worth forlorn.
But wild is the wailing of women as they fare to the place of the dead,
Where cold is Gudrun sitting mid the waste of Sigurd's bed.
Then they take the man belovèd, and bear him forth to the hall,
And spread the linen above him, and cloth of purple and pall ;
And meekly Gudrun followeth, and she sitteth down thereby,
But mute is her mouth henceforward, and she giveth forth no cry,

And no word of lamentation, though far abroad they weep
For the gift of the Gods departed, and the golden Sigurd's sleep.

Meanwhile elsewhere the women and the wives of the Niblungs wail
O'er the body of King Guttorm and array him for the bale,
And Grimhild opens her treasure and bears forth plenteous gold
And goodly things for his journey, and the land of Death acold.

So rent is the joy of the Niblungs; and their simple days and fain
From that ancient house are departed, and who shall buy them again?
For he, the redeemer, the helper, the crown of all their worth,
They looked upon him and wondered, they loved, and they thrust him forth.

Of the mighty Grief of Gudrun over **Sigurd dead.**

Of old in the days past over was Gudrun blent with the dead,
As she sat in measureless sorrow o'er Sigurd's wasted bed,
But no sigh came from her bosom, nor smote she hand in hand,
Nor wailed with the other women, and the daughters of the land;
Then the wise of the Earls beheld her, smit cold with her dread intent,
And they rose one after other, and before the Queen they went;
Men ancient, men mighty in battle, men sweet of speech were there,
And they loved her, and entreated, and spake good words to hear:
But no tears and no lamenting in Gudrun's heart would strive
With the deadly chill of sorrow that none may bear and live.

Now there were the King-folk's daughters, and wives of the Earls of war,
The fair, and the noble-hearted, the wise in ancient lore;
And they rose one after other, and stood before the Queen
To tell of their woes past over, and the worst their eyes had seen:
There was Giaflaug, Giuki's sister, she was old and stark to see,
And she said :

"O heavyhearted, they slew my King from me:
Look up, O child of the Niblungs, **and** hearken mournful things
Of the woes of living man-folk and **the** daughters of the Kings!
Dead now is the last of my brethren; **to the dead my sister went;**
My son and my little daughter in the earliest days were spent:
On the earth am **I** living loveless, long past are the happy **days,**
They lie with things departed and vain and foolish praise,
And **the hopes of hapless people: yet I** sit with the people's **lords**
When **men are hushed to hearken** the least of all my **words.**   [wrought,
What else is the wont of the Niblungs? why else by the Gods were they
Save to wear down lamentation, and make all **sorrow nought?"**

No word of woe gat Gudrun, nor had she **will to weep,**
Such weight of woe was on **her for the golden Sigurd's sleep:**
Her heart was cold and dreadful; nor good from ill she **knew**
For the love they had taken from her, and the day **with nought to do.**

Then troth-plight maids forsaken, and **never-wedded ones,**
And they that mourned dead husbands and **the hope of unborn sons,**
These told of their bitterest trouble and **the worst their eyes had seen;**
"Yet all **we live to** love thee, and the glory of the Queen.
Look **up, look up, O Gudrun! what rest for them that wail**
If the **Queens of men shall tremble, and the God-kin faint and fail?"**

No voice gat Gudrun's sorrow, no care she had to **weep;**
For the deeds of the day she knew not, nor the dreams of Sigurd's sleep:
Her heart was cold and dreadful; nor good from ill she **knew,**
Because of her love departed, and the day with nought **to do.**

Then spake a Queen of Welshland, and Herborg hight **was she:**
"**O** frozen heart of sorrow, the **Norns** dealt **worse** with me:
Of old, in the days departed, were my brave ones under shield,
Seven sons, and the eighth, my husband, and they fell in the Southland field:

Yet lived my father and mother, yet lived my brethren four,
And I bided their returning by the sea-washed bitter **shore :**
But the winds and death **played with them, o'er** the wide sea swept the wave,
The billows beat on the bulwarks and took what the battle gave :
Alone I sang above them, alone I dight their gear
For the uttermost journey of all men, in the harvest of the year :
Nor wakened spring from winter ere I left those early dead ;
With bound hands and shameful body I went as the sea-thieves led :
Now I sit by the hearth of a stranger ; nor have I weal nor woe,
Save the hope of the Niblung masters and the sorrow of a foe."

No wailing word gat **Gudrun, no thought** she had to weep
O'er the sundering tide of Sigurd, **and the loved lord's lonely sleep :**
Her heart was cold and dreadful ; **nor good from** ill she knew,
Since her love was taken from her **and the day of** deeds to do.

Then arose a maid of the Niblungs, and **Gullrond was her** name,
And betwixt that Queen of Welshland and Gudrun's grief she came :
And she said : " O foster-mother, O wise in the wisdom of old,
Hast thou spoken a word to the dead, and known them hear and behold ?
E'en so is this word thou speakest, and the counsel of thy face."

All heed gave the maids and the warriors, and hushed was the spear-thronged
As she stretched out her **hand to** Sigurd, and swept the linen away [place,
From the lips **that** had holpen the people, and the eyes that had gladdened
She set her hand unto Sigurd, and turned the face of **the dead**   [the day ;
To the moveless knees of Gudrun, **and** again she spake and said :

" O Gudrun, look **on** thy loved-one ; **yea,** as if he were **living** yet
Let his face by thy face be cherished, and thy lips on **his** lips be set !"

Then Gudrun's eyes fell on it, and she saw the bright-one's hair
All wet with **the** deadly dew-fall, and she saw the great eyes stare

At that cloudy roof of the Niblungs without a smile or frown ;
And she saw the breast of the mighty and the heart's wall rent adown :
She gazed and the woe gathered on her, so exceeding far away
Seemed all she once had cherished from that which near her lay ;
She gazed, and it craved no pity, and therein was nothing sad,
Therein was clean forgotten the hope that Sigurd had :
Then she looked around and about her, as though her friend to find,
And met those woeful faces but as grey reeds in the wind,
And she turned to the King beneath her and raised her hands on high,
And fell on the body of Sigurd with a great and bitter cry ;
All else in the house kept silence, and she as one alone
Spared not in that kingly dwelling to wail aloud and moan ;
And the sound of her lamentation the peace of the Niblungs rent,
While the restless birds in the wall-nook their song to the green leaves sent ;
And the geese in the home-mead wandering clanged out beneath the sun ;
For now was the day's best hour, and its loveliest tide begun.

Long Gudrun lay on Sigurd, and her tears fell fast on the floor
As the rain in midmost April when the winter-tide is o'er,
Till she heard a wail anigh her and how Gullrond wept beside,
Then she knew the voice of her pity, and rose upright and cried

"O ye, e'en such was my Sigurd among these Giuki's sons,
As the hart with the horns day-brightened mid the forest-creeping ones ;
As the spear-leek fraught with wisdom mid the lowly garden grass ;
As the gem on the gold band's midmost when the council cometh to pass,
And the King is lit with its glory, and the people wonder and praise.
—O people, Ah thy craving for the least of my Sigurd's days !
O wisdom of my Sigurd ! how oft I sat with thee
Thou striver, thou deliverer, thou hope of things to be !
O might of my love, my Sigurd ! how oft I sat by thy side,
And was praised for the loftiest woman and the best of Odin's pride !
But now am I as little as the leaf on the lone tree left,

When the winter wood is shaken and the sky by the North is cleft."

Then her speech grew wordless wailing, and no man her meaning knew;
Till she hushed her swift and turned her; for a laugh her wail pierced through,
As a whistling shaft the night-wind in some foe-encompassed wood;
And lo, by the nearest pillar the wife of Gunnar stood;
There stood the allwise Brynhild 'gainst the golden carving pressed,
As she stared at the wound of Sigurd and that rending of his breast:
But she felt the place fallen silent, and the speechless anger set
On her own chill, bitter sorrow; and the eyes of the women met,
And they stood in the hall together, as they stood that while ago,
When they twain in Brynhild's dwelling of days to come would know:
But every soul kept silence, and all hearts were chill as stone
As Brynhild spake:
                    "Thou woman, shall thine eyes be wet alone?
Shalt thou weep and speak in thy glory, when I may weep no more,
When I speak, and my speech is as silence to the man that loved me sore?"

Then folk heard the woe of Gudrun, and the bitterness of hate:
" Day cursed o'er every other! when they opened wide the gate,
And Kings in gold arrayed them, and all men the joy might hear,
As Greyfell neighed in the forecourt the world's delight to bear,
And my brethren shook the world-ways as they rode to Brynhild's bower,
—An ill day—an evil woman—a most untimely hour!"

But she wailed: "The seat is empty, and empty is the bed,
And earth is hushed henceforward of the words my speech-friend said!
Lo, the deeds of the sons of Giuki, and my brethren of one womb!
Lo, the deeds of the sons of Giuki for the latter days of doom!
O hearken, hearken Gunnar!   May the dear Gold drag thee adown,
And Greyfell's ruddy Burden, and the Treasure of renown,
And the rings that ye swore the oath on! yea, if all avengers die,
May Earth, that ye bade remember, on the blood of Sigurd cry!

Be this land as waste as the trothplight that the lips of fools have sworn !
May it rain through this broken hall-roof, and snow on the hearth forlorn !
And may no man draw anigh it to tell of the ruin and the wrack !
Yea, may I be a mock for the idle if my feet come ever aback,
If my heart think kind of the chambers, if mine eyes shall yearn to behold
The fair-built house of my fathers, the house beloved of old !"

Then she waileth out before them, and hideth her face from the day,
And she casteth her down from the high-seat and fleeth fast away ;
And forth from the Hall of the Niblungs, and forth from the Burg is she gone,
And forth from the holy dwellings, and a long way forth alone,
Till she comes to the lonely wood-waste, the desert of the deer
By the feet of the lonely mountains, that no man draweth anear ;
But the wolves are about and around her, and death seems better than life,
And folding the hands and forgetting a merrier thing than strife ;
And for long and long thereafter no man of Gudrun knows,
Nor who are the friends of her life-days, nor whom she calleth her foes.

But how great in the hall of the Niblungs is the voice of weeping and wail!
Men bide on the noon's departing, men bide till the eve shall fail,
Then they wend one after other to the sleep that all men win,
Till few are the hall-abiders, and the moon is white therein,
And no sound in the house may ye hearken save the ernes that stir o'erhead,
And the far-off wail o'er Guttorm and the wakeners o'er the dead :
But still by the carven pillar doth the all-wise Brynhild stand
A-gaze on the wound of Sigurd, nor moveth foot nor hand,
Nor speaketh word to any, of them that come or go
Round the evil deed of the Niblungs and the corner-stone of woe.

Of the passing away of Brynhild.

Once more on the morrow-morning fair shineth the glorious sun,
And the Niblung children labour on a deed that shall be done.
For out in the people's meadows they raise a bale on high,
The oak and the ash together, and thereon shall the Mighty lie ;
Nor gold nor steel shall be lacking, nor savour of sweet spice,
Nor cloths in the Southlands woven, nor webs of untold price :
The work grows, toil is as nothing ; long blasts of the mighty horn
From the topmost tower out-wailing o'er the woeful world are borne.

But Brynhild lay in her chamber, and her women went and came,
And they feared and trembled before her, and none spake Sigurd's name ;
But whiles they deemed her weeping, and whiles they deemed indeed
That she spake, if they might but hearken, but no words their ears might heed ;
Till at last she spake out clearly :
                    " I know not what ye would ,
For ye come and go in my chamber, and ye seem of wavering mood
To thrust me on, or to stay me ; to help my heart in woe,
Or to bid my days of sorrow midst nameless folly go."

None answered the word of Brynhild, none knew of her intent ;
But she spake : " Bid hither Gunnar, lest the sun sink o'er the bent,
And leave the words unspoken I yet have will to speak."

Then her maidens go from before her, and that lord of war they seek,
And he stands by the bed of Brynhild and strives to entreat and beseech,
But her eyes gaze awfully on him, and his lips may learn no speech.
And she saith :
                    " I slept in the morning, or I dreamed in the waking-hour,
And my dream was of thee, O Gunnar, and the bed in thy kingly bower,
And the house that I blessed in my sorrow, and cursed in my sorrow and shame,

The gates of an ancient people, the towers of a mighty name:
King, cold was the hall I have dwelt in, and no brand burned on the hearth;
Dead-cold was thy bed, O Gunnar, and thy land was parched with dearth:
But I saw a great King riding, and a master of the harp,
And he **rode** amidst of the foemen, and the swords were bitter-sharp,
But his hand in the hand-gyves smote not, and his feet in the fetters were fast,
While many a word **of mocking at** his speechless face was cast.
Then I heard **a voice in the world :** 'O woe for the broken **troth,**
And the heavy Need of the Niblungs, and the Sorrow of Odin the Goth !
Then I saw the halls of the strangers, and the hills, and the dark-blue **sea,**
Nor **knew of** their names and their nations, for earth was afar from me,
But brother rose up against brother, and blood swam over the board,
And women smote and spared not, and the **fire was master and lord.**
Then, then was the moonless mid-mirk, and **I** woke to the day and the deed,
The deed that earth shall name not, the day of its bitterest need.
Many **words** have I said in my life-days, and little more shall I say
Ye have heard the dream of a woman, deal with **it as ye may :**
For meseems the world-ways sunder, and the **dusk and the dark is mine,**
Till I come to the hall of Freyia, where the **deeds of the mighty shall shine.'"**

So **hearkened** Gunnar the Niblung, that her words he understood,
And **he knew she was set on the death-stroke, and** he deemed it nothing good:
But he said: "I have hearkened, and heeded thy death and mine in thy words:
I have done the deed and abide **it,** and my face shall laugh on the swords ;
But thee, woman, **I** bid thee abide here till thy grief of soul abate ;
Meseems nought lowly nor shameful shall be the Niblung fate ;
And here shalt thou rule and be mighty, and be queen of the measureless Gold,
And abase the kings and upraise them ; and anew **shall** thy fame be told,
And as fair shall thy glory blossom **as** the fresh **fields** under the spring."

Then he casteth his arms about her, and **hot** is the heart of the King
For the glory of Queen Brynhild and the hope of her days of gain,
And he clean forgetteth Sigurd and the foster-brother slain :

But she shrank aback from before him, and cried: " Woe worth the while
For the thoughts ye drive back on me, and the memory of your guile !
The Kings of earth were gathered, the wise of men were met ;
On the death of a woman's pleasure their glorious hearts were set,
And I was alone amidst them—Ah, hold thy peace hereof !
Lest the thought of the bitterest hours this little hour should move."

He rose abashed from before her, and yet he lingered there ;
Then she said : "O King of the Niblungs, what noise do I hearken and hear?
Why ring the axes and hammers, while feet of men go past,
And shields from the wall are shaken, and swords on the pavement cast,
And the door of the treasure is opened, and the horn cries loud and long,
And the feet of the Niblung children to the people's meadows throng?"

His face was troubled before her, and again she spake and said :
" Meseemeth this is the hour when men array the dead ;
Wilt thou tell me tidings, Gunnar, that the children of thy folk
Pile up the bale for Guttorm, and the hand that smote the stroke ?"

He said : " It is not so, Brynhild ; for that Giuki's son was burned
When the moon of the middle heaven last night toward dawning turned."

They looked on each other and spake not ; but Gunnar gat him gone,
And came to his brother Hogni, the wise-heart Giuki's son,
And spake : " Thou art wise, O Hogni ; go in to Brynhild the queen,
And stay her swift departing ; or the last of her days hath she seen."

" It is nought, thy word," said Hogni ; " wilt thou bring dead men aback,
Or the souls of kings departed midst the battle and the wrack?
Yet this shall be easier to thee than the turning Brynhild's heart ;
She came to dwell among us, but in us she had no part ;
Let her go her ways from the Niblungs with her hand in Sigurd's hand.
Will the grass grow up henceforward where her feet have trodden the land ?"

"O evil day," said Gunnar, "when my queen must perish and die!"

"Such oft betide," saith Hogni, "as the lives of men flit by;
But the evil day is a day, and on each day groweth a deed,
And a thing that never dieth; and the fateful tale shall speed.
Lo now, let us harden our hearts and set our brows as the brass,
Lest men say it, 'They loathed the evil and they brought the evil to pass.'"

So they spake, and their hearts were heavy, and they longed for the morrow
And the morrow of tomorrow, and the new day yet to be born.   [morn,

But Brynhild cried to her maidens: "Now open ark and chest,
And draw forth queenly raiment of the loveliest and the best,
Red rings that the Dwarf-lords fashioned, fair cloths that queens have sewed,
To array the bride for the mighty, and the traveller for the road."

They wept as they wrought her bidding and did on her goodliest gear;
But she laughed mid the dainty linen, and the gold-rings fashioned fair:
She arose from the bed of the Niblungs, and her face no more was wan;
As a star in the dawn-tide heavens, mid the dusky house she shone:
And they that stood about her, their hearts were raised aloft
Amid their fear and wonder: then she spake them kind and soft:

"Now give me the sword, O maidens, wherewith I sheared the wind
When the Kings of Earth were gathered to know the Chooser's mind."

All sheathed the maidens brought it, and feared the hidden blade,
But the naked blue-white edges across her knees she laid,
And spake: "The heaped-up riches, the gear my fathers left,
All dear-bought woven wonders, all rings from battle reft,
All goods of men desired, now strew them on the floor,
And so share among you, maidens, the gifts of Brynhild's store."

They brought them mid their weeping, but none put forth a hand
To take that wealth desired, the spoils of many a land :
There they stand and weep before her, and some are moved to speech,
And they cast their arms about her and strive with her, and beseech
That she look on her loved-ones' sorrow and the glory of the day.
It was nought ; she scarce might see them, and she put their hands away
And she said : " Peace, ye that love me ! and take the gifts and the gold
In remembrance of my fathers and the faithful deeds of old."

Then she spake : "Where now is Gunnar, that I may speak with him ?
For new things are mine eyes beholding and the Niblung house grows dim,
And new sounds gather about me, that may hinder me to speak
When the breath is near to flitting, and the voice is waxen weak."

Then upright by the bed of the Niblungs for a moment doth she stand,
And the blade flasheth bright in the chamber, but no more they hinder her
Than if a God were smiting to rend the world in two :   [hand
Then dulled are the glittering edges, and the bitter point cleaves through
The breast of the all-wise Brynhild, and her feet from the pavement fail,
And the sigh of her heart is hearkened mid the hush of the maidens' wail.
Chill, deep is the fear upon them, but they bring her aback to the bed,
And her hand is yet on the hilts, and sidelong droopeth her head.

Then there cometh a cry from withoutward, and Gunnar's hurrying feet
Are swift on the kingly threshold, and Brynhild's blood they meet.
Low down o'er the bed he hangeth and hearkeneth for her word,
And her heavy lids are opened to look on the Niblung lord,
And she saith :
              " I pray thee a prayer, the last word in the world I speak,
That ye bear me forth to Sigurd, and the hand my hand would seek ;
The bale for the dead is builded, it is wrought full wide on the plain,
It is raised for Earth's best Helper, and thereon is room for twain :
Ye have hung the shields about it, and the Southland hangings spread,

There lay me adown by Sigurd and my head beside his head:
But ere ye leave us sleeping, draw his Wrath from out the sheath,
And lay that Light of the Branstock, and the blade **that** frighted death,
Betwixt my side and Sigurd's, as it lay that while agone,
When once in one bed together we twain were laid alone:
How then when **the flames** flare upward may I be left behind?
How then **may the road he wendeth** be hard for my feet to **find?**
How **then in the gates of** Valhall **may the door of the gleaming ring**
Clash **to on the heel of Sigurd, as I follow on my king?"**

Then she raised herself on her elbow, but again **her eyelids sank,**
And the wound by the sword-edge whispered, as her heart from the iron shrank,
And she moaned: "O lives of man-folk, for unrest all overlong
By the Father were ye fashioned; **and what hope** amendeth wrong?
Now at last, O my belovèd, all is gone; none else is near,
Through the ages of all ages, never sundered, shall **we wear."**

Scarce more than a sigh was the word, as back **on the bed she fell,**
Nor was there need in the chamber of **the passing of Brynhild to tell;**
And no **more their** lamentation might the maidens hold aback,
But the **sound of their** bitter mourning was as if red-handed wrack
Ran **wild in the Burg of the Niblungs, and** the fire were master of all.

Then the voice of **Gunnar** the war-king cried out o'er the weeping **hall:**
" Wail on, O women forsaken, **for the** mightiest woman **born!**
Now the hearth is cold and **joyless,** and the waste **bed lieth forlorn.**
Wail on, but amid your weeping **lay** hand to the glorious dead,
That not alone for an hour may **lie** Queen Brynhild's **head:**
For here have been heavy tidings, **and the Mightiest under shield**
Is laid on the bale high-builded in **the** Niblungs' hallowed field.
Fare forth! for he abideth, and **we do** Allfather wrong,
If the shining Valhall's pavement await their **feet** o'erlong."

Then they took the body of Brynhild in the raiment that she wore,
And out through the gate of the Niblungs the holy corpse they bore,
And thence forth to the mead of the people, and the high-built shielded bale;
Then afresh in the open meadows breaks forth the women's wail
When they see the bed of Sigurd and the glittering of his gear;
And fresh is the wail of the people as Brynhild draweth anear,
And the tidings go before her that for twain the bale is built,
That for twain is the oak-wood shielded and the pleasant odours spilt.

There is peace on the bale of Sigurd, and the Gods look down from on high,
And they see the lids of the Volsung close shut against the sky,
As he lies with his shield beside him in the Hauberk all of gold,
That has not its like in the heavens, nor has earth of its fellow told;
And forth from the Helm of Aweing are the sunbeams flashing wide,
And the sheathèd Wrath of Sigurd lies still by his mighty side.
Then cometh an elder of days, a man of the ancient times,
Who is long past sorrow and joy, and the steep of the bale he climbs;
And he kneeleth down by Sigurd, and bareth the Wrath to the sun
That the beams are gathered about it, and from hilt to blood-point run,
And wide o'er the plain of the Niblungs doth the Light of the Branstock glare,
Till the wondering mountain-shepherds on that star of noontide stare,
And fear for many an evil; but the ancient man stands still
With the war-flame on his shoulder, nor thinks of good or of ill,
Till the feet of Brynhild's bearers on the topmost bale are laid,
And her bed is dight by Sigurd's; then he sinks the pale white blade
And lays it 'twixt the sleepers, and leaves them there alone—
He, the last that shall ever behold them,—and his days are well nigh done.

Then is silence over the plain; in the noon shine the torches pale
As the best of the Niblung Earl-folk bear fire to the builded bale:
Then a wind in the west ariseth, and the white flames leap on high,
And with one voice crieth the people a great and mighty cry,
And men cast up hands to the Heavens, and pray without a word,

As they that have seen God's visage, and the face of the Father have heard.

They are gone—the lovely, the mighty, the hope **of the ancient Earth :**
It shall labour and bear the burden as before that day **of their birth :**
It shall groan in its blind abiding **for the day that Sigurd hath sped,**
And the hour that Brynhild hath hastened, and the dawn that waketh the dead:
It shall yearn, and be oft-times holpen, and forget their deeds no more,
Till the new **sun** beams on Baldur, and the **happy sealess shore.**

BOOK IV.

GUDRUN.

HEREIN IS TOLD OF THE DAYS OF THE NIBLUNGS AFTER THEY SLEW
SIGURD, AND OF THEIR WOEFUL NEED AND FALL IN THE HOUSE OF
KING ATLI.

King Atli wooeth and weddeth Gudrun.

HEAR now of those Niblung war-kings, how in glorious state they dwell;
 They do and undo at their pleasure and wear their life-days well ;
They deal out doom to the people, and their hosts of war array,
Nor storm nor wind nor winter their eager swords shall stay :
They ride the lealand highways, they ride the desert plain,
They cry out kind to the Sea-god and loose the wave-steed's rein :
They climb the unmeasured mountains, and gleam on the world beneath,
And their swords are the blinding lightning, and their shields are the shadow
        of death :
When men tell of the lords of the Goth-folk, of the Niblungs is their word,
All folk in the round world's compass of their mighty fame have heard :
They are lords of the Ransom of Odin, the uncounted sea-born Gold,
The Grief of the wise Andvari, the Death of the Dwarfs of old,
The gleaming Load of Greyfell, the ancient Serpent's Bed,
The store of the days forgotten, by the dead heaped up for the dead.
Lo, such are the Kings of the Niblungs, but yet they crave and desire
Lest the world hold greater than they, lest the Gods and their kindred be
                                        [higher.
Fair, bright is their hall in the even ; still up to the cloudy roof
There goeth the glee and the singing while the eagles chatter aloof,

And the Gods on the hangings waver in the doubtful wind of night;
Still fair are the linen-clad damsels, still are the war-dukes bright;
Men come and go in the even; men come and go in the morn;
Good tidings with the daybreak, fair fame with the glooming is born:
—But no tidings of Sigurd and Brynhild, and whoso remembereth their days
Turns back to the toil or the laughter from his words of lamenting or praise,
Turns back to the glorious Gunnar, casts hope on the Niblung name,
Doeth deeds from the morn to the even, and beareth no burden of shame.

Well wedded is Gunnar the King, and Hogni hath wedded a wife;
Fair queens are those wives of the Niblungs, good helpmates in peace and in
Sweet they sit on the golden high-seat, and Grimhild sitteth beside,   [strife,
And the years have made her glorious, and the days have swollen her pride;
She looketh down on the people, from on high she looketh down,
And her days have become a wonder, and her redes are wisdom's crown.
She saith: Where then are the Gods? what things have they shapen and made
More of might than the days I have shapen? of whom shall our hearts be afraid?

Now there was a King of the outlands, and Atli was his name,
The lord of a mighty people, a man of marvellous fame,
Who craved the utmost increase of all that kings desire;
Who would reach his hand to the gold as it ran in the ruddy fire,
Or go down to the ocean-pavement to harry the people beneath,
Or cast up his sword at the Gods, or bid the friendship of death.

By hap was the man unwedded, and wide in the world he sought
For a queen to increase his glory lest his name should come to nought;
And no kin like the kin of the Niblungs he found in all the earth,
No treasure like their treasure, no glory like their worth;
So he sendeth an ancient war-duke with a goodly company,
And three days they ride the mirk-wood and ten days they sail the sea,
And three days they ride the highways till they come to Gunnar's land;
And there on an even of summer in Gunnar's hall they stand,

And the spears of Welshland glitter, and the Southland garments gleam,
For those folk are fair apparelled as the people of a dream.

But the glorious Son of Giuki from amidst the high-seat spoke:
" Why stand ye mid men sitting, or fast mid feasting folk?
No meat nor drink there lacketh, and the hall is long and wide.
Three days in the peace of the Niblungs unquestioned shall ye bide,
Then timely do your message, and bid us peace or war."

But spake the Earl of Atli yet standing on the floor:
" All hail, O glorious Gunnar, O mighty King of men !
O'er-short is the life of man-folk, the three-score years and ten,
Long, long is the craft for the learning, and sore doth the right hand waste:
Lo, lord, our spurs are bloody, and our brows besweat with haste ;
Our gear is stained by the sea-spray and rent by bitter gales,
For we struck no mast to the tempest, and the East was in our sails ;
By the thorns is our raiment rended, for we rode the mirk-wood through,
And our steeds were the God-bred coursers, nor day from night-tide knew :
Lo, we are the men of Atli, and his will and his spoken word
Lies not beneath our pillow, nor hangs above the board ;
Nay, how shall it fail but slay us if three days we hold it hid?
—I will speak to-night, O Niblung, save thy very mouth forbid :
But lo now, look on the tokens, and the rune-staff of the King."

Then spake the Son of Giuki : " Give forth the word and the thing,
Since thy faithfulness constraineth : but I know thy tokens true,
And thy rune-staff hath the letters that in days agone I knew."

" Then this is the word," said the elder, "that Atli set in my mouth :
'I have known thee of old, King Gunnar, when we twain drew sword in the
In the days of thy father Giuki, and great was the fame of thee then: [south
But now it rejoiceth my heart that thou growest the greatest of men,
And anew I crave thy friendship, and I crave a gift at thy hands,

That thou give me the white-armed Gudrun, the queen and the darling of lands,
To be my wife and my helpmate, my glory in hall and afield;
That mine ancient house may blossom and fresh fruit of the King-tree yield.
I send thee gifts moreover, though little things be these,
But such is the fashion of great-ones when they speak across the seas.'"

Then cried out that earl of the strangers, and men brought the gifts and the
White steeds from the Eastland horse-plain, fine webs of price untold,   [gold;
Huge pearls of the nether ocean, strange masteries subtly wrought
By the hands of craftsmen perished and people come to nought.

But Gunnar laughed and answered : " King Atli speaketh well ;
Across the sea, peradventure, I too a tale may tell :
Now born is thy burden of speech ; so rejoice at the Niblung board,
For here art thou sweetly welcome for thyself and thy mighty lord :
And maybe by this time tomorrow, or maybe in a longer space,
Shall ye have an answer for Atli, and a word to gladden his face."

So the strangers sit and are merry, and the Wonder of the East
And the glory of the Westland kissed lips in the Niblung feast.

But again on the morrow-morning speaks Gunnar with Grimhild and saith :
" Where then in the world is Gudrun, and is she delivered from death ?
For nought hereof hast thou told me : but the wisest of women art thou,
And I deem that all things thou knowest, and thy cunning is timely now ;
For King Atli wooeth my sister ; and as wise as thou mayst be,
What thing mayst thou think of greater 'twixt the ice and the uttermost sea
Than the might of the Niblung people, if this wedding come to pass ?"

Then answered the mighty Grimhild, and glad of heart she was :
" It is sooth that Gudrun liveth ; for that daughter of thy folk
Fled forth from the Burg of the Niblungs when the Volsung's might ye broke :
She fled from all holy dwellings to the houses of the deer,

And the feet of the mountains deserted that few folk come anear:
There the wolves were about and around her, and no mind she had to live;
Dull sleep she deemed was better than with turmoiled thought to strive:
But there rode a wife in the wood, a queen of the daughters of men,
And she came where Gudrun abided, whose might was minished as then,
Till she was as a child forgotten; nor that queen might she gainsay;
Who took the white-armed Gudrun, and bore my daughter away
To her burg o'er the hither mountains; there she cherished her soft and sweet,
Till she rose, from death delivered, and went upon her feet:
She awoke and beheld those strangers, a trusty folk and a kind,
A goodly and simple people, that few lords of war shall find:
Glorious and mighty they deemed her, as an outcast wandering God,
And she loved their loving-kindness, and the fields of the tiller she trod,
And went 'twixt the rose and the lily, and sat in the chamber of wool,
And smiled at the laughing maidens, and sang over shuttle and spool.
Seven seasons there hath she bided, and this have I wotted for long;
But I knew that her heart is as mine to remember the grief and the wrong,
So the days of thy sister I told not, in her life would I have no part,
Lest a foe for thy life I should fashion, and sharpen a sword for thine heart:
But now is the day of our deeds, and no longer durst I refrain,
Lest I put the Gods' hands from me, and make their gifts but vain.
Yea, the woman is of the Niblungs, and often I knew her of old,
How her heart would burn within her when the tale of their glory was told.
With wisdom and craft shall I work, with the gifts that Odin hath given,
Wherewith my fathers of old, and the ancient mothers have striven."

"Thy word is good," quoth Gunnar, "a happy word indeed:
Lo, how shall I fear a woman, who have played with kings in my need?
Yea, how may I speak of my sister, save well remembering
How goodly she was aforetime, how fair in everything,
How kind in the days passed over, how all fulfilled of love
For the glory of the Niblungs, and the might that the world shall move?
She shall see my face and Hogni's, she shall yearn to do our will,

And the latter days of her brethren with glory shall fulfil."

Then Grimhild laughed and answered : " Today then shalt thou ride
To the dwelling of Thora the Queen, for there doth thy sister abide."

As she spake came the wise-heart Hogni, and that speech of his mother he
And he said : "How then are ye saying a new and wonderful word,   [heard,
That ye meddle with Gudrun's sorrow, and her grief of heart awake ?
Will ye draw out a dove from her nest, and a worm to your hall-hearth take?"

" What then," said his brother Gunnar, " shall we thrust by Atli's word ?
Shall we strive, while the world is mocking, with the might of the Eastland
While the wise are mocking to see it, how the great devour the great?"   [sword,

" O wise-heart Hogni," said Grimhild, "wilt thou strive with the hand of fate,
And thrust back the hand of Odin that the Niblung glory will crown ?
Wert thou born in a cot-carle's chamber, or the bed of a King's renown?"

" I know not, I know not," said Hogni, "but an unsure bridge is the sea,
And such would I oft were builded betwixt my foeman and me.
I know a sorrow that sleepeth, and a wakened grief I know,
And the torment of the mighty is a strong and fearful foe."

They spake no word before him ; but he said : " I see the road ;
I see the ways we must journey—I have long cast off the load,
The burden of men's bearing wherein they needs must bind
All-eager hope unseeing with eyeless fear and blind :
So today shall my riding be light ; nor now, nor ever henceforth
Shall men curse the sword of Hogni in the tale of the Niblung worth."
                                                                [cried
Therewith he went out from before them, and through chamber and hall he
On the best of the Niblung earl-folk, for that now the Kings would ride :
Soon are all men asembled, and their shields are fresh and bright,

Nor gold their raiment lacketh; then the strong-necked steeds they dight,
They dight the wain for Grimhild, and she goeth up therein,
And the well-clad girded maidens have left the work they win,
To sit by the Mother of Kings and make her glory great:
Then to horse get the Kings of the Niblungs, and ride out by the ancient gate;
And amidst its dusky hollows stir up the sound of swords:
Forth then from the hallowed houses ride on those war-fain lords,
Till they come to the dales deserted, and the woodland waste and drear;
There the wood-wolves shrink before them, fast flee the forest-deer,
And the stony wood-ways clatter as the Niblung host goes by.
Adown by the feet of the mountains that eve in sleep they lie,
And arise on the morrow-morning and climb the mountain-pass,
And the sunless hollow places, and the slopes that hate the grass.
So they cross the hither ridges and ride a stony bent
Adown to the dale of Thora, and the country of content;
By the homes of a simple people, by cot and close they go,
Till they come to Thora's dwelling; but fair it stands and low
Amidst of orchard-closes, and round about men win
Fair work in field and garden, and sweet are the sounds therein.

Then down by the door leaps Gunnar, but awhile in the porch he stands
To hearken the women's voices and the sound of their labouring hands;
And amidst of their many murmurings a mightier voice he hears,
The speech of his sister Gudrun: his inmost heart it stirs,
And he entereth glad and smiling; bright, huge in the lowly hall
He stands in the beam of sunlight where the dust-motes dance and fall.

On the high-seat sitteth Gudrun when she sees the man of war
Come gleaming into the chamber; then she standeth up on the floor,
And is great and goodly to look on mid the women of that place:
But she knoweth the guise of the Niblungs, and she knoweth Gunnar's face,
And at first she turneth to flee, as erewhile she fled away
When she rose from the wound of Sigurd and loathed the light of day:

But her father's heart rose in her, and the sleeping wrong awoke,
And she made one step from the high-seat before Queen Thora's folk ;
And Gunnar moved from the threshold, and smiled as he drew anear,
And Hogni went behind him and the Mother of Kings was there ;
And her maids and the Earls of the Niblungs stood gleaming there behind:
Lo, the kin and the friends of Gudrun, a smiling folk and kind !

In the midst stood Gudrun before them, and cried aloud and said :
"What ! bear ye tidings of Sigurd? is he new come back from the dead?
O then will I hasten to greet him, and cherish my love and my lord,
Though the murderous sons of Giuki have borne the tale abroad."

Dead-pale she stood before them, and no mouth answered again,
And the summer morn grew heavy, and chill were the hearts of men
And Thora's people trembled : there the simple people first
Saw the horror of the King-folk, and mighty lives accurst.

All hushed stood the glorious Gunnar, but Hogni came before,
And he said : "It is sooth, my sister, that thy sorrow hath been sore,
That hath rent thee away from thy kindred and the folk that love thee most:
But to double sorrow with hatred is to cast all after the lost,
And to die and to rest not in death, and to loathe and linger the end :
Now to day do we come to this dwelling thy grief and thy woe to amend,
And to give thee the gift that we may ; for without thy love and thy peace
Doth our life and our glory sicken, though its outward show increase.
Lo, we bear thee rule and dominion, and hope and the glory of life,
For King Atli wooeth thee, Gudrun, for his queen and his wedded wife."

Still she stood as a carven image, as a stone of ancient days
When the sun is bright about it and the wind sweeps low o'er the ways.
All hushed was Gunnar the Niblung and knew not how to beseech,
But still Hogni faced his sister, nor faltered aught in his speech :

"Thou art young," he said, "O sister; thou wert called a mighty queen
When the nurses first upraised thee and first thy body was seen :
If thou bide with these toiling women when a great king bids thee to wife,
Then first is it seen of the Niblungs that they cringe and cower from strife:
By the deeds of the Golden Sigurd I charge thee hinder us not,
When the Norns have dight the way-beasts, and our hearts for the journey
                                                        [are hot !"

She answered not with speaking, she questioned not with eyes,
Nought did her deadly anger to her brow unknitted rise,
Then forth came **Grimhild** the Mighty, and the cup was in her hand,
Wherein with the sea's dread mingled was the might and the blood of the land ;
And the guile of the summer serpent and the herb of the sunless dale
Were blent for the deadening slumber that forgetteth joy and bale ;
And cold words of ancient wisdom that the very Gods would dim
Were the foreshores of that wine-sea and the cliffs that girt its rim :
Therewith in the hall stood Grimhild, and cried aloud and spake :

"It was I that bore thee, daughter ; I laboured once for thy sake,
I groaned to bear thee a queen, I sickened sore for thy fame :
By me and my womb I command thee that thou worship the Niblung name,
And take the gift we would give thee, and be wed to a king of the earth,
And rejoice in kings hereafter when thy sons are come to the birth
Lo, then as thou lookest upon them, and thinkest of glory to come,
It shall be as if Sigmund were living, and Sigurd sat in thine home."

Nought answered the white-armed Gudrun, no master of masters might see
The hate in her soul swift-growing or the rage of her misery.
But great waxed the wrath of Grimhild ; there huge in the hall she stood,
And her fathers' might stirred in her, and the well-spring of her blood ;
And she cried out blind with anger : "Though all we die on one day,
Though we live for ever in sorrow, yet shalt thou be given away
To Atli the King of the mighty, high lord of the Eastland gold :
Drink now, that my love and my wisdom may thaw thine heart grown cold ;

And take those great gifts of our giving, the cities long builded for thee,
The wine-burgs digged for thy pleasure, the fateful wealthy lea,
The darkling woods of the deer, the courts of mighty lords,
The hosts of men war-shielded, the groves of fallow swords!"

Nought changed the eyes of Gudrun, but she reached her hand to the cup
And drank before her kindred, and the blood from her heart went up,
And was blent with the guile of the serpent, and many a thing she forgat,
But never the day of her sorrow, and of how o'er Sigurd she sat:
But the land's-folk looked on the Niblungs as the daughter of Giuki drank,
And before their wrath they trembled, and before their joy they shrank.

Then yet again spake Gudrun, and they that stood thereby,
—O how their hearts were heavy as though the sun should die!
She said: "O Kings of my kindred, I shall nought gainsay your will;
With the fruit of your fond desires your hearts shall ye fulfil;   [old,
Bear me back to the Burg of the Niblungs, and the house of my fathers of
That the men of King Atli may take me with the tokens and treasure of gold."

Then the cry goeth up from the Niblungs, and no while in that house they
Forth fare the Cloudy People and the stony slopes they ride,   [abide;
And the sun is bright behind them o'er queen Thora's lowly dale,
Where the sound of their speech abideth as an ancient woeful tale.
But the Niblungs ride the forest and the dwellings of the deer,
And the wife of the Golden Sigurd to the ancient Burg they bear;
She speaks not of good nor of evil, and no change in her face men see,
Nay, not when the Niblung towers rise up above the lea;
Nay, not when they come to the gateway, and that builded gloom again
Swallows up the steed and its rider, and sword, and gilded wain;
Nay, not when to earth she steppeth, and her feet again pass o'er
The threshold of the Niblungs and the holy house of yore;
Nay, not when alone she lieth in the chamber, on the bed
Where she lay, a little maiden, ere her hope was born and dead:

Yea, how fair is her face on the morrow, how it **winneth all** people's praise,
As the moon that forebodeth nothing on the night of the last of days.

Nought tarry the lords of King Atli, and the Niblungs stay them nought ;
The doors of the treasure are opened and the gold and the tokens are brought;
And all men in the hall are assembled, where Gunnar speaketh and saith :

"Go hence, O men of King Atli, and tell of our love and our faith
To thy master, the mighty **of** men : go take him this treasure of gold,
And show him how we have hearkened, and nought from his heart may with-
Nay, not our best and our dearest, nay, not the crown of our worth,　[hold,
Our sister, **the** white-armed Gudrun, the wise **and** the Queen of the earth."

Then arose the cry of the people, and that Duke of Atli spake :
" **We** bless thee, O mighty Gunnar, for the Eastland Atli's sake,
And his kingdom as thy kingdom, and his men as thy men shall be,
And the gold in Atli's treasure is stored **and** gathered for thee."

So spake he amid their shouting, and the Queen from the high-seat stept,
And Gudrun stood with the strangers, and there were women who wept,
But she wept no more than she smiled, nor spake, nor turned again
To that place in the ancient dwelling where once lay Sigurd slain.
But she mounteth the wain all golden, and the Earls to the saddle leap,
And forth they ride in the morning, and adown the builded steep
That hath no name for Gudrun, save the place where Sigurd fell,
The strong abode of treason, the house where murderers dwell.

Three days they ride the lealand till they come to the **side** of the sea :
Ten days they sail the sea-flood to the land where they would be :
Three days they ride the mirk-wood to **the** peopled country-side,
Three days through a land of cities and plenteous tilth they ride ;
On **the** fourth **the** Burg of Atli o'er the meadows riseth up,
And the houses of his dwelling fine-wrought as a silver cup.

Far off in a bight of the mountains by the inner sea it stands,
Turned away from the house of Gudrun, and her kindred and their lands.
Then to right and to left looked Gudrun and beheld the outland folk,
With no love nor hate nor wonder, as out from the teeth she spoke
To that unfamiliar people that had seen not Sigurd's face.
There she saw the walls most mighty as they came to the fencèd place:
But lo, by the gate of the city and the entering in of the street
Is an host exceeding glorious, for the King his bride will greet:
So Gudrun stayeth her fellows, and lighteth down from the wain,
And afoot cometh Atli to meet her, and they meet in the midst, they twain,
And he casteth his arms about her as a great man glad at heart;
Nought she smiles, nor her brow is knitted as she draweth aback and apart,
No man could say who beheld her if sorry or glad she were;
But her steady eyes are beholding the King and the Eastland's Fear,
And she thinks: Have I lived too long? how swift doth the world grow worse,
Though it was but a little season that I slept, forgetting the curse!

But the King speaks kingly unto her and they pass forth under the gate,
And she sees he is rich and mighty, though the Niblung folk be great;
So strong is his house upbuilded, so many are his lords,
So great the hosts for the murder and the meeting of the swords;
And she saith: It is surely enough and no further now shall I wend;
In this house, in the house of a stranger shall be the tale and the end.

Atli biddeth the Niblungs to him.

There now is Gudrun abiding, and gone by is the bloom of her youth,
And she dwells with a folk untrusty, and a King that knows not ruth:
Great are his gains in the world, and few men may his might withstand,
But he weigheth sore on his people and cumbers the hope of his land;
He craves as the sea-flood craveth, he gripes as the dying hour,
All folk lie faint before him as he seeketh a soul to devour:

Like breedeth like in his house, and venom, and guile, and the knife
Oft lie 'twixt brother and brother, and the son and the father's life :
As dogs doth Gudrun heed them, and looks with steadfast eyes
On the guile and base contention, and the strife of murder and lies.

So pass the days and the moons, and the seasons wend on their ways,
And there as a woman alone she sits mid the glory and praise :
There oft in the hall she sitteth, and as empty images
Are grown the shapes of the strangers, till her fathers' hall she sees : ·
Void then seems the throne of the King, and no man sits by her side
In the house of the Cloudy People and the place of her brethren's pride ;
But a dead man lieth before her, and there cometh a voice and a hand,
And the cloth is plucked from the dead, and, lo, the beloved of the land,
The righter of wrongs, the deliverer, yea he that gainsayed no grace :
In a stranger's house is Gudrun and no change comes over her face,
But her heart cries : Woe, woe, woe, O woe unto me and to all !
On the fools, on the wise, on the evil let the swift destruction fall !

Cold then is her voice in the high-seat, and she hears not what it saith ;
But Atli heedeth and hearkeneth, for she tells of the Glittering Heath,
And the Load of the mighty Greyfell, and the Ransom of Odin the Goth :
Cold yet is her voice as she telleth of murder and breaking of troth,
Of the stubborn hearts of the Niblungs, and their hands that never yield,
Of their craving that nought fulfilleth, of their hosts arrayed for the field.
—What then are the words of King Atli that the cold voice answereth thus?

"King, so shalt thou do, and be sackless of the vengeance that lieth with us:
What words are these of my brethren, what words are these of my kin ?
For kin upon kin hath pity, and good deeds do brethren win
For the babes of their mothers' bosoms, and the children of one womb :
But no man on me had pity, no kings were gathered for doom,
When I lifted my hands for the pleading in the house of my father's folk ;
When men turned and wrapped them in treason, and did on wrong as a cloak:

l have neither brethren nor kindred, and I am become thy wife
To help thine heart to its craving, and strengthen thine hand in the strife."

Thus she stirred up the lust of Atli, she, unmoved as a mighty queen,
While the fire that burned within her by no child of man was seen.

There oft in the bed she lieth, and beside her Atli sleeps,
And she seeth him not nor heedeth, for the horror over her creeps,
And her own cry rings through the chamber that along ago she cried,
And a man for his life-breath gasping is struggling by her side,
Yea, who but Sigurd the Volsung; and no man of men in death
Ere spake such words of pity as the words that now he saith,
As the words he speaketh ever while he riseth up on the sword,
The sword of the foster-brethren and the Kings that swore the word.
Lo, there she lieth and hearkeneth if yet he speak again,
And long she lieth hearkening and lieth by the slain.

So dreams the waking Gudrun till the morn comes on apace
And the daylight shines on Atli, and no change comes over her face,
And deep hush lies on the chamber , but loud cries out her heart :
How long, how long, O God-folk, will ye sit alone and apart,
And let the blood of Sigurd cry on you from the earth,
While crowned are the sons of murder with worship and with worth ?
If ye tarry shall I tarry ?   From the darkness of the womb
Came I not in the days passed over for accomplishing your doom ?

So she saith till the daylight brightens, and the kingly house is astir,
And she sits by the side of Atli, and a woman's voice doth hear,
One who speaks with the voice of Gudrun, a queenly voice and cold :
" How oft shall I tell thee, Atli, of the wise Andvari's Gold,
The Treasure Regin craved for, the uncounted ruddy rings ?
Full surely he that holds it shall rule all earthly kings :
Stretch forth thine hand, O Atli, for the gift is marvellous great,

And I am she that giveth ! how long wilt thou linger and wait
Till the traitors come against thee with the war-torch and the steel,
And here in thy land thou perish, befooled of thy kingly weal ?
Have I wedded the King of the Eastlands, the master of numberless swords,
Or a serving-man of the Niblungs, a thrall of the Westland lords ? "

So spake the voice of Gudrun ; suchwise she cast the seed
O'er the gold-lust of King Atli for the day of the Niblungs' Need.

Who is this in the hall of King Gunnar, this golden-gleaming man ?
Who is this, the bright and the silent as the frosty eve and wan,
Round whom the speech of wise-ones lies hid in bonds of fear ?
Who this in the Niblung feast-hall as the moon-rise draweth anear ?

Hark ! his voice mid the glittering benches and the wine-cups of the Earls,
As cold as the wind that bloweth where the winter river whirls,
And the winter sun forgetteth all the promise of the spring :
" Hear ye, O men of the Westlands, hear thou, O Westland King,
I have ridden the scorching highways, I have ridden the mirk-wood blind,
I have sailed the weltering ocean your Westland house to find ;
For I am the man called Knefrud with Atli's word in my mouth,
That saith : O noble Gunnar, come thou and be glad in the south,
And rejoice with Eastland warriors ; for the feast for thee is dight,
And the cloths for thy coming fashioned my glorious hall make bright.
Knowst thou not how the sun of the heavens hangs there 'twixt floor and roof,
How the light of the lamp all golden holds dusky night aloof ?
How the red wine runs like a river, and the white wine springs as a well,
And the harps are never ceasing of ancient deeds to tell ?
Thou shalt come when thy heart desireth, when thou weariest thou shalt go,
And shalt say that no such high-tide the world shall ever know.
Come bare and bald as the desert, and leave mine house again
As rich as the summer wine-burg, and the ancient wheat-sown plain !
Come, bid thy men be building thy store-house greater yet,

And make wide thy stall and thy stable for the gifts thine hand shall get !
Yet when thou art gone from Atli he shall stand by his treasure of gold,
He shall look through stall and stable, he shall ride by field and fold,
And no ounce from the weight shall be lacking, of his beasts shall lack no head,
If no thief hath stolen from Gunnar, if no beast in his land lie dead.
Yea henceforth let our lives be as one, let our wars and our wayfarings blend,
That my name with thine may be told of when the song is sung in the end,
That the ancient war-spent Atli may sit and laugh with delight
O'er thy feet the swift in battle, o'er thine hand uplifted to smite."

So spake the guileful Knefrud mid the silence of the wise,
Nor once his cold voice faltered, nor once he sank his eyes :
Then spake the glorious Gunnar :
                              "We hear King Atli's voice,
And the heart is glad within us that he biddeth us rejoice :
Yet the thing shall be seen but seldom that a Niblung fares from his land
With eyes by the gold-lust blinded, with the greedy griping hand.
When thou farest aback unto Atli, thou shalt tell him how thou hast been
In the house of the Westland Gunnar, and what things thine eyes have seen :
Thou shalt tell of the seven store-houses with swords filled through and
Gold-hilted, deftly smithied, in the Southland wave made blue :   [through,
Thou shalt tell of the house of the treasures and the Gold that lay erewhile
On the Glittering Heath of murder 'neath the heart of the Serpent's guile :
Thou shalt note our glittering hauberk, thou shalt strive to bend our bow,
Thou shalt look on the shield of Gunnar that its white face thou mayst know :
Thou shalt back the Niblung war-steed when the west wind blows its most,
And see if it over-run thee ; thou shalt gaze on the Niblung host
And be glad of the friends of Atli ; thou shalt fare through stable and stall,
And tell over the tale of the beast-kind, if the night forbear to fall ;
Through the horse-mead shalt thou wander, through the meadows of the sheep,
But forbear to count their thousands lest thou weary for thy sleep ;
Thou shalt look if the barns be empty, though the wheat-field whiteneth now,
In the midmost of the summer in the fields men cared to plough ;

Thou shalt dwell with men that lack not, and the tillers fair and fain ;
Thou shalt see, and long, and wonder, and tell thy King of his gain ;
For in all that here thou beholdest hath he portion even as we ;
Sweet bloometh his love in our midmost, and the fair time yet may be,
When we twain shall meet and be merry; and sure when our lives are done
No more shall men sunder our glory than the Gods have rent the sun.
Sit, mighty man, and be joyous : and then shalt thou cast us a word
And say how fareth our sister mid the glory of her lord."

Then Knefrud looked upon Gunnar, and spake, nor sank his eyes :
" Each morn at the day's beginning when the sun hath hope to arise
She looketh from Atli's tower toward the west part and the grey,
To see the Niblung spear-heads gleam down the lonely way :
Each eve at the day's departing on the topmost tower she stands,
And looketh toward the mirk-wood and the sea of the western lands :
There long in the wind she standeth, and the even grown acold,
To see the Niblung war-shields come forth from out the wold."

Then Gunnar turneth to Hogni, and he saith : " O glorious lord,
What saith thine heart to the bidding, and Atli's loving word ? "

[rough,
" I have done many deeds," said Hogni, " I have worn the smooth and the
While the Gods looked on from heaven, and belike I have done enough,
And no deed for me abideth, but rather the sleep and the rest.
But thou, O Son of King Giuki, art our eldest and our best,
And fair lie the fields before thee wherein thine hand shall work :
By the wayside of the greedy doth many a peril lurk ;
Full wise is the great one meseemeth who bideth his ending at home
When the winds and the waves may be dealing with hate that hath far to
[come."

" I hearken thy word," said Gunnar, " and I know in very deed
That long-lived and happy are most men that hearken Hogni's rede.

Hear thou, O Eastland War-god, and bear this answer aback,
That nought may the earth of my people King Giuki's children lack,
And that here in the land am I biding till the Norns my life shall change;
Howbeit, if here were Atli, his face were scarce more strange
Than that daughter of my father whom sore I long to see :
Let him come, and sit with the Niblungs, and be called their king with me.'

Then spake the guileful Knefrud, and his word was exceeding proud
" It is little the wont of Atli to sit at meat with a crowd ;
Yet know, O Westland Warrior, that thy message shall be done,
Since the Cloudy Folk make ready new lodging for the sun."

He laughed, and the wise kept silence, and Gunnar heeded him nought :
On the daughter of his people was set the Niblung's thought,
So sore he longed to behold her ; for his life seemed wearing away,
And the wealth and the fame he had gathered seemed nought by the earlier
The day of love departed, and of hope forgotten long.   [day,

But Hogni laughs with the stranger, and cries out for harp and song,
And the glee rises up as a river when the mountain-tops grow clear,
When seaward drift the rain-clouds, and the end of day is near ;
As of birds in the green groves singing is the Niblung manhood's voice,
And the Earls without foreboding in their mighty life rejoice.
Glad then grows the King of the people, and the sweetness filleth his heart,
And he turneth about a little, and speaketh to Knefrud apart :
" What sayest thou, lord of the Eastland, how with Gudrun's heart it fares ?
Is she sunk in the day of dominion and the burden that it bears,
Or remembereth she her brethren and her father and her folk ? "

Then Knefrud looked upon Gunnar, and forth from the teeth he spoke :
" It is e'en as I said, King Gunnar : all eves she stands by the gate
The coming of her kindred through the dusky tide to wait :
Each day in the dawn she ariseth, and saith the time is at hand

When the feet of the Niblung War-Kings shall tread King Atli's land :
Then she praiseth the wings of the dove, and the wings of the wayfaring crane
'Gainst whom the wind prevails not, and the tempest driveth in vain ;
And she praiseth the waves of the ocean, how they toil and toil and blend,
Till they break on the strand belovèd, and the Niblung earth in the end."

He spake, and the song rose upward and the wine of Kings was poured,
And Gunnar heard in the wall-nook how the wind went forth abroad,
And he dreamed, and beheld the ocean, and all kingdoms of the earth,
And the world lay fair before him and his worship and his worth.

Then again spake the Eastland liar: "O King, I may not hide
That great things in the land of Atli thy mighty soul abide ;
For the King is spent and war-weak, nor rejoiceth more in strife ;
And his sons, the children of Gudrun, now look their first on life :
For this end meseems is his bidding, that no worser men than ye
May sit in the throne of Atli and the place where he wont to be."

In the tuneful hall of the Niblungs that Eastland liar spake,
And he heard the song of the mighty o'er Gunnar's musing break,
And his cold heart gladdened within him as man cried out to man,
And fair 'twixt horn and beaker the red wine bubbled and ran.

At last spake Gunnar the Niblung as his hand on the cup he laid :
" A great king craveth our coming, and no more shall he be gainsayed :
We will go to look on Atli, though the Gods and the Goths forbid ;
Nought worse than death meseemeth on the Niblungs' path is hid,
And this shall the high Gods see to, but I to the Niblung name,
And the day of deeds to accomplish, and the gathering-in of fame."

Up he stood with the bowl in his right-hand, and mighty and great he was,
And he cried : " Now let the beakers adown the benches pass ;
Let us drink dear draughts and glorious, though the last farewell it be,

And this draught that I drink have sundered my father's house and me."

He drank, and all men drank with him, and the hearts of the Earls arose,
As of them that snatch forth glory from the deadly wall of foes :
With the joy of life were they drunken and no man knew for why,
And the voice of their exultation rose up in an awful cry ;
—It is joy in the mouths that utter, it is hope in the hearts that crave,
And think of no gainsaying, and remember nought to save ;
But without the women hearken, and the hearts within them sink ;
And they say : What then betideth that our lords forbear to drink,
And wail and weep in the night-tide and cry the Gods to aid ?
Why then are the Kings tormented, and the warriors' hearts afraid ?

Then the deadened sound sweeps landward, and the hearts of the field-folk fail,
And they say : Is there death in the Burg, that thence goeth the cry and the wail?
Lo, lo, the feast-hall's windows ! blood-red through the dark they shine :
Why is weeping the song of the Niblungs, and blood the warrior's wine ?

But therein are the torches tossing, and the shields of men upborne,
And the death-blades yet unbloodied cast up 'twixt bowl and horn,
And all rest of heart is departed as men speak of the mirk-wood's ways,
And the fame of outland countries, and the green sea's troublous days.

But Gunnar arose o'er the people, as a mighty King he spake :
"O ye of the house of Giuki that are joyous for my sake,
What then shall be left to the Niblungs if we return no more ?
Then let the wolves be warders of the Niblungs' gathered store !
On the hearth let the worm creep over where the fire now flares aloft !
And the adder coil in the chambers where the Niblung wives sleep soft !
Let the master of the pine-wood roll huge in the Niblung porch,
And the moon through the broken rafters be the Niblungs' feastful torch !"

Glad they cried on the glorious Gunnar ; for they saw the love in his eyes,

And with joy and wine were they drunken, and his words passed over the wise,
As oft o'er the garden lilies goes the rising thunder-wind,
And they know no other summer, and no spring that was they mind.

But Hogni speaketh to Knefrud: "Lo, Gunnar's word is said:
How fares it, lord, with Gudrun? remembereth she the dead?"

Then the liar laughed out and answered: "Ye shall go tomorrow morn;
The man to turn back Gunnar shall never now be born:
Each day-spring the white Gudrun on Sigurd's glory cries,
All eves she wails on Sigurd when the fair sun sinks and dies!"

"Thou sayest sooth," said Hogni, "one day we twain shall wend
To the gate of the Eastland Atli, that our tale may have an end.
Long time have I looked for the journey, and marvelled at the day,
With what eyes I shall look on Sigurd, what words his mouth shall say."

Then he raiseth the cup for Gunnar, and men see his glad face shine
As he crieth hail and glory o'er the bubbles of the wine;
And they drink to the lives of the brethren, and men of the latter earth
May not think of the height of their hall-glee, or measure out their mirth:
So they feast in the undark even to the midmost of the night,
Till at last, with sleep unwearied, they weary with delight,
And pass forth to the beds blue-covered, and leave the hearth acold:
They sleep; in the hall grown silent scarce glimmereth now the gold:
For the moon from the world is departed, and grey clouds draw across,
To hide the dawn's first promise and deepen earthly loss.
The lone night draws to its death, and never another shall fall
On those sons of the feastful warriors in the Niblungs' holy hall.

*How the Niblungs fare to the Land of **King Atli**.*

Now when the house was silent, and all men in slumber **lay,**
And yet two hours were lacking of the dawning-tide of day,
The sons of his foster-mother doth the heart-wise Hogni find ;
In the **dead night,** speaking softly, he showeth them his mind,
And they wake **and** hearken and heed him, and arise from the bolster **blue,**
Nor aught **do their** stout hearts falter at the deed he bids them do.
So he and they go softly while all men slumber and sleep,
And **they enter the treasure-houses, and come to their** midmost heap ;
But so rich in the night it glimmers that **the** brethren hold their breath,
While Hogni laugheth upon it :—long it lay **on** the Glittering Heath,
Long it lay in the house of Reidmar, long it lay 'neath the waters wan ;
But no long while hath it tarried in the houses and dwellings of man.

Nor long these linger before **it** ; they **set** their hands to the toil,
And uplift the Bed of the Serpent, the Seed of murder and broil ;
No **word** they speak in their labour, **but bear out load on load**
To great wains that out in the fore-court for the coming Gold **abode :**
Most huge were the men, far mightier than the mightiest **fashioned now,**
But the salt sweat dimmed their eyesight and flooded cheek and brow
Ere half the work was accomplished ; and by then the laden wains
Came groaning forth from the gateway, dawn drew on o'er the plains ;
And the ramparts of the people, those walls high-built of old,
Stood grey as the bones of a battle in a dale few folk behold :
But in haste they goad the yoke-beasts, and press **on and make** no speech,
Though the hearts are proud within them and their eyes laugh each at each.

No **great** way down from the burg-gate, anigh to the hallowed field,
There lieth a lake in the river as round as Odin's shield,
A black pool huge and awful : ten long-ships of the most
Therein might wager battle, and the sunken should be lost

Beyond all hope of diver, yea, beyond the plunging lead ;
On either side its rock-walls rise up to a mighty head,
But by green slopes from the meadows 'tis easy drawing near
To the brow whence the dark-grey rampart to the water goeth sheer :
'Tis as if the Niblung River had cleft the grave-mound through
Of the mightiest of all Giants ere the Gods' work was to do ;
And indeed men well might deem it, that fearful sights lie hid
Beneath the unfathomed waters, the place to all forbid ;
No stream the black deep showeth, few winds may search its face,
And the silver-scaled sea-farers love nought its barren space.

There now the Niblung War-king and the foster-brethren twain
Lead up their golden harvest and stay it wain by wain,
Till they hang o'er the rim scarce balanced : no glance they cast below
To the black and awful waters well known from long ago,
But they cut the yoke-beasts' traces, and drive them down the slopes,
Who rush through the widening daylight, and bellow forth their hopes
Of the straw-stall and the barley : but the Niblungs turn once more,
Hard toil the warrior cart-carles for the garnering of their store,
And shoulder on the wain-wheels o'er the edge of the grimly wall,
And stand upright to behold it, how the waggons plunge and fall.

Down then and whirling outward the ruddy Gold fell forth,
As a flame in the dim grey morning, flashed out a kingdom's worth,
Then the waters roared above it, the wan water and the foam
Flew up o'er the face of the rock-wall as the tinkling Gold fell home,
Unheard, unseen for ever, a wonder and a tale,
Till the last of earthly singers from the sons of men shall fail :
Then the face of the further waters a widening ripple rent
And forth from hollow places strange sounds as of talking went,
And loud laughed Hogni in answer ; but not so long he stayed
As that half the oily ripple in long sleepy coils was laid,
Or the lapping fallen silent in the water-beaten caves;

Scarce streamward yet were drifting the foam-heaps o'er the waves,
When betwixt the foster-brethren down the slopes King Hogni strode
Toward the ancient Burg of his fathers, as a man that casteth a load:
No word those fellows had spoken since he whispered low and light
O'er the beds of the foster-brethren in the dead hour of the night,
But his face was proud and glorious as he strode the war-gate through,
And went up to his kingly chamber, and the golden bed he knew,
And lay down and slept by his help-mate as a play-spent child might sleep
In some franklin's wealthy homestead, in the room the nurses keep.

Nought the sun on that morn delayeth, but light o'er the world's face flies,
And awake by the side of King Hogni the wedded woman lies,
And her bosom is weary with sighing, and her eyes with dream-born tears,
And a sound as of all confusion is ever in her ears:
Then she turneth and crieth to Hogni, as she layeth a hand on his breast:
"Wake, wake, thou son of Giuki! save thy speech-friend all unrest!"

Then he waketh up as a child that hath slept in the summer grass,
And he saith: "What tidings, O Bera, what tidings come to pass?"

She saith, "Wilt thou wend with Gunnar to Atli over the main?"

Said Hogni: "Hast thou not heard it, how rich we shall come again?"

"Ye shall never come back," said Bera, "ye shall die by the inner sea."

"Yea, here or there," said Hogni, "my death no doubt shall be."

"O Hogni," she said, "forbear it, that snare of the Eastland wrong!
In the health and the wealth of the sunlight at home mayst thou tarry for long:
For waking or sleeping I dreamed, and dreaming, the tokens I saw."

"Oft," he said, "in the hands of the house-wife comes the crock by its fatal flaw:

An hundred earls shall slay me, or the fleeing night-thief's shaft,
The sickness that wasteth cities, or the unstrained summer draught :
Now as mighty shall be King Atli and the gathered Eastland force
As the fly in the wine desired, or the weary stumbling horse."

She said : " Wilt thou stay in the land, lest the noble faint and fail,
And the Gods have nought to tell of in the ending of the tale ?
O King, save thou thine hand-maid, lest the bloom of Kings decay ! '

He said : " Good yet were the earth, though all we should die in a day :
But so fares it with you, ye women : when your husband or brother shall die,
Ye deem that the world shall perish, and the race of man go by."

" Sure then is thy death," she answered, " for I saw the Eastland flood
Break over the Burg of the Niblungs, and fill the hall with blood."

He said : " Shall we wade the meadows to the feast of Atli the King ?
Then the blood-red blossoming sorrel about our legs shall cling."

Said Bera : " I saw thee coming with the face of other days ;
But the flame was in thy raiment, and thy kingly cloak was ablaze."

" How else," said he, " O woman, wouldst thou have a Niblung stride,
Save in ruddy gold sun-lighted, through the house of Atli's pride ? "

She said : " I beheld King Atli midst the place of sacrifice
And the holy grove of the Eastland in a king's most hallowed guise :
Then I looked, as with laughter triumphant he laid his gift in the fire,
And lo, 'twas the heart of Hogni, and the heart of my desire ;
But he turned and looked upon me as I sickened with fear and with love,
And I saw the guile of the greedy, and with speechless sleep I strove,
And had cried out curses against him, but my gaping throat was hushed,
Till the light of a deedless dawning o'er dream and terror rushed ;

And there wert thou lying beside me, though but little joy it seemed,
For thou wert but an image unstable of the days before I dreamed."

Quoth Hogni, "Shall I arede it ?   Seems it not meet to thee
That the heart and the love of the Niblungs in Atli's hand should be,
When he stands by the high Gods' altars, and uplifts his heart for the tide
When the kings of the world-great people to the Eastland house shall ride?
Nay, Bera, wilt thou be weeping ? but parting-fear is this ;
Doubt not we shall come back happy from the house of Atli's bliss :
At least, when a king's hand offers all honour and great weal,
Wouldst thou have me strive to unclasp it to show the hidden steel ?
With evil will I meet evil when it draweth exceeding near ;
But oft have I heard of evil, whose father was but fear,
And his mother lust of living, and nought will I deal with it,
Lest the past, and those deeds of my doing be as straw when the fire is lit.
Lo now, O Daughter of Kings, let us rise in the face of the day,
And be glad in the summer morning when the kindred ride on their way ;
For tears beseem not king-folk, nor a heart made dull with dreams,
But to hope, if thou mayst, for ever, and to fear nought, well beseems."

There the talk falls down between them, and they rise in the morn, they twain,
And bright-faced wend through the dwelling of the Niblungs' glory and gain.

Meanwhile awakeneth Gunnar, and looks on the wife by his side,
And saith : "Why weepest thou, Glaumvor, what evil now shall betide ?"

She said : " I was waking and dreamed, or I slept and saw the truth ;
The Norns are hooded and angry, and the Gods have forgotten their ruth."
                                                                [kind ;
" Speak, sweet-mouthed woman," said Gunnar, "if the Norns are hard, I am
Though even the King of the Niblungs may loose not where they bind."

She said : " Wilt thou go unto Atli and enter the Burg of the East ?

Wilt thou leave the house of the faithful, and turn to the murderer's feast?"

"It is e'en as certain," said Gunnar, "as though I knocked at his gate,
If the winds and waters stay not, or death, or the dealings of Fate."

"Woe worth the while!" said Glaumvor, "then I talk with the dead indeed:
And why must I tarry behind thee afar from the Niblungs' Need?"

He said: "Thou wert heavy-hearted last night for the parting-tide; ·
And alone in the dreamy country thy soul would needs abide,
And see not the King that loves thee, nor remember the might of his hand;
So thou falledst a prey unholpen to the lies of the dreamy land."

"Ah, would they were lies," said Glaumvor, "for not the worst was this:
There thou wert in the holy high-seat mid the heart of the Niblung bliss,
And a sword was borne into our midmost, and its point and its edge were red,
And at either end the wood-wolves howled out in the day of dread;
With that sword wert thou smitten, O Gunnar, and the sharp point pierced
And the kin were all departed, and no face of man I knew: [thee through:
Then I strove to flee and might not; for day grew dark and strange,
And no moonrise and no morning the eyeless mirk would change."

"Such are dreams of the night," said Gunnar, "that lovers oft perplex,
When the sundering hour is coming with the cares that entangle and vex.
Yet if there be more, fair woman, when a king speaks loving words,
May I cast back words of anger, and the threat of grinded swords?"

"O yet wouldst thou tarry," said Glaumvor, "in the fair sun-lighted day!
Nor give thy wife to another, nor cast thy kingdom away."

"Of what king of the people," said Gunnar, "hast thou known it written or told,
That the word was born in the even which the morrow should withhold?"

"Alas, alas!" said Glaumvor, "then all is over and done!
For I dreamed of the hall of the Niblungs at the setting of the sun,
How dead women came in thither no worse than queens arrayed,   [laid,
Who passed by the earls of the Niblungs, and their hands on thy gown-skirt
And hailed thee fair for their fellow, and bade thee come to their hall.
O bethink thee, King of the Niblungs, what tidings shall befall!"

"Yea, shall they befall?" said Gunnar, "then who am I to strive
Against the change of my life-days, while the Gods on high are alive?
I shall ride as my heart would have me; let the Gods bestir them then,
And raise up another people in the stead of the Niblung men:
But at home shalt thou sit, King's Daughter, in the keeping of the Fates,
And be blithe with the men of thy people and the guest within thy gates,
Till thou know of our glad returning to the holy house and dear
Or the fall of Giuki's children, and a tale that all shall hear.
Arise and do on gladness, lest the clouds roll on and lower
O'er the heavy hearts of the people in the Niblungs' parting hour."

So he spake, and his love rejoiced her, and they rose in the face of the day,
And no seeming shadow of evil on those bright-eyed King-folk lay.

Thus stirreth the house of the Niblungs, and awakeneth unto life;
And were there any envy, or doubt that breedeth strife,
'Twixt friends or kin or brethren, 'twas healed that self-same morn,
And peace and loving-kindness o'er all the house was borne,

Now arrayed are the earls and the warriors, and into the hall they come
When the morning sun is shining through the heart of their ancient home;
And lo, how the allwise Grimhild is set in the golden seat,
The first of the way-fain warriors, and the first of the wives to greet;
In the raiment of old she sitteth, aloft in the kingly place,
And all men marvel to see her and the glory of her face.

So all is dight for departing and the helms of the Niblung lords
Shine close as a river of fire o'er the hilts of hidden swords :
About and around are the women; and who e'er hath been heavy of heart,
If their hearts are light this morning when their fairest shall depart ?
They hear the steeds in the forecourt ; from the rampart of the wall
Comes the cry and noise of the warders as man to man doth call ;
For the young give place to the old, and the strong carles labour to show
The last-learned craft of battle to their fathers ere they go.
There is mocking and mirth and laughter as men tell to the ancient sires
Of the four-sheared shaft of the gathering, and the horn, and the beaconing
        fires.
Woe's me ! but the women laugh not : do they hope that the sun may be
And the journey of the Niblungs a little while delayed ?   [stayed,
Or is not their hope the rather, that they do but dream in the night,
And that they shall awake in a little with the land's life faring aright ?
Ah, fair and fresh is the morning as ever a season hath been,
And the nourishing sun shines glorious on the toil of carle and quean,
And the wealth of the land desired, and all things are alive and awake ;
Let them wait till the even bringeth sweet rest for hearts that ache.

Lo now, a stir by the doorway, and men see how great and grand
Come the Kings of Giuki begotten, all-armed, and hand in hand :
Where then shall the world behold them, such champions clad in steel,
Such hearts so free and bounteous, so wise for the people's weal ?
Where then shall the world see such-like, if these must die as the mean,
And fall as lowly people, and their days be no more seen ?
They go forth fair and softly as they wend to the seat of the Kings,
And they smile in their loving-kindness as they talk of bygone things.
Are they not as the children of Giuki, that fared afield erewhile
In hope without contention, mid the youth that knew no guile ?
Their wedded wives are beside them with faces proud and fair,
That smile, if the lips smile only, for the Eastland liar is there.
Fain the women are of those Brethren, and they seem so gay and kind.

That again the hope upspringeth of their lords abiding behind.

But Hogni spake to his brother, and they looked on the liar's son,
And clear ran King Gunnar's laughter as the summer waters run ;   [breath,
Then the Queens' hearts fainted within them, and with pain they drew their
For they knew that the King was merry and laughed in the face of death.

Fair now on the ancient high-seat, and the heart of the Niblung pride,
Stand those lovely lords of Giuki with their wedded wives beside,
And Gunnar cries : "O maidens, let the cup be in every hand,
For this morn for a little season we leave our fathers' land,
And love we leave behind us, and love abroad we bear,
And these twain shall meet in a little, and their meeting-tide be fair :
Rejoice, O Niblung children, be glad o'er the parting cup !
For meseems if the heavens were falling, our spears should hold them up."

Then he leaped adown from the high-seat and amidst his men he stood,
And the very joy of God-folk ran through the Niblung blood,
And the glee of them that die not : there they drink in their mighty hall,
And glad on the ancient fathers, and the sons of God they call :
The hope of their hearts goes upward in the last most awful voice,
And once more the quivering timbers of the Niblung home rejoice.

But exceeding proud sits Grimhild, and so wondrous is her state
That men deem they have never seen her so glorious and so great,
And she speaks, when again in the feast-hall is there silence save of the mail
And the whispered voice of women, as they tell their latest tale :

"Go forth, O Kings, to dominion, and the crown of all your might,
And the tale from of old foreordered ere the day was begotten of night.
For all this is the work of the Norns, though ye leave a woman behind
Who hath toiled and toiled in the darkness, the road of fate to find :
Go glad, O children of Giuki ; though scarce ye wot indeed

Of the labour of your mother to win your glory's meed.
Farewell, farewell, O children, till ye get you back again
To her that bore you in darkness, and brought you forth in pain !
Cast wide the doors for the King-folk, ring out O harpstrings now !
For the best e'er born of woman go forth with cloudless brow.
Be glad O ancient lintel, O threshold of the door,
For such another parting shall earth behold no more !'

She ceased, and no voice gave answer save the voice of smitten harps,
As the hands of the music-weavers went o'er their golden warps ;
Then high o'er the warriors towering, as the king-leek o'er the grass,
Out into the world of sunlight through the door those Brethren pass,
And all the host of the warriors, the women's silent woe,
The steel, and the feet soft-falling o'er the ancient threshold go,
While all alone on the high-seat the god-born Grimhild sits :
There hearkeneth she steeds' neighing, and the champing of the bits,
And the clash of steel-clad champions, as at last they leap aloft,
And cries and women's weeping 'mid the music breathing soft ;
Then the clattering of the horse-hoofs, and the echo of the gate
With the wakened sword-song singing o'er departure of the great,
Till the many mingled voices are swallowed up and stilled,
And all the air by seeming with an awful sound is filled,
The cry of the Niblung trumpet, as men reach the unwalled space :
So whiles in a mighty city, and a many-peopled place,
When the rain falls down 'mid the babble, nor ceaseth rattle of wheels,
And with din of wedding joy-bells the minster steeple reels,
Lo, God sends down his thunder, and all else is hushed as then,
And it is as the world's beginning, and before the birth of men.

Long sitteth the god-born Grimhild till all is silent there,
For afar down the meadows with the host all people fare ;
Then bitter groweth her visage, in the hush she crieth and saith :

"O ye—whom then shall I cry **on, ye that hunt my sons unto death,**
And overthrow our glory, and bring our labour to nought—
Ye Gods, ye had fashioned the greatest, **and** to make them greater I wrought,
And to strengthen your hands for the battle, and uplift your hearts for the end:
But ye, ye have fashioned confusion, and the great with **the** little ye blend,
Till no more on the **earth shall be living** the mighty that **mock at your** death,
Till like the leaves **men tremble, like the dry** leaves quake at a breath.
I **have wrought for your lives and** your glory, and for **this have I**
     strengthened my guile,
That **the earth your** hands uplifted might endure, nor pass in a while
Like the clouds of latter morning that melt in the **first of the night.**"

She rose up great and dreadful, **and stood on the floor** upright,
And cast up her hands to the roof-tree, and cried aloud and said:

"Woe to you that have made me for nothing! for the house of the Niblungs is
Empty and dead as the desert, where the sun is idle and vain   [dead,
And no hope hath the dew to cherish, and **no deed abideth the rain** !"

She falleth aback in the high seat, and the eagles cry from aloof,
While Grimhild's eyes wide-open stare up at the Niblung roof:
But they see **not,** nought are they doing to feed her fear or desire;
And her heart, the forge of sorrow, dead, cold, is its baneful fire;
And her **cunning hand** is helpless, for her hopeless soul is gone;
Far off belike **it drifteth from the** waste her labour won.

Fair now through midmost ocean King Gunnar's dragons run,
And the green hills round about them gleam glorious with the sun;
The keels roll down the sea-dale, **and welter up the steep,**
And o'er the brow hang quivering ere again they take the leap;
For the west wind pipes behind them, and no **land** is on their lea,
As the mightiest of earth's peoples sails down the summer sea:
And as eager **as the** west-wind, no duller than **the foam**

They spread all sails to the breezes, and seek their glory home :
Six days they sail the sea-flood, and the seventh dawn of day
Up-heaveth a new country, a land far-off and grey ;
Then Knefrud biddeth heed it, and he saith : " Lo, the Eastland shore,
And the land few ships have sailed to, by the mirk-wood covered o'er."

Then riseth the cry and the shouting as the golden beaks they turn,
For all hearts for the land of cities, and the hall of Atli yearn :
But a little after the noontide is the Niblung host embayed,
And betwixt the sheltering nesses the ocean-wind is laid :
No whit they brook delaying : but their noblest and their best
Toss up the shaven oar-blades, and toil and mock at rest :
Full swift they skim the swan-mead till the tall masts quake and reel,
And the oaken sea-burgs quiver from bulwark unto keel
It is Gunnar goes the foremost with the tiller in his hand,
And beside him standeth Knefrud and laughs on Atli's land :
And so fair are the dragons driven, that by ending of the day
On the beach by the ebb left naked the sea-beat keels they lay :
Then they look aloft from the foreshore, and lo, King Atli's steeds
On the brow of the mirk-wood standing, well dight for the warriors' needs,
The red and the roan together, and the dapple-grey and the black ;
Nor bits nor silken bridles, nor golden cloths they lack,
And the horse-lads of King Atli with that horse-array are blent,
And their shout of salutation o'er the oozy sand is sent :
Then no more will the Niblungs tarry when they see that ready band
But they leap adown from the long-ships, and waist-deep they wade the strand,
And they in their armour of onset, beshielded, and sword by the side,
E'en as men returning homeward to their loves and their friends that abide.
The first of all goeth Gunnar, and Hogni the wise cometh after,
And wringeth the sea from his kirtle ; and all men hearken his laughter,
As his feet on the earth stand firm, and the sun in the west goeth down,
And the Niblungs stand on the foreshore 'twixt the sea and the mirk-wood
                                                            [brown.

For no meat there they linger, and they tarry for no sleep,
But aloft to the golden saddles those Giuki's children leap,
And forth from the side of the sea-flood they ride the mirk-wood's ways.
Loud then is the voice of King Hogni and he sets forth Atli's praise,
As they ride through the night of the tree-boughs till the earthly night prevails,
And along the desert sea-strand the wind of ocean wails.

There none hath tethered the dragons, or inboard handled the oars,
And the tide of the sea cometh creeping along the stranger-shores,
Till those golden dragons are floated, and their unmanned oars awash
In the sandy waves of the shallows, from stem to tiller clash :
Then setteth a wind from the shore, and the night is waxen a-cold,
And seaward drift the long-ships with their raiment and vessels of gold,
And their Gods with mastery carven : and who knoweth the story to tell,
If their wrack came ever to shoreward in some place where fishers dwell,
Or sank in midmost ocean, and lay on the sea-floor wan
Where the pale sea-goddess singeth o'er the bane of many a man ?

Atli speaketh with the Niblungs.

Three days the Niblung warriors the ways of the mirk-wood ride
Till they come to a land of cities and the peopled country-side,
And the land's-folk run from their labour, and the merchants throng the street
And the lords of many a city the stranger kings would meet.
But nought will the Niblungs tarry ; swift through Atli's weal they wend,
For their hearts are exceeding eager for their journey's latter end.
Three days they ride that country, and many a city leave,
But the fourth dawn mighty mountains by the inner sea upheave.
Then they ride a little further, and Atli's burg they see
With the feet of the mountains mingled above the flowery lea,
And yet a little further, and lo, its long white wall,
And its high-built guarded gateways, and its towers o'erhung and tall ;

And ever all along them the glittering spear-heads run,
As the sparks of the white wood-ashes when the cooking-fire is done.

Then they look to the right and the left hand, and see no folk astir,
And no reek from the homestead chimneys ; and no toil of men they hear
But the hook hangs lone in the vineyard, and the scythe is lone in the hay,
The bucket thirsts by the well-side, the void cart cumbers the way.
Then doubt on the war-host falleth, and they think : Well were we then,
When once we rode in the Westland and saw the brown-faced men
Peer through the hawthorn hedges as the Niblung host went by.
Yet they laugh and make no semblance of any fear drawn nigh.
Yea, Knefrud looked upon them, and with chilly voice he spake :

"Now his guests doth Atli honour, and yet more will he do for your sake,
Who hath hidden all his people, and holdeth his vassals at home
On the day that the mighty Niblungs adown his highway come,
Lest men fear as the finders of Gods, and tremble and cumber the ways,
And the voice of the singers fail them to sing of the Niblungs' praise."

Men laughed as his voice they hearkened, and none bade turn again,
But the swords in the scabbards rattled as they rode with loosened rein.

Now they ride in the Burg-gate's shadow from out the sunlit fields,
Till the spears aloft are hidden and Atli's painted shields ;
And no captain cries from the rampart, nor soundeth any horn,
And the doors of oak and iron are shut this merry morn :
Then the Niblungs leap from the saddle, and the threats of earls arise,
And the wrath of Kings' defenders is waxing in their eyes ;
But Knefrud looketh and laugheth, and he saith :
                                                  "So is Atli fain
Of the glory of the Niblungs and their honour's utmost gain :
By no feet but yours this morning will he have his threshold trod,
Nay, not by the world's most glorious, nay not by a wandering God."

Then Hogni looked on Knefrud as the bodily death shall gaze
On the last of the Kings of men-folk in the last of the latter days,
And he caught a staff from his saddle, a mighty axe of war,
And stood most huge of all men in face of Atli's door,
And upreared the axe against it with such wondrous strokes and great,
That the iron-knitted marvel hung shattered in the gate :
Through the rent poured the Niblung children, and in Atli's burg they stood,
With none to bid them welcome, or ask them what they would.

But Hogni turned upon Knefrud, and spake : " I said, time was, ·
That we twain should ride out hither to bring a deed to pass :
And now one more deed abideth, and then no more for thee,
And another and another, and no more deeds for me."

'Gainst the liar's eyes one moment flashed out the axe-head's sheen,
And then was the face of Knefrud as though it ne'er had been,
And his gay-clad corpse lay glittering on the causeway in the sun.

No man cried out on Hogni or asked of the deed so done,
But their shielded ranks they marshalled and through Atli's burg they strode :
There they see the merchant's dwelling, the rich man's fair abode,
The halls of doom, and the market, the loom and the smithying-booth,
The stall for the wares of the outlands, the temples high and smooth :
But all is hushed and empty, and no child of man they meet
As they thread the city's tangle, and enter street on street,
And leave the last forgotten, and of the next know nought.

So through the silent city by the Norns their feet are brought,
Till lo, on a hill's uprising a huge house they behold,
And a hall with gates all brazen, and roof of ruddy gold :
Then they know the house of Atli, and they trow that sooth it is
That the Lord of such a dwelling may give his guest-folk bliss :
Then they loosen the swords in their scabbards, and upraise a mighty shout,

And the trumpet of the Niblungs through the lonely street rings out
And stilleth the wind in the wall-nook : but hark, as its echoes die,
How forth from that hall of the Eastlands comes the sound of minstrelsy,
And the brazen doors swing open : but the Niblungs are at the door,
And the bidden guests of Atli o'er the fateful threshold pour ;
There the music faileth before them, till its sound is over and done,
And fair in the city behind them lies the flood of the morning sun :
No man of the Niblungs murmureth, none biddeth turn aback
And still their hands are empty, and sleep the edges of wrack.

Huge, dim is the hall of Atli, and faint and far aloof,
As stars in the misty even, yet hang the lamps in the roof,
And but little daylight toucheth the walls and the hangings of gold :
No King and no earl-folk's children do the bidden guests behold,
Till they look aloft to the high-seat, and lo, a woman alone,
A white queen crowned, and silent as the ancient shapen stone
That men find in the dale deserted, as beneath the moon they wend,
When they weary even to slumber, and the journey draws to an end.
Chill then are the hearts of the warriors, for they know how they look on a
That Gudrun well-belovèd of the days that once have been ;   [queen,
Then were men that murmured on Sigurd, and as in some dream of the night
They looked, but the left hand failed them, and there came no help from the
                                                                [right.
But forth stood the mighty Gunnar, and men heard his kingly voice
As he spake : "O child of my father, I see thee again and rejoice,
Though I wot not where I have wended, or where thou dwellest on earth,
Or if this be the dead men's dwelling, or the hall of Atli's mirth !"

She stirred not, nothing she answered : but forth stood Hogni the King,
Clear, sharp, in the house of the stranger did the voice of the fearless ring :
"O sister, O daughter of Giuki, O child of my mother's womb,
By what death shall the Niblungs perish, what day is the day of their doom ?"

Forth then from the lips of Gudrun a dreadful voice was borne :
" Ye shall die to-day, O brethren, at the hands of a King forsworn. "

As she spake the outer door-leaves clashed to with a mighty sound,
And the outer air was troubled with a new noise gathering around :
As of leaves in the midmost summer ere the dusk of the even warm,
When the winds in the hillsides gathered go forth before the storm ;
Men abode, and a wicket opened on the feast-hall's inner side
And the Niblungs looked for the coming of King Atli in his pride :
But one man entered only, and he thin and old and spare,
A swordless man and a little—yet was King Atli there.
He looked not once on the Niblungs, but forth to the high-seat went,
And stood aloof from Gudrun with his eyes to the hall-floor bent :
Thence came a voice from his lips, and men heard, for the hush was great,
And the hearts of the bold were astonished 'neath the overhanging fate.

" Ye are come, O Kings of the Niblungs, ye are come, O slayers of men !
But how great, and where is the ransom that shall buy your departure again?"

Then spake the wise-heart Hogni : " Do the bidden guests so long
To depart to the night and the silence from the fire and the wine and the song?
Fear not ! the feast shall be merry, and here we abide in thine hall,
Till thou and the great feast-master shall bid the best befall."

There were cries of men in the city, there was clang and clatter of steel,
And high cried the thin-voiced Atli, the lord of the Eastland weal :
" Ye are come in your pride, O Niblungs ; but this day of days is mine :
Will ye die? will ye live and be little?   Hear now the token and sign !"

Great then grew the voices without, with one name was the city filled,
Yea, all the world it might be, and all sounds of the earth were stilled
With that cry of the name of Atli : but Gunnar stood for a space
Till the cry was something sunken, then he put back the helm from his face

And spread out his hands before him, and his hands were empty and bare
As he stood in the front of the Niblungs like a great God smiling and fair ·

"We shall live and never be little, we shall die and be masters of fame :
I know not thy will, O Atli, nor what thou wouldst with thy name."

"Ye shall know my will," said Atli, "ye shall do it, or do no more
The deeds of the days of the living : ye shall render the garnered store,
Ye shall give forth the Gold of Sigurd, the wealth of the uttermost strand."

"To give a gift," cried Hogni, "we came to King Atli's land :
Tomorn for a little season thou shalt be the richest fool
Of all kings ever told of ; and the rest let the high Gods rule."

"O King of the East," said Gunnar, "great gifts for thee draw nigh,
But the treasure of the Niblungs in their guarded house shall lie. '

" What then will ye do ?" quoth Atli ; "have ye seen the fish in the net ? "

" Eve telleth of deeds," said Gunnar, "and it is but the morning as yet."

Said Atli : " Yea, will ye die ? are there no deeds left you to do ? "

"We shall smite with the sword," said the Niblung, "and tomorn will we
[journey anew."
" Craftsmaster Hogni," said Atli, "where then are the shifts of the wise ?"

Said Hogni : "To smite with the sword, and go glad from the country of lies."

"So died the fool," said Atli, "as Hogni dieth today."

"Smote the blind and the aimless," said Hogni, "and Baldur passed away."

Said Atli : " Yet may ye live in the wholesome light of the sun,
And your latter days be as plenteous as the deeds your hands have done."

" Dost thou hearken, O sword," said Gunnar, " and yet thou liest in peace ?
When then wilt thou look on the daylight, that the words of the mocker may
                                               [cease ? "
" Thou, Hogni the wise," said Atli, " art thou weary of wisdom and lore,
Wilt thou die with these fools of the sword, and be mocked mid the blind
                                               [of the war ? "
" Many things have I learned," said Hogni, " but today's task, easy it is ;
For men die every hour and they wage no master for this.
—Get hence, thou evil King, thou liar and traitor of kings,
Lest the edge of my sword be thy portion and not the ruddy rings ! "

Then Atli shrank from before him, and the eyes of his intent,
And no more words he cast them, but forth from the hall he went,
And again were the Niblung children alone in the hall of their foes
With the wan and silent woman : but without great clamour arose,
And the clashing of steel against steel, and the crying of man unto man,
And the wind of that summer morning through the Eastland banners ran :
Then so loud o'er all was winded a mighty horn of fight,
That unheard were the shouts of the Niblungs as Gunnar's sword leapt white.
But Hogni turned to the great-one who the Niblung trumpet bore,
And he took the mighty metal, and kissed the brass of war,
And its shattering blast went forward, and beat back from the gable-wall
And shook the ancient timbers, and the carven work of the hall :
Then it was to the Niblung warriors as their very hearts they heard
Cry out, not glad nor sorry, nor hoping, nor afeard,
But touched by the hand of Odin, smit with foretaste of the day,
When the fire shall burn up fooling, and the veil shall fall away ;
When bare-faced, all unmingled, shall the evil stand in the light,
And men's deeds shall be nothing doubtful, nor the foe that they shall smite.

In the hall was the voice of the trumpet, but therein might it nowise abide,
But over burg and lealand it spread full far and wide,
And strong men quaked **as they heard** it in the guarded **chamber of stone**.
And the lord of weaponed kinsfolk was as one that sitteth alone
In a land by the foeman wasted, and no man to his neighbour spoke,
But they thought on the death of Atli and the slaughter of the folk.

Of the Battle in Atli's Hall.

Ye shall know that in Atli's feast-hall on the side that joined the house
Were many carven doorways whose work was glorious
With marble stones and gold-work, and their doors of beaten brass :
Lo now, in the merry morning how the story cometh to pass !
—While the echoes of the trumpet yet fill the people's ears,
And Hogni casts by the war-horn, and his Dwarf-wrought sword uprears,
All those doors aforesaid open, and in pour the streams of steel,
The best of the Eastland champions, the bold men of Atli's weal :
They raise no cry of battle nor cast forth threat of woe,
And their helmed and hidden faces from each other none may know :
Then a light in the hall ariseth, and the fire of battle runs
All adown the front of the Niblungs in the face of the mighty-ones ;
All eyes are set upon them, hard drawn is every breath,
Ere the foremost points be mingled and death be blent with death.
—**All eyes** save the eyes of Hogni ; but e'en as the edges meet,
He turneth about for a moment to the gold of the kingly seat,
Then aback to the front of battle ; there then, as the lightning-flash
Through the dark night showeth the city when the clouds of heaven clash,
And the gazer shrinketh backward, yet he seeth from end **to end**
The street and the merry market, and the windows of his friend,
And the pavement where his footsteps yestre'en returning trod,
Now white and changed and dreadful 'neath the threatening voice of God ;
So Hogni seeth Gudrun, **and the** face he used to know,

Unspeakable, unchanging, with white unknitted brow,
With half-closed lips untrembling, with deedless hands and cold
Laid still on knees that stir not, and the linen's moveless fold.

Turned Hogni unto the spear-wall, and smote from where he stood,
And hewed with his sword two-handed as the axe-man in a wood :
Before his sword was a champion and the edges clave to the chin,
And the first man fell in the feast-hall of those that should fall therein.
Then man with man was dealing, and the Niblung host of war
Was swept by the leaping iron, as the rock anigh the shore
By the ice-cold waves of winter : yet a moment Gunnar stayed,
As high in his hand unbloodied he shook his awful blade ;
And he cried :
                    "O Eastland champions, do ye behold it here,
The sword of the ancient Giuki ?   Fall on and have no fear,
But slay and be slain and be famous, if your master's will it be !
Yet are we the blameless Niblungs, and bidden guests are we :
So forbear, if ye wander hood-winked, nor for nothing slay and be slain ;
For I know not what to tell you of the dead that live again."

So he saith in the midst of the foemen with his war-flame reared on high,
But all about and around him goes up a bitter cry
From the iron men of Atli, and the bickering of the steel
Sends a roar up to the roof-ridge, and the Niblung war-ranks reel
Behind the steadfast Gunnar : but lo, have ye seen the corn,
While yet men grind the sickle, by the wind-streak overborne
When the sudden rain sweeps downward, and summer groweth black,
And the smitten wood-side roareth 'neath the driving thunder-wrack ?
So before the wise-heart Hogni shrank the champions of the East
As his great voice shook the timbers in the hall of Atli's feast.   [stopped ;
There he smote and beheld not the smitten, and by nought were his edges
He smote and the dead were thrust from him ; a hand with its shield he lopped ;
There met him Atli's marshal, and his arm at the shoulder he shred ;

Three swords were upreared against him of the best of the kin of the dead ;
And he struck off a head to the rightward, and his sword through a throat
        he thrust,
But the third stroke fell on his helm-crest, **and he stooped to the ruddy dust,**
And uprose as the ancient Giant, and **both his hands were wet :**
Red then was the world to his eyen, as his hand to the labour he set ;
Swords shook and fell in his pathway, huge bodies leapt and fell,
Harsh grided shield and war-helm like the tempest-smitten bell,
And the war-cries ran together, and no man his brother knew,
And the dead men loaded the living, as he went the war-wood through ;
And man 'gainst man was huddled, till no sword rose to smite,
And clear stood the glorious Hogni in an island of the fight,
And there ran a river of death 'twixt the Niblung and his foes,
And therefrom the terror of men and the wrath of the Gods arose.

Now fell the sword of Gunnar and rose up red in the air,
And hearkened the song of the Niblung, as his voice rang glad and clear,
And rejoiced and leapt at the Eastmen, and cried as it met the rings
Of a giant of King Atli, and a murder-wolf of kings ;
But it **quenched** its thirst in his entrails, and knew the heart in his breast,
And hearkened the praise of Gunnar, and lingered not to rest,
But fell upon Atli's brother and stayed not in his brain ;
Then he fell and the King leapt over, and clave a neck atwain,
And leapt o'er the sweep of a pole-axe and thrust a lord in the throat,
And King Atli's banner-bearer through shield and hauberk smote ;
Then he laughed on the huddled East-folk, and against their war-shields drave
While the white swords tossed **about** him, and that **archer's** skull he clave
Whom Atli had bought in the Southlands for many a pound of gold ;
And the dark-skinned fell upon Gunnar and over his war-shield rolled
And cumbered his sword for a season, and the **many** blades fell on,
And sheared the cloudy helm-crest and **rents in his** hauberk won,
And the red blood ran from Gunnar ; till that Giuki's sword outburst,
As the fire-tongue **from the smoulder** that the leafy heap hath nursed,

And unshielded smote King Gunnar, and sent the Niblung song
Through the quaking stems of battle in the hall of Atli's wrong:
Then he rent the knitted war-hedge till by Hogni's side he stood,
And kissed him amidst of the spear-hail, and their cheeks were wet with blood

Then on came the Niblung bucklers, and they drave the East-folk home
As the bows of the oar-driven long-ship beat off the waves in foam:
They leave their dead behind them, and they come to the doors and the wall,
And a few last spears from the fleeing amidst their shield-hedge fall:
But the doors clash to in their faces, as the fleeing rout they drive,
And fain would follow after; and none is left alive
In the feast-hall of King Atli, save those fishes of the net,
And the white and silent woman above the slaughter set.

Then biddeth the heart-wise Hogni, and men to the windows climb,
And uplift the war-grey corpses, dead drift of the stormy time,
And cast them adown to their people: thence they come aback and say
That scarce shall ye see the houses, and no whit the wheel-worn way
For the spears and shields of the Eastlands that the merchant city throng:
And back to the Niblung burg-gate the way seemed weary-long.

Yet passeth hour on hour, and the doors they watch and ward,
But a long while hear no mail-clash, nor the ringing of the sword;
Then droop the Niblung children, and their wounds are waxen chill,
And they think of the Burg by the river, and the builded holy hill,
And their eyes are set on Gudrun as of men who would beseech;
But unlearned are they in craving and know not dastard's speech.
Then doth Giuki's first-begotten a deed most fair to be told,
For his fair harp Gunnar taketh, and the warp of silver and gold;
With the hand of a cunning harper he dealeth with the strings,
And his voice in their midst goeth upward, as of ancient days he sings,
Of the days before the Niblungs, and the days that shall be yet;
Till the hour of toil and smiting the warrior hearts forget,

Nor hear the gathering foemen, nor the sound of swords aloof :
Then clear the song of Gunnar goes up to the dusky roof,
And the coming spear-host tarries, and the bearers of the woe
Through the cloisters of King Atli with lingering footsteps go.

But Hogni looketh on Gudrun, and no change in her face he sees,
And no stir in her folded linen and the deedless hands on her knees :
Then from Gunnar's side he hasteneth ; and lo, the open door,
And a foeman treadeth the pavement, and his lips are on Atli's floor,
For Hogni is death in the doorway : then the Niblungs turn on the foe,
And the hosts are mingled together, and blow cries out on blow.

Still the song goeth up from Gunnar, though his harp to earth be laid ;
But he fighteth exceeding wisely, and is many a warrior's aid,
And he shieldeth and delivereth, and his eyes search through the hall,
And woe is he for his fellows, as his battle-brethren fall ;
For the turmoil hideth little from that glorious folk-king's eyes,
And o'er all he beholdeth Gudrun, and his soul is waxen wise,
And he saith : We shall look on Sigurd, and Sigmund of old days,
And see the boughs of the Branstock o'er the ancient Volsung's praise.

Woe's me for the wrath of Hogni ! From the door he giveth aback
That the Eastland slayers may enter to the murder and the wrack :
Then he rageth and driveth the battle to the golden kingly seat,
And the last of the foes he slayeth by Gudrun's very feet,
That the red blood splasheth her raiment ; and his own blood therewithal
He casteth aloft before her, and the drops on her white hands fall :
But nought she seeth or heedeth, and again he turns to the fight,
Nor heedeth stroke nor wounding so he a foe may smite :
Then the battle opens before him, and the Niblungs draw to his side ;
As Death in the world first fashioned, through the feast-hall doth he stride.
And so once more do the Niblungs sweep that murder-flood of men
From the hall of toils and treason, and the doors swing to again.

Then again is there peace for a little within the fateful fold ;
But the Niblungs look about them, and but few folk they behold
Upright on their feet for the battle : now they climb aloft no more,
Nor cast the dead from the windows ; but they raise a rampart of war,
And its stones are the fallen East-folk, and no lowly wall is that.

Therein was Gunnar the mighty : on the shields of men he sat,   [ran,
And the sons of his people hearkened, for his hand through the harp-strings
And he sang in the hall of his foeman of the Gods and the making of man,
And how season was sundered from season in the days of the fashioning,
And became the Summer and Autumn, and became the Winter and Spring;
He sang of men's hunger and labour, and their love and their breeding of broil,
And their hope that is fostered of famine, and their rest that is fashioned of toil:
Fame then and the sword he sang of, and the hour of the hardy and wise,
When the last of the living shall perish, and the first of the dead shall arise,
And the torch shall be lit in the daylight, and God unto man shall pray,
And the heart shall cry out for the hand in the fight of the uttermost day.

So he sang, and beheld not Gudrun, save as long ago he saw
His sister, the little maiden of the face without a flaw :
But wearily Hogni beheld her, and no change in her face there was,
And long thereon gazed Hogni, and set his brows as the brass,
Though the hands of the King were weary, and weak his knees were grown,
And he felt as a man unholpen in a waste land wending alone.

Now the noon was long passed over when again the rumour arose,
And through the doors cast open flowed in the river of foes :
They flooded the hall of the murder, and surged round that rampart of dead ;
No war-duke ran before them, no lord to the onset led,
But the thralls shot spears at adventure, and shot out shafts from afar,
Till the misty hall was blinded with the bitter drift of war :
Few and faint were the Niblung children, and their wounds were waxen acold,
And they saw the Hell-gates open as they stood in their grimly hold :

Y

Yet thrice stormed out King Hogni, thrice stormed out Gunnar the King,
Thrice fell they aback yet living to the heart of the fated ring ;
And they looked and their band was little, and no man but was wounded sore,
And the hall seemed growing greater, such hosts of foes it bore,
So tossed the iron harvest from wall to gilded wall ;
And they looked and the white-clad Gudrun sat silent over all.

Then the churls and thralls of the Eastland howled out as wolves accurst,
But oft gaped the Niblungs voiceless, for they choked with anger and thirst ;
And the hall grew hot as a furnace, and men drank their flowing blood,
Men laughed and gnawed on their shield-rims, men knew not where they
And saw not what was before them ; as in the dark men smote,   [stood,
Men died heart-broken, unsmitten ; men wept with the cry in the throat,
Men lived on full of war-shafts, men cast their shields aside
And caught the spears to their bosoms ; men rushed with none beside,
And fell unarmed on the foemen, and tore and slew in death :
And still down rained the arrows as the rain across the heath ;
Still proud o'er all the turmoil stood the Kings of Giuki born,
Nor knit were the brows of Gunnar, nor his song-speech overworn ;
But Hogni's mouth kept silence, and oft his heart went forth
To the long, long day of the darkness, and the end of worldly worth.

Loud rose the roar of the East-folk, and the end was coming at last ;
Now the foremost locked their shield-rims and the hindmost over them cast,
And nigher they drew and nigher, and their fear was fading away,
For every man of the Niblungs on the shaft-strewn pavement lay,
Save Gunnar the King and Hogni : still the glorious King up-bore
The cloudy shield of the Niblungs set full of shafts of war ;
But Hogni's hands had fainted, and his shield had sunk adown,
So thick with the Eastland spearwood was that rampart of renown ;
And hacked and dull were the edges that had rent the wall of foes ;
Yet he stood upright by Gunnar before that shielded close,
Nor looked on the foemen's faces as their wild eyes drew anear,

And their faltering shield-rims clattered with the remnant of their fear ;
But he gazed on the Niblung woman, and the daughter of his folk,
Who sat o'er all unchanging ere the war-cloud over them broke.

Now nothing might men hearken in the house of Atli's weal,
Save the feet slow tramping onward, and the rattling of the steel,
And the song of the glorious Gunnar, that rang as clearly now
As the speckled storm-cock singeth from the scant-leaved hawthorn-bough
When the sun is dusking over and the March snow pelts the land.
There stood the mighty Gunnar with sword and shield in hand,
There stood the shieldless Hogni with set unangry eyes,
And watched the wall of war-shields o'er the dead men's rampart rise,
And the white blades flickering nigher, and the quavering points of war.
Then the heavy air of the feast-hall was rent with a fearful roar,
And the turmoil came and the tangle, as the wall together ran :
But aloft yet towered the Niblungs, and man toppled over man,
And leapt and struggled to tear them ; as whiles amidst the sea
The doomed ship strives its utmost with mid-ocean's mastery,
And the tall masts whip the cordage, while the welter whirls and leaps,
And they rise and reel and waver, and sink amid the deeps :
So before the little-hearted in King Atli's murder-hall
Did the glorious sons of Giuki 'neath the shielded onrush fall :
Sore wounded, bound and helpless, but living yet, they lie
Till the afternoon and the even in the first of night shall die.

Of the Slaying of the Niblung Kings.

Lo now, 'tis an hour or twain, and a labour lightly won
By the serving-men of Atli, and the Niblung blood is gone
From the golden house of his greatness, and the Eastland dead no more
Lie in great heaps together on Atli's mazy floor :
Then they cast fair summer blossoms o'er the footprints of the dead,

They wreathe round Atli's high-seat and the benches fair bespread,
And they light the odorous torches, and the sun of the golden roof,
Till the candles of King Atli hold dusky night aloof.

So they toil and are heavy-hearted, nor know what next shall betide,
As they look on the stranger-woman in the heart of Atli's pride.

Now stand they aback for the trumpet and the merry minstrelsy,
For they tremble before King Atli, and golden-clad is he,
And his golden crown is heavy and he strides exceeding slow,   [woe.
With the wise and the mighty about him, through the house of the Niblungs'
There then by the Niblung woman on the throne he sat him down,
And folk heard the gold gear tinkle and the rings of the Eastland crown:
Folk looked on his rich adornment, on King Atli's pride they gazed,
And the bright beams wearied their eyen, by the glory were they dazed;
There the councillors kept silence and the warriors clad in steel,
All men lowly, all men mighty, that had care of Atli's weal;
Yea there in the hall were they waiting for the word to come from his lips,
As they of the merchant-city behold the shield-hung ships
Sweep slow through the windless haven with their gaping heads of gold,
And they know not their nation and names, nor hath aught of their errand
                                                                [been told.
But King Atli looketh before him, and is grown too great to rejoice,
And he speaks and the world is troubled, though thin and scant be his voice:

" Bring forth the fallen and conquered, bring forth the bounden thrall,
That they who were once the Niblungs did once King Hogni call."

So they brought him fettered and bound; and scarce on his feet he stood,
But men stayed him up by the King; for the sword had drunk of his blood,
And the might of his body had failed him, and yet so great was he
That the East-folk cowered before him and the might of his majesty.

Then spake the all-great Atli : " Thou yielded thrall of war,
I would hear thee tell of the Treasure, **the Hoard of** the kings of yore !"

But words were grown heavy **to** Hogni, and scarce he **spake with a** smile :
" Let the living seek their desire ; for indeed thou shalt live **for a** while."

" Wilt thou speak **and live," said Atli, "nor pay** for the blood **thou hast
[spilt ?"**
Said he : **" Thou art** waxen so mighty, thou mayst **have the Gold when thou
[wilt."**
Said the King : " I will give thee thy life, and forgive thee measureless woe."

" It was gathered for thee," said Hogni, "and fashioned long **ago."**

" Speak, man o'ercome," quoth Atli : " **Is life so little a** thing ?'

"Art thou mighty? put forth thine hand and gather the Gold !" said the King.

" Wilt thou tell of the Gold," said the East-King, " the desire of many eyes ?"

" Yea, once on a day," said Hogni, "when the dead from the sea shall arise."

Said he : **" So great** is my longing, that, O foe, I would have thee live,
Yea, live and **be** great as aforetime, if this word thou yet wouldst give."

Said the Niblung : **" Thee shall I** heed, or the longing of thy pride ?
I, who heeded Sigurd nothing, who thrust mine oath aside,
When the years were young and goodly and the summer bore increase !
Shall I crave my life of the greedy and pray for days of peace ?
I, who whetted the sword for Sigurd, and bared the blade in the morn,
And smote ere the sun's uprising, and left my sister forlorn :
'Yea I lied,' quoth the God-loved Singer, 'when the will of the Gods I told !'
—Stretch forth thine hand, O Mighty, and take thy Treasure of Gold !"

Then was Atli silent a little, for anger dulled his thought,
And the heaped-up wealth of the Eastland seemed an idle thing and nought:
He turned and looked upon Gudrun as one who was fain to beseech,
But he saw her eyes that beheld not, and her lips that knew no speech,
And fear shot across his anger, and guile with his wrath was blent,
And he spake aloud to the war-lords:

                                      "O ye, shall the eve be spent,
Nor behold the East rejoicing? what a mock for the Gods is this,
That men ever care for the morrow, nor nurse their toil-won bliss!
Lo now, this hour I speak in is the first of the seven-days' feast,
And the spring of our exultation o'er the glory of the East:
Draw nigh, O wise, O mighty, and gather words to praise
The hope of the King accomplished in the harvest of his days:
Bear forth this slave of the Niblungs to the pit and the chamber of death,
That he hearken the council of night, and the rede that tomorrow saith,
And think of the might of King Atli, and his hand that taketh his own,
Though the hill-fox bark at his going, and his path with the bramble be
                                                     [grown."
So they led the Niblung away from the light and the joy of the feast,
In the chamber of death they cast him, and the pit of the Lord of the East:
And thralls were the high King's warders; yet sons of the wise withal
Came down to sit with Hogni in the doomed man's darkling hall;
For they looked in his face and feared, lest Atli smite too nigh
The kin of the Gods of Heaven, and more than a man's child die.

But 'neath the golden roof-sun, at beginning of the night,
Is the seven-days' feast of triumph in the hall of Atli dight;
And his living Earls come thither in peaceful gold attire,
And the cups on the East-King's tables shine out as a river of fire,
And sweet is the song of the harp-strings, and the singers' honeyed words;
While wide through all the city do wives bewail their lords,
And curse the untimely hour and the day of the land forlorn,
And the year that the Earth shall rue of, and children never born.

But Atli spake to his thrall-folk, and they went, and were little afraid
To take the glorious Gunnar, and the King in shackles laid :
They deemed they should live for ever, and eat and sleep as the swine,
To them were the tales of the singers no token and no sign ;
For the blossom of the Niblungs they rolled amid the dust,
That well-renownèd Gunnar 'neath Atli's chair they thrust ;
The feet of the Eastland liar on Gunnar's neck are set,
And by Atli Gudrun sitteth, and nought she stirreth yet.

Outbrake the glee of the dastards, and they that had not dared
To meet the swords of the Niblungs, no whit the God-folk feared :
They forgat that the Norns were awake, and they praised the master of guile
The war-spent conquering Atli and the face without a smile ;
And the tumult of their triumph and the wordless mingled roar
Went forth from that hall of the Eastlands and smote the heavenly floor.

At last spake Atli the mighty : "Stand up, thou war-won thrall,
Whom they that were once the Niblungs did once King Gunnar call !"

From the dust they dragged up Gunnar, and set him on his feet,
And the heart within him was living and the pride for a war-king meet ;
And his glory was nothing abated, and fair he seemed and young,
As the first of the Cloudy Kings, fresh shoot from the sower sprung.
But Atli looked upon him, and a smile smoothed out his brow
As he said : "What thoughtest thou, Gunnar, when thou layst in the dust
                                  [e'en now ?"
He said : " Of Valhall I thought, and the host of my fathers' land,
And of Hogni that thou hast slaughtered, and my brother Sigurd's hand."

Said Atli : " Think of thy life, and the days that shall be yet,
And thyself, maybe, as aforetime, in the throne of thy father set."

" O Eastland liar," said Gunnar, " no more will I live and rue."

Said Atli : "The word I have spoken, thy word may yet make true."

"I weary of speech," said the Niblung, "with those that are lesser than I."

"Yet words of mine shalt thou hearken," said Atli, "or ever thou die."

"So crieth the fool," said Gunnar, "on the God that his folly hath slain."

Said Atli : "Forth shall my word, nor yet shall be gathered again."

"Yet meeter were thy silence ; for thy folk make ready to sing."

"O Gunnar, I long for the Gold with the heart and the will of a king."

"This were good to tell," said Gunnar, "to the Gods that fashioned the
                                                              [earth !"
"Make me glad with the Gold," said Atli, "live on in honour and worth !"

With a dreadful voice cried Gunnar : "O fool, hast thou heard it told
Who won the Treasure aforetime and the ruddy rings of the Gold?
It was Sigurd, child of the Volsungs, the best sprung forth from the best :
He rode from the North and the mountains and became my summer-guest,
My friend and my brother sworn : he rode the Wavering Fire
And won me the Queen of Glory and accomplished my desire ;
The praise of the world he was, the hope of the biders in wrong,
The help of the lowly people, the hammer of the strong :
Ah, oft in the world henceforward shall the tale be told of the deed,
And I, e'en I, will tell it in the day of the Niblungs' Need :
For I sat night-long in my armour, and when light was wide o'er the land
I slaughtered Sigurd my brother, and looked on the work of mine hand.
And now, O mighty Atli, I have seen the Niblungs' wreck,
And the feet of the faint-heart dastard have trodden Gunnar's neck ;
And if all be little enough, and the Gods begrudge me rest,

Let me see the heart of Hogni cut quick from his living breast,
And laid on the dish before me : and then shall I tell of the Gold,
And become thy servant, Atli, and my life at thy pleasure hold.
O goodly story of Gunnar, and the King of the broken troth
In the heavy Need of the Niblungs, and the Sorrow of Odin the Goth !"

Grim then waxed Atli bemocked, yet he pondered a little while,
For yet with his bitter anger strove the hope of his greedy guile,
And as one who falleth a-dreaming he hearkened Gunnar's word,
While his eyes beheld that Treasure, and the rings of the Ancient Hoard.

But he spake low-voiced to his sword-carles, and they heard and understood,
And departed swift from the feast-hall to do the work he would.
To the chamber of death they gat them, to the pit they went adown,
And saw the wise men sitting round the war-king of renown :
Then they spake : "We are Atli's bondmen, and Atli's doom we bring :
We shall carve the heart from thy body, and thou living yet, O King."

Then Hogni laughed, for they feared him ; and he said : " Speed ye the work !
For fain would I look on the storehouse where such marvels used to lurk,
And the forge of fond desires, and the nurse of life that fails.
Take heed now ! deeds are doing for the fashioners of tales."

But they feared as they looked on the Niblung, and the wise men hearkened
And bade them abide for a season, yea even for Atli's sake,　　[and spake,
For the night-slaying is as the murder ; and they looked on each other and
For Atli's bitter whisper their very hearts had heard :　　　　　[feared,
Then they said : "The King makes merry, as a well the white wine springs,
And the red wine runs as a river ; and what are the hearts of kings,
That men may know them naked from the hearts of bond and thrall ?
Nor go we empty-handed to King Atli in his hall."

So the sword-carles spake to each other, and they looked and a man they saw,

Who should hew the wood if he lived, and for thralls the water should draw,
A thrall-born servant of servants, begetter of thralls on the earth :
And they said : ' If this one were away, scarce greater were waxen the dearth
That this morning hath wrought on the Eastland ; for the years shall eke out his
And no day his toil shall lessen, and worse and worse shall he grow."   [woe,

They drew the steel new-whetted, on the thrall they laid the hand ;
For they said : " All hearts be fashioned as the heart of the King of the land."
But the thrall was bewildered with anguish, and wept and bewailed him sore
For the loss of his life of labour, and the grief that long he bore.

But wroth was the son of Giuki and he spake : " It is idle and vain,
And two men for one shall perish, and the knife shall be whetted again.
It is better to die than be sorry, and to hear the trembling cry,
And to see the shame of the poor : O fools, must the lowly die
Because kings strove with swords ?   I bid you to hasten the end,
For my soul is sick with confusion, and fain on the way would I wend."

But the life of the thrall is over, and his fearful heart they set
On a fair wide golden platter, and bear it ruddy wet
To the throne of the triumphing East-King ; he looketh, and feareth withal
Lest the house should fail about him and the golden roof should fall :
But Gunnar laughed beside him, and spake o'er the laden gold :

" O heart of a feeble trembler, no heart of Hogni the bold !
A gold dish bears thee quaking, yet indeed thou quakedst more
When the breast of the helpless dastard the burden of thee bore."

The great hall was smitten silent and its mirth to fear was turned,
For the wrath of the King was kindled, and the eyes of Atli burned,
And he cried as they trembled before him : " Let me see the heart of my foe !
Fear ye to mock King Atli till his head in the dust be alow ! "

Then the sword-carles flee before him, and are angry with their dread,
For they fear the living East-King yet more than the Niblung dead:
They come to the pit and the death-house, and the whetted steel they bear;
They are pale before King Hogni; as winter-wolves they glare
Whom the ravening hunger driveth, when the chapmen journey slow,
And their horses faint in the moon-dusk, and stumble through the snow.

But Hogni laughed before them, and he saith: "Now welcome again,
Now welcome again, war-fellows! Was Atli hood-winked then?
I looked that ye should be speedy; and, forsooth, ye needs must haste,
Lest more lives than one this even for Atli's will ye waste."

About him throng the sword-men, and they shout as the war-fain cry
In the heart of the bitter battle when their hour is come to die,
And they cast themselves upon him, as on some wide-shielded man
That fierce in the storm of Odin upreareth edges wan.

With the bound man swift is the steel: sore tremble the sons of the wise,
And their hearts grow faint within them; yet no man hideth his eyes
As the edges deal with the mighty: nor dreadful is he now,
For the mock from his mouth hath faded, and the threat hath failed from his
And his face is as great and Godlike as his fathers of old days,   [brow,
As fair as an image fashioned in remembrance of their praise:
But fled is the spirit of Hogni, and every deed he did,
The seed of the world it lieth, in the hand of Odin hid.

On the gold is the heart of Hogni, and men bear it forth to the King,
As he sits in the hall of his triumph mid the glee and the harp-playing:
Lo, the heart of a son of Giuki! and Gunnar liveth yet,
And the white unangry Gudrun by the Eastland King is set:
Upriseth the soul of Atli, and his breast is swollen with pride,
And he laughs in the face of Gunnar and the woman set by his side:
Then he looks on his living earls, and they cast their cry to the roof,

And it clangs o'er the woeful city and wails through the night aloof;
All the world of man-folk hearkeneth, and hath little joy therein,
Though the men of the East in glory high-tide with Atli win.

But fair is the face of Gunnar as the token draweth anigh;
And he saith: "O heart of Hogni, on the gold indeed dost thou lie,
And as little as there thou quakest far less wert thou wont to quake
When thou lay'st in the breast of the mighty, and wert glad for his gladness'
And wert sorry with his sorrow; O mighty heart, farewell!   [sake,
Farewell for a little season, till thy latest deed I tell."

Then was Gunnar silent a little, and the shout in the hall had died,
And he spoke as a man awakening, and turned on Atli's pride.
"Thou all-rich King of the Eastlands, e'en such a man might I be
That I might utter a word, and the heart should be glad in thee,
And I should live and be sorry; for I, I only am left
To tell of the ransom of Odin, and the wealth from the toiler reft.
Lo, once it lay in the water, hid, deep adown it lay,
Till the Gods were grieved and lacking, and men saw it and the day:
Let it lie in the water once more, let the Gods be rich and in peace!
But I at least in the world from the words and the babble shall cease."

So he spake and Atli beheld him, and before his eyes he shrank:
Still deep of the cup of desire the mighty Atli drank,
And to overcome seemed little if the Gold he might not have,
And his hard heart craved for a while to hold the King for a slave,
A bondman blind and guarded in his glorious house and great:
But he thought of the overbold, and of kings who have dallied with fate,
And died bemocked and smitten; and he deemed it worser than well
While the last of the sons of Giuki hangeth back from his journey to Hell:
So he turneth away from the stranger, and beholdeth Gudrun his wife,
Not glad nor sorry by seeming, no stirrer nor stayer of strife:
Then he looked at his living earl-folk, and thought of his groves of war,

And his realm and the kindred nations, and his measureless guarded store:
And he thought: Shall Atli perish, shall his name be cast to the dead,
Though the feeble folk go wailing? Then he cried aloud and said:

"Why tarry ye, Sons of the Morning? the wain for the bondman is dight;
And the folk that are waiting his body have need of no sunshine to smite.
Go forth 'neath the stars and the night-wind; go forth by the cloud and the
      moon,
And come back with the word in the dawning, that my house may be merry
                              at noon!"
Then the sword-folk rise round Gunnar, round the fettered and bound they
As men in the bitter battle round the God-kin over-strong;   [throng,
They bore him away to the doorway, and the winds were awake in the night,
And the wood of the thorns of battle in the moon shone sharp and bright;
But Gunnar looked to the heavens, and blessed the promise of rain,
And the windy drift of the clouds, and the dew on the builded wain:
And the sword-folk tarried a little, and the sons of the wise were there,
And beheld his face o'er the war-helms, and the wavy night of his hair.
Then they feared for the weal of Atli, and the Niblung's harp they brought,
And they dealt with the thralls of the sword, and commanded and besought,
Till men loosened the gyves of Gunnar, and laid the harp by his side.   [cried,
Then the yoke-beasts lowed in the forecourt and the wheels of the waggon
And the war-thorns clashed in the night, and the men went dark on their way,
And the city was silent before them, on the roofs the white moon lay.

Now they left the gate and the highway, and came to a lonely place,
Where the sun all day had been shining on the desert's empty face;
Then the moon ran forth from a cloud, the grey light shone and showed
The pit of King Atli's adders in the land without a road,
Digged deep adown in the desert with shining walls and smooth
For the Serpents' habitation, and the folk that know not ruth.
Therein they thrust King Gunnar, and he bare of his kingly weed,
But they gave his harp to the Niblung, and his hands of the gyves they freed;

They stood around in their war-gear to note what next should befall
For the comfort of King Atli, and the glee of the Eastland hall.

Still hot was that close **with the sun, and thronged with the** coiling folk,
And about the feet of Gunnar their hissing mouths awoke :   [ran,
But he heeded them not nor beheld them, and his hands in the harp-strings
As he sat him down in the midmost on a sun-scorched rock and wan :
And he sighed as one who resteth on a flowery bank by the way
When the wind is in the blossoms at the even-tide of day :
But his harp was murmuring low, and he mused: Am I come to the death,
And I, who **was** Gunnar the Niblung? nay, nay, how I draw my breath,
And love my life as the living ! **and so** I ever shall do,
Though wrack be loosed in the heavens and the world be fashioned anew.

But the worms were beholding their prey, and they drew around and nigher,
Smooth coil, and flickering tongue, and eyes as the gold in the fire ;
And he looked and beheld them and spake, nor stilled his harp meanwhile:
" What will **ye,** O thralls of Atli, **O images of guile ?"**

Then he rose at once to his feet, and smote the harp with his hand,
And it rang as if with a cry in the dream of a lonely land ;
Then he fondled its wail as it faded, and orderly over the strings
Went the marvellous sound of its sweetness, like the march of Odin's kings
New-risen for play in the morning when o'er meadows of God-home they wend,
And hero playeth with hero, that their hands may be deft in the end.
But the crests of the worms were uplifted, though coil on coil was stayed,
And they moved but as dark-green rushes by the summer river swayed.

Then uprose the Song of Gunnar, and sang o'er his crafty hands,
And told of the World of Aforetime, unshapen, void of **lands ;**
Yet it wrought, for its memory bideth, and it died and abode its doom ;
It shaped, and the Upper-Heavens, and the hope came forth from its womb.

Great then grew the voice of Gunnar, and his speech was sweet on the wild,
And the moon on his harp was shining, and the hands of the Niblung child:

"So perished the Gap of the Gaping, and the cold sea swayed and sang,
And the wind came down on the waters, and the beaten rock-walls rang;
Then the Sun from the south came shining, and the Starry Host stood round,
And the wandering Moon of the heavens his habitation found;
And they knew not why they were gathered, nor the deeds of their shaping
        they knew:
But lo, Mid-Earth the Noble 'neath their might and their glory grew,
And the grass spread over its face, and the Night and the Day were born,
And it cried on the Death in the even, and it cried on the Life in the morn:
Yet it waxed and waxed, and knew not, and it lived and had not learned;
And where were the Framers that framed, and the Soul and the Might that
        [had yearned?

"On the Thrones are the Powers that fashioned, and they name the Night
        and the Day,
·And the tide of the Moon's increasing, and the tide of his waning away:
And they name the years for the story; and the Lands they change and change,
The great and the mean and the little, that this unto that may be strange:
They met, and they fashioned dwellings, and the House of Glory they built;
They met, and they fashioned the Dwarf-kind, and the Gold and the Gifts
        [and the Guilt.

"There were twain, and they went upon earth, and were speechless unmighty
        and wan;
They were hopeless, deathless, lifeless, and the Mighty named them Man:
Then they gave them speech and power, and they gave them colour and
        breath;
And deeds and the hope they gave them, and they gave them Life and
        Death;
Yea, hope, as the hope of the Framers; yea, might, as the Fashioners had,
Till they wrought, and rejoiced in their bodies, and saw their sons and were
        glad:

And they changed their lives and departed, and came back as the leaves of
    the trees
Come back and increase in the summer :—and I, I, I am of these ;
And I know of Them that have fashioned, and the deeds that have blossomed
    and grow ;
But nought of the Gods' repentance, or the Gods' undoing I know."

Then falleth the speech of Gunnar, and his lips the word forget,
But his crafty hands are busy, and the harp is murmuring yet.

And the crests of the worms have fallen, and their flickering tongues are still,
The Roller and the Coiler, and Greyback, lord of ill,
Grave-groper and Death-swaddler, the Slumberer of the Heath,
Gold-wallower, Venom-smiter, lie still, forgetting death,
And loose are coils of Long-back ; yea, all as soft are laid
As the kine in midmost summer about the elmy glade ;
—All save the Grey and Ancient, that holds his crest aloft,
Light-wavering as the flame-tongue when the evening wind is soft :
For he comes of the kin of the Serpent once wrought all wrong to nurse,
The bond of earthly evil, the Midworld's ancient curse.

But Gunnar looked and considered, and wise and wary he grew,
And the dark of night was waning and chill in the dawning it grew ;
But his hands were strong and mighty and the fainting harp he woke,
And cried in the deadly desert, and the song from his soul out-broke :

"O Hearken, Kindreds and Nations, and all Kings of the plenteous earth,
Heed, ye that shall come hereafter, and are far and far from the birth !
I have dwelt in the world aforetime, and I called it the garden of God ;
I have stayed my heart with its sweetness, and fair on its freshness I trod ;
I have seen its tempest and wondered, I have cowered adown from its rain,
And desired the brightening sunshine, and seen it and been fain ;
I have waked, time was, in its dawning ; its noon and its even I wore ;

I have slept unafraid of its darkness, and the days have been many and more:
I have dwelt with the deeds of the mighty; I have woven the web of the sword;
I have borne up the guilt nor repented; I have sorrowed nor spoken the word;
And I fought and was glad in the morning, and I sing in the night and the end:
So let him stand forth, the Accuser, and do on the death-shoon to wend;
For not here on the earth shall I hearken, nor on earth for the dooming shall
     stay,
Nor stretch out mine hand for the pleading; for I see the spring of the day
Round the doors of the golden Valhall, and I see the mighty arise,
And I hearken the voice of Odin, and his mouth on Gunnar cries,
And he nameth the Son of Giuki, and cries on deeds long done,
And the fathers of my fathers, and the sons of yore agone.

"O Odin, I see, and I hearken; but, lo thou, the bonds on my feet,
And the walls of the wilderness round me, ere the light of thy land I meet!
I crave and I weary, Allfather, and long and dark is the road;
And the feet of the mighty are weakened, and the back is bent with the load."

Then fainted the song of Gunnar, and the harp from his hand fell down,
And he cried: "Ah, what hath betided? for cold the world hath grown,
And cold is the heart within me, and my hand is heavy and strange;
What voice is the voice I hearken in the chill and the dusk and the change?
Where art thou, God of the war-fain? for this is the death indeed;
And I unsworded, unshielded, in the Day of the Niblungs' Need!"

He fell to the earth as he spake, and life left Gunnar the King,
For his heart was chilled for ever by the sleepless serpent's sting,
The grey Worm, Great and Ancient—and day in the East began,
And the moon was low in the heavens, and the light clouds over him ran.

The Ending of Gudrun.

Men sleep in the dwelling of Atli through the latter hours of night,
Though the comfortless women be wailing as they that love not light
Men sleep in the dawning-hour, and bowed down is Atli's head
Amidst the gold and the purple, and the pillows of his bed :
But hark, ere the sun's uprising, when folk see colours again,
Is the trample of steeds in the fore-court, and the noise of steel and of men
And Atli wakeneth and riseth, and is clad in purple and pall,
And he goeth forth from the chamber and meeteth his earls in the hall
A king full great and mighty, if a great king ever hath been ;
And over his head on the high-seat still sitteth Gudrun the Queen.
                                                                    [East
Then he said : "Whence come ye, children ? whence come ye, Lords of the
Shall today be for evil and mourning or a day of joyance and feast ?"

They said : "Today shall be wailing for the foes of the Eastland kin ;
But for them that love King Atli shall the day of feasts begin :
For we come from the land deserted, and the heath without a way,
And now are the earth's folk telling of the Niblungs passed away."

Then King Atli turned unto Gudrun, and the new sun shone through the door,
The long beams fell from the mountains and lighted Atli's floor :
Then he cried : "Lo, the day-light, Gudrun ! and the Cloudy Folk is gone ;
There is glory now in the Eastland, and thy lord is king alone."

But Gudrun rose from the high-seat, and her eyes on the King she turned ;
And he stood rejoicing before her, and his crown in the sunlight burned,
With the golden gear was he swaddled, and he held the red-gold rod
That the Kings of the East had carried since first they came from God :
Down she came, and men kept silence, and the earls beheld her face,
As her raiment rustled about her in the morning-joyous place :

So she stood amidst of the sun-beams, by King Atli's board she stood,
And men looked and wondered at her, would she speak them ill or good:
She wept not, and she sighed not, nor smiled in the stranger land,
But she stood before King Atli, and the cup was in her hand.

Then she spake: "Take, King, and drink it! for earth's mightiest men prevail,
And to thee is the praise and the glory, and the ending of the tale:
There are men to the dead land faring, but the dark o'er their heads is deep,
They cry not, they return not, and no more renown they reap;
But we do our will without them, nor fear their speech or frown;
And glad shall be our uprising, and light our lying-down."

She said: "A maid of maidens my mother reared me erst;
By the side of the glorious Gunnar my early days were nursed;
By the side of the heart-wise Hogni I went from field to flower,
Joy rose with the sun's uprising, nor sank in the twilight hour;
Kings looked and laughed upon us as we played with the golden toy:
And oft our hands were meeting as we mingled joy with joy."

More she spake: "O King command me! for women's knees are weak,
And their feet are little steadfast, and their hands for comfort seek:
On the earth the blossom falleth when the branch is dried with day,
And the vine to the elm-bough clingeth when men smite the roots away."

Then drank the Eastland Atli as he looked in Gudrun's face,
And beheld no wrath against him, and no hate of the coming days;
Then he spake: "O mighty woman, this day the feast shall be
For the heritance of Atli, and the gain of mine and me:
For this day the Eastland people such great dominion win,
That a world to their will new-fashioned 'neath their glory shall begin.
Yet, since the mighty are fallen, and kings are gone from earth,
Let these at the feast be remembered, and their ancient deeds of worth.
So I bid thee, O King's Daughter, sit by Atli at the feast,

To praise thy kin departed and Atli's weal increased ;
And the heirship-feast and the death-feast today **shall be** as one ;
And then shalt thou wake tomorrow with all thy mourning done,
And all thy will accomplished, and thy glory great and sure,
That for ever and for ever shall the tale thereof endure."

He spake in the sunny morning, and Gudrun answered and said :
"Thou hast bidden me feast, O Atli, and thy will shall be obeyed :
And well I thank thee, great-one, for the gifts thine hand would give ;
For who shall gainsay the mighty, and the happy Kings that live ?   [thee :
Thou hast swallowed the might of the Niblungs, and their glory lieth in
Live long, and cherish thy wealth, **that the world may** wonder and see !"

Therewith to the bower of queens the Niblung wendeth her way,
And in all the glory of women the folk her body array :
Forth she comes with the crown on her head and the ivory rod in her hand,
With queens for her waiting-women, and the hope of many a land :
There she goes in that wonder of houses when the high-tide of Atli is dight,
And her face is as fair as the sea, and her eyen **are glittering bright.**

By Atli's side she sitteth, o'er the earls they twain are set,
And shields of the ancient wise-ones on the wall are hanging yet,
And the golden sun of the roof-sky, the sun of Atli's pride,
Through the beams where day but glimmers casts red light far and wide :
The beakers clash thereunder, the red wine murmureth speech,
And the eager long-beard warriors cast praises each to each
Of the blossoming tree of the Eastland :—and tomorrow shall be as today,
Yea, even more abundant, and all foes have passed away.

It **was** then in the noon-tide moment ; o'er the earth high hung the sun,
When the song o'er the mighty Niblungs in a stranger-house was begun,
And their deeds were told by the foemen, and the names of hope they had
Rang sweet in the hall of the murder to make King Atli glad :

It is little after the noon-tide when thereof **they sing no** more,
Nor tell of the strife that has been, **and the** leaping flames of war,
And the vengeance lulled for ever and the wrath **that shall never awake** :
For where is the kin of Hogni, and who liveth for Gunnar's sake?

So men **in the hall make** merry, nor note the afternoon,
And the time when men grow weary with the task that ends not soon ;
The sun falls down unnoted, and night and her daughter are nigh,
And a dull grey mist and awful hangeth over the east of the **sky,**
And spreadeth, though winds are sleeping, and riseth higher and higher ;
But the clouds hang high in the west as a sea of rippling fire,
That the face of the gazer is lighted, if unto the west ye gaze,
And white walls in the lonely meadows grow ruddy under the blaze ;
Yet brighter e'en than the cloud-sea, far-off and clear **serene,**
Mid purple clouds unlitten **the light** lift lieth between ;
And who looks, save the lonely shepherd on the brow of the houseless hill,
Who hath many a day seen no man to tell him of good or of ill ?

Day dies, and the storm-threats perish, and the stars to the heaven are come,
And the white moon climbeth upward and hangs o'er the Eastland home ;
But no man in the hall of King Atli shall heed the heavens without,
For **Atli's** roof is their heaven, and thereto they cast the shout,
And this, the glory they builded, is become their God to praise,
The hope of their generations, the giver of goodly days :
No more they hearken the harp-strings, no more they hearken the song ;
All the might of the deedful Niblungs is a tale forgotten long,
And yester-morning's murder is **as** though it ne'er had been ;
They heed not the white-armed Gudrun, the glorious Stranger-Queen,
They **heed not** Atli triumphant, **for** they also, **they** are Kings,
They are brethren of the God-folk and the fashioners of things ;
Nay, the **Gods,—and** the Gods have sorrow, and these shall rue no more,
These world-kings, these prevailers, these beaters-down of war :
What golden house shall hold them, what nightless shadowless heaven ?

—So they feast in the hall of Atli, and that eve is the first of the seven.

So they feast, and weary, and know not how weary they are grown,
As they stretch out hands to gather where their hands have never sown;
They are drunken with wine and with folly, and the hope they would bring
Of the mirth no man may compass, and the joy that never was,   [to pass
Till their heads hang heavy with slumber, and their hands from the wine-cup fail,
And blind stray their hands in the harp-strings and their mouths may tell
                                                           [no tale.

Now the throne of Atli is empty, low lieth the world-king's head
Mid the woven gold and the purple, and the dreams of Atli's bed,
And Gudrun lieth beside him as the true by the faithful and kind,
And every foe is departed, and no fear is left behind:
Lo, lo, the rest of the night-tide for which all kings would long,
And all warriors of the people that have fought with fear and wrong.

Yet a while;—it was but an hour and the moon was hung so high,
As it seemed that the silent night-tide would never change and die;
But lo, how the dawn comes stealing o'er the mountains of the east,
And dim grows Atli's **roof-sun** o'er yestereven's feast;
Dim yet in the treasure-houses lie the ancient heaps of gold,
But slowly come the colours to the Dwarf-wrought rings of old:
Yet a while; and the day-light lingers: yea, yea, is it darker than erst?
Hath the day into night-tide drifted, the day by the twilight nursed?
Are the clouds in the house of King Atli? Or what shines brighter that morn,
In helms and shields of the ancient, and swords by dead kings borne?
Have the heavens come down to Atli?   Hath his house been lifted on high,
Lest the pride of the triumphing World-King should fade in the world and die?

Lo, lo, in the hall of the Murder where the white-armed Gudrun stands,
Aloft by the kingly high-seat, and nought empty are her hands;
For the litten brand she beareth, and the grinded war-sword bare:
Still she stands for a little season till day groweth white and fair

Without the garth of King Atli; but within, a wavering cloud
Rolls, hiding the roof and the roof-sun; then she stirreth and crieth aloud:

"Alone was I yestereven: and alone in the night I lay,
And I thought on the ancient fathers, and longed for the dawning of day:
Then I rose from the bed of the Eastlands; to the Holy Hearth I went;
And lo, how the brands were abiding the hand of mine intent!
Then I caught them up with wisdom, with care I bore them forth,
And I laid them amidst of the treasures and dear things of uttermost worth;
'Neath the fair-dight benches I laid them and the carven work of the hall;
I was wise, as the handmaid arising ere the sun hath litten the wall,
When the brands on the hearth she lighteth that her work betimes she may
That her hand may toil unchidden, and her day with praise begin.   [win,
—Begin, O day of Atli! O ancient sun, arise,
With the light that I loved aforetime, with the light that blessed mine eyes,
When I woke and looked on Sigurd, and he rose on the world and shone!
And we twain in the world together! and I dwelt with Sigurd alone."

She spake; and the sun clomb over the Eastland mountains' rim
And shone through the door of Atli and the smoky hall and dim,
But the fire roared up against him, and the smoke-cloud rolled aloof,
And back and down from the timbers, and the carven work of the roof;
There the ancient trees were crackling as the red flames shot aloft
From the heart of the gathering smoke-cloud; there the far-fetched hangings
The gold and the sea-born purple, shrank up in a moment of space,   [soft,
And the walls of Atli trembled, and the ancient golden place.
                                                          [stirred,
But the wine-drenched earls were awaking, and the sleep-dazed warriors
And the light of their dawning was dreadful; wild voice of the day they heard,
And they knew not where they were gotten, and their hearts were smitten
       with dread,   [dead,
And they deemed that their house was fallen to the innermost place of the
The hall for the traitors builded, the house of the changeless plain;

They cried, and their tongues were confounded, and none gave answer again:
They rushed, and came nowhither; each man beheld his foe,
And smote as the hopeless and dying, nor brother brother might know,
The sons of one mother's sorrow in the fire-blast strove and smote,
And the sword of the first-begotten was thrust in the father's throat,
And the father hewed at his stripling; the thrall at the war-king cried,
And mocked the face of the mighty in that house of Atli's pride.

There Gudrun stood o'er the turmoil; there stood the Niblung child;
As the battle-horn is dreadful, as the winter wind is wild,
So dread and shrill was her crying and the cry none heeded or heard,
As she shook the sword in the Eastland, and spake the hidden word:

"The brand for the flesh of the people, and the sword for the King of the
[world!"
Then adown the hall and the smoke-cloud the half-slaked torch she hurled
And strode to the chamber of Atli, white-fluttering mid the smoke;
But their eyen met in the doorway and he knew the hand and the stroke,
And shrank aback before her; and no hand might he upraise,
There was nought in his heart but anguish in that end of Atli's days.

But she towered aloft before him, and cried in Atli's home:
"Lo, lo, the day-light, Atli, and the last foe overcome!"
And with all the might of the Niblungs she thrust him through and fled,
And the flame was fleet behind her and hung o'er the face of the dead.

There was none to hinder Gudrun, and the fire-blast scathed her nought,
For the ways of the Norns she wended, and her feet from the wrack they
Till free from the bane of the East-folk, the swift pursuing flame, [brought
To the uttermost wall of Atli and the side of the sea she came:
She stood on the edge of the steep, and no child of man was there:
A light wind blew from the sea-flood and its waves were little and fair,
And gave back no sign of the burning, as in twinkling haste they ran,

White-topped in the merry morning, to the walls and the havens of man.

Then Gudrun girded her raiment, on the edge of the steep she stood,
She looked o'er the shoreless water, and cried out o'er the measureless flood:
"O Sea, I stand before thee; and I who was Sigurd's wife!
By his brightness unforgotten I bid thee deliver my life
From the deeds and the longing of days, and the lack I have won of the earth,
And the wrong amended by wrong, and the bitter wrong of my birth!"

She hath spread out her arms as she spake it, and away from the earth she leapt,
And cut off her tide of returning; for the sea-waves over her swept,
And their will is her will henceforward; and who knoweth the deeps of the
And the wealth of the bed of Gudrun, and the days that yet shall be? [sea,

Ye have heard of Sigurd aforetime, how the foes of God he slew;
How forth from the darksome desert the Gold of the Waters he drew;
How he wakened Love on the Mountain, and wakened Brynhild the Bright,
And dwelt upon Earth for a season, and shone in all men's sight.
Ye have heard of the Cloudy People, and the dimming of the day,
And the latter world's confusion, and Sigurd gone away;
Now ye know of the Need of the Niblungs and the end of broken troth,
All the death of kings and of kindreds and the sorrow of Odin the Goth.

THE END.

PRINTED BY BALLANTYNE, HANSON AND CO.
EDINBURGH AND LONDON

2 A

A CATALOGUE

OF THE

PUBLICATIONS

OF

MESSRS. REEVES & TURNER,

5, *Wellington Street, Strand,*

LONDON, W.C.

(Removed from 196, Strand.)

November, 1893

Catalogue of Books

SOLD BY

REEVES & TURNER,

5, Wellington Street, Strand,

LONDON, W.C.

	s.	*d.*
Anderson (A. A.) **On a Hitherto unsuspected Second Axial Rotation of Our Earth**, Second Edition, with additional matter, post 8vo, cloth	6	0
Andrews (William) **Historic Yorkshire**, reprinted from the *Leeds Express*, 210 pp., 8vo, cloth, gilt edges	8	6
Anglo-Saxon.—Analecta Anglo-Saxonica : A Selection in Prose and Verse from the Anglo-Saxon Authors of various ages, with a Glossary, designed chiefly **as a** first book for students, by Benj. Thorpe, a new edition, with corrections and improvements, post 8vo, cloth	7	6
Anglo-Saxon.—Bosworth (Rev. Jos.) **A Compendious Anglo-Saxon and English Dictionary**, 278 pp., *closely printed in treble columns*, 8vo, reduced to	6	0
- —— Bosworth (Rev. Jos) **Four Versions of the Holy Gospels**, viz.: In Gothic, A.D. 360 ; Anglo-Saxon, 995 ; Wycliffe, 1389 ; and Tyndall, 1526, in parallel columns, with Preface and Notes, by Rev. Dr. Bosworth, assisted by Geo. Waring, M. A., 622 pp., 8vo, cloth, reduced to	6	0

s. d.

Anglo-Saxon.—**The Anglo-Saxon Poems of Beowulf:**
The Scop or Gleeman's Tale, and the Fight at Finnes-
bury, with a literal Translation, Notes, and copious
Glossary, by Benj. Thorp, 366 pp., post 8vo, cloth
reduced to **5 0**

Anglo-Saxon.—**The Conquest of Britain by the Saxon;**
a Harmony of the "Historia Britonum," The Writings
of Gildas, The "Brut" and the Saxon Chronicle,
with reference to the Events of the Fifth and Sixth
Centuries, by D. H. Haigh, 8vo, cloth 1861 **15 0**

Biblia Innocentium, being the Story of God's Chosen
People before the Coming of the Lord Jesus Christ
upon **Earth,** and written anew for Children by J. W.
Mackad, **post** 8vo, gilt top **6 0**

Boutell (C.) **Arms** and **Armour in Antiquity** and the
Middle **Ages;** also a Descriptive Notice of Modern
Weapons, **from** the French of M. P. Lacombe, and
with a Preface, and Notes, one Additional Chapter on
Arms and Armour **in** England, by C. Boutell, 60 *wood-
cuts*, 312 pp., post **8vo,** cloth **5 0**

———— **English Heraldry,** specially prepared for the **use of**
Students, 460 *woodcuts in the text, engraved* **by R.**
Utting, Fifth Edition, **367** pp., post 8vo, cloth **3 6**

Byne (Elwin) Gather'd Fragments, A Collection of **Poems,**
12mo, cloth **3 0**

Large Edition, 913 pp., Imp. 8vo.

Chaffers (Wm.) **Marks and Monograms on European**
and **Oriental Pottery and Porcelain,** with Historical
Notices of each Manufactory, preceded by an Introductory Essay on the Vasa Fictilia of the Greek,
Romano-British, and Mediæval Eras, ornamental cloth **42 0**
Seventh edition, revised and considerably augmented, with upwards of
3,000 Potters' Marks and Illustrations.

Seventh Edition, considerably Augmented and carefully Revised by the Author.

—·—— **Hall Marks on Gold and Silver Plate,** Illustrated
with **Revised Tables of Annual** Date Letters em-
ployed **in the** Assay **Offices of the** United Kingdom,
316 pp., roy. 8vo, cloth **16 0**
This edition contains a History **of** the Goldsmith s trade in France, with
extracts from the decrees relating thereto, and engravings of the standard
and other Marks used in that country as well as in other foreign states. The
Provincial Tables of England and Scotland contain many hitherto un-
published Marks; all the recent enactments are quoted. The London Tables
which have never been surpassed for correctness) may now be considered

s. d.

complete. Many valuable hints to Collectors are given, **and cases** of fraud alluded to, etc.

Chaffers (W.) **Collector's Handbook of Marks and Monograms on Pottery and Porcelain, of the Renaissance and Modern Period**, selected from his larger work, Tenth Thousand, 204 pp., post 8vo, cloth, gilt   6 0

The Companion to " Hall Marks on Gold and Silver Plate."

Chaffers (W.) **Gilda Aurifabrorum**, a History of English Goldsmiths and Plateworkers and their Marks stamped on Plate, copied in *facsimile* from celebrated Examples and the earliest Records preserved at Goldsmiths' Hall. London, **with their** names, addresses, and dates of entry, 2,500 *illustrations ;* also Historical Account of the Goldsmiths' Company and their Hall Marks and Regalia ; the Mint Shop Signs **a** Copious Index, etc., 267 pp., roy. 8vo, cloth   12 0

Christian (E. B. V.) **The Lays of a Limb of the Law**, by the late John Popplestone, edited with a Memoir and Postcript, by Edmund B. V. Christian, *frontispiece by J. J. Proctor*, 12mo, cloth   2 6

Cobbett (W.) **Rural Rides** in the Counties of Surrey, Kent, Sussex, Hants, Wilts, Gloucestershire, &c., edited with Life, New Notes, and the addition of **a** copious Index, by PITT COBBETT, *map and portrait*, 2 vols., cr. 8vo., xlviii. and 806 pp., cloth, gilt   12 6

Cobbett's " Rural Rides " is to us a delightful book, but it is one which few people know. We are not sure that up to the present time it was impossible to get a nice edition of it. We are therefore glad to see that Messrs. Reeves & Turner's recently published edition is a **very** creditable production, two handy, well-filled volumes.—*Gardening*, July, 25. 1885

Condorcet (Marquis de) **Means for Learning how to Reckon Certainly and Easily**, with the Elementary Ideas of Logic, translated **by** J. Kaines, 12mo, sewed 1882   1 0

Cory's Ancient Fragments of the Phœnician, Carthagenian, Babylonian, Egyptian **and** other Authors, **a new** and enlarged edition, the translation carefully **revised** and enriched with Notes, Critical and Explanatory, with Introduction to the several Fragments, &c., by E. RICHMOND HODGES, 250 pp., 8vo, cloth   7 6

Crests, Book of Family, comprising nearly every Bearing and **its** Blazonry, Surnames, of Bearers, Dictionary of Mottoes, British and Foreign Orders of Knighthood, Glossary of Terms, *and upwards of 4,000 engravings* illustrative of Peers, Baronets, and nearly every Family

	s.	d.

Bearing Arms in England, Wales, Scotland, Ireland, and the Colonies, &c., 2 vols, 750 pp., 12mo, cloth — 12 6

Deal, Past and Present, a full and Comprehensive History of this Neighbourhood, by H. S. Chapman, 4to, cloth, 1890 — 8 6

Dickens (Chas.) Sunday Under Three Heads, a reproduction in exact facsimile of the rare original, 12mo, wrapper — 1 0

Erasmus in Praise of Folly, NEW EDITION, *illustrated by 80 plates from designs by Hans Holbein, beautifully printed in large type, on hand-made paper*, 220 pp., demy **8vo,** cloth — 12 0

———————— **Ditto,** new half calf, gilt top — 14 0

Eyton (R. W.) Notes on Domesday, reprinted from the Transactions of the Shropshire Archæological Society, 1877, **8vo** — 1 0

Fairfax (Walter) Robert Browning and the Drama, a Note by W. F., 8vo, wrappers — 1 0

Fleay (F. G.) Biographical History of the English Drama (1559 to 1642) containing lives of all the Dramatists, 2 large 8vo vols, hf. roxburgh — 30 0

Works on Freemasonry.

	s.	d.

An Investigation into **the** Cause of the **Hostility** of the Church of Rome **to** Freemasonry, **and** an Inquiry into Freemasonry **as** it Was and Is, etc., by the author of " The Text Book of Freemasonry," 8vo, sewed — 1 0

Carlile (Richd.) Manual of Freemasonry: Part **I.** The First Three Degrees, with an Introductory Key-stone to the Royal Arch—Part II. The Royal Arch and Knights Templar, Druids, &c.—Part III. The Degrees of Mark Man, Mark Master, &c., with an Explanatory Introduction to the Science, &c., 323 pp., post 8vo, red cloth, gilt — 3 6

	s.	*d*
Fellowes (J.) **Mysteries of Freemasonry,** or an Exposition of the Religious Dogmas and Customs of the Ancient Egyptians, shewing their Identity with the Order of Modern Masonry, &c., *with numerous illustrative woodcuts*, 366 pp., blue cloth, gilt	3	6
Fox (T. Lewis) **Early History of Freemasonry** in England with Illustrations of the Principles and Precepts advocated by that Institution, 12mo, cloth	2	0
Freemasonry, Paton's Origin of Freemasonry, 8vo, sewed	1	0
——— ditto, **Three** Tracing **Boards in** 12mo, cloth line	1	6
——— **ditto,** larger size, roy. **8vo, 4 plates**	1	6
——— **ditto,** ditto, coloured	2	6
Jachin and Boaz, or an Authentic Key to the Door of Freemasonry, both Ancient and Modern, cr. 8vo, wrapper	1	0
Text Book of advanced Freemasonry, containing, for the Self-Instruction of Candidates, the Complete Rituals of the Higher Degrees, viz., Royal Ark Mariners, Mark Masters, Royal Arch, Red Cross of Rome and Constantine, **or** Perfect Prince Mason, Knights Templar, and **Rose** Croix, also Monitorial Instructions **in** the 30th **to** the 33rd and last Degree of Freemasonry, to which are added Historical Introductions and Explanatory Remarks, compiled from the best Authorities, 278 pp., cr. 8vo, red cloth, also calf gilt	10	0
The Ritual, and Illustrations of **Freemasonry,** *with numerous engravings*, and a Key to Phi Beta Kappa, 254 pp., uniform with the last two, green cloth, gilt	3	6
The Text Book of Freemasonry : A complete Handbook of Instruction to all the Working in the Various Mysteries and Ceremonies of Craft Masonry, with the whole of the THREE LECTURES ; also the Supreme Order of the Holy Royal Arch, and **a** Selection of Masonic Songs and Odes, by a Member of the Craft, *four engravings of the tracing board*, REVISED EDITION, 270 pp., 12mo, blue cloth, red edges	5	0
Copies can now be had printed upon thin hard opaque paper and bound in blue leather with tuck, in a very convenient form for the pocket	5	0
The Three Distinct Knocks at the Door of the most Ancient Freemasonry, cr. 8vo, wrapper	1	0

s. d.

Halliwell's (J. O.) **Dictionary of Archaic and Provincial Words**, Obsolete Phrases, Proverbs, and Ancient Customs, from thoroughly, from the Reign of Edward I., 2 vols, **8vo, over** 1,000 **pp.,** closely printed in double columns, **cloth**   21 0

Hamilton, **Parodies of English and American Authors**, collected and annotated by Walter Hamilton. Parodies of the following Authors have appeared:—Lord Tennyson, Poet-Laureate; Henry W. Longfellow; Thomas Hood; Bret Harte; Miss Taylor's poem, "My Mother"; Edgar Allan Poe; Wolfe's "Not a Drum was heard"; and Hamlet's Soliloquy, &c., &c. Six volumes are **now** ready, completing the work, sm. 4to, cloth gilt   *Each* 7 6

—— Æsthetic **Movement in** England: The Pre-Raphaelites, **The Germ, John** Ruskin, W. Morris, A. C. Swinburne, THIRD EDITION, small 8vo, cloth   2 6

—— A Lyttel **Parcell** of Poems and Parodyes in Praise of Tobacco, contaying Divers Conceited Ballades, and Pithie Sayinges all newly collected by Walter Hamilton, 180 pp., 12mo   5 0

Hone (W.) **Apocryphal New Testament**, being all the Gospels, Epistles, **and** other pieces now extant (attributed in the first four centuries to Jesus Christ, His Apostles, and their Companions), and not included in the New Testament, now first printed for WM. HONE, 265 pp., 8vo, cloth   8 6

Hone (W.) **Ancient Mysteries Described**, especially the ENGLISH MIRACLE PLAYS founded on Apocryphal New Testament Story, including Notices of Ecclesiastical Shows, &c., *with illustrations*, 300 pp., 8vo, cloth   8 0

How to Speak **Extempore**, by an Old Platform Orator, 12mo, cloth   1886   1 0

Irsoy (J. E.) **Verses of Love and Life**, 12mo, cloth   1892   2 0

Jones (J. M.) **Naturalist in Bermuda**, a Sketch of the Geology, Zoology, and Botany of that remarkable Group of Islands, together with Meteorological Observations, *map and woodcuts in the text*, post 8vo., cloth   7 6

Keats (John) **The Poetical Works of John Keats**, given from his own Editions and other Authentic Sources, and collated with many Manuscripts, edited by H. Buxton Forman, *portrait*, THIRD EDITION, 628 pp., cr. 8vo, buckram   8 0

SECOND EDITION.

	s.	*d.*

Keats (John) **The Poetical Works and other Writings** of JOHN KEATS, now first brought together, including Poems and numerous Letters not before published, edited with Notes and Appendices, and over 200 pp. of new matter, by H. Buxton Forman, *numerous ports. of Keats, facsimiles, etchings etc.*, 4 vols, 8vo, buckram **52 6**

——— **Poetry and Prose**, by John Keats, a Book of Fresh Verses and New Readings—Essays and Letters lately found, **and** Passages formerly Suppressed, edited by H. B. Forman, *with port.*, **8vo**   **10 6**

This is incorporated with the Second Edition.

Kerslake (Thomas) **The Liberty of Independent His-torical Research**, 66 pp., 8vo, wrappers   **1 0**

——— Caer **Pensauelcoit**, a Long-Lost Unromanised British Metropolis, a Reassertion, *map*, 45 **pp.**, 8vo, wrappers   **1 0**

Leno (J. Bedford) **The Last Idler, and other** Poems, 126 pp., 12mo   **3 0**

——— Kimburton, **a Story of** Village **Life,,** 8vo, wrappers, 52 pp.   **1 0**

Lissagaray (H.) **History of the Commune of Paris**, 1871, translated from the French by E. MARX AVELING, 8vo, 500 pp., cloth   **10 6**

The only reliable history of the Commune. Of the general impartiality of the present historian, and of the care he has taken to sift evidence, there is no doubt.—*Time*, Sept. '86.

Long (W. H.) **A Dictionary of the Isle of Wight Dialect**, and of Provincialisms used in **the** Island, with Illus-trative Anecdotes, and Tales, etc., Songs sung **by** the Peasantry, forming a Treasury **of** Island Manners and Customs Fifty Years Ago, 182 pp., post 8vo, cloth   **3 6**

——— Ditto, printed on Thick and LARGE PAPER **8vo**, cloth   **6 0**

" *The Library of Old English Authors.*"

*A series of well-selected re-issues of the Works of Famous Authors of past times, tastefully printed in very legible type upon superior paper, and neatly bound in cloth in an uniform style, and offered **at a** greatly reduced published price, post 8vo.*

	s.	*d.*
Amadis of Gaul.—**The Renowned Romance of Amadis of Gaul,** by **Vasco** Lobeira, translated from the Spanish version **of** Garciodonez de Montalvo, by Robert Southey, a new edition, in 3 vols	12	0

Amadis of Gaul is among prose, what Orlando Furioso is among metrical romances—not the oldest of its kind, but the best.

	s.	*d.*
Ascham (Roger) **Whole Works,** now first collected and revised, with Life **of** the Author, by the Rev. Dr. Giles, 4 vols	16	0
Aubrey (John, *The Wiltshire Antiquary*) **Miscellanies,** new edition, with Additions and Index, to which is now added for the first time Sir T. Browne's Hydriotaphia or Urn Burial, *embellished with a fine portrait, and curious woodcuts.*	4	0
Camden (William) **Remains concerning Britain,** *portrait*	4	0
Carew (Thos.) **Poems and Masques,** edited with Indexes by Rev. J. W. Gibsworth	4	0
Crawshaw (Richard) **Poetical Works of,** Author of " Steps **to** the Temple," " Sacred Poems, with other Delights of the Muses," **and** " Poemata," now first collected, edited by **W. B.** Turnbull	4	0
Drayton (Michael) **Poetical Works** (comprising the Polyolbion and Harmony **of the** Church), edited by Hooper, 3 vols	12	0
Drummond (William, *of Hawthornden*) **Poetical Works** entire; edited by W. B. Turnbull, *fine portrait*	4	0

        s. d.

Hearne (Thomas) **Diaries of the Antiquary**, edited by Dr. Bliss, 3 vols, *port.*   12 0

Herrick (Robert) **Hesperides**, the Poems and other remains of Robert Herrick, a New Edition, carefully revised and re-edited by W. C. Hazlitt, with additions, *fine portrait frontispiece, **after** the original by Marshall,* 2 vols   8 0

Homer's Batrachomyomachia, Hymns and Epigrams. Hesiod's Works and Days, Musæus' Hero and Leander, Juvenal's Fifth Satire, translated by George Chapman, New Edition, with Introduction and Notes by Rev. Richard Hooper   4 0

Lilly's (John) **Dramatic Works** with Notes, Life, and Some Account of His Writings, by Fairholt, **2** vols, portrait   1892   8 0

Lovelace (Richard) **Poems**, now first edited, and the text carefully revised, with Life and Notes by W. Carew Hazlitt, *with 4 plates*   4 0

Margaret, Duchess of Newcastle's Autobiography, and Life of Her Husband, edited by M. A. Lower, *fine port.*   4 0

Mather (Dr. Cotton) **Wonders of the Invisible World,** being an Account of the Trials of several Witches lately executed in New England, with Dr. Increase Mather's Further Account of the Tryals, and Cases **of Conscience** concerning Witchcrafts, 1693, with an Introductory Preface, *portrait*   4 0

Mather (Dr. Increase) **Remarkable Providences of the Earlier Days of American Colonization,** with Introductory Preface by George Offor, *fine portrait*   4 0

Remains of the Early Popular Poetry of England, collected and Edited by W. Carew Hazlitt, 4 vols, *with many curious woodcut facsimiles*   16 0

Sackville (Thomas) **Poetical and Dramatic Works,** *port.*   4 0

Sandy (George) **Poetical Works,** now first collected, edited by the Rev. R. Hooper, 2 vols, *port.*   8 0

Selden (John) **Table Talk,** edited with a biographical Preface and Notes by S. W. Singer, *portrait,* New Edition. to which is now added for the first time Eden Warwick's "Spare Minutes"   4 0

Suckling (Sir John) **Poems, Plays and Other** Pieces, edited with Notes, Appendixes, **and Life, by** W. Carew Hazlett, 2 vols, portrait   .

The History of King Arthur and the Knights of the

s. d.

Round Table, compiled by Sir T. Malory, edited from the edition of 1634, with Introduction and Notes by T. Wright, Third Edition, 3 vols   12 0

The Iliads of Homer, Prince of Poets, truly translated, with a Comment **on some** of his chief Places, done according to the Greek by George Chapman, with Notes by the Rev. Richard Hooper, 2 vols, *portrait of Chapman and front.*   8 0

The Odysseys of Homer, translated according **to the** Greek by George Chapman, with Introduction **and** Notes by the Rev. Richard Hooper, 2 vols, **with** *facsimile of the rare original front.*   8 0

The Vision and Creed of Piers Ploughman, edited by Thomas Wright; **a** new edition, revised, with Addition to the Notes and Glossary, 2 vols   8 0

Webster (John) Dramatic Works, Edited, **with** Notes, **etc., by** William Hazlitt, **4** vols   16 0
This **is the most** complete edition, containing **two** more plays than in Dyce's edition.

Wither (George) Hymns and Songs of the Church, edited, with introduction, by Edward Farr, also the Musical Notes, composed by Orlando Gibbons, *with port. after Hole*   4 0

Wither (George) Hallelujah; or, Britain's Second Remembrancer, in Praiseful and Penitential Hymns, Spiritual Songs, and Moral Odes, with Introduction by Edward Farr, *port.*   4 0

Mackay (Eric) **A** Choral Ode to Liberty, **Author** of "Love Letters of **a** Violinist," 20 pp., 4to   1 0

Mackay (Eric) Gladys the Singer, other Poems, 113 pp., cr. 8vo, cloth   6 0

Malthus (T. R.) **An** Essay on the Principle of Population, or **a** View **of** its Past and Present Effects on Human Happiness, with an Inquiry into our Prospects respecting the Future Removal or Mitigation of the Evils which it Occasions, Ninth Edition, 567 **pp.**, 8vo, cloth   8 0

Mumby (A. J.) Faithful Servants being several Hundred Epitaphs on Faithful Servants, Male and Female,

	s.	d.
with **Records** of these Services edited **and** partly collected by, post 8vo 1891	5	0
Mumby (A. J.), **Vulgar Verses**, post 8vo	2	6
—— Susan, a Poem of Degree, sm. 8vo, only 159 printed	2	6
Murray (Miss Alma), as Juliet, by Frank Wilson, **8vo**, sewed	1	0
—— (Miss Alma) **As Beatrics Cenci, by B. L. Mosley,** 8vo, sewed	1	0

Works of William Morris.

	s.	d.
LIBRARY EDITION, 4 **vols**, cr 8vo, cloth.		
Morris (William) **The Earthly Paradise,** a poem **in Four** Parts	40	0
The Vols Separately :—		
Vols 1 and 2, Spring and Summer, 677 pp.	16	0
Vol 3, Autumn, 526 pp., Seventh Edition	12	0
Vol 4, Winter, 442 pp., Seventh Edition	12	0
Popular Edition.		
—— **The Earthly** Paradise, in 10 parts, post 8vo, cloth each	2	6
—— The Earthly **Paradise, complete** in one vol, 8vo, in a gilt binding designed by the Author, also in gilt binding, **full morocco**	10	6
—— Ditto, in 5 vols, **post 8vo,** cloth each	5	0
—— Hopes and Fears **for Art,** Five Lectures delivered in Birmingham, London, &c., in 1878—1881, Fourth Edition, 218 pp., post 8vo, **cloth**	4	6
—— The Æneids of Virgil, Done into English **Verse,** Second Edition, 382 pp., **sq.** post 8vo, cloth	14	0
——The Defence of Guenevere, and other Poems. Reprinted without alteration from the Edition of 1858, 256 pp., post 8vo, cloth	8	0
——The Life **and** Death of Jason : a **Poem, Eighth** Edition, 376 pp., sq. **post** 8vo, cl.	8	0

	s.	*d.*
Morris (Wm.) The Story of Sigurd the Volsung, **and the** Fall of the Niblungs, 345 pp., sq. post 8vo, cl.	6	0
———— Love is Enough, or the Freeing of Pharamond, a Morality, Third Edition, *with design on side in gold,* 134 pp., sq. post 8vo, cloth	7	6
———— The Odyssey **of** Homer, done into English Verse, Second Edition, sq. post 8vo, **450 pp.**	6	6
———— A Dream of John Ball, and a King's Lesson, Cheap Edition, 143 **pp., 12mo, cloth**	1	6
———— Ditto, Ditto, **wrappers**	1	0
———— Signs of Change, Seven Lectures delivered on various occasions, post 8vo., cloth, 202 pp.	4	6
———— A **Tale of** the House of the Wolfings, and all the Kindreds **of** the Mark, **written** in Prose and in Verse, **2nd Ed., sq. post 8vo,** 200 pp., **cloth**	6	0
———— **The Roots of the** Mountains, wherein is told **somewhat of the Lives** of the Men of Burgdale, written in Prose and **Verse,** 424 pp., post 8vo	8	0
———— News from Nowhere; or, An Epoch of Rest. Being some Chapters from **a** Utopian Romance, Second Edition, 238 pp., **cloth**	1	6
———— Ditto, Ditto, wrappers	1	0
———— Poems by the Way, post 8vo, buckram 1892	6	0
———— Story of the Glittering Plain, or the Land of Living Men, or the Acre of the Undying, post 8vo, buckram 1892, nett	5	0

IN THE PRESS.

Morris (Wm.) **Well at the World's End,** a New Romance, 2 vols, 8vo

———

	s.	*d.*
Nares (Archdeacon) Glossary, or Collection of Words, Phrases, Customs, Proverbs, etc., particularly Shakespeare and his Contemporaries, a New Edition with Considerable Additions, both of Words and Examples, by James O. Halliwell and Thos. Wright, M.A., 2 thick vols, 8vo, cloth	21	0
Public Houses, Hints to Beginners in the purchase and Management of, by S. Brown, 12mo, cloth. 1892		6
Rose (Henry) The Poetical Works of, collected edition, *with portrait and 9 Illustrations* 8vo, cloth, gilt	7	6

Shelley's Works.

THE BEST LIBRARY EDITION.

	s.	*d.*
Shelley's (Percy Bysshe) **Entire Works, Prose and Verse,** with Notes by Harry Buxton Forman, 8 vols, 8vo, cloth, gilt top, *with many etchings, facsimiles, etc.*	100	0
—— **New Edition of the Poetical Works,** with all Mrs. Shelley's Notes, in addition to Mr. Forman's numerous etchings, facsimiles, etc., 4 vols, 8vo, cloth	50	0
Shelley (Percy Bysshe) **The Poems,** in large type, without Notes, *and illustrated with two etchings,* Second Edition, 2 vols, 1265 pp., post 8vo, buckram, with a design on the side in gold, by Gabriel Rossetti	16	0
Shelley Library (The), An Essay in Bibliography, **by H.** Buxton Forman, Shelley's Books, Pamphlets and Broadsides, Posthumous Separate Issues, and Posthumous Books, wholly or mainly by him, 127 pp., 8vo, part 1, wrappers	8	6
Shelley Primer (A), by H. S. Salt, boards, 128 pp.	2	6

The Shelley Society's Publications.

	s.	*d.*
A Proposal for Putting Reform to the Vote throughout the Kingdom, by the Hermit of Marlow (Percy Bysshe Shelley). Facsimile of the Holograph Manuscript, with an Introduction **by** H. B. Forman, 4to, boards	10	0
Hellas, a Lyrical Drama, by P. B. Shelley. **London 1822.** A facsimile reprint, on hand-made **paper, together** with **Shelley's** Prologue to Hellas, and **Notes by Dr.** Garnett **and** Mary W. Shelley, edited, **with an intro-** duction, by T. J. Wise	8	0

	s.	*d.*
Hellas, Cheap edition, **for the performance of the Drama, may be had, paper**	2	0
—— ditto **Choruses set to Music, by W. Christian Selle, paper**	4	0
The Mask of Anarchy, written **on** the occasion of the Massacre at Manchester, by Percy Bysshe Shelley. Facsimile of the Holograph Manuscript, with Introduction by H. B. Forman, 4to, boards	10	0
The Wandering Jew, a Poem, by P. B. Shelley, edited by B. Dobell, 8vo, 500 printed	8	0

Shakespeare (W.) **Hamlet, Prince of Denmark, with In-**troduction and Notes, by David Maclachlan, 189 pp., post 8vo, cloth	8	6
Solomon (G.) **Jesus of History and Jesus of Tradition** Identified, 297 pp., demy 8vo, cloth	7	6
Smith (H. A.) **Stellar Songs and other Poems with** an Introductory Essay **on** Science and Poetry, *portrait and illustrations*, 280 pp., **cr.** 8vo, cloth Net	5	0
Stealing of the Mare, translation of this celebrated **romance of the** Original **Arabic,** by Lady Annie Blunt, **and done into** verse by **W. S.** Blunt, sq. post 8vo, buckram, 1892 Nett	5	0
Theosophical.—**Man;** Fragments **of** Forgotten History, by Two **Chelas** in the Theosophical Society, Second Edition, 191 pp., post 8vo, cloth	4	0
The Life of James Thomson, with a Selection from his Letters, and a Study of his Writings, by H. S. Salt, 8vo, cloth, *with portrait*, 340 pp.	7	6
Thomson's (James B.V.) **Poetical Works,** complete in 2 vols, post 8vo		
Wagner (Richard), Tristan and Isolde, English Words in the mixed illiterative and Rhyming Metres of the Original, by Alfred Forman, post 8vo, paper 1891	2	0

NEW TEMPLE PRESS, 17, Grant Road, Addiscombe.